THE LONG NIGHT

The Library of Alabama Classics,

reprint editions of works important

to the history, literature, and culture of

Alabama, is dedicated to the memory of

Rucker Agee

whose pioneering work in the fields

of Alabama history and historical geography

continues to be the standard of

scholarly achievement.

THE

LONG NIGHT

Andrew Lytle

with an Introduction by

FRANK L. OWSLEY, JR.

THE UNIVERSITY OF ALABAMA PRESS
TUSCALOOSA   LONDON

Published Originally in 1936 by
The Bobbs-Merrill Company

Introduction Copyright © 1988 by
The University of Alabama Press
Tuscaloosa, Alabama 35487

Library of Congress Cataloging-in-Publication Data

Lytle, Andrew Nelson, 1902–
The long night

I. Title.
PS3523.Y88L66 1988   813'.52   88-12101
ISBN 0-8173-0413-4 (alk. paper)
ISBN 0-8173-0415-0 (pbk. : alk. paper)

British Library Cataloguing-in-Publication Data available

THIRD PAPERBACK PRINTING, 1994

Contents

INTRODUCTION

by Frank L. Owsley, Jr.

The Long Night, a novel of honor and revenge, begins in the late antebellum period in Georgia. Cameron McIvor, a man of honor and duty, was goaded into a fight that ended in his adversary's death, and the subsequent court case cost McIvor most of his property. As author Andrew Lytle says, "In those days when a man was ruined, he set out for Texas." McIvor took what little remained of his worldly goods and followed the trail to Texas. While passing through Alabama he was offered and accepted a position managing a plantation near Wetumpka, a job he viewed as an opportunity to recoup his fortune.

Upon learning that his landlord, a Mr. Lovell, was engaged in stealing horses and slaves, McIvor felt obliged to report this information to the authorities. Unfortunately, Lovell and his accomplices soon became aware that McIvor had discovered their activities. When they could not persuade him to continue on his journey to Texas, they murdered him.

The author depicts Lovell as the leader of a group similar to the Murrell gang, an infamous and powerful band of slave and horse thieves in the South of that time. Believing that McIvor, who had come to the area alone, had no family, Lovell calculated that his death would end the incident. In fact, much emphasis was placed on possible retaliation should McIvor have relatives who might try to avenge his death.

Lovell felt confident not only because McIvor seemed to be alone but also because his gang controlled the entire community. In fact Lytle suggests that the gang *was* the community to such an extent that the sheriff, district attorney, and judge were all part of the operation. Lovell and his band of criminals were grievously mistaken in their belief that McIvor did not have a large family. Lytle elucidates throughout the novel the magnitude of this error.

McIvor's extended family gathered from as far away as Kentucky and met secretly to determine their course of action, but they delayed making a decision until the court had opportunity to settle the case justly. When the court failed to convict the murderers, the family did what they viewed as the only honorable thing: they set forth to avenge McIvor's death. Lytle makes clear that this would be the only acceptable choice in such a frontier setting of the time. A family would be expected to settle matters of honor.

At this point in the novel Lytle describes a significant period of transition in the life of the South. At an earlier date the family might simply have sought revenge rather than attempt to use legal institutions. Indeed, in an earlier time or in a less developed area even closer to the frontier, Cameron McIvor might either have ignored Lovell's criminal activities by moving on, or, if he still felt that honor required some action, might have called in his family and friends to punish Lovell. As it developed McIvor apparently planned to seek the aid of the sheriff and the community, and it is clear that Lytle's McIvor is a man who believed in the legal institutions. The transition from family revenge to institutional justice is once more demonstrated when the family comes together after the murder. A heated debate takes place within the family as to whether they should seek revenge on their own or justice through the local enforcement people, and those favoring legal action emerged as winners.

The court's failure to punish the culprits signaled the beginning of the family's understanding of the area's corrupt legal system. At last they saw the court as part of the gang and decided to pursue the path of vengeance. When the law failed them, the McIvor family reverted to older customs by defending their family honor in the only other way they knew. The novel depicts, without approval or disapproval, the methods by which folk justice was accomplished. For Lytle the transitional period when people first began to turn to institutional law enforcement proves the perfect vehicle to show clearly the workings of a folk culture. Here he allows the reader to contrast the old with the new.

The beginning of the Civil War sees revenge put aside as most of the men in the family joined the Confederate service. Cameron's son, Pleasant, after a brief stint in the service, continued to seek retaliation for his father's murder. Pleasant had by this time become a lone hunter, a solitary seeker. His quest for vengeance had reached the point where he was outside of both community and family. Finally even Pleasant could take no more blood. Seeing the battles of the war and the death of many friends and family finally quenched his desire for revenge.

Lytle leads his reader to believe that Pleasant suffered a crisis in re-

3

examining his own values, with the result that his earlier objectives seemed less important. Perhaps he had gone too far and come to recognize his own sins. In any case, Pleasant took refuge in the remote woods of Winston County, Alabama, where the reader may believe that he found repentance and salvation.

Like much of Lytle's writing, *The Long Night* has an underlying theme of mysticism and religion. There is never any doubt about the existence of good and evil in this novel; but it is difficult, as in real life, to separate good from evil or to identify the villain, or to determine whether Pleasant might not be the most wicked of all. In the end Lytle gives his reader a hero who has repented his sins and gone into the wilderness to cleanse himself.

The story could have had another ending. Pleasant easily could have continued his quest, spending the rest of his life as an overzealous seeker of revenge. Instead Lytle chose not to make him a complete monster or simply a killing machine. With so many examples of fanatics in the world, Pleasant could easily have followed this model; and had he done so Lytle would have allowed evil to triumph and *The Long Night* would have no hero. The author humanizes his character and eventually allows Pleasant to choose between salvation and revenge.

Lytle's novel skillfully depicts life in antebellum Alabama. His descriptions of the people and times are well drawn and beautifully written. The McIvors are typical of the highly loyal, closely related families who settled the southern frontier. Their response to the murder of one of their own was the anticipated behavior of the clan-like groups who in other circumstances might have engaged in a lengthy feud with another family. Lytle relates their behavior to the clans of the Scottish Highlands; and whether southerners were of a predominantly Celtic heritage as some historians have suggested, there was a strong Celtic influence in the frontier states of the lower South where many Scots, and especially Scots-Irish, settled. That the McIvors behaved like a Highland clan should surprise no one.

The Long Night is based on a true story. While Lytle made substantial changes, many of the incidents are real and the basis for the story is fact. The author researched both the language and settings of frontier Alabama in the 1850s and 1860s, reproducing them with remarkable accuracy. In addition, Lytle tells a good story with believable personalities who are a part of the setting. His figures, while fitting well into the frontier environment, are universal enough to have lived at any time.

4

The scenes in *The Long Night* not only are accurate in their descriptions of the lifestyle of the time, but also have the unusual quality of interpreting the values and feelings of the time. Lytle gives his characters nineteenth-, not twentieth-, century convictions. While it is not likely that one can enter the mind of another, especially in another time period, the reader of this novel is able to identify with the McIvors and feel their sense of honor, love, and frustration. It has been said that the character of people has never changed over the entire history of mankind, and that the only variable is in the physical world around them. This view may very well be true, but society changes and brings out new facets of human personality. This novel describes a very real southern folk character close to the frontier who lived in a society filled with a strong sense of loyalty and honor.

The Long Night is a complex book. There are stories within stories and value conflicts within value conflicts. A good example of these conflicting ideals can be found in the relationship of family to class. The McIvor extended family consisted of people who were obviously of different social and economic backgrounds, and yet family solidarity is clearly far more important than any class difference. And while the interest in family was probably all important, community was also of great consequence. Lytle has done an unusually fine job of showing the values and loyalties of both family and community, especially where they come into conflict.

The author develops the effects of good and evil on his people, a characteristic of most good literature. However, only the best writers can maintain a balance between complex and sometimes contradictory values and still make the characters act realistically. This is the quality of writing that gives life to the printed page and marks the difference between literature and ordinary fiction.

The Long Night can be enjoyed not only by the reader who likes a good, fast-moving story of action but also by the historian. This story, while fiction, describes real events narrated with precision. But it is the novel's social and intellectual insights that make it most useful to historians. Perceptions and ideals are difficult to capture in historical narrative, and thus we rely on the novelist to deal with these issues. Nevertheless, if historians are to give their work life and meaning, they must understand the convictions of the people about whom they are writing; and for this purpose, novels like *The Long Night* are extremely useful tools.

Andrew Lytle, one of the youngest of the Vanderbilt Agrarians, was raised on a large farm in North Alabama. He also has strong family connections in Tennessee, where he has lived much of his life. Most of his writing deals with his native rural middle South, Alabama and Tennessee. Aware that this area developed a distinctive folk heritage, Lytle has become an informed student of this culture. It is within this framework that he is able to develop portrayal of the cultural and religious conflicts that refine the unique nature of his beloved midsouth.

The Long Night is valuable for anyone wishing to gain insight into the antebellum South, especially Alabama. It portrays a folk tradition fast changing and disappearing in the modern world, a tradition which based much of its value system on ideals of honor and family and community obligation. While the people of the area sought a good life complete with material comforts, duty and honor merited more importance to them than did the materialism usually associated with the class-conscious society of the classic Old South.

Frank Owsley, Esquire,
Dear Frank:

It has been over a year now since you told me the story of
your Uncle Dink. You had stopped over at Cornsilk, you
will remember, on your way to South Alabama, and we were
sitting on the porch in the cool of the evening waiting for
supper. It would be hard to say exactly what started you on
the history of his exploits. It may have been that your journey
to the old neighborhood brought it to mind. But I like to
think that stories come naturally at such a time and at such a
place, for certainly if it be true that the crowded town is
necessary to the arts as a place where the artist may mingle
with other artists and learn the conscious practice of his craft,
I am sure that it is no less true that but for the country there
would be few good stories left to tell. It is not only that in a
healthy country society man finds himself in his right relation
to nature. It is, more explicitly, that neither man nor the arts
can long flourish after the country loses its vigor, for this
vigor sustains in one way or another all the social practices,
making it possible for the town to intensify, give form and expression to the common life.

I cannot in this note defend this assumption at any great
length, except to say that the country is still a place where
both work and play move at a leisurely pace. It is still, to a
great extent, free from the rapid tempo of modern affairs. It
largely lacks the artificial pleasures which the towns and even
the villages now seek, leaving men to find the greatest pleasure
in their own society. This condition brings about, among
other things, a preoccupation with people's behavior and a lasting interest in character. And so, inevitably and naturally you
get stories, the tall tales of a winter's evening or the discussion
through the hot afternoon of the idiosyncrasies and high deeds
of some kinsman, now long dead. You get, which is more to

the point, the account of the life and passion of such a pro-
tagonist as your great-uncle. When you proposed that I try
to do something with his story, I very eagerly took you up,
and here at last it is. You will find that Pleasant McIvor's
long night does not follow as closely as we had intended the
performance of the original character. Perhaps this is in-
evitable. It is impossible, I believe, even if it is desirable, to
make a fiction adhere too strictly to life. But, at any rate, your
part in this story is a very great one, for it would not have been
written but for your help and suggestions, and, do I need to
say, your encouragement. Now, having put upon you a share
of the responsibility, I had better let you get on with the story.

Affectionately yours,

A. L.

Cornsilk Plantation
August, 1936.

THE LONG NIGHT

*To My Father
and to the Memory of
My Mother*

1

To be at ease in the

dark. To know what

the long night meant.

That was the secret

of vengeance.

THE LONG NIGHT

His voice stopped suddenly, as a clock might stop. I remember the room for a moment seemed to hang in a hiatus
of time, in such a hiatus as only the body can know when the
heart's last stroke sounds down the blood stream. For twelve
hours, from sun till sun, I had listened to Pleasant McIvor.
By degrees the steady fall of his words had beat all the warmth
out of my senses, until terror crept over my body, leaving it
defenseless in the grip of rigid nerves. For hours my will had
been the creature of that voice, rising and falling in its cease-
less monotony. Now it had stopped. The gray of his eyes
which had spread out and covered the world in an opaque
light that was no light contracted. My senses returned; and
there before me sat Pleasant McIvor, my father's brother, with
the same gray eyes circling the same dark pupils, giving again
that enigmatic appearance to the broad white face of the
genial old man who had met me at his door a few days before.

The cold light of a winter's dawn lay upon the puncheon
floor and streaked the hearth like a ghost's mark. I had last
remembered a room filled with dark shadows and a fire curling
over the back stick into the dark suck of the chimney's mouth.
Now the ends of the sticks had stabbed the white ashes, and
a faint red glowed among the coals. A light gust from the
chimney littered the hearth, and I shivered into the chair. It
was the middle of February, but a cold sweat was soaking to
the tops of my shoes.

He looked at me eagerly, unwearied. I did not move.

Instead I looked away from the fixed inquiry of those eyes
I would never forget. I might almost say patient inquiry, except that an animal's patience does not carry the human meaning of the word, and there was about my uncle at that moment the look of an animal—the cold scrutiny of power.

13

Scarcely a week had passed since I received his letter which had brought me to Winston County. I had just received my degree from an Arkansas college and was leaving for home to marry and take up those responsibilities which a young man is eager to assume. I had paid my debts and with tender remonstrances of lasting affection bade farewell to friends and acquaintances. Just as the hack drove up to take me to the train my landlady called my name. There was a letter, she said. In the confusion of my departure she had almost forgotten.

Five minutes more, and I might never have learned this story of my family, so strangely hidden it had been. But for the letter that brought me to Winston I would never have pieced the whole thing together. I read it hurriedly; then read it again. I had known that my father had had a younger brother Pleasant—Pleas he called him; but he had disappeared shortly after the Civil War, and the family had thought he came to some violent end in old Mexico, where so many went after the fall of the Confederacy. We knew little about him, except that the sudden death of Grandfather McIvor in the 'fifties had for a time bereft him of his senses. So when I finally understood who had written me, I felt the curious sensation, although there was nothing obviously mystifying about the letter, that I had had communication from the other world.

Dear Nephew Lawrence:—

You will soon be leaving for South Alabama, and I am writing to ask you to stop over and spend some time with me in Winston County. Besides the gratification your company will give me, I have something to relate which should be of interest to you, the oldest of your Grandfather McIvor's issue. You have never seen me, but I have known you since you were a small boy playing with your little sister upon the rough boards of your sainted mother's cabin in Coosa County. You will go to Florence and there find directions to my place from Squire Hicks.

Your devoted uncle,
PLEASANT McIVOR.

Three days later I stepped out of Squire Hicks' buggy onto the soft crunching sand of Winston County. Behind lay the scattering settlements which widened, as they drew northward, into the rich lands watered by the Tennessee. Before me stood the rough wilderness mountain within whose confines lay somewhere my uncle's place.

"Well, young man, this is as fur as we go together," said the squire. "I've give you as well as I'm able the directions to Pleas's farm. If you stumble off the way, ask a fox or a crow to set you right. Them's the only smart critturs you'll run into up thar."

He broke into laughter at his own humor, which seemed so strange in such a place and at such an hour—it was barely light—that his flea-bitten mare quivered and sharpened her ears. He restored her habitual docility, and his own, with a stream of abuse the weight of his authority and two hundred and twenty pounds called for. He did not long show resentment at this rebellion. His small black eyes soon drowned their resentment in watery sockets. They were so small, so hard and black, and stuck so close together that, as I looked, I had the curious feeling the mass of flesh and chins was slowly but surely closing about them. Quickly falling into the attitude of Pleasant McIvor's old friend doing his duty by that friendship, he drew himself into the dignity of this relationship and gave good luck to the rest of my journey. That this dignity was that which an enormous meal sack might have the squire could not judge, for the squire had long forgotten the surfeit of the flesh in contemplation of things of the spirit.

"I'd try to stumble the rest of the way with you if the business of the court didn't compel me to be in Moulton by ten o'clock. I'm railly taking a chance bringing you this far, fer the railroads air trying to take advantage of the people; and as the people's representative, I've got to fergit my own pleasure in their service. Tell Pleas not to fail to put up with me next fall when he comes down to sell his corn. Tell him I'll take it hard if he don't."

Turning the buggy with a scraping noise, he trotted back

toward his duty with an alacrity unusual to the guardians of the public weal; and I was left to finish my journey of some thirty miles on foot. As I turned my back on the squire's equipage, I did so with reluctance. It was perfectly clear that the squire never let his official duty interfere in any way with his pleasure; and it was natural to think that he would take this opportunity to visit with an old friend, especially on such an occasion. The only motive which occurred to me was an impure one, but it was obvious the squire's public life was above reproach. If he refused to attend closely to the minor duties of his office, it was because he left such matters to the lesser talents of the court. For him there must be an adversary worthy of his strength and courage, and in the 'eighties and 'nineties anything beneath a railroad failed to arouse him. Since the affairs of the county were never troubled by these corporations, the squire's great talents wasted away in coon hunts or behind the stoves where the groceries kept their barrels of fine liquors. As I did not believe in his excuse, I wondered what powerful reason led him so quickly to retrace his steps. I had noticed in his protestations of friendship an undue haste. I could not quite put my finger on it, but there was a look about him when he spoke of Uncle Pleas that did not spring from affection. Then I remembered the reference in my uncle's letter to Squire Hicks was more in the nature of a command than the entreaty of a favor. Indeed, the letter to me was a command.

And so it was with reluctance that I faced the road which entered the wilderness before me. Most roads defy an unsettled country, bringing as they do the order of law and civilized habits. But this sandy trail left no such impression. It seemed to be on sufferance of the high-towering forest and steep low mountains which at any moment threatened to press together the trees and retake it. And I had the absurd feeling that it was only waiting for my entrance to close behind and trap me. As the reassuring sun lifted, I threw off the weight, as I then thought, of these morbid thoughts and started out, southeast by east. After an hour I began to climb the sharp slopes of the miniature mountain. What fears I had left vanished in the exertions of the climb. A good sweat will do wonders for a man.

About an hour or so before sundown I came to a point where the road suddenly dropped. For some time the plateau of sand had been dipping before me. I sank against a large boulder to view the sight that spread itself below me. That feeling of trembling fatigue, which makes the body dry as well as empty, went away leaving me refreshed. A tremor of excitement told me I was at my journey's end. Almost at my feet lay a pocket of some several hundred acres of cleared ground. It was spread in fan fashion before a story and half hewn log house. To the west and left of the house the fan had closed up to a steep gorge tumbling with fresh hill water, while eastward the farm land bulged into the pocket's side, as if a stave had broken. Toward the north, where I was, the woods circled it in a ragged way, a fan much raveled with use.

The only entrance was by the road I would presently descend. At the base the gorge dropped in a series of falls, turning sharply to the west where it disappeared noisily through the pines and mountain growth. The road came to an end at a bridge which spanned the gorge. The whole pocket had the air of a feudal retreat an outlaw might well defend indefinitely. I quickly dismissed the inevitable drift of my thoughts, for I was too tired to think. But why should Pleasant McIvor withdraw himself from a society he must have loved and hide out so far from his connections and kin? Such questions shook off the soothing rest my body was giving way to. I set out with a good stride, eagerly curious and meaning that this curiosity should be satisfied.

I reached the cabin unannounced. It was first dark. The cabin backed into the side of the plateau, and from a raised rock foundation spring water ran out. It looked heavy and secure, like a small fortress. Smoke rose straight up from the chimneys, and I could smell bacon cooking. There is no smell in the open air that will so quickly bring the juice to a hungry man's stomach. I hallooed.

All movement in the house stopped. After a short silence, a man appeared in the dog-run, entering from the left-handed crib. He was of medium height and squarely built. Black hair streaked with white fell thickly down to the collar of his coat, but he gave little impression of age. The tremendous power of his body hung lightly about him, making his stiff homespun clothing look as soft as carded wool. Indeed, in the dark falling quickly about us, I saw no lines upon broad forehead and weathered face. I knew at once who it was. The family resemblance was too plain. Before I could speak, he called to me in tones so genial and pleasant my heart was filled with warmth.

"Nephew Lawrence!"

As he spoke, he came down to meet me.

"Step into the house. I didn't look for you until tomorrow. Martha, here's Brother William's boy."

"I got your letter, and here I am," I said.

"I had no notion you wouldn't come," he replied.

As we stepped into the run, Aunt Martha stood in the door wiping her hands on her apron. She was a small woman, and the years hadn't treated her kindly; but there was no complaint to be seen in the look she gave me.

"I'm glad you've come," she said. "Mr. McIvor won't be so restless now."

She stood respectfully aside as we entered. A young girl about fourteen years of age waited shying in the opening between the family room and an ell which held the kitchen and dining room. At any moment I expected her to run off and hide, but her father told her to come and speak to her cousin. She obeyed him instantly; then disappeared.

"The child of my forties," said he simply.

I was soon made comfortable. The oldest girl bathed my feet in a pan of warm water, and she rubbed a salve made from suet on my blisters. Later the boys came in with bags of game; then supper was put on the table. They ranged themselves around the table, and Uncle Pleas sat at the head like a lord. The women stood by to wait on us, or bring warm food from the kitchen. I was seated in the place of honor, next my uncle. The greatest deference was paid me. I was treated not so much as a cousin whom nobody had seen, but as the eldest son returned from a long journey. My earlier doubts and half-expressed fears soon vanished, and I found myself falling into the rôle I was expected to play. I was twenty-two at the time, and Uncle Pleas's oldest boy was scarce fifteen.

They sent me off to bed immediately after supper, and I sank to sleep in the middle of a feather bed. For several days the condition of my feet didn't allow me to stir about out-of-doors, and I was able to observe all things closely. It was apparent that I was living under the roof of a benevolent patriarch. He did no work of any sort but directed all things with the air of a man who has done great deeds, and his family sustained this state with the most perfect discipline and pride.

My entertainment went on for several days with no mention of the grave family matter which had occasioned this visit. I was beginning to grow restive—after all I had a bride waiting for me in Montgomery County—when one evening as we sat about the fire the family, as if by signal, rose silently and went off to bed. Julian, the oldest, lingered hungrily in the doorway looking first at me then toward his father. But Uncle Pleas did not notice him, and he closed the door softly. We were left alone with the comfortable cheer only a February night can give to a warm room. Presently the old gentleman bent over and threw a stick on the fire. It blazed and popped and the sparks crackled up the chimney and out over the hearth. He watched them a moment before he resumed his seat. For a while we sat in silence and watched the twisting heat.

"I have brought you here," he finally began, "for reasons unknown to anyone but myself. What I have to say is not a thing I can tell my wife and children. But it is a thing that must be told." He paused. "And you are next of kin."

He leaned over the hearth to pick up a live coal and set his pipe going. The sharp smell of home-cured tobacco soon drifted my way. I turned away and let my eyes fall upon the cheering fire, for I could see that the memory of some misfortune was still green in his mind. Once I shifted in the leather-bottomed chair for an easier position and waited, as I innocently thought, for him to recover his composure. But as I was looking at the flames, they suddenly lost their cheer, the room its comfort; and I could feel stealing into my senses like a noxious gas that unknown fear which had followed me—almost literally—into the wilderness. Desperately I looked at my uncle for reassurance. But my quick head was frozen as it turned. Pleasant McIvor had dropped the mask from his face. He sat rigidly in the chair, leaning slightly forward. A shadow from the big kettle cut across his neck and chest, and his square white face seemed to hang in darkness, free from its body. But it was the eyes which were worst of all. I knew they were cold gray—I had seen them in all their guarded mildness—but now they were ruby red and churning in their sockets. I pushed against the chair, and they spitted me there.

There was a moment which I thought would never end, and then:

"In the late 'fifties," came the voice, "our family had its seat in Georgia. Your grandpa, Cameron McIvor, was the head of the family, and he had prospered. But when he reached his middle years, trouble began. The thing that led to our humiliation took place at a militia muster."

From what he told me that night and from what I could learn from other sources, I was able to piece the story together, and of course you must understand that, at this late date, I cannot tell which words are his and which are mine. . . .

2

You're too young to remember militia musters, but in my boyhood they were mighty fine gatherings. It was one of those days, I remember, when a man didn't care what happened so long as he could feel his strength or try his skill. Pa had some business to attend to, and we got to town before most. I was fourteen at the time and, of course, set up over being allowed to go. I was up and about before day to see the wagons roll in. Eli was with me. He was my uncle by rights, but our ages ran so close together people often took us for brothers. From childhood we had taken a strong fancy to each other.

It wasn't long until riders from every section of the county came in, some of the younger and more spirited men shouting and taking on. But you'd see sober gentlemen of middle years, sitting straight in their saddles, ride by in a running walk as if they rode to musters every day. Those too poor to own stock, although there were not many of this condition, straggled in on foot. I saw one fellow jump from his mule, leap high in the air, strike his heels, then throw his arms about a friend and hug him like a bear. Kin would meet that hadn't seen one another for a year or more; and the women had hardly run through the ailments of children and servants, with just a running start on the marriages and baptizing, when the muster came to an end.

Such jollification you never saw. There were dinners on the ground, and red-mouth barbecue pits. The groceries knocked out the tops of their liquor barrels, and red whisky ran down gullets like rain after a dry spell. There was no great drinking until after the drills. The colonel was a temperance man; and as he was a popular gentleman, the men tried to stay on their feet so that they could wheel properly. Temperance colonels were rare articles in those days.

23

This day there was more speech-making and standing for drinks than common. Everybody felt good and there was great rivalry at the games. One or two were cut up right smart, but nobody got involved in a killing. Men settled their disputes in those days with their fists. When it came time for the wrestling, Judge Taliaferro looked for pa. Pa had the name of being the best wrestler in western Georgia. He was a well-built man and light on his feet. Up to the time he left Georgia he had an outstanding wager of a thousand dollars he could outrun any horse a hundred yards and back. Eli and I swelled out, for we didn't believe anybody could whip him. I was timid, like a well-brought up boy of fourteen ought to be; but I pushed up close, jostling the crowd a little. After a while they came up together. Pa was shaking his head, the judge was arguing, not in a judicial way either. I had thought it strange that somebody had to go look for him. He was always by, standing off a little from the crowd but never out of calling distance.

There was an old man from the piny country near me. He wore a dirty cotton smock and leather stockings. His head hadn't been touched since the day his mammy left off washing him, and I've my doubts if it was washed much then, and his face was black from sleeping around pine torches. He had a right rank odor too, but he was known for his prowess as an Indian scout in the old days. I suppose he never was able to learn the ways of civilization. "Thar comes a rale man," he sang out, when he saw my father walk that way. "Me and Cam McIvor fit the Indians together. I remember once him and another man in camp couldn't git along. There warn't no reason. They jest couldn't bear to look at one another. Everybody saw that blood war bound to spill; and everybody war a-wanten to see some, since we'd been a-hunten the Injuns for a month without runnen into so much as a squaw. The other man's name was Jeff. He stood Cam as long as he could, and one mornen come up and come right out with 'I don't like the way your ha'r hangs.' I marked off the line. In them days we didn't have yer fancy meetens. Will you be pleased

to meet me right sharp after sun at sich and sich a tree? I
would consider hit an honor to put a slug through your heart.
No. We done it different in the woods. I stuck a knife in
the ground, straight as the sun at dinner, and stepped off the
line—one hundred paces each way. Cam, haven the name of
a runner, he give Jeff twenty paces on him. The companies
lined up on either side. After waiten ontell I figgered everybody had placed their bets, I toed em to the line. Blowed my
horn. Away they went. Did you ever see a wild turkey Tom
gitten away from where he seen you a-slippen up on him?
That's the way Cam McIvor made up them twenty paces he'd
give Jeff. A streak of greased lightnen warn't in it, fer you
can see that. But I don't know yit whe'r or not I seen Cam
that day. He grabbed the knife jest in time to spit Jeff,
a-holden him for everybody to see before he pitched him into a
pile of bresh."

You may well know with what pride I overheard such en-
comiums passed upon your grandfather's prowess and with
what eagerness I looked forward to another such display of his
strength and skill. But instead Eli and I heard those fatal soft-
spoken words—that he had concluded not to wrestle any
more, that it was no longer becoming for a man of his years
so to disport himself, especially since he had several grown
boys who, if they were still so unfortunate as to remain bach-
elors, might any day make him a grandfather. The assembled
crowd protested, but they did not shake his stubborn resolu-
tion. I remember to this day how keen was my disappointment; and as I think on it, how sly and innocent-sounding were
those words destined to change the whole course of my life.

Two young men among us were particularly insistent that
he try his skill with them. They went so far as to use unseemly
taunts, but pa smiled pleasantly and turned away. Eli and I
were so disturbed that we prepared to challenge them ourselves, but fortunately for us others stepped in the ring and
saved us that public embarrassment. These two boys, or
young men rather, for they were twin brothers nearing that
prime state of manhood which twenty-five years marks, had

been in our part of Georgia only two years. They both had
a roving eye and a loose foot. They made little pretense at
earning their bread and keep. How they lived I would hesitate to say, but I do remember that people regarded them with
great circumspection. I find myself referring to them as one
person, and indeed the Caruthers brothers were more than
twins. Their love was nearer what a man holds to himself.
Sympathy was so close that their physical movements, even,
were the same. If one would toss his head or throw a foot
forward, the other unconsciously imitated the movement.
They dressed well and exactly alike and strangely the only difference between them was about clothes. Job, the elder, was
very hard on his garments and wore them through first. He
had the habit of slipping out of bed earlier than Mebane and
leaving the discarded apparel for him to put on. Once after
a long spree the younger got so provoked that in a scuffle he
stabbed his brother. His remorse was extreme, and he nursed
him back to health. His care, I've been told, was as tender
as any woman's might be. They were great lovers of games
and were popular with the young blades of the county, and
some said they taught them most of their meanness; but I've
found you don't have to teach people meanness. They inherit
that along with blue eyes or gimber jaws. They even held their
women in common, a singular taste enough and one which pre-
vented any prospects of marriage, even if they ever considered
such permanent separation. Job was the more forward of the
two, and it was said among the women that Mebane, if left
to himself, would make an excellent helpmeet, since his natural
temper was gentle and kindly. Of this I do not know, for
my knowledge of the brothers is of another sort.

A day or so later, pa was in the fields directing the work
of the hands. Job rode up and again demanded the scuffle.
He was put off in a gentlemanlike way, but the twin used such
language as no man can tolerate, especially before his servants,
who were looking around their hoes at their master. I was not
there; but Cæsar, the black driver, told me afterward. Pa
must have weighed twenty pounds more than his challenger.

He was square-set, something like myself; but of course he was much older than the younger man and the decay of age had eaten away at his strength. I privately believed this to have been the reason for his withdrawal at the muster. Defeat has always been particularly bitter to the McIvor men, and pa was no exception; although I now believe that this consideration had little or nothing to do with his decision.

Job's arms were long, his flanks clean and rangy. He had hands pretty to look at and ribs that dropped like those blinds in a New Orleans house. I thought then and I still think he was as handsome a man as ever I saw. Right quick he grabbed pa and lifted him off the ground. He meant to make short work of it. The hands dropped their hoes. Old Cæsar listened for his master's ribs to cave in. I can't say what happened, but I believe pa let him squeeze until his first strength winded, for before anybody could see how it was done, he had Caruthers on his hip. With a sudden heave and jerk he threw him over the fence, and there the twin lay with his arm broken in three places and a hole jabbed in his head. Some of the people carried him to the house, and there he remained until he got on his feet again. Mebane was away at the time on some sort of speculation, and he didn't return until Job was well enough to leave. We all thought the affair was ended, for Job left in the friendliest way. But Mebane was cold and sullen and barely civil.

"I don't like the looks of things, Mr. McIvor," said ma.

"Nonsense, Susanne."

She shook her head. "The boy Mebane's heart stings for his brother's humiliation. Anybody can see, that is, any woman can see a dangerous jealousy there."

There were two fine horses on the place that pa had raised from colts. They had fine heads and were very broad between the eyes. As soon as the crop was sold, he had intended buying a carriage for his wife. A many a trader tried to get them. Ma would often laugh and say, "Mr. McIvor, I do believe you'd as soon swap off two of the children as those horses." Then a wrinkle'd come in his eyes. "Well, Miss Susanne, I know the breeding of those mares on both sides for nine generations, while as to your children I can make out the papers for sure only on one line." She used to pretend that made her awful mad. She was a French woman, out of the Vine and Olive colony settled by refugees from Napoleon's armies. He met her on a trading journey into Alabama; and since the Frenchmen made a poor out at raising either olives or grapes, he used to tease her about them not being what they represented themselves to be.

One day Job and Mebane asked to borrow these horses to go courting. Pa didn't want to loan them, but he was afraid the twins would take it the wrong way. He had no notion what they had in mind. Four hours later they drove those fine mares back dripping wet with sweat and wind broke. They were a pitiful sight to see. This was Mebane's jealous vengeance. It was deliberate, for two shotguns lay in the bottom of the buggy. Pa went crazy. He grabbed up a gun he had just cleaned for the hunt and, before they could get out of the buggy, shot both men. Job died instantly. The horses ran away with Mebane, and pa reloaded to follow him, but ma ran from the back of the house and laid her hands on him. It's a pity she held him back, for the charges Mebane brought practically ruined us. It dragged through the courts two years. Pa was released, but he had to sell the home place and fifteen niggers to pay fees and costs. Without his brother, Mebane was lost. I learned long afterward that he shut himself up with his grief and drank himself to death.

In those days when a man was ruined, he set out for Texas. And that's what pa decided to do. On the day set for leave-taking our friends and near of kin gathered at the home place. Many had decided to leave with us, my three young uncles and several cousins. In this way they proposed to show their loyalty to the family head and their disgust with the way of justice which allowed an innocent man to suffer while defending himself against premeditated injury. Others, I believe, would have joined our caravan, if they had been able to dispose of their property to advantage. A many a tear was shed and many a silent handclasp was given in farewell. To turn west in those days was to turn away forever. We were delayed a day by another addition to our party, John McIvor, the brother next in years to pa. As soon as he drove up, all was put in order. There was a flurry of putting away the breakfast things. Babies squalling. Little children running about, the women calling sharply at them. By sun the wagon-teams stood hitched. Pa sat his speckled mare by the front gate, and a silence fell upon man and beast, upon those going and upon those being left behind. Susanne, dressed in brown calico, a little pale, walked out of the front door, down the steps, and out the front gate. Pa got down from his mount, lifted his hat, and helped her in the wagon. He rode to the front of the line and gave the word to move out. Whips cracked, the men spoke to the mules; and all was drowned in the last confusion of good-bys. Not once did ma turn back her eyes upon the place where she had been brought, twenty years before, a bride.

Brother William, the oldest son, drove the first wagon. Ma and little Levi sat with him. Lucius drove the second. Eli and I rode with him. The negro women were spread out between the two and in a cart behind. The men walked and looked after the cattle. Uncle John and the rest of the kin brought up the rear with their families, that is, those that had them. I will not recount to you our troubles on the road: how two mules went lame, nor how we labored to push through mud often over the axles. These troubles passed when we struck the Georgia plank road. This was the mail and stage route. I can still recall those thundering planks as the stage galloped by, rolling away in the distance, swinging and swaying on its springs as if at any moment it would hurl itself into the trees and somehow leaving the tall hard pines more silent for the clatter. We traveled for hours at a time through the deep stillness which sifted out of the forests. Sometimes a lone horseman would come suddenly upon us from a bend in the road, and we stopped to pass the time of day. It was a real pleasure to meet up with a traveler on the Georgia plank road.

There was one camp ground, about half a day out of Opelika. By this time everybody had accustomed themselves to the habits of the road, and there was right good cheer in all the wagons. Word had gone about that the women had to wash. It was such a day as I will never forget. Spring seemed to break all at once. I looked up from the collar of the lead mule and saw that all the buds had suddenly burst open. The woods were full of song birds, and the air soft and the least bit dampish. The great pines seemed not so lonesome. Pa gave the word and we pulled up in a clearing near an abandoned cabin. A wet weather spring fell out of the bottom of a rise not two hundred yards away, and it was near this we pitched camp. The little negroes were sent into the woods for fat pine. Fires were soon blazing and the coffee pots unslung from the axles. The stock was hobbled in the cane and a boy put to watch. All was bustle and the cheerful voices of the women made a pleasant noise as they went about supper. It was an hour or so before dark, and the men slipped into the woods with their guns. They came back, most of them, empty-handed. I really believe they didn't care whether they shot anything or not. The guns were an excuse to get away and stretch their legs.

Eli and I got off by ourselves. We came to a fine grove edging some flat prairie. We had a game we liked to play. We'd pick out a spot where the pines broke into a stand of oak and hickory, climb up and race for a sapling. We were pretty well matched, and the pines stood close together. We reached the sapling about the same time, but I was the quickest to jump. It stood off about six feet and forty feet from the ground. I jumped and caught. Eli jumped and caught me by the waist and down we came like a bullet, a-whooping and a-hollowing like young Indians. The sapling cracked, but it broke our fall and we tumbled to the ground in a wrestle. Over and over we rolled, our arms tight and our feet kicking for holts. We felt as good as two young colts that day. We would have been powerful outdone if anybody had seen us, for we both thought we were too old for any such goings-on.

That night everybody felt in a frolicsome mood, and you wouldn't want anything better than pine straw for a breakdown. Uncle John was a fine hand to make music, and a place was quickly cleared for the dance. This was the first time ma showed any lightness since we had left. She never complained, but we could see it had hurt her bad to leave the home place. She got out her sweet herbs and spices and made up a mighty fine punch. The men stood by and watched her, holding out their cups to taste it. When they'd got done tasting, she had to make up another bowl. Eli edged up behind and poked his cup up. They crowded around her in the shadows so close she filled him up several times before she knew who it was. She gave him a crack over the noggin and he set up a howl. That punch got him in trouble, or it may have been the spring air. Later that night he made eyes at a cousin of ours and held her tight in the swing. When the ladies cheated, she always swung him. The big fires leaped up after their shadows and reddened the faces and brightened the eyes of the dancers. The niggers hung on the outer edge passing comment, and their flat toes patted the straw dust; and the women shook their shoulders as they went to pass about the punch. Pa stood and watched the young folks for a while, and after a spell bowed low to ma: "Miss Susanne, will you favor me?" She blushed and told him to go 'long, she had business to do, but he was feeling the soft air blowing through the pine straw. He would dance one set anyway, he told her. They saluted to *Cotton-eyed Joe* and were soon moving as easy as the youngest to Uncle John's fiddle, stepping quick, dipping, heads up, with no break above the hips. When the prompter called, Swing the girl you love best, he swung her off the ground. It was a mighty fine frolic, and that night as me and Eli rolled up in our quilt and watched the dark settle down on the fires, I commenced to think of home and how they were breaking the land there now, our land we'd had to give up for no good cause. And for the first time I got to studying about how things take hold of a man, just as the night was taking the light out of the big fires. Directly I felt Eli's hand slipping over to see if I was awake.

"Pleas?"

"What?"

"I think some of them are talking about stopping off at Opelika."

"Who?"

"Cousin Cassius and some of them."

"They are?"

"That is, if they like the country. They say it being break-ing time it would be better to make a crop and then push on to Texas. Cousin Cassius is short on corn."

I knew what he was thinking about—that giddy-headed girl of Cousin Cassius. I started to tease him, but thought better of it, and we turned over and went to sleep.

2

All but our immediate family stopped off at Opelika. With some reluctance we pushed on toward Wetumpka. As the shortened caravan passed hands breaking in the fields, pa restlessly cast his eye in their direction. And when we drove into East Wetumpka, the center of spring bustle, Old Cæsar, the driver, hinted that the land looked mighty good in these parts. And it was. We made camp back in the direction of Tallassee, and pa rode to town to reconnoiter. He took me with him. For some reason I was his favorite. In every generation it has been a family habit for the father to single out one son for his especial confidence and affection. By rights it should have been Brother William, as he was the oldest; but Brother William didn't take after any of our people. He was a quiet man and something of a scholar. He didn't look like any of our kin. Our build is square, while he was tall and spare, with a shock of dark hair and sensitive brown eyes. He

was a fine horseman but didn't take to hunting or any of the
country sports. He had the curious notion that no animal
ought to be trapped and killed unless there was need of the
meat. He must have picked that up out of some book. He
didn't believe in settling disputes of honor with firearms either,
said that nothing was ever settled that way. Don't misunderstand me—he was not a coward, and he was not a weakling.
He just warn't a McIvor. Little Levi came pretty close to
worship where he was concerned. He trotted after him when
he could no more than walk good. He went everywhere with
him, to the woods or to the fields. Brother William used to let
him hold the plow lines. One day pa rode up to where they
were working in the fields and said, "William, what will you
give me for that least boy there? I've got more than I can
well feed." Levi was wide-eyed and hanging upon the answer.
Brother William smiled and asked if five coppers was too much.
"It's a trade," said pa. That young scoundrel rammed his
hand in his pantaloon pocket and brought out a copper. "Here
de money, Bre'r William." They both laughed loud, and pa
swung him up on his saddle and rode to the house to tell ma.

Lucius was ma's favorite. He was a wild boy, always into
trouble of some sort, and generally disobedient. He always
had the little niggers into some meanness; and when pa
whipped him along with them, he stood there and took it without crying. Once he grabbed pa's hand and bit it. When
he grew up, he had a mighty slick tongue and was as polite
as honey to the ladies. I suppose this was what decided ma
to make him a preacher. I never thought he was filled with
the godly reverence for the teachings of our Lord Jesus that
a preacher ought to have, but soon after we settled around
Wetumpka, pa gave him a horse, saddle, and bridle and enough
silver to put him in Princeton. He didn't show much interest in helping us raise the houses and get ready for the fields,
but would be off to town dressed fine and jaunty. He always
came back with his pockets jingling, and once when he
sprawled on the porch to sun himself, I saw him grab up two
articles that looked awful like dice before ma could see what

they were. And he made an excellent preacher. His silver tongue brought a many a sinner to grace, and after the war it was said he would be a moderator sure. But as mischance would have it, as he rode to meeting one Sunday, his horse shied under a limb and knocked a brand new stovepipe hat into the mud. He cussed so loud the leading elder heard him, and the Synod asked for his resignation. He finally switched to the law, but never gave up preaching altogether. And it was a mighty fine thing to fall back on in hard times; so I don't suppose you could rightly say his time was wasted at Princeton, as it would have been wasted at home. He certainly was no help to us.

So it naturally came about that I was my father's favorite child. He taught me how to hunt and trap and follow a trail, and he always talked things over with me, even when I was too little to know how to answer him. I tell you this, as it will make you understand why I took the lead in what was to follow. As we neared Wetumpka, we met a gentleman on a tall strong horse riding our way. As men will do when they first meet, they eyed one another's mounts, their trappings, and then one another. The gentleman's appraisal was quicker than ours, for he had got done with both our mounts before we'd passed judgment on him. He pulled up and stopped. So did we. I looked at him good. His eyes were set close together, but the right eye was larger than the left. He seemed to be a handsome man, until you examined each feature separately; then you got the impression he wasn't one man, but a lot of different men slung together. He was large in size, but his feet didn't fit; and when he knocked a fly from his nose, I got the odd feeling that somebody else was doing it for him. This quality, whatever it was, was confusing. It made you feel alone. If you weren't careful, you would find yourself taking him into confidences you wouldn't say to the closest of friends. I decided later that this was the secret of his great influence with men and of his power over them. He drew his foot out of the stirrup and threw it over the pommel of the saddle. I looked at it. The foot was small like a woman's and all out of proportion to the calf and thick, heavy thigh.

"Good day to you, gentlemen."

"Good day to you, sir," replied pa.

"Strangers, I take it."

"On our way from Georgia to Texas."

"Texas is a great piece off, sir. You ought to look our country over. Below our little city here and above it is mighty fine planting ground. The confluence of the Coosa and Tallapoosa Rivers forms just below the town, an easy channel for our produce. We are in direct touch with our capital, Montgomery, and that great southern port of Mobile."

"I had thought some of stopping over, for a season at any rate." This was news to me, and I glanced at pa.

"A fine decision, if I may take the liberty to say so, sir. Lovell's my name."

"I am Cameron McIvor. This is my son."

"Pleased to meet you both. Always glad to meet such fine-looking gentlemen. There can't be enough gentlemen in any community. Your stock and slaves?"

"Yes, sir."

He eyed our niggers and stock awful close. "Four prime field hands, an old driver good for five more years, five choppers, one cook, one maid, one woman, two men too old to work. Eight good mules, one saddle mare. Tools a plenty, wagons." He spoke as if aloud to himself, as a man does taking inventory. "That about right, sir?"

"You are quick to judge, sir," replied my father.

"Have to be. Otherwise never get done. I've a proposition to make to you, Mr. McIvor. I've more land than I can work. I've a plantation near the falls and in the edge of the hills above Wetumpka. Five hundred acres. You manage it; furnish your hands and what tools you have. In chopping time I'll lend you enough hoes to work it out. We'll split the crop. Is it a trade?"

"I'll consider the proposition . . . after I see the location and the land."

"Come then. We'll go to Wetumpka, have a toddy or two, ride up to my place and look it over. You can come back in the morning."

And that was how we came to settle in Alabama. The plantation had some right good cotton land on it, and the bottoms made fifty bushels of corn to the acre. We moved in the second day of April, and the hands commenced to break the day after. The neighborhood had a plain cast to it, with a few scattering plantations. The big places began on the other side of the river and stretched all the way to Montgomery. It didn't take us long to run up a few shacks for the hands, and there was a right good double log house for the family. It leaked in places; but the work in the fields was pressing, and we never got time to patch any but the worst leaks. Brother William married two months after we had moved and went in to town to clerk for his father-in-law. We were so busy up to August that we rarely left the place. Every morning before sun pa stepped onto the porch and raised the horn to his lips. It was breakfast by first light, down to the fields, in to dinner; then to bed by dark. After we had got caught up with the crop, we were able to look around a little and ride into town.

It wasn't long before we all noticed that Mr. Lovell's actions seemed a little out of the way. He would spend a good deal of time at his upper plantation, which was only a few miles away, without visiting us. Strange men would be seen for a day or two, rough-looking men they were too, about his house, then disappear as suddenly as they had appeared. I came on the hands talking together once. They hushed right up and went on hoeing. We always made it a rule never to mix in their private affairs, but I could see they were uneasy about something. I began to think somebody might be tampering with them. Planters had missed a good many of their people and blamed it on the underground railway, but stealing was pretty general among work stock too; and that didn't look like the work of abolitionists, although it was no telling what fool notions they might take up. Anybody that would call a nigger his brother, might claim kin with a mule.

Mr. Lovell did a considerable stock business. His barn always had one or two strange mules to be fed. Once there were as many as eight to be put away. I never thought much about it at this time, except that it did seem queer that there was so much secrecy about the business. Then one night about laying-by time, we missed Old Blue. Pa took it up with Mr. Lovell, and he made a fuss about hunting for him. But I tracked him north, through an old Indian trace; and it was curious that none of Mr. Lovell's men hunted in that direction.

I told pa what I had found. He could find his way about in the woods and tell a trail and how cold it was. He learned that in his Indian fighting days in middle and west Georgia and in Florida. He taught me something about it, but I was never able to learn the markings as well or as quick as he. The trace was a grown-over bridle path, and we rode single file through the woods. Our mules were unshod. This let us go along fast without making any noise. About ten miles out he held up his hand at a small stream. He spoke low to me.

"Son, they've pulled off here and gone up this stream. See that pine straw, where it's been disturbed?"

We hid our mounts in the bushes. About a quarter to the west, near a tall sycamore, a rough shack stood in the bushes. We dropped to the ground and crawled to a dirt mound that had been thrown up by an uprooted tree. In front of the shack's door, well covered by undergrowth, we saw two men. They were talking in low tones and appeared nervous and jumpy. We couldn't make out at first who they were; but after an hour or two, a squirrel missed his limb and fell to the ground. They jumped in that direction with guns. It was the Wilton brothers, neighbors of ours. They laughed sheepishly; one spoke to the other, and they went in the house. At a motion from pa I squirmed my way to the rear of the place, going straight back of the place two hundred yards before I moved down on it. I looked back and saw he had it covered with old Maybelle, a squirrel rifle that had been in our family for a long time. She was a beautiful and trusted piece, with the stock embossed in silver carvings. She talked pretty too. Holding my breath, I squirmed like a snake up to a loose chink. None of the logs was well chinked. There were cracks as wide as two inches. My knees were covered with the green blood of the leaves and grass I had crushed, for I had crawled the last hundred yards. I had two heavy bushes sticking in the back of my boots to cover my face. Through the chinking I could see the Wiltons at the table eating a snack. Every now and then they'd stop and listen as if they were expecting somebody. Over in the corner crouched two niggers. Their clothes were torn and muddy. Jeems Wilton pitched them some cold pone. They ate it down to the crumbs. I waited about ten minutes, until I saw they wouldn't say anything before the niggers, then hurried back to pa's stand. Before I left, I noticed fresh manure in a lean-to on the far side, but no sign of the mule. We got out, covering our tracks as well as we could and turned our animals' heads for home.

After riding well out of hearing distance, I said, "Don't you think we ought to tell Mr. Lovell about this?"

"By no means, my son, speak to anybody about what we've just seen."

We rode on in silence, and he spoke again, more to himself than to me. "The Wilton brothers are seen often in Lovell's company."

"You don't reckon, do you . . ." I interrupted.

"I do not mean to reckon," and he drew in his chin.

When we got into the open, a number of horsemen galloped in our direction. They turned out to be some of our plain neighbors, with Mr. Lovell at their head.

We met, and they pulled up. "Where've you been, McIvor?" asked Mr. Lovell too abruptly to suit me.

"On a wild-goose chase," answered pa. He paused to let that sink in. "My son here and I thought we might find some sign of the mule up that trace." He spoke easily, but his voice was hard.

"How'd you know there was a trace there?" Lovell sat up in his saddle.

"I was an Indian fighter once," came pa's reply. "But that's neither here nor there. A horse thief," he emphasized those ugly words, "a horse thief who knew these old trails could make a quick departure." He paused again, and I felt somehow great suspense in that body of men. I scratched my back where my pistol was. It was getting late, and we were in a lonesome part of the country. Mr. Lovell eyed both of us close, and his eyes warn't easy to stand. At certain moments they had a swelling, hypnotic look. But pa didn't seem in any way disturbed. He sat his mount easily as if he were talking to a neighbor about the weather. Finally Lovell blurted out:

"Well, did you find anything?"

"Not our mule," pa's voice bounced in reply.

"Not your mule? Well, did you find anything else?"

Pa shot right back: "Anything else? What do you mean?" He watched Lovell's confusion. He had let himself be drawn into showing suspense about that trace.

"I thought," continued Lovell with deliberate casualness, "you might have found evidence of this band of speculators that's been stealing niggers and work stock."

"There is a band then?" Pa opened his mouth in slight surprise.

"That's the supposition, sir. Of course, I'm like everybody else. I don't know." Lovell's voice was sharp and ugly.

"Of course not. A man in your station would immediately turn such information over to the Grand Jury." I heard my father put something in his voice that had never been there before.

"Yes, of course. If I had absolute proof. But that's a hard thing to get, McIvor. And nobody knows the full extent of these speculators' operations, or their power. I've heard it said they have secret agents everywhere. It has been suggested, even, that one of Murrell's chief lieutenants heads it. We who own slaves must be very careful not to arouse their anger needlessly. As for you, you've been in this country only a

short time. You are without friends or kin, so far as I know.
I would advise you to be very circumspect about what you
see."

"You believe I ought to give up hunting for the mule?"

"There's no mule worth a man's life," Lovell replied.

"That's true, Mr. Lovell. I wouldn't lose a wink's sleep
over the death of the man or men who have stolen my best
mule!"

"You misunderstand me, sir. You don't get the drift of my
remarks."

"The drift of mine is clear, though, ain't it?"

I kicked my mule and rode away, as nobody appeared to
have any more to say. Pa bade good day to the neighbors and
followed. Neither of us spoke until we reached the house, but
both of us were doing a good deal of straight thinking.

"Take the mules to the barn, son. Stay at home and watch
things close tonight. I won't be here."

As I was returning from the barn, he stepped out of the
house dressed in an old pair of moccasins and his scouting
clothes. Our house sat close to the woods. He looked carefully about him before he slipped behind the trees. It was
first dark, and he was headed north. He would need all his
speed that night, I thought as I stepped into the run to stretch
out and rest before supper.

Several days later as I was on my way back from a visit to
Brother William's, I passed Mr. Lovell in the big road. His
mount went by me in a walk so slow as to be unnatural. I
looked up from mount to man; and although we passed within
a foot of each other, his two-colored eyes were so full of
meanness, he didn't see me. When I rode in the gate and up
to the house, pa and ma were talking together.

"What's the matter with Mr. Lovell?" I asked.

"The gentleman," I can see the curl to his lip now as he
used that word, "the gentleman has picked a quarrel over
the wages due my hands. Furthermore, he says we must be
moved by the first."

"You mean to move?"

"The first is a week off. There's plenty of time to decide."

I could see I had interrupted a conversation—so I went in the house and hung up my saddle just outside my door. My parents sat on the porch in a short silence. I heard pa say, "I had hoped, my dear, this year's crop would set us on our feet here or send us to Texas in better shape. Now this trouble has come up, there's no telling where it may end. The hardships of our young days are not a thing for you to take on now, Susanne."

She turned toward him with a look that only a woman can give who has received for twenty-five years the full and steady love of her husband. "I have been happy with you, Cameron, because I knew you were a man who would mind his own business and expect others to mind theirs. That's a great comfort to a woman who has a family to raise." There was a short silence between them.

"If we call the dog, as they say, and pull out for Texas, it means losing this year's crop and a good mule to boot."

"Why?" she asked with precision.

"It happens that Lovell is the head of a band of speculators, and he suspects that I know it."

"A rich planter like Mr. Lovell steal slaves?"

"Maybe that's why he's rich."

"What do you intend to do?"

"Lovell advised me to hit for Texas."

She looked at him squarely. "It shan't be said that my husband was robbed and run out of the country."

Those were the words he had wanted to hear from her. The small woman rose and walked to the end of the porch and put her hand to the bell rope to ring the workers in from the fields. There had been such a spirit to her walk that as she stood away from him with only the air heavy with July heat between them, I think he must have felt the years suck back to that day when he first met her. It had happened as those things often happen. He had just ridden out of the woods into the open, his mind on anything but wiving. There she stood, so neat and trim, driving chickens off the porch. At that moment he knew he had met his wife, although it was a year before he came back courting. He suddenly felt the heat from his body rise about his face and with it the wind-dried smell of his leather clothes, that familiar smell that had hung sweet about him on that memorable day, now so far away. He was so shaken he did not notice that the bell had stopped and that she had turned and was walking toward him. The light from the sun ate away what gray was over her slick black hair, and he did not see the lines and wrinkles which had cut away at her youth. He rose up and took her by the hand, and they went into dinner without words.

3

The first of August came and went. The early morning of the second, the household was aroused by the clatter of a good many horses' hoofs. When I jumped into my breeches and grabbed a gun, pa was standing in the run with his pants pulled up over his nightshirt, talking to the center horseman. He was asking pa if he knew anything about two missing slaves. Judge Imboden below Montgomery had lost two the day before. Pa answered the man sharply, as there was an ugly insinuation to his voice. I had a good chance to look him over. He was a big man, and his clothes creased where the fat had rolled; but there was plenty of bone and meat mixed in with his lard. He had dangerous-looking elephant eyes and jowls that dropped an inch or two. Just as I was thinking he was as unwholesome a man as ever I saw, somebody kicked in the door to the smokehouse and called out, "Here they are, sheriff." And sure enough there were two prime field hands squatting in behind our meat. Just as they were about to take pa off to gaol, Mr. Lovell rode up. He was as sweet as pie. Said he reckoned there was some mistake. He couldn't believe his partner, a slave owner, had had anything to do with any such speculation. He'd go to town and make his bond. Curtly and with the blood mounting his cheekbones, pa declined this accommodation, and the posse galloped off with their prisoner. I saddled up and followed them. I didn't like the looks of things at all.

When I reached the town, I saw a mob of men assembled about the square. I edged up to hear what was being said. They were talking about stringing pa up, at the least tarring and feathering him. I sent Levi to Brother William to tell him what was going on. He might be able to raise a few of his wife's kinfolks. His father-in-law, Mr. Malcolm Holcombe, had taken a strong fancy to pa and he was a well-respected merchant in those parts. I also learned that in the dark some men had come out of the hills and run away with the slaves. That looked bad too. It was plain whoever was behind this ruse didn't want the thing to come to trial, as it wouldn't with the evidence missing. This wasn't long after the John Brown raid, and feeling was bound to run high; and the band of speculators would be able to dispose of pa in a better way, without the danger to themselves which a regular court trial would entail. After an hour or two the crowd dispersed, as they couldn't find pa. Most of them gathered at the hotel bar to talk the situation over. I followed them over there, because I was getting desperate. It's a hard thing to be in a strange country without friends or kin. I stepped right up and called for straight whisky. I felt I was going to need it. I stayed in there about an hour, until I got a little drunk. The general tone of the place dropped its angry note as the men commenced to feel the liquor. They stood about in groups, some loud and red-faced, others sallow where the fever had been eating at their livers. A good many were at the tables, but most of them ranged up to the bar. It did a good business that morning. The thick smells of black tobacco smoke rolled about in the rank odor of unwashed men shut in a tight place. The golden juice ran down the tops of the brass spittoons that were polished so bright when

I came in. I turned to leave, as I had satisfied myself they had hit on no plan of action; but I hadn't moved two steps toward the door when I stopped dead in my tracks. The doors swung to and there stood pa.

Mr. Malcolm Holcombe once said that Cameron McIvor was the most lovable man he had ever known, except when he was drunk or mad. Then of all the men of his acquaintance he was the most to be feared. "When I used to hear that he had been drinking," he said, "I always left home and hid out in the woods, for he had a habit of coming to see me when he was in his cups. I never knew when he might turn on me, although he never did. He loved liquor but seldom drank it for fear of what it would do to him. Always when fits of depression came on him, he liquored up; and he would come to me because he thought I understood him. I did. I loved him like a brother; better than any brother, and I've always regretted that I used to hide from him. But when he got in one of those brooding spells, I got a cold feeling in the pit of my stomach."

That's where pa had gone after they turned him loose, and he had not found Mr. Holcombe at home. From there he came straight to the Coosa Inn bar and called for whisky. Conversation quickly subsided to a few tables in the far corners. As the silence traveled, men's voices hushed, as if they had been caught in something they ought not to be doing. A whisky bottle was set before him, and the men on either side slid elbow room away. The lulled conversation swung back into force with a steady hum. Pa looked at the little glass, his eyes sullen and his great head hanging over it. He raised up abruptly and spoke to the bartender, as if he'd been cheated. "Tumbler." Before the man could get it, he took up a beer glass just as the owner was about to reach for it and threw its contents over his shoulder. He filled it from the bottle until the red stuff spilled on the bar's smooth polish— and emptied it without a breath. I edged my way around behind him and put my hand on my pistol. He repeated this, drinking deep and slow. The voices had stopped again. A dandy, fitted out with great elegance, his stock spoiled with the amber liquid, was asking for satisfaction. Pa seemed not to hear the magpie repetition of the angry words. He drained his second tumbler. Without turning, without so much as glancing at the dandy at his elbow—he was regarding the bartender with cold appraisal—he picked up the empty tumbler and threw it. The barman dropped like an ox. With a continuous movement pa lifted and balanced the dandy; shot him like a bolster over the top of the heads. The pretty man fell on a corner table. There was a crash, a light echo of breaking bottles and glasses. In an instant knives and pistols were out. It was a free-for-all now. I saw pa moving before him with a table, dropping men like blades of oats. The top had been broken until it looked like a scythe. In five minutes the place was cleared but for one man, standing with his back to the bar, a derringer in his hand. That man was Tyson Lovell. Pa dropped his weapon and walked toward him. For once I saw fear on Lovell's face. The hand with the derringer trembled, but I raised my Colt. At that moment something hit me over the head.

What passed between those two men will never be known. When I came to, I was at our hitching stand. Pa, Levi, and Brother William were working with me. I was wet enough to have had a barrel of water poured over me. As I opened my eyes, I heard little Levi's voice, "Let's go git'm, pa. They've killed him. Let's go git'm." I'll never forget the tender worry in pa's eyes as he was bending over, nor the relief in them when I spoke, nor the whisky fumes. To this day that smell is as sweet to me as rose water. We went on home, and for the rest of the month of August kept careful watch for trouble. There were always loaded guns lying about handy. Brother William rode out every night, but nothing happened. A man, though, in that country and at that time might as well have been caught with two Black Republican abolitionists in his bed as with two stolen slaves in his smokehouse.

Lovell made no effort to move us, but he talked it about that pa was hard to get along with—a man too big for his breeches.

He was frequently heard to say, with a regretful shake of the head, that it was too bad he had to let McIvor go, as he was such a good overseer and so handy with the negroes; and when he said that last he looked significantly—"yes, too handy with the negroes." Then a rumor started that pa had been run out of Georgia for some desperate crime, and it wasn't long until report had it that he was head of the band of speculators who had taken so much property and that the band spread from Tennessee to Georgia. If it hadn't been for his behavior at the Coosa Inn bar, the people would have strung him right up, for to their excited state of mind there was more than enough proof. They feared pa personally and they feared the action of his supposed evil power, which by being in the dark made neighbors look distrustfully at one another. This was perfect strategy on the speculators' part. It threw such strong suspicion on our family that attention was diverted from their doings; and it isolated us in the community whose support we could have had if the truth was known.

About the time the strain of this situation was beginning to draw our nerves tight, the drift of the speculators' intentions became clearer. One morning as pa was testing a chopping ax he had just sharpened, the two Wilton brothers idled up and leaned on the fence posts.

"I see," said the oldest one, "you've been sharpening your chopping ax. Let me look at it. I don't believe I've seen one the shape of that."

Pa was slow to hand it over. He turned it several times and ran a straw over its sharp edge. "A good man," and pa looked their way; "a good man can sink it up to the eye." Very carefully he stepped back after it had changed hands. In this encounter he had the advantage of knowing their connections without their knowing he knew.

"So a good man can sink it up to the eye, can he?" There was mockery, just a trace of it, in Penter's voice. He went through the same inspection, a little more slowly and with much exaggeration to the movements. Pa stepped back toward the porch.

"Well, how about this, Mr. Cameron McIvor, you black-livered abolitionist?" And with that he brought the blade down on a rock. Raising up, he flung it at pa. Pa dropped, and it skimmed over his head. It hit and bounced through on the porch. Before it had stopped clattering, pa got to the porch in a single leap and reached for a gun. The whole business was so quick that the Wiltons hadn't run three paces before Penter was boosted along his way with a load of shot in the hind quarters. He yelled all the way home, "I'm kilt, he's got me. Old Man McIvor has kilt me." But his throat didn't sound like any dying man.

Pa was not far behind. Jeems had disappeared in the woods. At the house the Wilton women were a-hollering and taking on mightily. When they saw pa vaulting the front fence, they pitched their tune a higher key.

"Where is Penter?" he asked. Their mouths shut to like turtles. "If you won't tell me, I'll find out for myself."

He found him lying in bed rolled up in quilts, moaning and groaning something terrible. I don't know what they thought those quilts would do for him, but there he was. "Git away. You've kilt me. Now let me die in peace."

"Oh, no, Penter," said pa. "It will take more than bird-shot to do that." And with one jerk at the blankets, he rolled him onto the floor. Next, he undressed him. One young girl turned away her face, but the old women bent over mighty close.

"If you ladies will get your needles, you may pick him clean by dinner time. I wouldn't throw him in the pot, though, until I'd scoured him with a mixture of strong lye and ashes. The meat looks tough to me." Penter got up shamed, mad, and frightened. At the door pa turned and spoke.

"The next time you come for a neighborly visit, Wilton, I'll greet you with the left barrel. That carries buckshot."

This episode loosened the whole household, everybody but pa. He took me off and told me that the affair wasn't far from coming to a head. "I'm afraid they will get me, son.

Lovell has succeeded in blackening my character until I can have no recourse to local law."

I told him we didn't need any help from the courts, and that if they got him they'd have to dispose of me first.

"There are too many of them, son; Lovell is clever and corrupt. I don't know how far he has the support of the officials. But evidently the sheriff is his creature. Now this Wilton business. If that ax had struck me, no jury would have believed a member of my household. Penter would have come free. On the other hand, look how it stands. You watch now. They will try to arrest me for an attack on an innocent neighbor. And this time the evidence will not be run out of the country."

"Don't you think, sir, I'd better go over to Opelika and rally the family?" I asked.

"No. Under the circumstances it will be best not to involve them. If they come to my assistance, they will be taken for outlaws and thieves. There's one other chance. The United States District Attorney. You and I will take the *Coosa Belle* to Montgomery . . . tomorrow."

4

The distance between Wetumpka and the capital is not great. As soon as we landed, we went directly to the lawyer's office. My father, in black dusty boots, a light gray broadcloth coat well filled with bone and muscle, white vest crossed by a chain of heavy gold links, stepped across the threshold into the cool shadows of the attorney's office. He paused a moment before knocking; and there was a slight tremble to the hand that held the broad-brimmed black hat that so plainly told the caste to which its owner belonged. The attorney was giving instructions to a clerk as we entered, and we were able to look about and get our bearings. The room was large and pleasant. Around two of its walls stacks of Records and Reports stood in military formation, each shelf of leather faces rising above the other in solid unbroken uniformity. As if to defy the servant's daily attention, an invisible cement of dust lurked about the shelves, giving to the already solid appearance of the tomes the look of authority which age and the accumulated body of precedent gives to these things. Tall windows reaching to the floor opened on a wrought-iron balcony overlooking the street. The noises from the town lost their sharpness there. Over the fireplace hung the portrait of John Marshall, a plain austerity to the printed head which somehow seemed not to go with the robes of office. The hand was drawn back and an accusing finger pointed to the open Constitution unrolling itself magically upon a plush-covered table. My thoughts wandered a little. That head with its rough sharp features seemed better suited to watch the dirt fall over the plow's mold board, the hand grasping firmly the stock, and the finger not pointing toward the document of Union but wrapped around by the plow line. Blushing at such unseemly thoughts, I was brought to my senses by a nervous, slightly irritated voice.

"Well, sir, what can I do for you?"

I looked at the lawyer. His voice was hollow, his eyes were dry and burning. He might have been a corpse just resurrected.

"Sir, you can do nothing for me," answered pa, "but you can do a great deal for the public peace in my community."

"State your business, sir. The state of the public peace in this Southland is in a precarious position. The abolitionists, sir, the abolitionists are going to drive us out of the Union."

Pa proceeded to relate what he knew of the speculators, their names, his discovery of their meeting place, and his opinion of their probable extent and power.

"These are very grave charges, Mr. . . ."

"McIvor. Cameron McIvor."

"Tyson Lovell, Mr. McIvor, is a wealthy planter and a large

owner of slaves. It is not reasonable that he should be the head of a band of speculators."

"I would not have believed it, sir, if I didn't have definite knowledge."

"How long have you been in the community, Mr. McIvor?"

"Since spring."

"Unhhm. And you've been in partners with Mr. Lovell?"

"Yes."

"And you think many of the public officials are implicated?"

"That's my opinion," pa said.

He paused and looked hard at my father. "And he picked a quarrel with you over the settlement?"

"After he suspected my discovery." Pa's eyes were narrow.

"I see. Well, Mr. McIvor, I'll look into it. I'll look into it." He rose and bowed very stiffly. "You will have to excuse me now. The press of business, sir."

As we turned and left his chambers, anybody could see that help from that quarter was not to be looked for. When we got back to the place, Brother William was waiting for us. There was an air of restraint I didn't like a bit. Then it came out. The Wiltons, he told us, had sworn out a bench warrant for pa. Dead or alive. That's what it meant. Cameron McIvor had been outlawed.

This piece of news was greeted with silence. It was Mr. Lovell's last warning to get out of the country. Without once coming out into the open he had maneuvered us into this desperate position. It was really the sign of death, but not one of us, not even ma if she had had the mind to, could have mentioned the word Texas at that moment; and yet all of us were thinking if we had just gone on there and not stopped over. I could see it about to form under Brother William's mustache, but he was quick to sense a situation; and he turned away, pulling jerkily at its bristly ends.

Pa dropped his head on his chest, and I could feel the bitter thoughts form behind his eyes. I wanted to go up and do something, and my toes itched to kick at the post. Pa was thinking how step by step he had been outsmarted. Hog-tied and with a rope wound so easy he couldn't feel its plies until the knotted jerk. First the slaves in the smokehouse; his blow-up at the Coosa Inn bar; Lovell's air of being taken in; the rumors of mean and desperate actions; the Wilton visit and now the bench warrant. It was devilish clever. Every move that pressed us tighter in a corner made Lovell more secure. A man don't mind dying in a fair fight, but to have no come back . . .

Pa raised his head and looked out at the fields. Old Cæsar was easing the dirt up to some late corn with a Cary plow. The wood mold board was placing the dirt just right. Directly pa said:

"That's pretty work. That's as pretty a piece of work as I ever saw Cæsar do."

He stepped off the porch and went down the rows where the old nigger was. The sun was high. The rich, greasy-green corn struck him about the waist. There was a hush over the fields that comes in August and sometimes on a June afternoon. A light gust of wind shook the tops, and they rustled like heavy silk in ladies' dresses. He stopped and listened to the noise. It was a sweet sound, and one he had heard for forty years or more. He held perfectly still until the quiet returned. It all seemed so natural and peaceful, Cæsar talking to Kate in his low way, it didn't seem there could be the knowledge of death anywhere.

The next days we went about our work as if we weren't looking for a posse to gallop up. The house was in as good a state of defense as we could put it. The bell rang us up in the morning—in from the fields at dinner—and to the barn at taking-out time. A week like this passed and no posse. We began to have hope that they were afraid to try us. It made us feel good. It's a curious thing how people who are backed in a corner will take the worst signs for the best. Here we were expecting the thing to come to a showdown in the open, and after we had all seen the way Lovell's mind worked. On a Monday, it was, a strange boy came to the house and said Brother William's wife was down with the fever. Nobody stopped to think that there was anything out of the way in a stranger bringing such news. Brother William was packed off right away, and pa suggested that I go along with him for some supplies we had to have, such as more lead and powder. I didn't think I ought to leave, but I suppose pa wanted me to go along in case this was a trick. What we ought to have done was send Cæsar to see if Mary was really down with the fever; but when a man's young wife is in trouble, he naturally don't think of such things.

I hurried the best I could to get back before dark. I was so worried I didn't wait to find out if we had been tricked or not. When I came within a mile of the place, the sun went down. My horse was in a lather and I slowed down to keep from killing her. I didn't hear the shot that dropped her. The noise of the river's Staircase* to my left was ringing through my ears and the mare's gallop. The fall stunned me for a few seconds; and I lay there looking at my mare kick. When I got to my feet, I was surrounded.

They took me and chained me in a log church about five miles away from the house. Two of the speculators stood guard. I couldn't kick. I couldn't holler. I was so well tied I could scarcely squirm. The only thing I could do was lie there and think . . . that at that very moment they were slipping up on pa. I must help him now, or never do it. This thought nearly drove me out of my senses. I flung about like a flogging turkey until I had to lie still from weakness, the sweat from my head running down and smarting my eyes. After a while the moon rose, and I lay there and looked at the guards. I stared so hard I stared their masks off. It made them uneasy, for they tried to smile at each other. I would know those two men again if they ran to hell for a hiding-place. One of them I wanted to hurt so bad I forgot for the minute what he had done. I imagined all sorts of things. Sticking needles in his eyes and squeezing his privates with a red-hot

---

* Until several years ago the Coosa River for several miles above Wetumpka dropped in a series of falls—known as the Staircase. The roar of the water could be heard for miles.

poker tongs. Then the danger to pa would sweep all over me, and my head felt like it must break open.

After I had tried every way to get loose and couldn't I began to imagine Brother William and his wife's people coming to the rescue. I even saw our own kin gallop up from Opelika. This gave me a little comfort, but even while I was thinking these things I knew they couldn't happen. I gave up to despair.

After I don't know how long my guards spat out their tobacco and left. That meant just one thing. I had seen my father for the last time on this earth. If I could in some unknown way get loose now, it wouldn't make any difference to their plans. His ghost must have given me strength, for the muscles in my arms and legs swelled until they just but broke the bond. This last effort set me crazy. I ground my teeth against the gag. The bloody foam nearly choked me, and I was so out of my mind that I wondered how cotton could bleed and foam. It was the longest time before I realized it was my tongue I had hold of.

My head must have struck something hard, for when I came to it was broad light. A bell was ringing, and I tried to jump up and leave what I thought was a mare-tromped bed. When the ropes bit me afresh, it swept all over me where I was and what had happened. I shook with a chill and dripped with a fever and chewed at the gag like a man in his short rows. My tongue was so swollen I had to chew around it; but still it got in the way, and every time my teeth grazed it the pain shot right to the heart and made it stop. I saw I couldn't let my heart keep a-hanging like that; so I changed to chewing every other beat. After a while the pain got to be as sweet as love-making, and I didn't care how much it hurt. Finally the gag broke in two, and I hollered until my voice gave out. Somebody came in off the road and turned me loose. I must have fainted away, for the next thing I remember I was lying on the bed in Brother William's room.

In that part of the night when people sleep the hardest, our enemies slipped around the house as easy as smoke. Pa didn't hear them until they broke into his room. As he raised up in bed, Penter Wilton and his brother Jeems held him—ma saw them by the flash of the gun—while a man by the name of Fox shot his head off.

3

I

The August night was almost spent. Its brief darkness had cooled for a moment the hot dry world, but the air about the cracked earth quickly cankered, and over the fields, the woods, the barns and houses lay the stale warmth which shrivels the grain in the ear and curls the green leaves about the stalk. Over the McIvor house it gathered its sickly taint, but there its warning had come too late. In the empty bedroom lay the stilled form of Cameron McIvor. Across the run his wife Susanne sat in a pale hickory chair, ignorant of the weather. She sat, leaning slightly forward, listening to the sounds of her son's voice coming from behind the closed door of the boys' room. The dead man's four brothers, Washington, Clarke, John, and the youngest, Eli, filled out the room. Grave and still, under the shadow of the one light, they too listened. The stain of the long gallop was on them, and the smell of the road lingered in their clothes. And their old uncle, Thomas, with his black hat upon his broad wrinkled forehead, straighter than the stick which supported him, seemed to listen, but the brown lids hung down over his eyes like a screen. When he had heard of the trouble in his nephew's house, he had ridden hard with the others.

Presently Clarke, barely turning, barely speaking, asked, "How long, Susanne, has Pleasant gone on like this?"

"They brought him in yesterday morning," she answered slowly, as if she feared to divert her attention. "He asked where his father lay. I showed him."

When she found it hard to say more, Clarke urged her gently. "Yes, sister."

"He came right out and locked himself in the room there, without speaking to us, without asking how it happened."

Her bitter voice quavered slightly and rose, "Oh, the misery on that child's face . . . the misery."

At that moment the frantic mumbling rose sharply, broke off, and clearly the watchers heard the boy inside call his father's name. The four brothers moved restlessly in their chairs and looked at the bare walls as if they were shamed.

"He has gone on like this, off and on," continued the mother. "Sometimes we can hear him praying and crying. William and I have watched at the door. We were afraid." She paused to listen. "At first we couldn't understand him. Then we heard strange prayers, awful prayers."

There was a silence behind the locked door, and Clarke stood up. The other brothers, as if they feared to be left behind, moved away from their chairs. "It won't be long until light, sister," said Clarke.

Susanne faced her tall kinsman. "No, it won't be long," she repeated.

"We must leave you now."

She made no reply. She understood that her husband's nearest and dearest must leave in the dark like thieves. No words passed, but she knew and they knew she understood that their brother's murderers must not know he had kin. For a few seconds there was a stillness in the room where they were matching the silence of the locked door.

Clarke said, "After you bury Brother Cameron, sister, come to us as soon as you can."

She bowed her head, and the four brothers filed silently out of the house into the decaying air. The old man was slow to go. He waited facing the white-faced woman.

"You know, child, what it means for us to leave you alone with your troubles?"

"Yes, Uncle Thomas."

"My house will be empty against your coming," he said simply and followed the others. She went out to the small porch and watched him move with the deliberate care of age, watched him walk to his horse as if he were measuring the ground, saw him swing straight into the saddle and ride away before the others. She listened to the creaking saddle leather, heard the slow walk to the Wetumpka road, the quickened gallop, sharp for a spell, afterward fading, then silence. Suddenly she tasted the weak salt tears.

In time she went back into the house, where sorrow was. The coming day she knew by the signs was nigh, but her feelings were lost, and light seemed no nearer than the crack of doom. It had long been time for grief to loose, to flow and heal the bitter hurt, but her tears dried upon her cheeks. They did not melt the sullen, outraged heart, nor cleanse the shame from the ravished house, nor the empty bed defiled with her love's secret blood.

Nor did they stop her son's rapid tongue, growing more violent and distraught. Soon it must break into a brain fever. She turned to her oldest, her William. For two days and two nights he or she had waited by the locked door, and now he was standing, his head of bright hair rising almost up to the lintel, uncertain whether to press his square shoulders against the barrier and break it down. As he stood there in his uncertainty, the wild words from within the room slowly died away. William sought his mother's eyes. The vigil seemed ended, and rest must surely come. But Pleasant's voice was heard again, this time talking in a conversational tone. There were questions, pauses for answers. William pressed his ear against the door. He turned sadly away.

"He thinks he's talking to pa. He thinks pa is telling him who the murderers are."

Susanne, under the weight of this new trouble, bent to the chair nearest her. Lost in time she sat there until she heard the key turn in the lock. She looked up fearing to see. The door swung to, and Pleasant came out. He looked like a man who has been through a long and desperate illness, but he was calm and self-possessed. She looked anxiously for signs of madness. If his mind had strayed, there was no evidence of it. He sat down and talked quietly to his mother, and as she listened to this son who had been more than son to his father and to her, she saw he had changed. She could not understand it but she was glad. He was young, but his youth seemed gone. In its place there was a terrible patience and a terrible purpose, and at once she knew this younger son, grown so wonderfully strange, would take their shame away. Her knotted body unloosed itself and exhaustion, like a flood of nausea, swept through it.

Old Thomas McIvor, sitting high in his saddle, his long white hair curling in the wind of the gallop, with the beating hoofs of his nephews' animals behind him, led the way back over the road they had traveled the day before. As they pushed along, the half-dark world wore thin. Rents of light tore it like a ragged garment. By the roadside dogs slunk along, heading home from their secret prowls. At these signs of day the horsemen spoke to their mounts, and they spurted forward. But it was early afternoon before the brothers reached their uncle's plantation between Tallassee and Opelika. Dismounting, they waited long enough to take refreshment and get a change of horses.

Before parting, Washington, Clarke, John, and Eli stood respectfully before their uncle in the deep shadows of the long gallery which ran the full length of the low-country house. Old Thomas looked from the depths of the gallery at the heat stirring in the air like water about to boil. He said:

"That sun will scald man or beast."

The four men turned their heads, as if about to view some natural phenomenon for the first time, then turned again to their uncle.

Clarke said, "We'll take care of the horses, Uncle Thomas."

"It's not the horses, sir." The old man put the right shade of reproof into his voice. "It's the time."

Clarke inclined his head. Old Thomas waited a moment. When he spoke again, his voice struggled with the phlegm in his throat, rose forcefully:

"There were a great many desperadoes, I understand."

Without raising his voice, as if he must calm his uncle, John McIvor answered: "At least forty or more, sir."

"That's too many for us to handle well," Clarke said, almost casually.

Old Thomas's words came back, deliberate, slightly quavering: "You'd better ride to Georgia and tell the family what has happened." His lips flicked once when he came to the word, Georgia. He now spoke to the brothers in turn, beginning with Eli, the youngest:

"You'd better ride to Gray and Greensboro."

"All right, sir," Eli replied in a voice that was thick with emotion. The old man was turning toward Clarke, but at this display of feeling he sharpened his eyes and looked hard at the boy, as if he had suddenly shown himself unfit for his responsibility. Eli blushed and straightened up. The old man hesitated, then withdrew his eyes.

"Clarke," he said, "you go to Milledgeville and you, Washington, to Leesburg." The two brothers nodded.

"Where do you think I'd better go, Uncle Thomas," asked John.

"To Macon," he said absently.

The brothers stirred, ready to leave.

"Hold on a minute," the old man ordered. "I think, John, you'd better take the cars for Kentucky."

"For Kentucky, Uncle Thomas?"

The old man answered slowly: "It wouldn't be right not to let Armistead McIvor know, and the mails are uncertain. He's your brother's double first cousin, you know."

"That's right, sir. I forgot. It's been so long since I've seen Armistead."

"They were as close as any brothers," Old Thomas said with finality.

"I'll take the cars at Opelika."

The four brothers stepped into the yard and the heat. Their uncle's eyes followed them from the shaded gallery. He watched them take the bridles from the negroes' hands, turn once to salute him, and ride away. He raised his frail white hand in Godspeed, let it fall uncertainly to his side, then walked into the house.

2

It took two weeks for the kin to gather. But by that time all who could be reached had come in. Some arrived on horseback. Others took the cars as far as they went and finished the journey by stage. A few of the plainer relations who had been with Cameron in the Seminole Wars arrived in wagons, which they camped by in the front yard. Now they were gathered in the front parlor of Old Thomas's large house.

McIvors, Longs, Pritchards thrust their boot heels into the rooms, crossed them over tight kneecaps, or planted them grimly upon the flowers in the carpets. Some were dressed in fine broadcloth, others in butternut, and one rich old planter wore ancient gate breeches. Rich or poor, they had all come in because they had known and loved Cameron or because the memory of the long years was still fresh when, in the old country across the waters, they had stood up and fought the English who had crossed their borders.

The curtains were drawn in the musty rooms, and upon the hearths small fires blazed, for even in September a damp air clung to the parlor walls. The ceiling lamps cast a pale yellow light upon the somber faces, darkening the eyes and drawing heavy shadows down the weathered cheeks. Susanne greeted the family and connection quietly. Many who were present she had known. All she had known about. But Armistead of Kentucky, double first cousin and oldest friend, she had not seen since the last child came. She looked long and hard at his features, and he saw the pain gather in her eyes. He understood what this small kinswoman was thinking about. He leaned over impulsively and whispered, "He will be avenged."

"He will be avenged," she answered.

He pressed her hand and turned abruptly away.

As soon as the men had settled in their seats, gathered around Old Thomas who sat near the fire, grave and erect, wearing his hat even under his own roof as a mark of rank and dignity, Pleasant and William entered.

The rooms grew still, and Pleasant remembered that other stillness which crept through the house in Coosa County the day when they put his father in the ground. He felt again through the open doors the hot August air mix with the cooler shade inside and blow over his face. He could hear the fans strike in their regular beat the bosoms of the neighbor women, the constrained silence in the house where death is, the nervous cough, the heavy breathing, the men and women with the sweat rolling down their hot bodies, under the starched waists and stiff strange clothes; and, hanging above their heads, the sweet and stale odors mingling in the heat, the salt of blood wasting down cheeks, and at last the sudden chill of the parson's words.

He heard again the silence when the parson was done, the rise of the women's voices into the song, *Amazing Grace*. As the lines rose and fell, he had watched the faces there, and on only a few did he see the marks of sympathy. All looked about for the men who might belong to the dead man's band, and he thought how right it was that his uncles had left in the night. There were strangers a-plenty there that day, come to see if Cameron had any kin to avenge his death. He saw them look at one another and smile at the lack of mourners—only the family and Old Man Holcombe, Cameron's friend and William's father-in-law. When newspaper men from the Montgomery *Mail and Advertiser* questioned him about the *alleged* abolitionist, he spoke twice. "He was," he said, "the best man I have ever known." When they tried to trick him into giving information, he cut them short with, "That, sirs, I shall let those who are concerned find out for themselves." He stood by Susanne at the burying and turned when Lovell, hat in hand, came up to make a show of speaking to the widow. Her eyes stuck through Lovell like two briars, and he mumbled and slunk back into the crowd.

But now, under her kinsman's roof, were all those men the funeral lacked. Pleasant heard Old Thomas open his dry lips to speak.

"There's little need for me to tell you why we've come together, nor what to do. Our nephew and cousin shot down by thieves, in a strange state——" He paused, but there was no impatience among the kin, for they had already decided what was best to do. "Shot down for an abolitionist." The words came slow and with anger, and the men in the two parlors were silent with shame. He continued: "No such dishonor has been done us since we crossed the waters."

The sullen faces waited respectfully for the old man to say more, but he was done. Bob Pritchard listened a few moments, then stood up with a nervous jerk.

"Well, sir, we're ready to ride." He faced Cameron's sons.

There was an eager leaning forward in the parlors, and all eyes turned toward William. William was standing, as the chairs had all been taken when he came in. His great build made all those around him look small. The last two years had matured him, but his beard was still soft. He looked like his mother, and grief, instead of softening his features, made the lines stand out clean and sharp. He hesitated a moment.

"I think," he said slowly, "that we ought to make the two Wiltons and Fox stand trial."

The heavily armed men listened as if they had not heard aright. William continued:

"Nothing will bring my father back. As the oldest son, I claim the right to try the courts first. Then, if we can't get justice, we'll make our own."

This time there could be no mistaking his meaning. At this quiet assumption of authority in the face of his white-haired Great-Uncle Thomas a murmur of surprise and sudden indignation ran through the room.

Armistead McIvor got to his feet as soon as he had recovered from the shock. He was a heavy man, and the floor creaked under him. Marks of pleasure lined his eyes, but now he was grave and humorless.

"The courts, sir, are for land litigations and the punishment of the state's criminals."

William flushed at the implication. "The men who killed pa are criminals," he replied stubbornly.

Armistead advanced into the room as if he had been stung from behind.

"Why, son, if every family difference found its way to our judiciary, the dockets would be as tangled as the tail of a free nigger's mule."

The flush had left William's face. "I want to try the law first, sir," he repeated.

At his unyielding stand there was a baffled hush. Armistead went slowly to his seat. The tension might any moment break, for all felt William had betrayed them. At each ticking of the clock neighbor looked for neighbor to denounce him, but as the moments passed, nobody spoke his thought, for all were disgusted by what they did not understand and by William's grief.

Finally the old planter asked, "What have we come here for?" The voice was not pleasant.

"Yes, Will," asked Clarke McIvor, "why were we allowed to call our family together? They have come here with a great deal of trouble and inconvenience. They don't understand your position, nor can I say that I do."

William made no answer to this rebuke, for it was plain that he had seemed thankless and ungracious; and yet without giving ground, he saw no way to show how grateful he was for the family's display of loyalty.

When it was seen he had no answer to his uncle's question, Bob Pritchard pushed back his chair and with a nervous jerk stood up. He was a little older than William and as handsome. Down his nose and crossing his cheek an ugly scar ran. One of his eyes drooped from another cut. His features showed both hard and fair. He faced the crowded room, turning his back contemptuously on Cameron's sons. The few murmurings died away. Every man gave his attention, not so much to what Pritchard would have to say, but because he was a man that all men liked to look upon and because upon his reckless shoulders and youthful face, already hard with a life-time's violence, they saw the mark of early death.

"I don't know about the rest of you," came his scornful words, "but I mean to leave. It's plain that what's wanted here is lawing, and lawing is out of my line." He held a breath and then with insulting emphasis: "I never felt the need to study it."

He had barely turned when Old Thomas, rising gaunt and stern, stayed him.

"Tarry a while, young man," he said, as if he were speaking to a wayward child. Pritchard shot his restless eyes upon the old man, held them a moment, and dropped to his seat. Thomas waited patiently until he was down, and with the same patience turned upon William.

"Now, son, it's right that you should have your say, and it's right for us to consider it, for"—and here he addressed the others—"Cameron was his father." He waited for this to be considered, then: "But, William, you mustn't forget we all share this dishonor." He sat back down.

When William spoke, it seemed strange that such a gentle voice could come from such a large-framed man. He told his kin in simple words how much he valued their proffered help but that little could be done. Too many had surrounded his father's house that fatal night. Only the law might clear the stain. For the family to ride at this moment would be proof positive that Cameron was the leader of a band of thieves. So well had the speculators spread this rumor to cover their operations.

"Do you want to die as mule and nigger thieves?" he asked at the end.

In the silence which followed his appeal, Clarke turned his eyes toward Pleasant.

"You were more with your father than his other sons. Do you agree with your brother?"

At first there was no sign on Pleasant's face that he had heard his uncle. He was standing behind and a little away from his older brother. He seemed smaller than he was, coming only up to William's shoulders. And when the attention shifted, it did not fasten upon him. He appeared of no importance, almost lost as he was in the uncertain light of the room. But at his silence the members of the family who were farthest away gradually looked about to find him.

He made a short movement forward, and at once the attention which had wavered lost its casual interest and fastened upon him. The rooms grew still. He looked evenly at his uncle who was yet in his prime. The lift of the head, the turn of the hard eyes, strangely bright under his deep forehead, were so steady and direct that he seemed not to have made any movement at all. Quickly, in the unexplainable way such things seize a body of men, all felt they had found a way out of their embarrassments. Eagerly they waited to hear him speak, and each man felt in some way excited by the unnatural calm on a face so youthful.

He showed no knowledge of the sudden interest in himself, but with grave directness centered his complete attention upon his father's brother. The first words were flat and conversational.

"Uncle Clarke, it's not for me to interfere with Brother William."

At these words the interest began to fall.

"But," he continued, "those men Brother William wants to stand trial an't the only ones." His eyes began to catch on fire and his voice grew thin and shrill. "They an't even the chief ones. Fox and the Wiltons killed pa, but others had him killed." Now his voice dropped to a deadly whisper. "The Wiltons who held him, Fox who killed him, every one that had anything to do with it are going to die." He hesitated, leaned forward, and with deep reverence said, "I know."

The kin drew forward, but Pleasant closed his lips like a trap. The fires went out, a film drew over his eyes, and he stepped back to his brother's side.

Again the common hope had been balked and with it the patience, never too strong, of the McIvors. There was some show of irritation, and men turned to their neighbors with the great need to relieve their minds by speaking them. After a while Cyrus Long of Georgia rose and took the floor. His manner was so sure and suave that a respectful attention waited upon his words.

"Gentlemen, it's clear to me that this is no easy thing to settle. We are here to help our cousin's family, not to be contrary. If it was all in the open, we could act in the open, in the way our bold young connection," and he turned and bowed toward Bob Pritchard, with just a shade of irony, "has suggested. But if I understand things aright, we have to do with a dangerous and secret band whose corruption spreads pretty nigh over the Southwest, a thing almost beyond believing. We only know a pitiful few of them. By shooting these few down like the dogs they are, we'll spread the alarm to the others. But not only that—we'll play into their hands, for they have so guarded themselves with guile that any hasty action on our part will set us against our—God bless his memory—beloved kinsman's innocent neighbors. They'll shoot us, and we'll shoot them, and this scoundrelly band of mule thieves will laugh and jeer at our stupidity. If you mean to kill a snake, you've got to crawl on your belly. Let us meet guile with guile, secret death with secret death."

Before the speaker could return to his seat or discover the effect of his words, Pleasant, pale and exalted-looking, walked like a man in his sleep toward the center of the parlor and stood there like one possessed. His eyes were fixed on the speaker, but they peered beyond him. He seemed not so much to see as to be listening.

"Did you hear?" His voice cracked like a whip. "That was pa talking. He came to tell us what to do." He paused and his sight dulled. "He comes to me like that. Sometimes I can hear him out of the wind, sometimes through the trees, or in the middle of the night, out of the loft." His excitement passed, and the strange, incorruptible calm returned. "Secret death with secret death. That's the way it must be. That's the way it will be."

The words trailed off into a lull, but there was no break as he continued in a rising and falling cadence:

"They came to his burying to gloat, but I saw them, and that night I followed them. I won't tell you where I knew to go—that's between pa and me—but I followed and found them. It wasn't a bright night, for thin clouds had come up from the southeast all day, mares' tails with a fresh east wind blowing. I noticed a good many strange horses tied to the fence. Some of the animals I knew, the sheriff's gelding, and Judge Wilton's roan. I slipped among them, so that I'd know them again. I had ridden up not far behind Sheriff Botterall, and the dogs hadn't quit barking before I was up a tree and hiding near an open window. I could hear but I couldn't see, so I hung from my feet until I had made out all the faces. It was a hot night, like before a storm that breaks a dry spell. The speculators had set the lamp back in the corner of the room. The light brought them out plain, but it threw me into the shadows. But God kept'm away from the window. They laughed and talked about us having no kin, and one of them said——" Pleasant's voice choked, and for a moment he looked as if he might strangle. But he gained control and went on, speaking a word at a time, and as he spoke the veins swelled on his marble forehead. Tearing the words from his tongue, he dropped them into the room as if they were cornerstones:

"One of them said to his chief, 'I reckon you'll have—to—go—over—and—console—the widow.' "

Pleasant stopped, completely spent, and swayed. His brother grabbed his arm. The parlor rose to a man, and anger rattled in many throats. All gathered about him and in lowered voices pledged themselves. Some had their pistols out and some their knives to grip. Bob Pritchard stood like a crazy man. Suddenly he whirled and drove his dirk into the wall.

The room was now too close to hold the men, and they drifted into the open air. Pleasant, the four uncles, Armistead McIvor, and Bob Pritchard were left in the parlor. When they saw they were alone, they stood uncertain and listless. Then

Armistead, Cameron's double first cousin, jerked his head, and the dandruff shook out onto the shoulders of his fine broadcloth coat. Like an old bull among yearlings, he strode over to the brothers, threw one arm around William and the other about Pleasant, drew the closest of kin into an intimate circle. He spoke to them in his lusty voice. It was such a voice that might call hogs three miles away or charm the loose cattle in the distant woods-lot, or sound down a high wind, full-toned and rich, filling the wide outdoors.

Bob Pritchard, like all men of his nature, had sudden loyalties and sudden hatreds. He had found a man he would follow, but a shyness had seized him and he was about to follow the others from the room, unwillingly. Armistead saw him hanging about, saw him start to leave.

"Step over here, young man." Rolling through the parlor, his voice vibrated like an organ. "Join us, sir."

Pritchard came over and very simply offered his hand to Pleasant. As he looked at Pleasant, the scars which had twisted his face into its hard recklessness softened with boyish eagerness.

"I'm your man," he said, "if you'll take me."

Pleasant took his hand and on the instant understood the quality of his strength.

"I'd like to thank you," Pleasant said.

"That's fine, boys," spoke up Armistead. "Now I'm of the notion that what's to be done is going to be done by us right here in this room." He looked around significantly. "Too many hounds will spoil this chase." Then turning to William: "Son, I understand how you feel in this matter. You're a fine Christian boy, and we are going to support you. But if this thing don't work out like you think it will, you've got to help us. I had a younger brother such as you. He thought, poor fellow, that all the niggers would be better off free. People said mighty ugly things about him, but I understood his opinion and respected it, just as I do yours. But when you get older—he never lived to learn any better— you'll find that all we can do in this world is to be good neighbors, be kind to our inferiors, respect our betters, and let things go on like they ought to."

William answered with warmth, "Thank you, sir. I only . . ."

"I know, son," interrupted Armistead. "You needn't say any more. But we've got to look at this thing from a practical point of view. This attorney-general an't going to hang himself, and he an't going to hang his two cousins. You go through with the trial, and we'll wait. I don't mind waiting. I'd go mighty far and wait a long time to deal with the people who have killed your pa. We are double first cousins. I've got more of your pa's blood in my veins than you have. We played together, hunted together, stood by each other at our weddings, and I'm not going to desert him now, when he needs me the most." He paused to take hold of himself. When he spoke again, his voice had softened to a rumble, angry, threatening:

"I'll take care of this Judge Wilton."

Saying this, he sat them all down and gradually directed the conversation toward hunting, how to tell a good horse, what kind of land lies the right way, and matters pertaining to the state of the nation.

Pleasant took no part in this talk. He heard as a man in a light sleep hears the strange footfall. He was thinking how things had turned out—the family disposed of without offense, Brother William satisfied—and he left to do what he had to do.

3

Lawson Wilton, District Attorney and one-time circuit judge, stepped from his office into the shadows of the covered sidewalk. He paused by one of the grilled columns and pulled out his thick gold watch. From the dim light of the flicker-

ing street lamp he barely made out the hour—it was ten p.m.
He looked up and down the street with a nervous sweep of
his head. He was alone in the moist darkness. The planting
town had long closed its shutters and gone to bed. There was
only one place which held out against the night. The Coosa
River Inn bar flattened its feeble light against the mist. Its
hospitable doors stood ready to swing for the belated guest
who might want a nightcap against the foggy evening. And
the fog had blown off the river to settle quietly over the houses
and streets. Judge Wilton scowled at the thick atmosphere
and shuddered as he pulled his cape over his drooping shoulders.
Head down, he struck a brisk pace in the direction of the
frosty glow, as if he feared it would fade away before he
could reach it.

He was not a drinking man, but he dared not go to bed
without a stiff hot toddy. It made him sleep, he informed the
bartender, and he had been sleeping badly for the last month.
He assured himself it was the late hours his practice made him
keep. This excuse served as far as the bottom stair which led
to his chambers. But when the door closed behind him and
he laid his folded clothes across the chair, blew out the light, and
settled a body no longer youthful between the cool, white
sheets, something more desperate than a crowded docket
clawed at the covers and drove rest away.

Each evening his sleep had grown shorter, but the last evening, after a short doze, he had found himself bolt upright in
bed, grasping the sideboards, and a dry scream at the roof of
his mouth. Across from the foot slab stood a mahogany dresser, its slim, flat-surfaced mirror tilted to catch the bed's reflection. It had been placed where, the moment he woke, he
might refresh himself with the image of his handsome features:
the curling brown locks, the soft, matching eyes, now a little
dull and harried, the fair complexion, the full lip hanging
petulantly forward, and the nose—the one feature which
marred the whole, rough in texture and bulging coarsely. This
in time he came not to see. But in that horrible hour, with
the three-quarter moon lighting the mirror, the image reflected

upon the edge of darkness struck him with terror. He could make out only the white, broken face, lifted from the head which night had made its own. There was only one sound in the world, the flutter and beat of his heart, smothering under the dreadful gaze from the specter across the room. He tried to move, but his will, streaming like tears upon his body, had soaked into the covers. Directly the bed shook until it set the pins to creaking, and he fell back upon the pillows. The moon went under. The image disappeared, and he lay in utter darkness with the secret of damnation. This had been the night's vigil, to count over the monotony of waste and corruption. Never should that mirror throw another such reflection. To-morrow he would have the dresser moved from the room.

But now the morrow had come and passed, and the dresser remained in its appointed place by the wall. Somehow he must find a way to escape his thoughts, he whispered, as he pushed his way through the swinging doors of the Coosa River Inn bar.

"Same thing tonight, Judge?" asked the bartender.

"You name it, Sid." As he took off his cape, the warmth of the room sent a slight chill across his spine.

"Yes, sirree. I've got something special I shake up for a gentleman of a foggy evening."

"I'll just wait over here. I'm tired tonight."

"Right away, sir."

As Wilton turned, a large man with a tremendous shock of hair had risen and was bowing. "Won't you share my table with me, sir. It's late, and we are alone in the bar."

Wilton, as he looked at the man, pulled himself up straight. He felt a curious eagerness to join the stranger, a sense of relief, as if he had feared he might not find him there. When he had looked at his watch, he remembered that he had felt the need to hurry for fear of being late for a rendezvous.

"I never drink by myself if I can help it," continued the stranger in a lusty voice. "Drinking alone tarnishes the liver. And a tarnished liver makes for mighty shabby living. We have no recourse, sir, but in calomel. And of all the drugs known to medicine its humors are the worst."

Wilton looked eagerly at his host. He saw a great head of hair, greasy with sweet oil and falling about the shoulders. This man seemed to be in his middle fifties, yet the muscle and flesh stuck hard to the bone, and his complexion was that of all men who stay much in the wind. He was dressed in elegant fashion, in fine broadcloth from neck to ankle. There was not a crease to the pants from rounded stomach to small foot. Wilton caught himself wondering how so small a foot could hold up such a mass of weight. In a finishing glance he noticed that dandruff had fallen from the oil stains on the velvet collar as far out as the shoulders.

"Yes, sir," repeated the stranger, "there lies our joy—and our misery. If science wants to give a boon to mankind, let it find a way to polish the liver. God never meant for it to be squeezed like a sponge."

Wilton smiled in agreement. As had so often happened before, he found himself charmed by the stranger. There was so much honor upon his open face, so much comforting vigor to his body. He felt desperately in need of such comfort. Wilton waved him to a seat. The stranger bowed from the waist and spoke again:

"And might I know, sir, whose company I'm to be honored with? I make it a point never to sit at table until that small formality is got out of the way." The stranger's eyes sharpened, and for a second lost their mildness.

"Wilton's my name. I'm district attorney. And you, sir?"

There was the slightest pause. The drooping eyelids for a split second curtained the amiable bluff appearance on the large man's face. Only one who had a sharp sense for faces, the subtle changes of the countenance, would have attached any significance to the break, and Wilton was not at that moment disposed to be critical. The lids drew back.

"Armistead Weatherford. From Kentucky. On my way south to see my sister's factor. Leave in several days on the *Coosa Belle*." This was spoken loud enough for the bartender to overhear.

"Odd time of year for that, sir," Wilton said.

"It's an odd business I'm on," came the abrupt reply.

The drinks were brought, and the two men sat in a short silence, letting the aroma drift by their noses. Wilton sipped from his glass and set it down. Mr. Weatherford passed his several times before his nose and let a sigh rumble from his chest. He emptied half the glass and set it on the table.

"My boy,"—he turned toward the bar,—"if you were a nigger, I'd buy you. That's the finest punch I've had in two days. Stir me up another."

"Yes, sir, Colonel."

"If I wasn't afraid you'd spile it, I'd say put in just a touch more of the rum."

"A touch more it'll be, sir."

A broad smile settled over Mr. Weatherford's face. His heavy chin crushed the ruffles at his throat. "Mr. Wilton, throw that toddy away and let me order you a planter's punch."

Wilton felt his hand reach to do the other's bidding. To hear him speak the words describing the punch made it seem a nectar which would soothe all the burning edges of a man's mind. He smiled, instead, and shook his head.

"A toddy is all I allow myself, sir. Something to send me pleasantly to bed."

"You're a young man, Judge. And I can see, a sober-minded one. I look for you to stand at the top of your profession. It's me that ought to be drinking the toddy, and you the punch. But I've got a heap to fill. It takes a spiced drink to sizzle through this fat of mine."

"You do yourself an injustice, sir. I never saw a better turned out gentleman."

"Go long, sir. Go long."

The punch was finished and another brought. Wilton looked at his companion.

"I see you are a philosopher, Mr. Weatherford."

"Go long, sir. Go long. There an't been any philosophers in this country since Mr. Jefferson and Mr. Calhoun, God bless their memory, went to their rewards."

Wilton cleared his throat. "I myself like to reflect upon

the joys and miseries that trouble a man in his passage through life. In my profession I see, of course, more of the misery."

"To be sure, to be sure." Mr. Weatherford put his large fat hand upon the table. "I'm indeed fortunate in running upon such a gentleman. It's as singular as it's unexpected . . . to find in the heart of the cotton belt no mention of that article of commerce. Coming down I could hear of nothing else. I drank it, spat it, slept with it, smelled it. King Cotton is a tyrant, sir. He does nothing but put a flimsy shelter over our backs, and for this poor service we must fall down and grovel in the dust. I hope I an't offended you, Judge."

"Not at all, sir. Not at all. But I can see you're from a tobacco state."

"I am, Mr. Wilton. And proud of it. Tobacco is the gentleman among the plants. His rule is strict but modest. I can say without prejudice there's nothing better than the dark-fired leaf. He's got his poor kin, the worms that live off his broad back. He tones up the digestive system when he's chewed, and what can beat a good segar to turn a man's fancy upon those speculations which an't of the flesh."

"I've got a little cotton plantation on the Alabama River." Wilton under the influence of the stranger and the toddy was becoming expansive and confidential.

"That brings up another point," said Weatherford, interrupting. "Tobacco fits our peculiar institution so much better than cotton. A planter can't grow more'n fifty acres of tobacco very profitably. That calls for a twenty-nigger shift. While look at your white lice—that's what I call cotton. It spreads by the thousands of acres, breeding thousands of niggers. It's not going to be many years, Judge Wilton, before the niggers'll eat you people out of house and land. Then the cannibals will turn about and eat one another." He thrust his hand across the table, opened and closed his fingers like a ravenous mouth. Wilton watched the hand emptying the table of its population, spoke:

"Oh, I don't see such a dark future for our country, Mr.

Weatherford." Wilton pursed his lips, shook his head. "Our real danger is from the abolitionists."

"There now!" rolled Weatherford's voice, and he pounded the table. "They breed like hogs, sir."

"The Constitution's in danger, Mr. Weatherford." Wilton spoke earnestly. "Real danger," and he dropped his voice and clasped his hands on the table. "We don't know how desperate our situation is."

One might have thought from Wilton's manner, his voice, the look of fright in his eyes that it was not the Constitution but he personally who was in danger. Weatherford eyed him narrowly, rushed to break the pause:

"We see eye to eye on that, sir."

Wilton sat back in his chair, laughed uneasily, "You must excuse my overwrought condition. I get too easily worked up."

As if Wilton's too great concern had gone unnoticed, Weatherford spoke with studied regret:

"I thought Mr. Calhoun could bring us together, but his untimely death took the meat out of the Nashville convention."

Wilton seized upon this, carried it further:

"If we can't act in the Union, there's one desperate remedy left." He paused. "Secession."

Weatherford stood upon his small feet and raised the almost empty glass: "The South. May she get together before it's too late." The two men drained their glasses, lifted their hats, and parted for the night.

For the first time in weeks Lawson Wilton opened his eyes next morning with the sun streaming through the windows. He got up and dressed with special care; and when he went down to breakfast, his step was so quick and his look so fresh that he felt at once the workings of his old charm on the other boarders. He got through the work of the day quickly. In spite of the fact that his most important case would come up within the week he left the office an hour earlier to prepare for a supper engagement with his new companion.

In the warm fall evening Mr. Weatherford walked up and down the piazza of the Coosa River Inn. His small shining feet struck the brick floor softly as if they were stalking the grilled pillars at the end of the promenade. A long black stogey burned far from his mouth. The strong black smoke shot into the air or rose in clouds about his head. When he passed the lobby, the wash of light showed his eyes, now hard and cunning, hiding under their drooping lids. If the expected guest had seen him at that moment, he would have missed the frank genial expression which had given him so much comfort on the previous evening.

As Weatherford's hand was reaching for the heavy gold fob at his thigh, Lawson Wilton hailed him. He stepped into the light, turned out in gray broadcloth pants and a green velvet coat. At his throat a thin lace ruffle was caught by an amethyst stud. He lifted his tall silk hat, and the scent from his hair struck Weatherford's nose disagreeably. But he gave a hearty greeting and, taking Wilton by the arm, led him into the dining room. The white-coated waiters pulled back their chairs.

After the dishes had been removed, the decanter of brandy set between them, their cigars lighted, they settled back pleasantly in their chairs. Wilton broke the silence.

"You remember we touched, Mr. Weatherford, our first evening together, upon the joys and miseries in this world?"

"I do, sir. And if my mind don't deceive me, I put the secret to the liver," Weatherford replied in the tone of a man who tries to remember the subject of a casual conversation. "It's my solid opinion that science begins at the wrong end of man. The medical gentlemen ram a herb in your mouth and leave the rest to gravity. That's magic, sir. Black magic. If there was an ounce of imagination to their heads, which I may add are as empty as the skulls they tap, they'd look better after our innards. For there lies our joy and our troubles. I was a medical man once myself." He paused and lifted the heavy lids from his mild blue eyes. "An't that been your experience, sir?"

Wilton answered hurriedly with the haste of a man who wants the floor. There was a tremor to his first words, and Weatherford looked sharply toward him.

"I have known for some time a colleague of mine," he proceeded, "a man about my age, whose story might interest you."

"There's nothing better than a good story over a good segar. I'd be pleased to hear it," Weatherford said.

Wilton bowed slightly. "This friend—I say friend—this colleague, rather, is facing a crisis in his life, and I would give much to help him bring it to a happy conclusion. I thought maybe you could advise me."

"Judge, I've lived—well, if old Marster was to call me away tonight, I could have no complaint—and I've yet to meet the man who took any counsel but what counsel he wanted to hear."

Wilton smiled politely, hurried on with his story.

"Let us for the sake of convenience call my friend Purtle. He was born in Savannah, Georgia, of a prosperous merchant family. When he was seventeen, his father and mother were drowned at sea. What modest fortune his father had accumulated went down with the vessel. Against the advice of friends and distant connections he sold what little was left him, bought a horse, and decided to try his fortune in the West. At that time Alabama had just entered the Union, and she was emptying the old states of their citizens. His friends knew it was folly for one who had been raised so gently to try the hard fare of the West, but he was in no mood to listen to sound advice. He saw in Alabama a land of imagination: the vast green forests, the blue mountains, the pleasant fountains, and somewhere a miraculous fortune. His leavetaking showed how little he knew what lay before him. In green velveteen coat and broadcloth breeches, his horse pawing the western road, he turned back to view for the last time his native city; then whirling dramatically, galloped away.

"He hadn't been long on the road before his high spirits fell. The fifth day out the coarse food, the hard beds and their active vermin had wearied and disgusted him. Often he looked back over his shoulder, but when a man has once started West, there's no turning back. He sickened of loneliness. The wilderness frightened him, and the first night in he sat up against a tree and held to the horse's bridle more for comfort than as precaution against theft. Just at day, as he dropped off to sleep, a rough hand shook him to his senses. 'Boy, don't you know better than to sleep on a trail with a horse an Injun can smell ten miles off? Git up and come along with me.' He obeyed automatically, although his imperative companion looked none too savory. He was in that state where he would have welcomed the devil for company.

"They hadn't been together an hour before Purtle had given his complete devotion to the stranger. The boy was one of those fortunate or unfortunate people who must receive approval and sympathy no matter what company they keep. All day his tongue chattered like a girl's. To make the man think well of him he recounted a life history related to the facts about as closely as you and I are to Adam."

Weatherford flicked the ashes off his cigar. "That's mighty close kin sometimes, Judge."

Wilton missed the humor. He was now so lost in his tale he scarcely heard the interruption.

"To hear the boy tell it, he'd been a hell of a blade. As the hard-featured companion looked at the fuzz on his chin, a contemptuous smile lurked behind his dirty beard. Next day, when it was too late, Purtle remembered it. The sun was high when he batted his eyes. He sat up with a jerk and called for Tinker—that was the man's name. It took him several minutes to understand that he had been left alone in the wilderness. The fine brace of pistols, which he didn't know how to shoot, his horse, the companion, had disappeared. The small sack of gold that hung about his neck had been cut away. He sat perfectly quiet for ten or fifteen minutes. He was too sick at heart to eat the remains of the short breakfast left on the ground. After a while he felt thirsty, and he went down to the spring. He drank like a man whose belly is full of a big bait of salt meat. In some way he stumbled to the road. He was too desperate to make plans. He walked toward the West merely because he happened to turn that way.

"Late in the day, from the East, a small caravan of wagons rolled toward him. He trembled so he had to lean for support against a tree. He could not bring himself to speak until the first wagon and its outriders had passed. The immigrant he fixed upon was a hard-bitten man, low and heavy-set, with beard growing on neck and face like a bristly napkin. Beside him sat a raw-boned woman in a dirty calico dress. From under her slatted bonnet stood a snuff mop of slippery ellum. They were riding a two-wheeled cart. At the back hung a coop of chickens. A muley cow was tied to the axle. Purtle walked by the oxen and let the words tumble out of his mouth. The man spoke once. 'Git away.' Purtle turned desperately from the man to the woman and repeated his story. Out of her long face two small eyes showed a slight interest. He was a handsome youth. The rough wear and the open life had worn away much of his softness.

" 'Take the boy on, Dan'l,' said the woman.

" 'Ain't got vittles enough,' the man spat back.

"The oxen had stopped. Dan'l raised the black bull whip. It curled like a snake and cracked over their heads. The beasts swung their necks, and the cart rolled forward. The whip cracked again, and Purtle fell in the road. He closed his eyes with the pain—he never would learn to stand it—and when he opened them again the woman stood over him.

" 'Git up. I told my man to make room for ye.'

"Without other words she turned around and walked back to the cart. Purtle watched the frayed edges of her calico skirt catch the twigs in the road. As she put her foot on the shafts, the dust sifted from a torn hem down the buckskin stockings. He could not tell why, but the sight made him shudder. No other word passed between them until camp was made.

"After three days' travel Dan'l dropped out of the train. Purtle wanted to go on, but he lacked the courage to leave his benefactors. Dan'l gave him an ax, and in two weeks' time they had a pole crib of a sort standing in a small clearing.

For weeks the two men did nothing but girdle trees and clear away for a garden and a few corn patches. By the time the leaves began to turn, Purtle found new pleasures in the hard tasks Dan'l had set him. At first Purtle was shown less consideration than the oxen got. But as his muscles swelled and his shoulders grew heavy, he gradually resented the treatment and began demanding things.

"Unlike the other men who went West, he didn't enjoy the slow deaths of the great trees. There was one special grove he liked. He threw some skins on the pine straw and slept there rather than stay under the same roof with the others. One morning before the stars faded, he woke to the sound of an ax. Dan'l, knowing his pleasure in the spot, had set in to clear it away. He jumped to his feet and asked him what he was doing. Dan'l scarcely straightened up to answer,

" 'I'm cl'aring this piece. Git yer ax.' There was distinct malice in the words. Purtle felt his throat tighten with anger.

" 'If you cut that tree, I'll knock you down,' he said sharply. Dan'l dropped his ax in surprise. He slouched toward the boy.

" 'I'm feeden you too well,' he said.

"Purtle struck toward the beard, and Dan'l fell back into the pine straw. He got up slowly, and they closed. They fought a good while. At last the older man gave in and walked toward the pole crib. The woman had seen them. As they sat down to breakfast, Purtle noticed a strange disquieting look on her face. He took his bread and went outside to eat.

"After the short evening meal he wandered out to his grove, dropped his clothes and went down to the spring to wash. Whether it was fear of becoming like the man and woman, or whether it was from his own squeamish nature, the boy could never lie down with the day's sweat on him. It was the last of the full moon. As he idled back to his sleeping place, the light winds dried his body. He took some time in returning. The white light fell down the trees and broke among the bushes and about the shadows on the soft straw. The cold water had soothed his fatigue. He had been almost drugged

with sleep when he went to the spring, but as he lay down
upon the skins, he felt fresh and strangely excited. There
was a break in the trees above. The night was so bright he
could see the resin under his nails. He ran his hands down
his arms and rubbed off the thin stiffness which a wind-dry
leaves, looked at his flesh. It shone like satin. He lifted a leg
and stretched it, stretched his arms. Feeling the warm glow
under the skin, he let his eyes travel over his nakedness. For
the first time he knew the delight in the discovery of his body.
He sighed, and, after a little, with the sweet pine in his lungs
and the wind in his ears, dropped gently into sleep.

"How long he lay in the deep sleep which followed he had
no way of knowing. He remembered waking suddenly with
the feeling of vermin crawling over his body. He lay still
until he might collect his senses and throw off the hideous
dream. Then he felt pressure against his side and a stale odor
in the air, disagreeable and vaguely familiar. Something
crawled over his chest toward his neck. He leaped to his
knees in terror, but two rough arms caught and held him to
the pallet. A voice near his ear whispered:

" 'Lie down, purty boy. Hit's me, Dan'l's woman.'

"He shook her off and drew to the edge of the skins.

" 'What are you doing here?' he asked fiercely under his
breath. There was still some light in the woods, and he could
see the woman, with no more than some sort of a shift over her
angular bones. It was the first time he had seen a woman like
this. She drew toward him and caressed his arms.

" 'I seen ye whup him this mornen,' she whispered. The
words seemed coated in grease and the stale smell of onions.
She drew closer, pressing the warmth of her body against his.
Her touch was repulsive, but strangely fascinating, and he
found himself thinking how odd it was that she had warmth
and movement to her limbs. He let her take his arms and put
them about her.

"Later, after she left and slouched through the grove toward
the crib, he stood by a tree and vomited. For several days he
scrubbed in the spring, but he couldn't wash clean the smell

of stale snuff. It covered him like a plaster. In the heat of the day's work it would rise and almost smother him. The following nights he lay awake, dreading and desiring her return."

Mr. Weatherford cleared his throat. "Well, in his fix, she was better'n nothing; but I'd call it mighty poor pickings."

Wilton's voice had risen in the steady flow of his speech. Slight drops of perspiration gathered on his forehead. "For weeks," he continued, barely noticing his listener's comment, "he thought about running away, but he lacked the courage. At last he grew used to his paramour. In time he grew bold and together they shut old Dan'l up in the lean-to. He was now master in the house, but by laying-by time the tension had become unbearable. He was always on guard against the revenge which smoldered in Dan'l's eyes. So as soon as the corn was gathered and made into whisky, Purtle with the woman's help tied the old man to his bed, nailed up the crib, and drove away. The look of sullen hatred on the bearded face haunted him for days. It is still a scar on his memory. It would not let him rest, so the moment the liquor and cattle were sold, he bought a horse and abandoned the woman."

Wilton rose. "I've kept you up mighty late with this, Mr. Weatherford."

"Not a-tall, sir. I found it a mighty pretty story."

"Perhaps tomorrow, or next day, you will let me finish it."

"The *Coosa Belle* sails day after tomorrow, toward midnight," said Weatherford. "Have supper with me again."

"You must eat with me next time," and Wilton inclined his head.

Weatherford interrupted hurriedly. "No, I'll have my packing to do and my bill to settle. You furnish the tale, and I'll buy the victuals."

Weatherford took the cape, the stick, the tall silk hat from the servant and, bowing graciously, handed them to his guest. Wilton showed pleasure at this delicate attention. As he stepped into the night, Weatherford followed him out and lingered on the piazza until he had disappeared. At last he turned away. Upon his face night had left its dark patch, and his two eyes were as hard as marbles. As he walked through the lobby, the few loiterers shifted, followed his sure tread up the steps, its heavy purpose, and, attentive until released by the door slamming, slouched back into their vacancy.

On their last evening together a table had been set on the upper piazza of the Coosa River Inn. A brandy bottle and glasses were its only ornaments. The hotel backed upon the river's edge, and far down the line of warehouses the two men could see the *Coosa Belle* moored to her wharf. Her decks were being piled with the season's first cotton bales. Weatherford's baggage was already aboard. His bill had been settled. When the warning whistle blew, he had only to put on his hat, walk down the three flights of stairs and in ten minutes be across the gangplank. It was nine o'clock. The boat would leave sometime between ten and midnight. There was nothing to disturb Lawson Wilton and his companion as they took the air or talked together for the last time. A fresh breeze blew from the river and swept the smoke from the cigars into the blue evening. From a distance the steady-falling water from the Staircase roared like winds turning over in faraway caves. Weatherford had been unusually quiet, and there was a positive set to his features; but the man who looked on him as a friend, as more than a friend, did not notice the change. He had thought all evening only of the other's courage, the direction to his life which Wilton had at once sensed on their meeting in the bar, his simple, generous nature, the small vanities—all those virtues which Wilton saw in the older man had by their mere existence brought him to the verge of a coherent plan of action. He drained his glass. As he set it upon the table, his hand trembled slightly.

"It's your turn, Judge." There was the faintest shade of irony in Weatherford's voice. "Unless you're still hungry, my part of the bargain is over."

"You've more than done your part, Mr. Weatherford." With no other introduction, Wilton continued:

"The next period of my friend's life was vague. He threw himself into the coarse debaucheries of the frontier. He told himself it was to forget. And when his memory had grown dull, he sobered up and joined a trading expedition among the Indians. He went into that with an enthusiasm that brought him respect from his rough companions. But just when he had become clever at cheating and swapping, he lost interest and settled into heavy gloom. He came out of that to enter land speculation, but the same thing happened, and in the end he was robbed of his share of the profits. Year succeeded year as he fled from that thing in his character which had sent him West. Never was he able to keep to any fixed plan of action. He was always playing a part, always on the defensive. He could not make himself feel the lust for possession and destruction which those who grasped the wilderness had. He could only pretend to have the vast energy of these men. The stretches of forest and river which once filled his imagination with delight now made him afraid. He drifted into the law, to pick up their leavings; but even here, in a more tiresome way he must struggle with the same desire to take and to hold, to destroy and pass on."

"What a singular fellow," said Weatherford, flicking the ashes of his cigar into the river below.

"The day he turned thirty he suddenly realized that the hard-fisted brutality which settles a new country had passed in Alabama. All about him were prosperous towns and wide-stretching cotton plantations. The life he wanted to live, the material to feed his senses, lay all about him, but he was forbidden to enjoy it. His fortunes had advanced but little in the thirteen years; and yet he had suffered all the weary pain that piles up a frontier fortune. The knowledge of his predicament, or what he believed to be his knowledge, covered him in clouds of despair.

"Precisely at that moment when one day more would have meant ruin, he met the person who was to become the controlling influence in his life. C—— was a large planter, reputed to have property in land and slaves scattered all over the black belt. He began by giving Purtle a large part of his legal business. The fees were handsome, paid in cash, and always in fresh bank notes. Purtle paid little attention to this, as his patron had large affairs and was much in New Orleans where he might easily obtain new money. Even if he had realized what he was taking, it is doubtful whether he would have backed away from the career he was destined to follow, so cleverly did the other lead him into its toils.

"Soon the two men were boon companions. C—— flattered Purtle as a man his mistress. He showed genius in discovering his desires. They would go down the river to Mobile or to New Orleans and stay weeks at a time on a frolic. Each time C—— gave him some handsome gift. Once it was a costly gold-faced watch with a black velvet cord to hang it on. At another time an entire wardrobe from the best tailor in the city. Purtle delighted in clothes. The tones of the rich fabrics were chosen with elaborate care. Every movement of his body felt their caress. Until their newness wore away, he reeled in continual self-intoxication."

In the dark, upon Weatherford's face there crept the feeling of disgust a man feels when he has trod underfoot some soft, slimy object.

"On one occasion," continued Wilton, "—it might be called the fatal occasion of payment—C—— had taken a large house in New Orleans for their cavortings. Here and elsewhere in the city they met their friends. The frolic lasted for two weeks. It began in mild enough fashion, with the sampling of the choicest menus that famous city prepares so well. From there it proceeded, at an artfully regulated pace, to a grand and sustained climax of two days' debauchery, in which each of the five senses was gorged. Midway of the drama, C—— went off on some business of his own and left Purtle for an entire day to his own devices. This he could not tolerate. He sent a note to Yvonne, a fancy woman of their acquaintance, inviting her to dinner. When she arrived, she entered upon the arm of a mere lad, a robust fellow, with clean shanks, a clear eye, and sandy-colored hair. The moment Purtle saw him, he was pleased. Here was another world to conquer. But when he looked squarely at the innocent face above the black evening stock and the uncomfortable clothes—they were not ill-fitting, his discomfort was a lack of ease—he felt the luxury of a selfless emotion. He would appoint himself the boy's protector and disengage him from the reckless course his youth was bringing him to.

"Purtle sent the evening smoothly and quickly along. He carefully timed the wine, instructing the servant to under-fill the guest's glass. He measured his success by Yvonne's hostility, which increased as the evening wore along. She was not only angry; she was bored, for under the influence of the wine her escort had run away with the conversation. It kept strictly to one subject: himself. She became sullen. She had no interest in an adolescent's discovery that there was a vastly exciting experience awaiting his explorations. When he spoke about his family raising sugar on Bayou LaFourche, it seemed an extraordinary fact. The thought of his widowed mother and what he would do to anyone who might molest her brought tears to his eyes. But the villainy of their overseer was the climax to his narrative. 'He tried to come along with me,' the boy said thickly, 'and help sell the sugar.' In his voice was defiance, the youthful resentment of help from an elder. As he threw back his head, Purtle could scarcely control a smile, for it rolled with the wine. 'Told him to go to Hell. I could take care of myself.' Then suddenly the boy's already flushed face darkened. He remembered the woman. 'Excuse me, ma'm. I forgot there was a lady here.'

"It was no difficult matter for Purtle to persuade the lad to share their apartments. C—— welcomed him in the hearty bluff way he could assume so easily. The three of them rioted along together. Purtle's interest was completely absorbed in his self-appointed chaperonage. He taught the boy those things he must know with great skill, never allowing him to overload or dull his senses with improper excesses. On the last days he watched him perform with the pleasure of a crafts-man surveying a finished piece of work. He was so absorbed in the game he failed to notice the preliminary warning of disaster to himself.

"On the last night the great doors had been locked upon the guests, and C—— had pocketed the key. In mockery he announced himself King of Misrule and, taking no active part in what followed, watched and at times directed the advancing stages of the, shall I say, drama. When that point had been reached when only the strongest of the guests were on their feet, C—— took Purtle by the arm and led him toward the boy's chambers. They found him lying on the bed in that state when man is most defenseless. He raised up and leered at them. The woman, Yvonne, was sleeping in the fumes of wine. The boy looked at her and winked heavily, 'Ain't it fun?' he said thickly. Purtle reproached himself for his neglect.

" 'Dress him,' commanded C——. This was done with difficulty, as the boy kept repeating the monotonous phase, 'I don' want to go.' When his boots had finally been pulled on, C—— stood him on his feet and, coolly grasping him by the back of the neck, began to choke him. The boy struggled, but in his state he was no match for the other. They fell across the bed, and he kicked and squirmed for several minutes. Purtle could not move. He saw the fair face darken, saw the arms wave aimlessly about, clutch feebly at the flat thumb crushing in the windpipe.

"Purtle turned away, faint, with the squeeze of nausea at his stomach. At that moment steps could be heard outside the door. The handle turned, and a reveler stumbled in. Purtle, pale with fright, rushed toward him to thrust him out, when he heard C——'s voice, jovial and confidential, 'A nice place to leave the world from, eh, Edmonds?' Edmonds swayed about the door with a leer on his flabby mouth. Purtle turned his head and stared at C——. He must have shown fright, for he heard C—— say, as if the voice had traveled far, 'Pale with envy, Purtle?' Purtle glanced at the bed. The boy had been thrown, face down, across the body of the woman.

"Briskly, C—— walked toward Edmonds and said in the tones of an elder brother, 'Make way for us out there. I'm going to take the boy to his hotel.' Edmonds turned, still leering, and stumbled down the hall toward the ballroom.

"'Make way for the dead,' he shouted with the effort at mockery, 'make way for the dead.' C—— lifted the body over his shoulder, and as he did so the woman stirred. 'We must get out of here,' C—— spoke brusquely. 'Behind the wardrobe there's a carpetbag with ten thousand dollars in gold. Pick it up and follow me to the carriage.'

"Purtle, shaking and almost hysterical, did as he was told. In single file they marched through the revelers. Quickly passing into the courtyard, they found the carriage with its black driver in his box. The body was deposited between them, and Purtle heard the heavy wheels rumble upon the cobblestones as they rolled out into Dauphine Street. In an hour they were outside the city. Purtle kept his face straight before him upon a button in the cushions, but out of the corner of his eye he could not help seeing the slumped figure whose arms and head hung so stiffly forward. At some point on the Mobile road the carriage pulled up. C—— got out and ordered Purtle to follow. He did again as he was bid. There were two horses saddled and waiting. They mounted and galloped away. Up to this moment no explanation had been advanced, and Purtle had asked for none. There had been no need. He understood by instinct what must follow.

"They rode along in the night, made blacker by their silence. Purtle sank into a state of bitter despair. He was lost in the misery of one of his old fits. In the past year he had put them from his mind. He had never expected to be tortured again. Yet precisely when he felt the greatest security, when the future seemed clearest, this thing had happened. It could not be accident. It was a deliberate warning of that Fate which he at last felt would never leave off driving him toward the carefully concealed end it had prepared. C—— was its present instrument. As he turned with a feeling of surrender, the first marks of day blurred the gloom. C—— was whistling a soft gay tune, and he realized with horror that C—— had dismissed the recent past as a man might forget his breakfast.

"He cut short the tune and gave his horse the reins. The sky to the east snapped open like a colored fan. Purtle was tempted to flee, but without any motion of his he felt his animal jerk its head and spread its feet upon the road. He had the curious feeling that C—— tolled him along by an invisible halter. After a while C—— pulled in to a trot, then to a walk. Purtle rode up beside him, ready for what might happen. He did not have long to wait. The sky washed clean, and the red sun sliced the road. Purtle shuddered. It rose slowly like a molten door shutting off all escape. As it swung free of the earth, C—— turned and spoke.

" 'I've been testing you, Purtle, and you'll do.' C—— paused as if thinking how to phrase his words and continued. 'I'll tell you a secret. I'm head of a fine body of speculators. Land pirates, some call us. And I'm going to take you into the band.' He smiled like one who is conferring a great favor. 'And what's more you will take your place in the fourth realm.'

"You must understand, Mr. Weatherford, that the band was divided into four realms. At the top were C—— and two others. Purtle made the fourth. The fourth realm decides the strategy, gives the orders to the next below who perfect the plans in their districts and are responsible for their successful execution. They oversee those who do the detail work, who work, you might say, for their victuals and their board. There is the last division, the 'feelers.' They are men from all walks of life. It is their business to turn in the evidence and all information the others might need. If any of the workers are hard-pressed, it is their duty to hide them."

Weatherford leaned forward in his chair, and his voice hissed, "Yes, yes."

"At this point C—— leaned over in his saddle—I've a good memory and my friend was eloquent, Mr. Weatherford, as well he might be on this subject—C—— leaned very close to Purtle and said with a mad look in his eyes, 'Only two men know me for what I am. You will be the third. I've watched you. I can judge men just like that.' He snapped his thick fingers. 'I know you better than your mammy ever knew you. You ain't got the grit to destroy evidence.'

"As C—— looked at Purtle he felt he lacked the grit to do anything.

" 'Now take this ten thousand in gold.' C—— idly patted the heavy saddle-bags as if he were an old-field school-teacher emphasizing an obvious point. 'The Supreme Court of the United States can't take it away from me. Why? Because the *evidence* of the transfer is oozing its way to the unknown bottom of a swamp sink-hole. I make it a point never to let any man in on our speculations unless he's got the grit to get rid of the *evidence*. I'm making an exception in your case, for you will be useful to me in other ways. Already, although you don't know it, you've doubled my profits in six months.' Purtle looked astounded, and C—— smiled the smile of all great men at the lesser understanding of their inferiors. 'You remember that suit: Ames vs. McAnnelly, where your client had caught the runaway nigger and resold him. You made the distinction between stealing and selling the property out-right, which is a criminal offense, and recovering and selling it, after the runaway had been advertised in the papers, which made it a breach of trust and only a civil offense. I tell you, fellow, your wits are sharp. If you had a little grit, I'd make you my partner.' He looked at his companion and shook his head sadly. 'But you ain't.'

" 'Before you won that case, we could only steal a nigger once. Now we can steal him as many as four times, although three times is enough. It don't pay to be a hog in anything. By the fourth time he is too well advertised. It's not safe. Why, man, I made nine thousand dollars out of the sale of a blacksmith picked up in Lebanon, Tennessee, and would have made more except I had to take in some of our counterfeit on the last trade. Amusing, ain't it?'

" 'That black nearly got me in bad trouble. The man liked his marster and didn't want to run away. He'd been given a likely-looking mulatto wench for wife and he hadn't lived long with her. But I told him if he'd let us sell him a few times, we'd run him across to freedom and steal his wife for him later. I sometimes for the excitement entice the slaves away myself. You've no idea how lonesome I get with only my grand schemes for company.' He sighed and was silent a few seconds; then resumed rapidly. 'Well, this old nigger got mighty tired of being run all over the country. He got suspicious, too, for instead of selling him in Kentucky, we ran him south. In Arkansas he'd about made up his mind to talk. The yellow wench was terrible on his mind, and if it hadn't been for the cunning of one of my men, we would have got into considerable embarrassment. He told the old nigger his wife was waiting for him in a shack on the Mississippi, ready to be run across the line. My man took him in a boat and left him in the swamps. It set up raining and rained for three days without stopping. The nigger wandered around and got lost. When the marster's bloodhounds ran him down, he was stiff dead.'

"C—— suddenly dropped the subject of his speculations and cast his eyes at the woods and the sky. He seemed pensive and melancholy. Directly he spoke, and his voice was soft and brooding, 'I'm always up by first light. I am only myself this time of day, Purtle. The world is alone, and I'm alone. The sun is so close and strong. It refreshes and prepares me for my responsibilities.' He lifted his shoulders with a heavy sigh. 'Ah, when I was younger at the game, I had a heap more fun than I'm having now. Ambition takes away the pleasure in life. Here am I the greatest man in the Southwest, and hardly anybody knows it. Some day though . . . but never mind about that. When there were only two or three of us working together, I used to dress up like a preacher and hold camp meetings. I have a fascinating speaking voice and, with ten gallons of sorrow in my eyes, I let the simple fools have it. When the shouting got general and everybody was taken up with the sisters coming through, my companions were slipping about and unhitching the teams. We used to get away with considerable stock that way. I remember once in North Carolina I stole a man's whole flock of sheep and sold them back to him the same night. It's true he was avaricious and blind. That's the thing. Look for the weakness in a man. It takes that to go high up in this game. That's why so many bold and clever speculators have fallen by the way. They can't smell a man out. I always could. See the flaw. Think fast. Have grit.' He waved his hand toward Purtle and smiled contentedly. 'That's all there is to it.' "

Judge Wilton paused; knocked the ashes from his cigar stump and tossed it over the wrought-iron balcony into the river. A few clouds had blown over the sky, drawing a dark shade between the two men. In the distance the lights from the *Coosa Belle* swam the water like colored driftwood. Harsh voices of command rose in staccato tones above the stevedores' chant, and the chant had risen freely upon the air, telling of lighter burdens and the end of loading. Wilton poured another glass of brandy and gulped it down. The gentleman from Kentucky neither drank nor spoke. He was very still. He might have been asleep but for his quick heavy breathing. Wilton coughed and continued:

"It was in this fashion that my colleague became the creature of the most sinister figure in the entire Southwest. Willingly he allowed himself to be whirled into the center of the speculations. There was no complaint to be made from the partnership. Most of the ventures had been executed at a safe distance from his county. Mules stolen in Kentucky and Tennessee, slaves picked up everywhere, even unidentified murders Purtle could stomach—as long as his profits rolled in with pleasing regularity and he was free from any direct responsibility for the crimes. He soon began to persuade himself that he had no sort of responsibility, either direct or indirect. For a man of his nature this was not hard to do. He even thought of retiring, taking a wife and living the pleasant life of a cotton planter. His share of the profits had been enough to buy and stock a thousand-acre plantation on the Alabama River.

"Then one day his composure was shattered. He received an order to meet at an appointed place. It was on an old Creek trace, near the abandoned sight of a small Indian village, a depot used by those speculators whose business it was to run the stolen property out of the country. Here C—— announced his plans for the future. He had abandoned his earlier caution, as there must have been thirty men present. He told them he meant to set up an empire, a pirates' empire in the Southwest, and he would begin the first campaign by arousing the slaves to revolt. This would throw, so he argued, the states into chaos and allow his men to seize the strategic places, the banks, the rivers and turnpikes, the mint at New Orleans. With these things under his control, the blacks spreading murder and rapine through the land, he would raise the black flag at New Orleans, the city set out for his capital. As the plans for this insurrection were discussed, Purtle realized that he had become a pawn in the hands of a madman. He looked about him, hoping others had also come to the same conclusion, but that way of escape was closed. They were spellbound. Not a man there saw it for what it was—a maniac's dream, but a dream capable of spreading ruin and destruction.

"After this meeting Purtle went gradually to pieces. The members of the bar advised him to go to the springs for a rest. He couldn't tell them he dared not. *He had been ordered to perfect the plans of the slave insurrection.* He lay awake at night with the ravished faces of women and children hanging from the ceiling. The sins of his past returned to plague him, and the dark clouds of that unknown doom began to gather. This state of mind reached its lowest when he was ordered to take part in the murder of a gentleman from Georgia who had discovered by accident enough evidence to threaten exposure."

Weatherford leaned forward and his voice barked, "Did you say a gentleman from Georgia, Judge Wilton?"

"Yes, sir, and the Georgian was a bold and cunning man. But at last he was done away with in such a way that his family was left under a cloud. It was devilish clever, but Purtle feared its very boldness. Clever in this case failed to destroy his evidence. Why the Georgian's death should have affected Purtle so he could not say, unless it was that he lacked the grit to do the deeds himself. For he wasn't by nature a bad man. From this moment life became unbearable. His nights were tortures, and his days were haunted with the memory of his nights. Then suddenly, as miracles happen, he met a stranger who, unknown to himself, promised to come to Purtle's rescue." Wilton leaned forward and made his voice very distinct. "There was so much honor on the stranger's face and such obvious integrity that his very image gave Purtle the grit, if not enough to destroy evidence, at least enough to make up his mind to pull away from C—— and all his ventures. The moment he reached this decision his mind became clear. He recovered his composure. The horns of his dilemma crumbled in his hands. . . ."

The deep-toned whistle of the *Coosa Belle* sounded, moaning and quavering, down the night air. Both men gave a start as men do who, having forgotten the expected crisis, hear the fatal signal that must bring it on. Wilton rose abruptly and advanced with outstretched arms. His voice shook with emotion.

"Perhaps, if it is my good fortune for us to meet again, Mr. Weatherford, you shall hear the rest of my story. The ending, I know, will give you genuine pleasure."

But there was no answering pressure upon the outstretched hands. They fell, unclasped to his side. Wilton, like a man who feels a blow about to be delivered in the dark, staggered back against the balcony. The man he called his friend moved silently toward him.

"Weatherford? You mistake me, sir. My name's not Weatherford."

Wilton grasped the railing, and it rang dully as if it had been struck by a block of wood.

"My name . . ." The big man leaned forward and covered his voice with a whisper so low and terrible that it fell scarcely an inch behind Wilton's ear. "My name," he breathed, "is Armistead McIvor!"

Wilton stiffened and shook with a rigor. Helplessly he watched the great thigh draw back, saw the ridiculously small foot hang for a moment in the dark, grunted when it sprang forward and kicked him over the balcony.

Beside the stacks on the *Coosa Belle* a column of vapor, white and hot, shot upward. As Armistead McIvor lifted his hat to his head, the shrill thin boom of the whistle's last warning blew down the night. He turned and walked briskly toward the stair landing. Five minutes later he stepped from the gangplank, between the piled bales, onto the *Coosa Belle's* upper promenade.

4

Sheriff Botterall's place lay in the hills above Wetumpka. The hills were not high. They ended abruptly back of the town, lifting gradually northward around gaps, across creeks, to a slow plateau. Their broad wooded shoulders were bald where the small farms lay. Here and there, lonely plantations took up the richer spots. On the western border the waters of the Coosa Staircase cut their steep way for a stretch of miles, falling in graduated rapids to the town below. Beyond the warehouses which followed the banks the Coosa met the Tallapoosa, combined with it, and swept south as the Alabama. On the Staircase the water tumbled over the rapids to flow calmly, swiftly through deep pools, the watery landings. This alternation, rapids and pools, came to an end in the steamboat channel at the town. Some of the pools were as wide as small lakes.

In dry weather the banks were very high. Near the tops of these cliffs, a hundred yards above the water, dark scoops in the clay walls marked a line of caves that could not be reached except by way of the trees which screened their hollow dry mouths. A stranger sitting in the dog-run of the Botterall house, which sat a quarter back from the left bank, might easily look toward the other side and never know that the caves were there. For long stretches tall, great-trunked pines stood straight up from the edges of the pools, spreading their tops almost level with the fields above and brushing them in a wind. At a distance they looked like a fringe of green meadow, but a sinister meadow, for the noise of the Staircase rolled pounding through the green needles, carrying for miles around its steady solid warning.

At night, a head lifted slowly through the pasture's dark rim. It lifted so slowly it might have been the black shadow of the rising moon. It suddenly froze in the pine top, fixed on the sheriff's house, the still fields, his barn; then slowly disappeared beneath the tender branches. At this same hour, this same night six weeks before, men on horses had drawn a circle, close and ever closer, about Cameron McIvor who lay in his bed with eyes shut, to open once in violence, then shut forever.

The pine top shook, and a figure dropped to a limb which brushed the pasture, swung hand over hand to its end, dropped to the bank's sharp edge and lay there, holding to the bushes. Another figure, more clumsily, followed out the limb and dropped. Moving cautiously, it placed its mouth to the other's ear and whispered:

"What'll we do now, Pleas?"

"Circle the fields and slip up to Botterall's house from the south. The dogs will smell you and bark."

"Then what?"

"Draw'm off toward town. By that time I'll be at the barn and can reach the house."

"Reckon Botterall won't wake up?" Eli's voice carried some misgiving.

"I can walk on a may-pop and not bust it," Pleasant answered shortly.

"All right." Eli's voice quavered with excitement. "Here I go."

He reached for a bush to pull by. The other's hand detained him.

"Eli?"

"What?"

"You sure you know what to do, now?"

"As soon as I draw off the dogs, I'm to keep down the river road until I reach the creek."

The other nodded in the half-dark.

"That's right. Bob Pritchard will meet you there," said Pleasant.

"You watch out for yourself." Eli looked toward his nephew and friend.

"Tell Bob," Pleasant continued in a low voice, "I'll be in the loft of Botterall's house, over the space that joins the ell to the back porch."

Eli nodded.

"When you and Bob are done, you know where to meet me?"

"Yes. Got your snack, Pleas?" Eli asked. He seemed loath to go.

"Yes, in my breeches."

"Well, I'm gone."

Pleasant felt for his hand and pressed it. Both boys crawled to the top, reached their feet and, hanging over like bears, moved off in opposite directions.

At the edge of the woods Pleasant struck a cow path. It would lead, he knew, to the barn. He put his moccasin in the path, and the soft dust puffed up. This would never do. He picked up a piece of brush and covered the print left by his foot. This done, he walked, a dark brown shadow, along its edge until he reached the barn. The building was set partly in the woods. He noticed well its location before he stepped softly along the square-hewn log walls. In the darkness of their joints he waited for the signal. Presently the moon rose high, and he leaned as still as a saw-log, listening for the first suspicious growl from the dogs.

From his cave across the river he had made out the general positions of everything, but the small things that trip a man up he had been too far off to see. Now quickly his eye ran along the heavy barnlot fence. It was extra well built and he knew that there it was the sheriff kept his wild horses. The house itself stood not many yards away from the lot, a double log house built of deep yellow timbers hewn smooth and close, joined to its ell and covered by a slanting roof. The run between the cribs extended into another open space which tied the ell to the house. It was in this space that the eating table stood, so that the sheriff might feel the breezes during the hot months. Above the open space hung the loft. It was reached by a ladder in the wall. There was a scalding pot turned over in the ashes, an ash hopper to the side. In the rear the smokehouse squatted, and the drying clothes hung from there to the end of the ell. They hung in their stiff dry with no wind to shake them. The night was hot. As Pleasant felt the sweat itch his naked brown waist—he had let the sun turn him the color of clay as the surest disguise—he remembered it was wash day, and wash day was Monday, and Monday was the date set for the *Coosa Belle* to go down the river.

Pleasant grew a little nervous waiting. Everything was going well, but it was time to hear the sudden scramble from under the porch and the hounds' baying-bark. Only the night noises broke the stillness. Suddenly from behind he heard a loud squealing. It sent the blood to his ears. Then another, an unearthly sound to break upon the night's early silence. Then angry pawing. With quick relief he recognized the sound. The wild horses. The animals had discovered him. He had not calculated on any such threat to his plans. He must do something, and at once. The other horses were growing restless, stamping about in their stalls.

He vaulted over the fence, advancing in a running slouch toward the barn, stepped quickly inside and shut the door behind him. He waited a second to get his bearings. To his left was the gear room with harness and saddles hanging on racks or lying huddled on the floor, to the right the corn crib.

It was half full. Down the hall were the stalls made of good stout timbers. He stepped softy forward along the ammonia-soaked straw. He looked sharply at the manure droppings. No matter how pressing his emergency, he must leave no tracks.

The moon was now bright enough to throw an uncertain light through the cracks in the logs. On either side he saw restless heads reaching over the bars. The pawing increased and the low whinnies, but it was before a beautiful gray stallion that he stopped. He was pawing the straw, and it flew in dusty streams between his legs. Suddenly up shook the head and its bright silver mane, and through his teeth and quivering mouth sounded a long, frightened whinny. A mule answered the call of distress. The stallion swung his barb neck and looked at Pleasant. There was a killing look in his wide, bright eyes. In spite of his stress Pleasant could not help admiring the horse's points: the tapering head, the great width between the eyes, the thin-bellowsed nostrils, the deep chest.

In his fierce rage the stallion rose up and beat his hoofs against the fodder rack. They came down with a clatter into the feed box. Pleasant followed with his eyes and saw a small white hen roosting on top of the rack. Pressing her side, a dark shadow waved two evil circles of moist light. The horse's distress was apparent. The hen was his stall mate. The hungry owl had already pushed her near the end of the pole. With a final shove it would knock her off, swoop down and fix its claws in her back and fly away. The stallion had at last managed to rouse her. Now from the fowl's throat sang the long cawk of fear. Pleasant snatched a whip and cracked it. With one flap of its wings the bird of night swept down around the gray's shivering neck, dove upward through the barn, out under the open eaves, to disappear into the night.

This was no good omen. From all the stalls came whinnies and pawings. The noise by this time was bound to have reached the house. Pleasant slipped to the door and looked through a crack. He saw a light swinging low to the ground and coming toward the barn. There was another light in the front room of the house. If he slipped out and around the barn there was a chance of discovery. He did not mean to take such a chance. To make matters worse the dogs set up a barking. Whether they had scented Eli or whether it was the general disturbance made no difference now. His plans had gone astray. Or had they? Thinking quickly, Pleasant climbed to the loft and lay behind the fodder and dried grass. Presently he heard the heavy tread that must be Botterall's and his labored wheeze before the doors. Suddenly there were sharp, high-pitched words: "Now you stay back thar." Yes, that was Botterall's voice.

With a lingering creak the wide doors swung slowly back, and from the yellow light the grotesque likeness of a giant of a man fell across the opening. The sudden thrust of lantern ate it away, and Botterall's head peered around the logs. The mule's box was shaking with his rhythmic kicks. Still uncertain, Botterall advanced no farther than the gear room, throwing the lantern about with his left hand, for the right hung with a plainsman's Colt against his thigh. Then he advanced, giving quick glances at the stalls, softly calling as he slunk along:

"Thar now, my purty. Thar now, Lady Doll. You, sir. Thar now, my purties. Thar now."

Botterall's waist was uncovered, and the rolling mass of flesh fell about his homespun breeches like yeasty dough. He could not see into the loft, where he cast rolling furtive squints— his curly head sat too deep into the shoulders. He satisfied himself that there was no prowler about and planted himself before the stallion.

"Ye couldn't wait till day, hanh? Ye wanted to feel me back ye, hanh? If the moon was brighter, my purty man ..."

The other animals, excited by the mule, raised their hoofs until the barn shook. Botterall whirled quickly for a man his size and spoke aloud:

"Whar's my whup?" He reached for it—Pleasant could hear him feeling along the boards, knew it was missing from its place before he heard the snarl: "Somebody's been in hyar."

There was a pause, a chilling pause, and Pleasant knew that Botterall had found the whip where he had tossed it.

"Come out of that loft, or I'll plug ye." The horses had quieted now at the sound of his voice. "Come out . . ." Botterall raised the Colt and shot five times along the hay. Pleasant counted the cracks as they knocked up the fodder about him. He didn't move. There was still one charge left in the cylinder. He might with any degree of luck jump down upon his enemy. But he would wait. He settled back in the fodder and listened. Words, admonitions rushed through his mind. He must never be hasty, never rush at his enemies. They would in good time fall into his hands. One by one, when their times had come, they would deliver themselves, and he must wait. It was only natural that he wait. But he had learned one thing this night. He had been foolish to listen to Eli and Bob Pritchard, to let them come along. He would always know what to do about the unknown things that were bound to come up. But they . . . Would Eli hear the shots and think him cornered? Eli like all the family was reckless where he loved. If he came plunging toward the barn, all was ruined. And then as Pleasant thought of his young uncle, how they had played together, eaten, and slept together, how they had been closer than brothers, he suddenly realized that his own feelings had changed, that the thing he had to do had crowded everything else from his heart. He kept wishing over and over, hoping his wish might carry to Eli: "Get on down the big road to Bob."

The shots had brought fresh terror to Botterall's animals. For the moment Pleasant had forgotten where he was. He heard Botterall's running waddle and the sound of his whip against the stalls. "Heish, sir. You, sir. What do you mean, madam?" He heard him stop before the mule and pull himself up to beat the animal over the head. At another door he jabbed the ribs of a filly. But it was the sheriff's voice, gentle and commanding, softly promising corn, or a mad gallop that finally brought quiet to the barn. As Botterall went from stall to stall, Pleasant wondered at the power to his voice, that strange

power that all men have who are born to manage stock. As
before Botterall stopped near the stallion. There was a caress,
a reprimand, and the animal threw high his head and nickered.

"You kicked up all this commotion, sir. You wanted me to
back ye. That's what ye wanted. Ye couldn't wait ontel
mornen. You aim to throw me like you done yistiddy, hanh?
I'm a great mind to straddle ye now—what a purty sight we'd
make a-jumpen about in the night."

"You old fool, come on back to bed." The woman's voice,
tired and rasping, spoke from the entrance.

Pleasant crawled slowly from cover, where he could see
better. Botterall had turned and faced the woman. His
whole bearing had changed.

"Git on back to the house, Maude."

"I've never seed sich an old fool. Shooten at rats? Thar's
a plenty in hyar and a plenty at the house."

"I 'lowed somebody'd been snoopen amongst my beastes,"
Botterall answered in a low sullen voice.

"I've told ye foolen with these critturs'd addle your wits."

"You git to the house"—he spoke in sudden fury—" or I'll
lay this hide over yer back."

"No man'll ever tech me," the woman replied, and she lifted
an old hunting rifle across her arms, "long as I can tote Sally
Betts."

He made her no answer, and after a while, with the faintest appeal to her voice, she said, "Lemuel, I wish you'd let this
hyar hoss be. Wild Nelly didn't give me no peace, and now
I'll be bound this crittur'll stomp ye to death."

His voice softened a shade. "Now, git along, Maudy. I'm
a-comen."

She said stubbornly, "I heard ye name it to ride him tonight.
All you've spent on these critturs, I could 'a' had me some
niggers to help about the house."

"Don't like the smell of niggers," Botterall growled.

She made him no answer. As the man and woman faced
each other across the hall of the barn, there was nothing common in their lives but the bitterness of this ancient quarrel.

After a while a voice, not her own, dropped in low horror.
"You'd take the meal bread out'n our mouths, Lemuel, before they'd want."

There was a long wait, broken only by the sheriff's heavy wheezes and an occasional whinny from the restless horses; then, picking up his lantern, Botterall shuffled out of the barn, past the woman without a look her way. She turned and trailed behind him. They had had time to go ten paces when Pleasant dropped from the loft and followed. He knew they would not, in their anger, look back. By the time the couple had reached the porch, he was safely hidden behind the smoke-house. Soon one of the dogs gave a warning growl. With a sudden rush they ran barking toward town. Pleasant waited until he saw them clear the yard. He slid along the porch of the ell, reached the ladder, and climbed noiselessly to the loft.

Above he waited until the darkness left his eyes, then settled softly along the boards. The easy movements of his body, its muscular repose, filled him with a sense of secret strength. To feel the litter with his shoulder sent an even, unbroken flow along his side until, from hip to toe, the flesh fitted tenderly, caressingly, whatever object it touched. Turning his head in a quick, instinctive inspection, he saw his arm glide along a piece of quilt, his fingers fluttering about its edges like a snake's tongue. He watched it drop the cover under his head as if it were no part of his body, as if the hand had a will of its own. Then suddenly he remembered how once on a hunt as he lay under a wild turkey roost waiting for the flock to appear, embodied silence from the yellowing underbrush, he saw the long black body of a Coach whip speed over the greasy sod, movement without sound, lifting from the level earth the spear of its head and its dull frog eye in stately progress—the curving plunge at the scaley bark and the terror in the lizard's blue tail. Slowly he had watched the rigid stroke relax and the sullen spiral unwind to the brush, glide and bend through the crisp yellow leaves, never rustling nor shaking them until beneath their brittle cover it lay in fatal secrecy.

He had somehow sensed then the menace of secret places.

Now he knew. In the darkness of the loft he waited and thought how familiar he had become with the unknown parts of houses, the forbidden areas above the ceiling, beneath the floors. How easily he moved about them, while people slept in their beds, ignorant and helpless, trapped above or below, all of their strength wasted in the daylight. This was how his enemies lived—by the sun and open places, except for that one time when they had blundered about his father's cabin. Their very way of blundering, bringing many men to strike down one, gave their fears away. Pleasant almost laughed to himself. To be at ease in the dark. To know what the long night meant. That was the secret of vengeance. All at once he felt a great pity for the weakness of these men who would fall by his hand; the helplessness of Botterall lying in his troubled bed, the futile tenant of the house he held at his, Pleasant McIvor's, pleasure.

He broke from these thoughts to listen. Faintly, far down the Staircase, fading away at the drums of his ears, he thought he heard an alien sound. He raised himself like an animal and sharpened his ears. Again, after a minute, it sounded up the wind, stronger, less wavering. This time he did not mistake the sound. It was the thin echo of a steamboat whistle. It was the *Coosa Belle* sounding her last warning to the passengers. In a few minutes the fire would leap in the boilers, the black smoke roll from the chimney stacks, the heavy shafts move slowly backward, then lunging and plunging turn the paddle wheels over, churning the water, driving the boat out in the current with its cargo and passengers. His Cousin Armistead was now aboard.

Pleasant dropped from his crouching position. He felt he could not stand this rapid spasm in his chest. His bending ribs must, with the next gulp of air, rip through the skin and fling themselves over the loft. Presently his lungs grew calmer. Soon he was breathing in regular strokes. Upon his lips formed the image of words he dared not murmur even to himself. His eyes stared into the vacant darkness, and in a little while he was asleep.

5

The next morning Botterall, in a great hickory chair, sat at the head of his table. On either side of the square table ranged boys of varying ages. The dishes curved in half-moon around his plate. Thick slices of bacon, a hoe cake, biscuits large as saucers and puffed on top like feather pillows, a pitcher of molasses, fried eggs swimming in dark bacon grease, a bowl of gravy. In steady movement he lifted the food to his plate, from the plate to his mouth. All ate in silence. The smallest boy, toward the end of the meal, spoke once:

"Pap, air you a-goen to ride Gray today?"

Botterall looked up but made no answer. The women came silently from the kitchen with warm platters of bread and meat.

Botterall slid his knife under a fried egg, poised it midway between the plate and his mouth, and paused to listen.

"Somebody in a hell of a hurry," he growled through his food, then neatly ran the egg into his mouth. Before a third egg could be eaten, clear hard hoofbeats came over the rise near the house, slowed down, and a rider drew up his mount in the sand by the open run. The sheriff glanced over his shoulder, saw it was one of his deputies. He was a little man with a bright, shifty eye and a sharp face.

"Sheriff," he said, "Judge Wilton fell off the balcony at the Coosa River Inn and busted his brains out."

Botterall deliberately lifted the syrup pitcher and poured the dark liquid over his bread.

"They found him," continued the deputy, "lying there with his hand in the water. I saw it. The water had washed it plumb white. It was wrinkled like a old woman's hand."

Botterall slipped his knife through the middle prong of

the fork. With quick regular strokes he squared the bread.
"Sheriff, you better make haste."

Never lifting his eyes from the plate, Botterall spoke: "Expect me to bury him? I ain't his folks." The knife went rapidly from plate to mouth.

"It was cur'us to see the water run through his fingers." The deputy raised his hand in the air to demonstrate, bent his thick hairy fingers, squinted his eyes with sly triumph.

Botterall turned at last and looked squarely at his deputy. "If a dead man's hand is in the water," he said gruffly, "do you expect the river to run away from it?"

There was a loud guffaw from his eldest son, a gangling boy with large head set on a scrawny neck.

The deputy dropped his voice. "They say as how he might have been knocked off." As he spoke, the little man stuck his head forward like a ferret, to see whether this last piece of information would shake his superior's composure. But his watery eyes failed to keep the least direction, and he withdrew to the wall and looked out toward the fields. Botterall pushed the dishes away and, picking up a pitcher of buttermilk, washed his breakfast down. Very daintily, with the fourth finger of his right hand, he wiped away the white stains from his walrus mustache.

"Of course now," said the deputy with fresh courage, "thar it is. When a man drinks as much as Judge Wilton . . ."

The sheriff rose from the table, broke a straw from the broom, and picked his teeth in careful order.

"Never could abide a purty man," he reflected. "Never saw one yet could hold his licker."

After a little Botterall's horse was brought around. He swung into the seat with a large man's active grace, and the two men slow-loped toward Wetumpka. The boys got up from the table and the women sat down. Pleasant from his hiding-place above reached in his pocket and brought out a cold pone of bread. He ate it slowly, listening carefully to what was said below. The women might tell him something about Botterall's habits he wanted to know.

Late the same afternoon the hickory chairs were ranged in their usual places across the porch of the store at Buyckville. One chair, large and sturdy, alone stood empty. Its wide, sagging bottom was in the direct rays of the declining sun. The porch was full of men, but no one chose to dull the shiny amber seat. They preferred to lounge against the posts or sit without support of any kind, their shoulders hunched upon their chests, dangling their feet over the porch's sides, and whittling.

Mr. Quintus Harrison stepped from the cool shadows of his store into the open door and looked down the gradual slant of the red sandy pike. Shading his eyes—there was no need to shade them; they were turned to the south—he spoke absently:

"He's late today."

There came a pause to the loungers' conversation. After a little, as if the matter had been considered from every angle, Abner Buchanan broke the silence.

"Maybe he's found one hoss he's afraid to ride."

The faintest flicker of impatience shaded the storekeeper's thin lips. He pulled out his heavy gold watch. It lay for a moment in his fragile hand, and the black-ribboned fob dropped like a flag between the long bony fingers. The speaker took this gesture as a reprimand and said no more. Mr. Harrison lingered a few moments longer in the doorway. As long as he remained on the porch, there was silence from the loungers. Somehow his person never failed to bring a constraint to the idle talk, even upon the halts between stories. What it was about him that forced this reticence the people at Buyckville had often discussed and had as often left unresolved. His wife they could understand, with her head stuck high like a turkey hen's, and his son, "that Damon," wild in his ways and with the mad glint about his eyes that is so often found in overbred horses. These ways they could understand and set out of their minds. But in the eight years that Mr. Harrison had been in the neighborhood, moving up from the low country below Montgomery to set up in business among them, he had shown the slightest degree of intimacy with but one man—Lem Botterall.

It was not that he was disliked. It was rather that he was still a stranger, and a stranger from his own preference. He met everybody with the same gentle courtesy, never varying his bow, whether it was to child or old man. But the most curious thing about Mr. Harrison was the way he looked after his business or didn't look after it. He kept the store at a distance just as he kept people. Nobody had ever seen him sit down inside or hang about with the loafers on the porch. Always, whenever anybody came to buy, they found him standing quietly in the doorway or behind the counter, or walking impatiently to and fro like a customer in a hurry.

In time people took to waiting on themselves, making their own change and their own settlements at the end of the year. They even went so far as to hand him things to take to the house for his wife. Not long after he had set up business among them the sporting element at Buyckville was raised to a high pitch of excitement. They had discovered infinite possibilities in the storekeeper's strange habits. Very quietly bets were placed as to whether he "would ever set and rest himself." For months those who had money up, as well as a large body of spectators, gathered in the mornings as soon as the doors opened. They watched him evasively from the corner of their eyes. Always they found him the same, attired in snow-white linen, carefully folded stock, black slippers—only when he rode abroad did he wear boots—with the faintest stain of tobacco on his shirt, "standing like a man dressed for his own funeral," as Rod Heflin, who was known to bet on anything from a fly to a woman, put it bitterly. Rod had been the first man to see the betting possibilities of the merchant. At first he lost only a two-year-old hen, but that a man could show such indifference to his business and the porch's society was so contrary to Rod's knowledge of human nature that he grew reckless. No sooner had he lost the hen than he wagered a gallon of whisky; then his sorrel mule, and finally his crop.

In time Mr. Harrison was accepted as the hills were accepted. He was to be lived with but never understood. So on this particular afternoon as soon as the loungers saw him return to the back part of the store and heard his familiar steps among the whisky barrels, a small redheaded man threw his stick away, brushed the shavings from his homespun clothes, closed his knife and, leaning over on his left hip, dropped it down his long pocket. This was, as all knew, a prelude to a yarn.

"The worst beat I ever was at a trade," he said after he had commanded the proper attention, "was from a preacher"— he paused and winked—"a Campbellite preacher."

"Christian preacher, sir. Thar's no Campbellite faith." This sharp voice came from a lean, raw-boned old man, whose back was as stiff as his new homespun breeches. There were subdued smiles and winks, when the redheaded Abner continued solemnly:

"Now, that's puzzlen. In Tennessee where I was liven at the time, Brother Macon, unless my memory's gone plumb back on me, they was a big faith of Campbellites holding forth."

"That's what the ignorant call the Christians, Abner Buchanan. The ignorant and the unlettered."

"Now do tell. Well, I'm glad to know it." Abner winked broadly.

"You knew it all the time, sir," said Brother Macon sharply.

"Well, anyhow I was out hunten cattle, and a friend told me he wanted a special good milk cow. He offered me solid money if I could git him one. And it had been named to me that a Campbellite preacher by the name of Ezekiel Baugh had a herd of mighty fine cows—that's what this ignorant man called him, Brother Macon, a Campbellite preacher."

Brother Macon rose from his chair as if he would leave, spat, and sat back down in great indignation. After he had been thoroughly baited—it was known by all that Brother Macon had two loves, his church and a good story—Abner went on:

"Going out to his place, I met a man in the road and I

asked him if he knew this preacher. 'Why, to be shore. Ever-body knows Brother Baugh,' he said. 'I just passed him a mile back.' 'How'll I know him, stranger, I'm new to these parts?' The stranger thought a while, flicked a hoss fly from his mare's neck and lowed in a voice that sounded like a saw. 'Well,' he says, 'he's a little ornery-looken baldhead man, riden in an old woman's buggy and driving a hoss with his mane on the wrong side of the neck.'

"Of course I didn't have no trouble finden him after that description. I told him my trouble, and jest as polite as life he turned around and went back with me. 'A Christian duty,' he put it, 'to help a man out.' You never saw such a clever man. Everbody told me I could believe *anything he said*. The Campbellite, excuse me, Brother Macon, the Christian faith, don't allow a brother to take advantage of a heathen, like us Baptists. I soon found this out. He talked so purty about brotherly love, I could hardly wait to git back to town and take my letter out of the First Baptist and drag it over to his faith and say, 'Here's a lost sinner, take him in.' "

Abner waited for the run of snickers at Brother Macon's snort. All over the porch men began to draw their backs up and sit at attention.

"Well, men, we struck a pastur of as purty a bunch of milk cows as ever you saw. The preacher looked 'm over and with a wave of his hand said,"—Abner waved his own in a wide sweep that took in the universe—" 'You may have any cow in the pastur but one, and that's my wife's cow. Melissa's cow ain't for sale.' Well, I knew right off I had to have Melissa's cow. I was in a hurry and I jest knew that of all them good cows Melissa was bound to have the best-un. So, after looken about at this one and that one, I said in an offhanded way, 'Can't I jest take a look at Miss Melissa's milker, Brother Baugh? It won't do no harm.' 'No,' he lowed slow-like, 'I reckon it won't do any harm. But, mind you, she's not for sale.' 'Oh, I know that!' I said. 'I jest want to see what kind of a cow Miss Melissa milks.'

"We walked toward the back end of the pastur, and as we

went along I could see Brother Baugh looken awful gloomy. He sighed once or twice and shook his head and directly he said that if for some reason unknown to man, that *if* he ever was *tempted*, and when he named the word I smelt brimstone, to sell Melissa's cow, he didn't believe she'd ever let him set foot in the house ag'in, although they had grown and married chillun. He turned to me. 'Why, she thinks as much of that cow as she does of me, I do believe.' Well, knowen you could rely on a preacher's word, I made up my mind I was goen away with that cow if I had to stay until sundown. And sure enough she did look fine, with a big bag, rolling hindquarters and as purty a set of teats as ever you saw. I'd no more'n got one good look at her before he edged me away to show me a heifer. I reckon we must 'a' fooled away two hours looken at his herd, with me all the time bringen the conversation back to Miss Melissa.

"Finally when I could see the day was about gone, I come right out and told him I had to have her. He never said nothen. Jest shook his head right fast. Then I got down to collection-plate talk, and he looked back of him to see if Melissa could see him, and I thought she must have mighty powerful eyes to see what was in Brother Baugh's mind a quarter of a mile away. I pressed him hard, and he hollered out, 'Don't tempt me, man; don't tempt me.'

"Why, folks, I felt as mean as Old Scratch himself, driven this good Campbellite preacher agen his conscience."

By this time every knife had stopped and every jaw. Mr. Quintus Harrison had stepped to the door, but for once nobody heeded him. Brother Macon's face was torn between leaving in rage and hearing the end of the trade.

"Well, sir, in a minute Brother Baugh drew me behind a persimmon tree, looked to his right side and to the left, dropped his voice so low I had to stick my head close up to his mouth to hear. 'Mister Buchanan,' he said and, my, what a pitiful voice, 'Mister Buchanan, I believe the devil calls you his own.' By that time I'd come to think so too. 'You've tempted me beyond mortal endurance. I'll tell you what I'll do. I'll sell you that cow if you promise me one thing—you got the money with you?' I nodded I had. Then he give me a little talk about how dangerous it was to go about the country with so much money in my breeches. I promised I'd never do it agen, and I ain't, but not for the reasons Brother Baugh give me. . . .

" 'I'll tell you what I'll do. I'll sell you Melissa's cow on one condition.' 'What's that?' I popped back. 'You must promise never to come back here again.' I was mighty quick to promise, you can bet. 'Another thing, you must drive her away around to the back of the pastur and let down the bars of the fence and take her out that way. For if Melissa sees you, the trade's off.' Before he had done talken, I had the money out counten it, I was so afraid he would change his mind."

There was a long silence. The crowd waited for the last punching line. Brother Macon, driven beyond endurance, leaped up:

"Well, what about her, you money-changer, you forni-cator?"

Deliberately Abner answered:

"She was everthing, Brother Macon, Brother Baugh *said* she was. But there was one article of Campbellite faith I didn't know about."

"One article, sir. One article. I'm glad to hear you admit thar's one thing you don't know."

Abner dropped his head meekly.

"I give this for anybody who might want to trade with one of Brother Macon's faith. No Campbellite is obleeged to tell you what you don't ask him outright. When the time come to milk Miss Melissa's treasure"—he looked around the gathering—"she had two spoiled teats."

Before the laughter had reached its downward swing and the short reviving chuckles, before Brother Macon's rage could drive him to his saddle, Mr. Harrison said sharply: "There he is. There comes Lem Botterall."

The porch sat to attention, as if the voice had been one of

command. Every eye measured man and mount, the big-boned sorrel, her long strides, and the sheriff's steady seat. They watched him until he pulled up to the side of the porch and dismounted like a balloon in a slow wind. He waved a hand, and the chair creaked as he adjusted his haunches to the plaited bottom. A large fan lay conveniently by. The sheriff picked it up and cooled the sweat that ran from his face to collar his perspiring neck.

"Lem"—there was in Mr. Harrison's voice a tone of restrained excitement, and his eyes came alive in the dead face— "Lem, the boys heard you mean to ride that stallion this evening."

"Looks like"—the sheriff's wheeze broke with difficulty from his chest—"I won't ever git to ride that animule."

Mr. Harrison tried to hide his disappointment with a merry tone. "If you don't mind, Lem, the boys will be saying you've found one horse you can't back."

Botterall leaned forward, and the chair creaked. "Penter Wilton," he said, "has just been dragged to death by his nag." He spoke slowly, like a man who has lost his bearings.

6

It was good dark. The loungers had all gone home to their suppers, to their wives, and their beds. Lem Botterall had lingered to talk of everything but the something which was on his mind until he, too, went on his way. For an hour in the emptiness of the storehouse Quintus Harrison stood without moving. At last, like a man in a dream, he walked out and locked the doors; hesitated a second on the steps and walked the three hundred yards to his dwelling. He was met by his body servant who took his hat and with a great deal of ceremony, hung it on the deer horns in the run. Quintus looked vaguely about him.

"Marster," the negro said, "supper's been ready."

"Tell your mistress I'm here."

"She's washen herself. P'niny's done tole her."

Quintus breathed quickly and, squaring his shoulders, walked into the room on the left of the run. The room smelled strongly of lye, and as he entered, his servant's voice, its veiled reproach, carried into the room and, mingling with the sharp fresh odor, stung his nostrils. The floors had been scoured until they looked worn and white. He examined the room as if he were entering it for the first time. It was small and well-built. In its center, crowding the walls, a mahogany banquet table extended the entire length. The table was covered with a heavy linen cloth and down the long center heavy candelabra spread their silver branches. The tallow from the half-burned candles hung in dirty brown stalactites and dripped monotonously upon the cloth. At the far end a massive sideboard stood upon its claw feet. There was barely room to pass between its crotch sunburst and the master's chair.

Around the walls hung the family portraits. They leaned oppressively in the already overcrowded room, scowling at or regarding with self-contained gaze the heavy table and its ornaments. There was the eighteenth-century face of Captain Harrison, an officer of foot under Greene and the founder of the family in Georgia. He had sat for the picture in the buff and blue of the uniform of the Continental line. From his neck dropped the linen stock, and across the left chest the ribbon of the Order of the Cincinnati ran into the lapel of the coat. There was the faintest shadow of disdain spreading along the tight line of his mouth. His nose was large, the forehead high, running back into the silver hair. But it was the eyes that pulled the face together. From the dark cracks in the canvas they seemed alive, peering directly forward in the candlelight, clear and untroubled. Next hung the younger brother, the Ensign. Farther along, the oldest son of the captain and his buxom wife. The structure of this face was all bone. The hair stood on end, dry and bristling, and the glint to the eyes lay like a hard film over the dark, opaque iris. But for certain markings of blood, the son hanging beside the Revolutionary father might have belonged to another civilization. While the captain's image impressed itself clean across the room, it was necessary to stand immediately before the son to get a sense of his character. This was Quintus Harrison's father. He had taken up large bodies of land in Alabama, leaving to his eighteen children sufficient property to keep them in affluence all their days. His issue, their wives and children, covered the rest of the walls.

As Quintus Harrison waited by the door, not once did he notice this evidence of the past thrust in such obvious fashion within the limits of the small log room. Presently a tall woman stooped beneath the rough lintel and came into the room. From her long sensitive face watery blue eyes looked reproachfully at her husband. Without speaking, he handed her to her seat, moved down the long table and took his place at the opposite end.

After a moment she asked, "Where is your son, Mr. Harrison? There was no resonance to her voice. It was empty but for its bitter ring. She raised a bottle of smelling salts and waved it beneath her fine nostrils.

"I don't think we need wait for him," her husband answered quietly.

They ate in silence. The fare was plain, but she served herself liberally. The man ate a biscuit and drank a glass of milk. He looked at the cloth before him, ignoring the feast in his wife's plate, always to be followed as he knew by long days of famine. Presently, in a tone that was meant to be casual, he said:

"Don't you think, my dear, it's a little hard on the servants to use so much water this dry weather?" When she made no reply, he continued absently, "Our well is dry, you know, and the creek is some distance."

Her voice broke to pieces.

"You know, Mr. Harrison, the poor white smells of this house give me asthma. Of course, if you want me to choke to death."

Her speech was interrupted by the sound of a saddle dropping on the porch. Her face brightened, but only for a moment. Presently their son, Damon, came into the room. He kissed his mother on the forehead and dropped into the seat by his father.

"Sorry I'm late, mama;" then turning to the older man, he spoke excitedly. "I've just been over to the Wiltons'. Jeems thinks there's been foul play. Penter was too good a horseman to be killed in any such way."

Mr. Harrison brightened at the confidential tones of his son's voice.

"There was a big hole in the back of his head. He couldn't"—Damon dished the food to his plate to the servant's disapproval—"he couldn't fall off a horse."

His father laid a reproving hand on Damon's arm, let it linger, then withdrew it as he looked toward the other end of the table. The boy flushed. A sullen flicker passed through his reckless blue eyes, and he bent over his plate to finish the meal in silence. He had early learned that he must never mention before his mother any occurrence in the Buyckville world. He remembered with shame what he considered her lack of courage in the face of misfortune, how she had made this cabin her shell, never leaving it, pretending the up-country had no existence.

He was ten when the family left the low country. It had then seemed an adventure: the very cause for leaving appealed to his imagination. He remembered the fatal day, how one Sunday afternoon the family had gathered on the side piazza at Fair Meadows. He was lying stretched on the cool floor with his head on a saddle. The black house girl, Adelaide, was fanning the flies away. His father sat in the shade of a wisteria, planted by Aunt Janey when she was a little girl, the first year after the Meadows had been raised by his grandfather's servants. He was reading Burke's orations. His mother had stepped down to the quarters with a fly blister to put on old Ephraim's back. She had scarcely got out of sight of the house when Mr. Malcolm Buford, Cousin Letitia's husband, rode through the front gate. He had heard his mother say that Cousin Letitia was the only Harrison in twenty years to marry out of the connection.

A week never passed but the two men, his father and Mr. Malcolm, shot marbles together. He used to lie awake at night dreaming of the sack that was always in the lean man's pockets, hoping against hope that it would pass into his father's hands and some day to his. But it was not for marbles that the two older men shot their taws. Their stakes had to do with more substantial things. Until that Sunday their winnings and losses were about even, for the two were well matched.

"Get down and step in the shade here, Buford. It an't often we see you on Sunday."

Damon could hear now the grave gaiety of his father's voice.

"I got tired hearing Miss Letitia's flies buzzing. And I thought I'd come over and hear how yours sounded." Buford lighted from his claybank and sat gingerly in an empty rocker. " 'Y God, but wouldn't we get rich, Quint, if niggers bred as fast as flies.' "

"Or if they were as busy with their hoes."

The two men eyed each other. There was a faint challenge in Quint's look.

"You didn't come over for your game last Friday, Buford," he said slyly after a short silence. "Warn't the sign right?"

"Well, I thought"—here Buford stopped to clear his throat—"I thought we might have a little game this afternoon," he went on hurriedly, "just to take our minds off the insects."

"You know I never gamble on Sunday, Buford." The tone was excessively pious.

"Oh, I meant a friendly game. Just to hear the taws crack."

Quint flushed slightly at the reprimand and set the book by his chair.

"I'll tell you what I will do, Buford. I won't gamble with

you, but I'll lay one prime field hand, without blemish, you can't beat me."

"That's not fair, Quint. It's like taking a sugar teat away from a baby." He laughed, but the humor sounded a little forced. There was the suggestion of a taunt in the short dry cackles.

Quint waited until the other grew quiet; then he heard his voice sound arrogantly: "Well, then, if the stakes don't interest you, I'll raise the ante!" He spoke as if some other will were forming the words. "I'll bet you ten niggers I can beat you three straight games."

Buford narrowed his eyes and let his hands run into his pocket and roll the marbles about. The humor had left his voice, but the arrogant tones of his friend's lingered in his ears. This was not the first time, because his wife's land hung upon the edge of the Harrison holdings, that he had been made to feel their contempt.

"All right," he answered; "if you're such a fool, I'll shoot you."

They stepped into the yard, and Quint took out his gold taw and spun it in the dust. He picked it up and gently blew the dust away and spun it again. Buford with great deliberation drew the circle and placed the four large marbles at each corner and carefully, oh, so carefully, set the center one down, measuring the distance from the corners with quick accuracy. He glanced toward Quint who stood aloof, his proud head thrown back, rolling his little gold ball between the palms of his hands.

"Satisfied?" asked Buford.

Quint walked over and gave a quick look at the set-up. He nodded his head. "Satisfied."

"Let's shoot for position then."

They walked back to taw.

"I'll shoot first," said Quint as he knelt in the dirt.

At this last touch of arrogance Buford set his face. Damon stood by the post stiff with excitement. His father put eye and thumb in line, squinted once and shot. The small gold taw jumped forward, slowed, rolled within two inches of the line and stopped. He looked neither pleased nor displeased. Before the trail of dust had settled, Buford kneeled, aimed, and shot. His taw, a solid maroon-colored agate, leaped into the air. It hit the ground and, spinning, came to a stop beside his opponent's. The men picked up a stick and measured to the circle. It was a tie. They took it over. This time Buford split the boundary of the circle. The advantage was his.

He knelt, spun his taw in the dirt three times, and with a slow steady movement took position. There was a dart and a crack, and the center marble bolted from the circle. He looked at his opponent.

"There went your ten niggers," he said dryly.

"There's ten more where those came from."

"Well, I lay these first ten against them."

"No, we will play according to agreement."

Damon's breath swelled into his throat and caught there in lumps at this gesture.

Buford won the next three games. When Quint finally got the first shot, he appeared calm, but his hand trembled slightly. He knocked out two of the corners before he nailed the center. A cruel smile played about his opponent's mouth as he set the marbles back in the ring. Quint had not trusted himself to hazard the first shot at center. But the next game he was calmer. He aimed at the center and hit it, but the marble rolled barely without the circle.

"The game's yours, sir. I'm willing to call it quits," said Buford.

"Not at all. Not at all."

"Well, I think something of my conscience, too. We can't go on playing like this all day. Set a limit."

Damon felt he could not wait for his father's reply. He did not have long to wait. There was the flush on Quint's cheekbones, a sign of anger with all Harrisons.

"I'll beat you two out of three," he said.

No other word was spoken until the games were ended. When the two men rose from their knees, Buford called for

his horse and mounted. He turned to speak. In his voice
there was an overbearing ring that had never been there before.

"Of course, Quint, you understand that I can't take advantage of your vanity."

"I will send you the deeds Monday, Mr. Buford."

Malcolm Buford, as he rode away, did not notice his familiar
companion turn on his heel and step back to the piazza; he
did not see the few beads of sweat gathering on his pale forehead. He heard only his own heart sing with triumph and
sweet vengeance. In one afternoon he had returned arrogance for arrogance, contempt for contempt. He had given
back at one blow all that he had been forced to take from the
hands of all the Harrisons.

Quint was sitting quietly in his rocker when his wife returned from the quarters.

"I think old Eph will be all right now, though I'm afraid
of pneumonia." She hesitated.

"What's the matter, Mr. Harrison? You are pale. Are
you sick too?"

"You needn't trouble yourself about Ephraim any more."
Her husband's voice seemed to drag out forever. "He belongs to Malcolm Buford."

She looked at Quintus for further explanation, but he was
unable to answer her. Damon burst out excitedly:

"Mama, papa's just shot away all the niggers and Fair
Meadows."

For some seconds the words had no meaning and then suddenly she knew it was true. Thirty minutes ago she had
walked away from the house, mistress of two thousand acres
of land and seventy servants. On her return . . . she knew it
was true because it was more real than life. The fatal words
rang upon her ears as if she had heard them over many times.
The time, the place, the position of her husband and son on
the piazza seemed familiar like a constantly recurring dream.
Moving quickly, she crossed the piazza into the broad cool
hall, and the heavy door swung to behind her.

The husband and son could hear the retreating steps and follow them to her chamber, but they could not follow the bitter workings of her heart, nor could they know how a woman's despair may, falling steadily about the things she has loved, slowly wither the affections; nor how an old passion once betrayed may torture in hidden ways may eat backward until the secret things snap, and there is no decay but a dry emptiness.

This Damon with his years could never understand. He could only feel shame at the change he felt in his mother. This led him, as he grew up in the strange country, to drift farther away in sympathy from his mother, and more into the hill life about him. Her resentment of his behavior and his sullen persistence in finding the most reckless companions rarely came to the surface as it had on this evening. The meal came quickly to an end. The mother rose and went to her room. The boy and his father sat for a while in the cool of the evening. She listened with her ear to the window. She had known her son rioted around with the Wiltons, and she knew the Wiltons were no fit company for a boy of his disposition. As she pressed against the curtain, upon her face, exposed in the pale light, was a drawn look of dread.

7

The following Sunday a young horseman was moving along the soft road in a fast running walk when a sudden commotion sent his mount shying into the bushes. With sure ease the youth urged the animal forward, out into the clearing. He saw at once what the commotion was about. From a house set in the center of a large field the women were running in charging lines, hollering and beating on pans. One old woman held high her dress, tramping up the fields with her feet and ringing the dinner bell. Overhead a black swarm of bees circled, hesitating above the white sheet which was waving to attract its attention. Suddenly changing direction, it flew in solid formation toward the woods. A young girl dropped the sheet, snatched the bell from the old woman, and ran after them. The boy drew up his mount to watch the race. The bees, confused by the noise, still hung low to the ground.

The girl moved swiftly over the rough field. She was rapidly gaining. Her plaits flew behind her, and the blue gingham dress clasped her thighs. Her feet lifted as if she were running over smooth ground. The boy threw his leg over the saddle and watched in admiration. But soon he saw she would lose the race. She had almost caught up with the bees when the snake fence got in her way. The boy saw this, and he also saw the bees swing toward his position. Quickly he stood in the saddle and waved his hat and shouted. The swarm hung for a moment in the air, swung away from the newer noise, back into the field and hovering an instant above the ringing bell settled in the girl's outstretched apron.

"Wait a minute," the boy shouted, "I'll help you." He jumped down from his horse and threw the bridle over the stay post in the fence. His hands fumbled at the apron strings. "Hold still now," he said excitedly, "or they'll sting you."

"I'm not scared of them," she answered. "Hurry up and get the apron off." His hands still fumbled. In the chase the bow had become a knot. "Come around front," she called impatiently, "and hold the apron. I'll untie the strings."

He obeyed her instantly, took the outer ends of the apron and held it while she quickly undid the knot. The black confusion of bees seethed in their calico pocket—a few, as if they were struggling in molasses, crawled out upon his hands.

"Here, knock'm off," he said; "they're getting away."

She looked up and smiled. "Scared?"

"Who, me?" He blushed.

Deftly she gathered the four ends together. As she did so, their hands touched. For a moment she met his eyes. She saw the bold blue stare, the broken features, the impetuous mouth. Intuitively she understood the careless slouch of his shoulders. Even in the excitement of the swarm's capture she was aware of his arrogant swagger as he was hurrying to her relief.

He saw a girl of sixteen with a round smooth face, flushed from the chase, light auburn hair and eyes that fairly glittered. Now that the crisis was past she was quick to drop her gaze, murmur an embarrassed thanks and turn to go.

"Wait," he called, "let me help you."

She went slowly away. Scattered across the field, the old women were coming toward her in a fast walk, calling back to an old man to hurry with the hive. When she didn't answer, he ran in front and blocked her way.

"I'm Damon Harrison," he said. "What's your name?"

"Ruth Weaver," she answered shyly, hurrying away and leaving him standing there.

He watched the sure grace of her moving body, made more marked by her meeting with the old women who had hurried after her when they saw the swarm settle. Now they hovered around the girl, giving directions, shifting their stiff joints abruptly, unevenly. He saw one of them peer into the apron and throw up her head and step awkwardly back, tripping to her knees over the furrow. With amazement Damon realized that what he had taken to be a pasture was an old plowed-over field. He turned away and said to himself, "She'll know it when I offer to help her again." He climbed the fence and looked back out of the slant of his eye to see if she had turned to watch, but she was busy with the bees. He mounted and put the horse at once into a quick gallop, looking straight before him, with his head insolently high. Damon knew she would watch him get down the road. He would show her whether it made any difference to him whether she was polite or not.

The afternoon was hot, but he galloped most of the way to the sheriff's. Botterall had given out he would ride the Spanish stallion or burst. When his blood had cooled, Damon noticed his horse was pretty well blown. When he rode into the crowd of standing men, their appraising eyes mortified him. He greeted the older men distantly, and a voice from the gathering asked: "A booger git after you, Damon?"

He turned angrily and opened his teeth, but at that moment he caught sight of his father and saw his displeasure. He shut his mouth without replying and threw his leg over the saddle. He tried to hide his shame, for he imagined everybody knew exactly why he had run the horse.

He did not sit long in his misery. The barn doors soon opened, and a small two-year-old strawberry mule bucked into the lot. He pranced mightily on his slim legs, all the while throwing his head about, chewing the strange bit until small flecks of foam gathered in the mouth corners.

"Hyar's my first mule colt out of that wild stock," said Botterall. "He's the get of Colonel Bascom's thoroughbred, out of my Wild Nelly. I'll service free the man's mare that can break him." Botterall's voice had a happy ring. As he stood before the men, whip in hand, trousers stuck carelessly down the boot tops, stepping lightly about as only a large man can do, jerking his great head around his shoulders, his voice seemed to curl about the gathering and draw it to do his bidding. "Who would keer to try him?" he called again in his peculiar penetrating voice.

The crowd was silent. The mule, as if to show his mettle, dropped his head and sent his heels sparkling into the air.

"Why, shorely you all ain't fixed up on stock?" The heavy sarcasm stung the ears of the younger men.

A red-faced, tawny-haired man stepped out into the open.

"All right, Tim Bean," said the sheriff with malicious pleasure, "thar he is, as slick a piece of mule meat as ever you'll straddle." The sheriff stepped back to watch him mount.

There was a mild degree of interest as the holders pulled the halter loose. For a second the mule and rider held perfectly still; then, bucking and kicking, down the pasture they went. Tim Bean held on for two hundred yards, when the strawberry leaped upward, then downward, twisting his hindquarters and dropping his neck. Bean's legs took the air and he tumbled to the ground. Before he could reach his feet, the strawberry had pawed his shirt off. He beat at the mule with his hat like a man fighting bees and, rolling out of the way of the animal's hoofs, got to his feet and put one long leg before the other until he had reached a place of safety. The mule followed him a short distance, and broken waves of laughter greeted the strawberry's triumph.

As the animal was caught and brought back to position, the sheriff repeated his offer. He had less difficulty in getting riders now. A sporting instinct spread contagiously from man to man. There were several trials and several failures when Abner Buchanan, thinking that the mule was tired, asked for a chew of tobacco. This got the expected attention.

"I'll declare, Lem," he said with a twinkle in his eye, "I don't know what's got into our young men. If they can't break a measly crittur like that ar'n, I dunno how they'll git bread for our gals when we take to the chimney corner."

"Well, now, Ab," said the sheriff with obvious pleasure, "maybe you better show'm a p'int or two."

"Looks like one of us has got to," came the dry reply.

Abner straddled the animal gingerly; then, facing about, he waved his hand.

"All right, boys, turn him aloose." Lifting his hat, he called out, "Now, young-uns, watch your Uncle Abner."

The mule made one whirl, and Buchanan fell into the dirt, head foremost. The strawberry was greeted with loud cheers this time. He threw up his head and brayed. Abner stood up and wiped the dust from his face. He was not in the least abashed.

"That's the way to do it, boys. When you see a crittur's a-goen to throw you, git off."

After the amusement had restored general good feeling—the friends and kin of the unfortunate riders had felt disgruntled—somebody said:

"Hit's too bad now Jeems Wilton's not here. There's a mule-breaker from way back."

"He named it to me to come today, but I see he's not hyar."

This was spoken by Dee Day, overseer on Mr. Lovell's hill plantation. He was a curious-shaped man with a foul odor. It was said that his mother several months before his birth stepped down to the spring after a fresh bucket of water and, as she leaned over, a snapping turtle struck at her from under a rock. The kin claimed this marked the child, and his long neck and squat body, with shoulders slung forward like flippers, the bow legs, gave credit to the report. People came for miles around to see the baby, and for a while the mother took pleasure in the sensation, but when he was eight months old she turned against him and refused to nurse him. The woman's father raised him on pot licker and bread dipped in buttermilk. This old man was Dee Day's only intimate and, after he died, Dee Day raised himself. The other children refused to play with him, ran off and hid, so that early in life he took up with the stock. This gave him a way with animals, and when he grew to manhood he found he could always find work where there was stock to look after. Lovell picked him up at a livery stable in Montgomery and put him over the barns. After a while he turned the plantation over to his charge. He was found to be as good with negroes as with animals. The slaves showed a peculiar respect for his deformity, and his sharp biting voice drove the hoe hands better than a whip.

"Jeems named it to me he'd be hyar," he repeated, standing apart from the others. He spoke carefully with a tone that pretended great intimacy with Wilton. Damon was not far away, and the sound of the overseer's voice, the suggestion of familiarity with his friend, irritated him. He spoke up:

"Mr. Lem, let me try my hand."

"All right, my boy. If you've got any of your pappy in you, I look to work this mule come spring."

Quintus heard his son's impulsive offer. His feelings were mixed. He knew the boy had broken no sort of stock, much less a two-year-old combining the stubborn traits of an ass with the wild hard-breaking character of Botterall's Spanish strain. But his pale cheekbones grew pink and his eyes brightened for the contest. He had not felt his gambling instincts so strong in him since he had put them away with his other low-country habits.

Damon swaggered a little too much as he went forward for the breaking. It was evident that he was nervous, but he did not intend to humiliate his father. He mounted easily and took a firm seat. The holders stepped away, and at once the mule reared on its haunches and moved backward. As it darted forward, Quintus saw his son's long-muscled thighs clamp the animal's belly. At the pressure the strawberry ran for a distance, stopped suddenly, whirled, ran again; then dropped his feet to roll the hateful body off. Damon got easily out of his way and when the animal rose up, he rose with him. Quintus looked quickly at the crowd and saw their approval and turned back to the contest. The mule was running. The boy gave him the bit and kicked him in the flanks. After a while he rode back and with a ring in his voice said, "Whoa."

The strawberry, blown and dripping, obeyed. Damon got down and looked shyly at his father as he handed the reins to the sheriff. But the sheriff refused to take them.

"Boy, he's yours," he said.

Quintus rode toward them.

"No, Lem, that's not the agreement."

"You ain't got a thing to do with this, Quint Harrison. The mule's Damon's. Go 'long now. It's gitten late and I've got my own riden to do."

Botterall and the holders walked toward the barn. Every eye followed them, for it was the sheriff's high moment. After what seemed a long wait, four men rushed from the barn, dancing away from the paws of the gray beast. At the sight the sheriff's sallow flesh—he ordinarily looked as if the blood had dried up in his fat—burned to a slow bronze. The holders maneuvered the leaps and jumps toward the open gate. Once the stallion planted his feet and kicked around in a circle. He backed into the fence and tried to rub the blanket off. Finally he was got out of the lot into the open field. At the sight of his plunges every man thought to himself it would take a pearter man than Lem Botterall to back that horse.

Botterall motioned and two men came forward. He placed his hands upon their shoulders to be lifted to his seat. At that moment he lost all sense of his audience. The stallion's eyes had been covered against the approach of the men, but he sensed their movement and veered away.

"Easy, Gray; easy, boy."

The sheriff's strident wheeze was gone. The words were ordinary. But into the animal's cocked ears they poured soft command, magnetic, intimate sound. The gray held to a rigid stand, listening but at the moment of betrayal ready to flee.

Quintus Harrison had changed in the moment. He had come alive, and he leaned forward in the saddle like a young man. Of all those present he alone understood the desperate gamble his friend was about to make, for Lem Botterall was as unsure of the earth as a sailor and as lost upon it. He was the most skillful rider in the country but for one serious handicap. He could not, because of his size, mount from the ground. As Quintus saw the men hoist him and let him fall like a tub of butter upon the bare gray back, saw the small flat legs hug the flanks, the tremendous buttocks melt down over the backbone, the horse shake once with the weight and bound into the air, he whispered to himself, "Lem's done for if he's ever thrown." For once Botterall got beneath the stallion's hoofs he could never rise again. He knew this, and it was this reckless quality in Botterall that drew Quintus to him, the fearless pride that is able to stake life in a game that can bring no profit.

Quintus, bent stiffly from the waist, watched at each heaving spring the great body sink deeper around the stallion's back. It seemed that no man could stand the wild lunges; yet Botterall looked more of a shaggy hump than a man, and at last his friend thought him safe. But the horse had one last trick. Gathering his strength, which was running from his pores in streams, the stallion plunged through the air in a series of circles. Quintus, as he saw him touch the earth to leave it again, became vaguely aware of a restlessness in the crowd. He could hear an angry murmur and, for a moment, an excited voice. He was too busy with his eyes to look around, for at last the gray, dispirited by his unsuccessful plunging, had set off in a fast run. This was the first sure sign of conquest. With neck up and tail streaming to the rear, three times the wild horse sped around the hundred-acre field, kicking up the dirt, changing in color to a dirty brown as the sweat poured, until finally slowing, his gasping wind pumping from his chest, he carried his first master to a stop before the spectators.

For a few moments Botterall sat glued to the horse, the bridle hand trembling from the exertion, drenched and winded like his beast, as if man and animal had been transformed by the ordeal into one. In the flush of his private triumph a look of nobility suffused his features, deepening the marks of cunning and avarice until his face appeared almost heroic. But before his friend could ride forward and meet him, the expression had changed. Botterall saw that something had happened to the crowd. Some were mounting their horses to leave. Others were already in the road galloping away. Those that were still on their feet were milling in confusion. Nobody took notice of his victory. This did not offend him, for now that he had done the thing he had set out to do, it seemed of little moment; the wild stallion felt no different from any of his other mounts. He watched two of his deputies walk toward him with something like fear in their eyes.

"What's the matter hyar?" he growled suspiciously, laboring to make his short breath speak with authority.

"Mr. Tyson Lovell just sent word Jeems Wilton's been found shot dead in the big spring on his place."

"Shot dead." The sheriff spoke with effort. "Who by?" The deputies shook their heads.

"How come nobody knows?" Botterall's words were dull,

automatic. His heavy jowls dropped as he spoke. His eyes turned empty. They darkened briefly with a sense of dread; then settled back to their vacant expression. With a great effort he shook himself together.

"I deputize every man here . . ." The sudden energy of his speech died away. He looked about and saw that the crowd had melted away. Only Quint Harrison and the two deputies were near him. "Whar's everybody a-goen?" he asked rhetorically. Lifting his bridle reins, he said, "I guess we better go to the spring and look into this thing." His commands had changed to statement.

"Hadn't you better change horses, Lem?" cautioned his friend. "You haven't any saddle on that stallion."

The sheriff nodded and rode to the fence. He got onto the rails and waited until another mount could be saddled and brought around. He failed to turn his eyes as the gray was led away to his stall.

Quintus could not help but observe the sheriff's sudden change from elation to apathy, and as he looked at him perched upon the fence, at his sullen stare, he felt a curious sense of disgust. Without warning a chill ran down his spine, such as happens to a man when the sun goes under a cloud. He looked at the sky, but it was hot and blue clear. Nowhere could he see even a feather of a cloud. He was strangely disturbed by this delusion and after a little he heard Botterall speak as if in answer to a question of his own:

"I ain't got no notion what to think."

Quintus was too startled to do more than look at the other man.

"That makes three Wiltons, Quintus," Botterall said, and his voice was hard.

The horse was brought, and the four men rode slowly out of the field into the road. They had ridden some distance before the animals' hoofs struck the soft pike in a gallop.

8

Tyson Lovell stood with his back to the black, empty fireplace in the front room of his hill country plantation. He had waited there without speaking for some ten minutes until the atmosphere of the room, although it was a hot September night, seemed chill and desolate to the others gathered there. Botterall and Dee Day sat motionless in their chairs, uneasy at the silence and resentful. Behind them three bearded men they had never seen before leaned in the shadows of the wall. Lovell had spoken but once since his arrival. He had kept them waiting a long time, and when at last he opened the door and walked softly across the floor, he took position before the mantel, scarcely noticing their presence. He turned upon each man and let his eye slide across their faces like a plane, shaving away their sulky reticence.

"Where's Fox?" he asked at last.

No man answered, but each man dropped his naked sight in shame. After a while Lovell beat his riding whip against the leg of his boots, gently at first until it could barely be heard above Botterall's troubled wheeze. As time passed, the monotonous strokes increased in strength and speed. The angry rhythm seemed to snatch at the wheezes in the sheriff's chest. Minute by minute the tempo quickened. The breath gasped and rattled in Botterall's throat. As the lashes stung the leather, Dee Day winced at each downstroke, as if it had fallen across his back. The dim light from the lamp exposed no emotion upon Lovell's face. When at last he spoke again, his voice sounded thin and far away.

"I will wait no longer on Mr. Fox."

The words had the fatal ring of a death sentence, but they relieved the tension. Botterall felt his body fall wearily about the chair. He reached for his handkerchief and wiped his face and neck.

"Mr. Sheriff, I come up from my lower plantation and what do I find?" He paused as if for an answer. "Three of my best men dead—mysteriously disposed of."

"You can't hold it agen me, Tyson. Everybody knew the judge had taken to drink. I had the boys look around . . ."

Lovell continued, ignoring Botterall:

"Judge Wilton climbs up three stories to fall off a balcony. Penter, one of the easiest of riders, is dragged to death by his horse, and now his brother shoots himself . . . from grief I suppose." He paused and let his voice thicken with irony. "The Lord, I guess you figger, was running short on Wiltons. He had more need for'm than I did, I guess you figgered."

"No, sir. I commenced to git suspicious after Penter's death. I looked good for strangers."

Lovell cut across a long explanation like a basket knife.

"And now you're sure that strangers must be about. What did you do? Get in the big road and hail everybody that passed: 'Stranger, did you push Judge Wilton off the balcony of the Coosa River Inn?' . . . Or, 'Stranger, did you see Penter Wilton fall from his horse? Did you see his brother Jeems shoot himself?'"

"No, Lovell, I'm a-goen . . ."

"I'll tell you what you're going to do. You're going to comb this country with a rake, now, tonight."

"Well, now . . ."

"I've put men on the roads, at every creek. You get you a posse. Deputize every able-bodied man from Buyckville out and bring me the man or men who are laying for us."

A look of despair settled over the sheriff's features. Lovell saw it at once and changed his tone. When he spoke again, his voice was soft and coaxing:

"Now, Lem, what's the matter?"

"I'll tell you, Mr. Lovell, I just don't know who mought be a-doen this-here thing."

"You don't think it's ha'nts, do you? You don't believe

somebody's put a spell on the Wiltons? You don't believe
that, do you? Do you?"

Botterall blurted out, "Well, how can it be any of Old Man
McIvor's folks? He ain't got no kin. The widow and her
three boys, and them young, left the country."

Lovell answered slowly like a man thinking aloud:

"I never did like the way the widow slipped away from
here, in the night, going God knows where. She didn't wait,
even, for me to take her crop. It wasn't according to the
way she ought to have behaved. They were mighty set on
their rights, those McIvors. The woman had grit. We both
saw her at the Grand Jury. She never minded that people
thought her a nigger-stealer's widow. She meant for Fox
and the Wiltons to hang." He was silent for a few seconds.
"And the next day, and the next, and what niggers and stock
she had was gone from the country. I couldn't have done it
better myself."

"What do you think?" Botterall leaned forward in his
chair.

"It's not clear to my mind," Lovell answered like a man
thinking out loud. "I want you to find out."

The clock over the mantel struck nine times. The men in
the room listened to the last buzz of the spring, its halt before
the strike, the brassy ring die away.

"You better get on your way, sheriff," said Lovell.

As soon as Lovell heard Botterall's horse turn into the road,
he spoke to the men who had, during all this time, hung in
the shadows of the wall. He did not lift his voice but the
rapid commands were bitten off in a way that left no grounds
for misunderstanding.

"I've already showed you where to go. As soon as Botterall
collects his posse and *before*," he emphasized this word, "*before*
the posse begins scouring the woods, you will meet your niggers
and run'm in the regular way. That's all."

Lovell's confederates slunk out of the room.

"That's purty doens, Mister Ty," said Day.

Lovell took his pistols off the mantel and examined them.

"The public memory is short," he replied. "It needs a little prodding." He rolled the words over his tongue as if he liked their sound. "It needs a little prodding." Then he turned to go. "I'm going to follow Botterall. He might bungle things. You stay here."

Day's face paled.

"Don't you think, Mister Ty, I'd better go 'long with you. Something might . . ."

"Something what?" Lovell scowled at Day.

"Something might hurt ye."

Lovell's lip curled, "Why, the widow didn't see you, too, did she?"

"No, sir."

"You stay here and look after the place like you're hired to do."

Day followed him out to the road and watched him mount and disappear over the rise. He did not linger until the hoof-beats grew faint, but, looking quickly about, dropped his head and shuffled back toward the shelter of the house.

The hour seemed blacker than it was to a sight accustomed to the dim light of the room, and Dee Day had looked into the darkness around him as if he feared what the night held. His steps quickened as he neared the porch. But even if his glance had been less brief, he would not have seen the slow thrust of a head from beneath the puncheon floor, for, swaying as it emerged, it froze upon its neck the moment the over-seer turned. The darkness might have dripped to clot there beneath the window, for all the sharpest eye could tell; and there were no dogs to raise their voices in warning. They were baying a more familiar scent on the lower plantation.

Day passed the edge of the house. The head at once came to life. Swaying upward, it lifted along the wall and the body slid noiselessly after it. A hand felt the window sill; then the other. They gripped and the figure vaulted into the room recently vacated by Lovell and his men. Day's step sounded in the run. The figure drew erect, listening; and its moccasined feet slipped over the puncheons, quickly along the wall until, slowing, it advanced toward the door like a panther, suddenly moving, crouching.

The door opened out, and Dee Day shuffled in. He shut it behind him, locked it, turned. He fell away from the door and the fear streamed from his eyes. The figure remained perfectly still and looked at Day. The overseer turned his head away and reached for the key, but the brown fingers snatched it from the lock. The sweat broke out on Day's forehead, and he heard his dry voice ask, "Who are you?"

"Cameron McIvor's son."

"No." Then more hoarsely, "No."

Speaking, Day stumbled back toward the hearth, and as he retreated he left a foul sickening odor behind.

"I'll give you two minutes to make what peace you can with your Maker."

"I didn't do it. I was just in the yard. I went there because Mr. Lovell sent me."

Above Day's head on the mantel the clock ticked out the seconds. He listened in the stillness and watched the dark brown figure, the naked brown waist, the brown leather breeches, the brown moccasins. Upon his face Day could see, in spite of its effort at control, an increasing disgust.

"Git back, Pleas," he cried. "I didn't know ye at first. Git back. I know my stink is turrible. Git back. I won't run. I'll tell ye who done it."

Instead of answering, Pleasant looked up at the clock. The overseer saw his glance, and he turned helplessly about. His breath began to come faster.

"I don't know how to pray," he said desperately, as if this fact might instill mercy in the other's decision.

Once more his eyes fluttered, looking for some weapon. He saw a chair and darted for it, but Pleasant, scarcely shifting, caught him by the throat and pushed his back to the mantel. Slowly the hand relaxed its grip and for the next minute Day strained his ears to hear the steady sound of the clock. The pendulum swung out a minute to the second. The time had come. Before one final plea could be phrased upon the quivering mouth, the McIvor hands were at his throat. His flipper arms reached to break the hold, waved aimlessly upon the air; and his eyes, by nature popped, now streaked with congested blood. They stood out beside his nose like spinning marbles, while his legs tramped the floor, first desperately, then weakly, then not at all.

Pleasant released one hand and reached for the knife at his belt. Quickly he pushed the short thick blade under the ribs near the heart. The body fell to the hearth. He did not wait to hear the last rattle in the throat or see the final spasm. With precision he piled all the chairs and light furniture in the center of the room, glanced once at the inert body, at the dark pool slowly spreading upon the puncheons and, picking up the lamp, walked toward the window. Halfway across the floor he tossed the lamp into the pile of furniture. It exploded and the flames darted after the oil. He watched with composure the first bodiless flames licking the surface of the wood, saw them catch, waited until their pale scattered blaze lifted uncertainly above the pile, waited for the crackle, the surer leap, and the red jagged sheet of fire. Then, dragging the heavy walnut secretary up to the window, he threw its drawers upon the flames and slipped through the smoking window. Outside he closed the shutters and ran toward the cover of a woods near by. He turned to make sure of his work. Through the trees he could see the blinds. The green of each shutter was lined with amber light. At the top, visible in the reflection from the room, white sticky smoke curled to the eaves of the house. He turned about and listened. Faintly upon the wind he could hear to the southwest the roar of the Staircase. Facing in that direction, he trotted quickly off, and the night covered him.

He pressed toward his objective with long steady strides. From what he had heard lying under the puncheons that would shortly be destroyed by fire he knew that before he could reach his destination the roads and woods would be filling with men. But he showed no signs of flurry. Only a special alertness as his eyes swept the darkness, frequent stops to listen—otherwise with swinging rhythm, the soft pat of his moccasins kept surely the changing ground. But he was not at ease in his mind. It was only by accident he had learned of Lovell's purpose to throw a cordon around Buyckville. He was still able to dupe the neighborhood. Well, if men had little enough sense not to tell a scoundrel from an honest man, it was not his fault. But would Eli and Bob Pritchard run into them? Would they give the meeting place away? He had fired Lovell's house, but would that draw enough of the posse in the other direction? Would the negroes get together and put it out and discover the evidence of Day's death, undoing his plan to throw a spell of mystery about the deaths? He had emptied the rain barrels. Maybe the negroes, lacking direction, would be slow to rally and fight the fire. He had to take that risk. He halfway regretted the decision to make away with the overseer just at this time, but he could not ignore the chances of Providence. He had put himself in Its hands, and he must do what It told him to do.

He was coming to a side road that led to Buyckville. He slowed down, going from tree to tree, never moving from their shadows. The night was brighter. The late copper moon began to roll up the hill of the horizon, the unlucky love moon. He slipped around a tree and faced to the rear. What was that noise in the brush? As still as the trunk he pressed against, with his hand upon his knife, he waited. Then he saw a gray fox with a fresh brush trot into an open space not ten yards away. The animal did not recognize the dangerous odor. The wind was blowing toward the river. He stepped toward the road, listened, looked east and west; then darted across to the woods on the other side. A possum dropped dead before him. He stopped and listened again. Somewhere to the east he could hear the low thuds of hoofs striking the dry roadbed. The possum winked an eye, and Pleasant passed on.

The country, as it drew near the Staircase, became more broken. He traveled the ravines, but the light was only bright enough to be confusing. He had to stop more often to get his bearings by the sound of the Staircase. The bottoms of the ravines slowed his pace. He climbed their slippery sides, missed his step and sent rocks tumbling behind him. He could hear them roll noisily backward. He realized he was becoming a little anxious, and the pursuit had barely begun. For himself he was not afraid, but he must meet with the others before they committed some blunder. Eli had a reckless way, and he could not see well by night.

He lay down and put his ear to the ground, but it was no use. The country was too broken for sound to travel far. Before him a sharp knoll stood up and blocked his way. He hesitated a moment and, bending over, moved on hand and foot up its steep side, clutching the soft slick needled floor. At last on top he felt his brow. It was damp. The first sweat. His blood was warming up. The joints and muscles were oiled for the race. He put his hands around a slim, straight-standing pine and glanced at the sky. The large arms of the greater trees spread some forty feet above and in the dying wind fanned the air. Like a monkey, hand over hand, moccasin above moccasin, he climbed swiftly to the first extended limb, reached for it and swung away from the sapling. Surely, quickly, he worked his way to the needled top and thrust his head into the cooling air. At once he smelled the river. Looking around he saw he was on the ridge which rolled gradually downward toward the Staircase. To his left the wide, red glow of the burning house splotched the sky. Vaguely to his perch came muffled shouts and cries. The moon was before him. In the clearings he could make out a few houses. In some there were faint sparks. This meant the occupants were turning out, or had already turned out, for the posse. In the distance, near where he judged Botterall's farm must lie, he could make out, losing themselves, then showing themselves, the winking lights of fireflies. He looked long and hard. The flickers moved slowly toward the river. This was an unwelcome sight. Men with torches were beating the woods across his line of escape.

He might do one of two things. He might fall back to his rear and swing on a wide arc to the Staircase with little chance of meeting Botterall's deputies. That way was five miles and the crossing of the Staircase rough and uncertain at night. Or he might descend the ridge and go directly toward his cave. That was only two miles. It was shorter and he knew the ground better. But the danger was greater. He did not delay over the decision. Dropping down the tree to the lowest arm, he swung back to the sapling and scrambled to the ground. He must take the risk and join with Eli and Bob. He must know they were safe. So much depended upon their undiscovered return to the cave.

With his mind made up there was no time lost in debate. He set off in a straight line toward the sheriff's place. His pace increased. He climbed the hills and dropped down their descending sides with the minimum of effort, working always where there was a choice toward the right. After an hour he reached the bluffs. The place of descent opposite the sheriff's lay a quarter to his front. He could see the torches and hear the men walking heavily several hundred yards to his left. Their voices were indistinct. He paused and considered for a moment drawing within better range, but decided to move along. He was now at ease and contemptuous of his pursuers, those daytime men whose eyes needed fire to see by.

He broke into a trot. He had become a little careless of the noise he was making when, around a bend, he suddenly halted. Ten paces away, so close he had almost run into them, were three of the posse. He stepped back off-guard. As he did so, the dry brush crackled. The men were stooping over, with their backs turned. But they heard the noise. They raised their heads and listened. The foremost walked forward a few paces. Pleasant's heart pounded under his chest. He lay flat on his back behind a fallen log. If the man advanced, he was bound to see him, for the moon by this time rolled high in the heavens.

"Do you see ary thing?" came a voice from the rear, and after long seconds, "Nary thing."

"Well, I shore heared something. Go up and look around that bend."

Pleasant heard the heavy boots advance with supposed caution. He drew in his breath and pulled out his knife. The man reached the log and peered over it into the woods.

"Hell, I don't see nothing," he said. "Hurry up and git that fat pine lit." Saying this, he sat down upon the log. His broad back was not a foot from Pleasant's head. The man continued, "When we git to the road, I'm a-goen back to bed. Whoever done fer them Wiltons been gone from here. Never did like'm noway."

After a while another voice spoke up. "I've never seen Lem Botterall so worked up. He looks skeered to me."

"Well, jest because Lem's skeered ain't no good reason for me to leave my old woman this time o' night. How come he didn't do something when he found Jeems Wilton?"

There was another pause, and the rich pine flared up. Pleasant could hear the other two rise to their feet.

"Well, these hyar killens do look cur'ous. I don't like'm a-tall."

The man on the log stood up. "Come on then." His voice was disgruntled. He stepped over the dead tree, and his boot almost grazed Pleasant's chest. The others, blinded by the torch, which the forward man held in front of him until it caught good, stepped over below. This was another sign of Providence. If they had waited until the pine had flared high, they must have seen him lying at their feet. Pleasant waited until they were out of sight before he got up. Completely alert now, he worked his way slowly to the right.

It took him less than an hour to go the quarter. Never again would he be so foolish and abandon his precautions. He had learned his lesson. Reaching the sharp bank where he and Eli had parted a week ago, he sat down and slid slowly toward the tree they had come up on, holding himself back by the stubby bushes and loose roots. He swung out to the tree and caught a large grapevine. He knew its strength but tried it to make sure, then swiftly dropped to the bottoms below.

The undergrowth was thick, and he was slow to get to the place where the boat had been sunk. He frowned. Eli or

Bob had left their tracks. The boat would be gone, and he would have to swim. He put his hand into the water and washed away all signs of the tracks. He stripped, put what clothes he wore on top of his head, stepped softly into the water and waded into the pool. The river was low and the current none too swift. He reached the other side without much exertion and climbed to the cave. As he jumped lightly into its mouth, a pistol was shoved into his ribs.

"It's me," he said quickly, and Eli withdrew the nervous gun. They went to the back of the cave.

"Where's Bob?" he asked.

"He turned back to see if Old Man Fox was ready to join the others."

Pleasant thought a while before he spoke again.

"I'm afraid he's upset things."

"Why?"

"Old Man Fox's left the country."

"Got scared, did he?"

"Got smart. The whole country's turned out."

"We've got to go back and help him." Eli started toward the cave's mouth.

"No," came the reply. "We wouldn't know where to find him. Time's come to scatter. You pull out for Opelika. I'll follow in a few days. If they ask for me, tell about we got separated hunting."

"It an't right to go off and leave Bob like this," Eli said.

"Just one man can do what's got to be done now. Got any pone left? I'm growling empty."

"Here's a piece I stole." Eli offered the bread. Pleasant took it absently.

The two boys stood in the mouth of the cave. Eli turned and looked at his friend.

"Take care of yourself, Pleas."

"I'll take care of myself. Get along now. It's almost first light."

Pleasant watched his young uncle climb until he was lost in the dark clusters of pine needles. He heard the tree shake slightly, and he knew Eli had jumped to the ground above. He turned his head and looked to the northwest. The glow in the sky was dying away. He stood there for a while, peering through the night. He shook his head, then dropped to the floor of the cave. But it was bright day before he slept.

9

As the fire settled down to the ashes, with now and then streams of sparks beading the mulatto sky, the red glow flushed the faces of the men who had come too late to put it out. Lovell had ridden hard, but he had arrived only to see the chimneys standing away from the smoldering foundation.

"Where's Dee Day? Anybody seen Dee Day? Didn't he go with you, Mr. Lovell?"

At once the rumor spread that Dee Day was missing. Lovell sat his horse and looked hard at the dying flames. His dark face burned, but not altogether from anger. There was the sullen twinge of fear not yet admitted, yet lurking somewhere. For the first time in his life he felt he had met an enemy as dangerous, as subtle, as himself. The fire, coming at the moment when he took over the fight, was a direct challenge of no quarter. As he turned away from the ruins of his dwelling, the pyre of his servant, he began to feel something of the old excitement when he had traveled the roads with a few companions. The boredom of success and secret ambition fell from his shoulders like a rotten cloak. He lifted his hat and spoke to the murmuring crowd of men and slaves:

"Maybe this was an accident, gentlemen. Day was always clumsy, you know." The accent of his words was such that all said there is a gentleman who won't think hard of people until he's seen the proof. But somehow his voice left a warning that no house or barn in Buyckville was safe.

The news traveled to the posses riding up and down the roads, to the men with their pine torches staining the gloomy woods. It was evidence that the outlaws were still about. The man hunt settled down to serious business. Botterall rode as a man possessed. Once he pulled up close to the fire, looking hard at the hot coals. He saw what looked like bones, and the lard poured out of his body. By sun the cordon had drawn in several miles. Tired horses and tired riders stopped to blow. The women cooked up food and brought it out to the roads, sent it to the forest by the children. Reports came in that slaves were missing. Botterall rode down three horses, whipping up the lagging searchers carrying the news of the missing slaves. His high frenzy was catching. The mounts were driven until the foam gathered in their bits and the sweat poured down their flanks and bellies. Plenty of game was beat up, but no strange men. Rabbits scurried about, and the dogs wore out their high nervous voices until, dropping to the ground, they let their tongues hang dripping in the dust and trash.

By light the little dew there was had dried, and before the sun was up men were saying, "We'll sizzle in our own sweat today, buddies." The Senegalese driver on Lovell's place had poked in the hot ashes and stirred up a black-socketed skull.

Meanwhile Bob Pritchard, keeping at times to the woods and at times to the roads and paths, circled and backtracked to elude the live net that was closing in around him. After he had left Old Man Fox's empty house, he was surprised to find his way to the cave blocked. He fell back and lay about the brush, hoping to find some opening before day, but with the light the hunt took on a fresh heat. He thought at first it was only a coon hunt, then gradually he became aware of its true nature. At first he was contemptuous. Later he took pleasure in the commotion he had stirred up. But after he had traced the bank of the Staircase for two miles, a serious look settled upon his bold face. It was closely guarded all the way. Once after light he might have slipped through and made a break for it, but he knew he must have been seen.

"I'll be God-damned if I'll show these skunks where to throw their stink," he said to himself.

He fell back and kept to the thickest part of the woods, but the woods were strange to him, and he was always rooted out. Each time he moved, he fell farther away from the river and his way of escape. At first he was so absorbed in the chase he didn't notice how he had let himself be sucked toward the center of the cordon that was closing in on Buyckville. "I've been in many a fox hunt, but this is the first time I've played fox," he said half aloud, and a twisted smile curved down his mouth. But the humor was half-hearted. He looked up at the sun. It was three hours high. The woods were still except for the hum of the insects and the heat. How loud they sounded! A sign of a powerful hot day. Already the sweat on his face and neck was stinging with gnats. No matter where he lay now he could hear, either close or far away, the sound of hoofbeats. If only he could stay hidden until night. . . .

He crawled into a sassafras thicket and lay down on his back. He took out his pistol and examined it, just to make sure. . . . The feel of the gun was getting to be mighty comforting, the grip was so sure, the barrel so straight and cool. He sat up. What was that? And he found himself pointing to the rear, rigid and straining. Well, I'll be . . . A God-damned bird makes more noise in the woods than an elephant. . . . After this he couldn't rest. He hadn't eaten in thirty-six hours, and he'd been moving all night without sleep, but he couldn't rest. If a measly jay can upset a fellow . . . but the jay had given him the consciousness of the hunted feeling. He found his ears straining, listening for the slightest noise. He could not lie still. Every silence was an ambush. He must leave the hiding-place in the hollow. He must be where he could always hear the two-footed hounds. He climbed the ridge and looked about. Now if I cross that road down yonder and double back . . . Well, damned if I ain't a fox shore-'nough now.

Damon Harrison was riding along the narrow road with his

leg thrown over the saddle's pommel. He had left the others with some excuse. The truth was he was beginning to feel foolish riding up and down the roads and finding nothing. Now he discovered he had turned the horse's head down the road where the bee girl lived. "I'm Ruth Weaver," rang through his head in time to the feel of his mount. As he realized where he was going, he flushed and threw his leg back in the stirrup. He lifted the reins to turn back when he saw what looked like bushes rustling a hundred yards ahead. He put his animal into a trot. As he passed the spot which had aroused his suspicions, he kept his head straight to the front; but he saw out of the corner of his eye what seemed to be the figure of a man squatting. He did not increase his speed. He kept on down the road as if he had seen nothing. It was not long before he came out of the woods at the Weaver place. In front of the house five of the posse were drinking from a gourd, and she was handing the bucket around. She pretended not to see him as he rode up. "Just saw a man in the bushes about a quarter back," he shouted. He had planned to say it in an offhanded way, but his voice quivered like a little boy's bringing exciting news. He dropped his gaze from embarrassment. When he looked up, the men were starting off and calling to him for more exact information. He tried to slink away without seeing her.

"Don't you want a drink before you go?" As she spoke, he saw only the brightness of her eyes.

He drank hurriedly, spilling the water out of the gourd's sides. He looked toward her with what he believed masculine tenderness.

"Thank you, Miss Ruth." He dropped his voice and leaned down. "If I get out of this fracas alive, can I come talk to you sometime?" He could not suppress the ring of reckless, noble sentiment that he felt although he had wanted to be casual, like a man who was weary of hunting outlaws down.

She did not drop her eyes, but their gay brightness warmed as she said, "If you want to." As he lifted his reins to leave in a flourish, he heard her say, "Take care of yourself."

For the next thirty minutes he could think of nothing but this womanly show of concern, and it made him so reckless in his hunt that an older man had to call sharply to him to go to the rear.

Bob Pritchard had reached the road he had seen from the ridge. As he was about to cross, he saw a lone horseman with his leg thrown over the saddle slow-walking his way. He dropped quickly to cover. Maybe now if he dropped the rider, he might seize the critter and make his escape. He cocked the pistol and raised to his knees—he warn't any hand to shoot lying on his belly like a toad. The horse was stepping forward in a quick, handsome trot. He watched the legs shine in the sun as the beast threw them forward. He raised the gun. Hell, that was nothing but a kid in the saddle. He'd be damned if he'd sink so low as to shoot a boy not dry behind the ears. And anyway the old fox warn't ready to find his hole. But if he'd known a race was a-foot, he'd by all rights have stuck something between his ribs. Pull up the belt tighter and take a chew . . . a chew of tobacco is as filling as a chicken dinner anyway. . . .

He swallowed and stepped into the road and turned down it in the opposite direction from the way the boy had gone. The boy might have seen more than he let on. Anyway, the going in the woods was mighty rough. He was mortal tired, and the road didn't make a man stretch his legs so. It was plain and straight, noways tangled up. He'd just walk down it and, if he came to any obstruction, he'd shoot his way through. He'd be damned if a set of nigger stealers and hoss thieves would run him all over the country like a coon. It was queer now that he'd been walking a half an hour, and no sound or sight of anything or anybody. He dropped to the ground and put his ear to the red sandy road. Faintly a crunching struck his ears, but they were so full of blood maybe he didn't hear straight. He'd lie still a while to make sure. The road here was covered with trees and it was cool. A little rest wouldn't do him any harm. He lay until his body fell away from the bone and his

eyelids drooped. The whole chase was worth this piece of rest.
Somewhere in his mind he recollected trying to draw his muscles
together to get up; and, when his legs wouldn't move, he remembered thinking he had laid down in molasses. His
thoughts grew confused and he was watching a fly trying to
step up the sides of a sugar pot. . . .

A big cane-cutter, jumping across the road to his front,
brought him to his senses. He lay for a minute before he
could remember where he was and what had happened. He
must have fallen asleep. How long—he looked up at the sun.
He couldn't see it from where he was, but it left blotches of
heat waves as far up the road as he could see. Other rabbits
began to hop across in the clear—from both directions. That
was a bad sign. A few varmints slunk quickly by, paying him
no more mind than if he himself was a varmint. A rattler pilot
tailed its way, head up and tongue flickering, into the bushes.
No use taking to the woods now. Too late. It looked mighty
like he was trapped. Varmints don't run from themselves.
There was a rise near the bend in that road. Now if he could
make it, he might . . . anyway he could give lead ball for
lead ball.

He set off in a run, and as he reached the base of the rise, two
horsemen walked into view. They slouched in their saddles
and swept their eyes before them. He looked to his rear.
There were three more from that direction. How many more
men were in the woods God A'mighty knew but maybe the
devil would hold them until he could reach the top. So this
was the way it felt to be trapped. Now if he could climb that
topmost tree. No. He'd burn before he'd be treed like a coon.
He'd stand with his feet on the ground like a gentleman. Now
that the thing was coming to a showdown, it was amazing
how clear everything seemed. He noticed the bushes and the
sharp outlines of the trees, the slope of the ground, how they all
fitted neatly together and how the boulder to his left could not
be moved without throwing the whole setup out of joint. He
saw several twigs fall, and before he could wonder why, the
reports of guns shook the air. He stooped over and hurried up

the slope. He reached the top with only a nip at his boots. That seemed a little queer. Maybe now . . . No. All around the woods were shaking. He walked calmly around the top of the knoll as if he were sighting for a survey. The top wasn't so good after all. It was too wide to control. He picked out a broad-trunked pine and backed up against it. He took out his pistol, powder and shot, arranged the ammunition on the ground. He looked at it to see whether he had placed it handy enough, then stood up. He shifted his quid from one jaw to the other and waited. Now let the tail-wagging, belly-dragging sons of bitches come on.

At once, from all sides, the reports of rifles cracked from the cover of the woods. The twigs fell, and the dirt jumped up. A rock leaped from the ground and twanged by his head. It had come. He drew himself up until his head sat high, with his eyes at a point on the green foliage. Fifty yards or so to the front he saw the bushes move. Automatically his pistol arm raised and fired. A loud yell followed the report. He shook his head. Missed by a burn. No dead man hollers. He waited a long minute. All around, in an uneven line, he could see the spent powder rising, spreading among the tall branches like a blue web. This gave him a general sense of their advancing positions. In the silences he could hear boots crunching.

Out of the corner of his right eye he saw some bushes quiver, part, and show the whites of two eyes. He let the second bullet fly. The bushes went down and a man fell through, spouting blood from his neck. Bob smiled grimly. He had become accustomed now to the sound and smell of powder, to the zipping of the lead bees about his head. Unconsciously his ears were registering and classifying the dangerous sounds. He had felt behind him a man running from tree to tree. He had timed the pauses in the runner's advance. Suddenly he turned and fired. The third shot caught the lean man in the stomach. He flung his beard in the air, stumbled over his boots, caught himself, and fell slowly to the earth, burying his head like a heathen.

As Bob was watching the startled look on the falling man's

face, the forest behind him crackled afresh and the bullets stung the air. Not until he turned to face this danger did he feel the burn run straight through his back to his lungs. He caught a limb to steady himself, and his mouth filled with blood. He tried to swallow it, thinking maybe if he could just keep it down . . . but his jaws fell open, and it ran through his teeth, spilling from beneath the chin, blotting out the wide white checks on his shirt. He hung by the limb a little longer, gripping the round smooth bark convulsively, his pistol hand shooting up the ground at his feet. Another volley shook his clothes. The hand turned loose and, squatting on his haunches, he dropped to his knees. He felt his legs spread apart, felt the jar as his butt struck the rock, the bump of the head, and then, for a moment, there was nothing between his wide blue eyes and the narrow blue sky but the still trees and their green branches.

10

Dusty boots climbed the steps to the long run between the four rooms at the Weaver house, creaking as their owners attempted to put them lightly down. Other men stood in the yard, talking in lowered voices, while late-comers were taking out and feeding the teams with corn and fodder they had brought along, knowing Old Man Weaver would be short, as it was the end of the crop year and not yet gathering time. The women had already gone back to the ell to sit with the women or help in the kitchen. In the front room, together on the double bed, Brother Macon and Alf Weaver, the casualties of the afternoon, lay stretched beneath the sheet. The sun had gone down, but it was still light.

About first dark Abner Buchanan rode up on his pacing mule. He slipped down and tied him to the fence. There was a pause in the conversation of a small group of his friends as they waited for him to join them.

"Has anybody washed the dead?" he asked as he entered their circle. His voice was pitched to a pious key.

"Some of the boys washed Alf Weaver"—around the speaker's eye there lurked the suspicion of a twinkle—"but everybody said 'twarn't right to wash Brother Macon ontell you come up."

"Until I come up?" He looked sharply at his friends.

"Didn't anybody rightly know how a Campbellite ought to be fixed for burying."

"You wash'm same as you do a Baptist or a Methodist." He spoke crisply.

"We all figgered you'd know where the artickles would say wash."

Buchanan could smell the strong fumes of liquor, but every face wore a solemn, respectful look. The suspicion upon Abner's face melted into a pious gravity.

"I feel the honor powerful, but that duty belongs to his kin. I ain't nothing but a pore sinner."

"You know, Abner, Brother Macon ain't got no kin in this country." The voice carried a gentle reprimand.

Joe Beatty spoke up. "If that outlaw hadn't turned to plug Brother Macon, Abner, it might 'a' been you Brother Macon would be called on to scrub. You wouldn't deny sech a little service to the man who had saved your life."

At that moment a voice from the run, lowered to the proper key, called, "Brother Buchanan, oh, Brother Buchanan."

Abner turned his head. "All right, you got me. But I deputize all of you chief mourners—to hand me things and bile the water."

"The water's bilen in there now," Ed Johnston said matter-of-factly.

"Well, I'll need you to hand me things."

He turned toward the house and the others followed. Damon Harrison was sitting in the run. As he passed by, Abner said:

"Son, fetch me some water in the laying-out room."

The boy nodded and got up with pleasure. He had been hanging around hoping to see Ruth. Now he had a good excuse to go near the kitchen, where she would be helping the women. He lingered over the water buckets as long as he could, but his backward glances into the long kitchen showed only the older women moving about in the glow from the open fire. He ambled to the well, drew two buckets and was carrying them to the house when he heard a woman's voice:

"Now whar'd them buckets git to?"

He saw his chance. "Here they are, ma'm," and he stepped onto the porch.

He was met by a large woman with her waist drawn tight and her stomach rolling from under the dark calico apron. The light was fading fast, but the eyes in her brown, wrinkling face were kind.

"I'm perishing for a drink," she said.

"This is fresh drawn," and Damon, as he spoke, held up the bucket.

"Son, whose boy are you?" she asked, dropping the dipper back in the water.

"Mr. Quintus Harrison's. My name's Damon."

"Lawd, I've heard about him, but this is the fust I've seen any of his folks. I'll just take them buckets. We're setten about making the coffee."

"It sure smells good." He hesitated.

"I always did say the smell of roasten beans makes a body eat more. There'll be plenty et tonight, but they won't need coffee to make them hongry what with traipsing all over the woods and toddying in the sitting-up room. They'll need it to keep thar heads from rolling, though. But," as she reached for the buckets, "I don't begrudge it to'm this time. Now that outlaw fellow's been killed and strung up maybe a body can sleep without looken for her man to turn up dead. Maybe it'll larn the others to mind their business."

Damon held to the buckets.

"I'll just carry these in there for you, ma'm. They need me

to fetch water. They're going to wash Brother Macon."

"All right, sonny. I'll git something to empty it in. Pore Brother Macon, I've heared he was a godly man."

He followed her into the kitchen. It was a pleasant, sociable-looking room. At the moment a long hand-made table stood pushed against the wall, closing the door into the family room where the Weavers had gone to rest, leaving the watch of the dead to their neighbors. Already the table was loaded with food. At each end, rising from their drippings, two brown hams sent with Mr. Lovell's compliments rolled in their platters. Down the center four freshly baked cakes stood high upon their glass-legged dishes, the thick icings looking rich in the friendly glow from the big fireplace. Loaves of flour bread sat to the front, and there was more baking in the small ovens lying on the hearth buried under hot coals and ashes. The dishes of the neighborhood were stacked in tiers and beside them, neatly piled, lay the silver.

Damon looked hastily at the table and at the women. At the moment there were four in the kitchen. One, in her middle years, was at the biscuit block, a tall white oak stump planted before a window. She was making up egg bread in a large wooden mixing bowl. Her sleeves had been rolled up and her hands, thrust in up to the wrists, mixed the batter. Near by, in regular jerky swings an old woman, her shoulders curving around her flat breasts, was turning the coffee mill. Her arm was nothing but hanging bones held together by a tight wrapping of skin. Any moment the mill might jerk it away from her shoulder and break it into a thousand pieces against the solid puncheon floor. Standing on the hearth, a shy young woman with blood in her cheeks was leaning over and stirring the big pot. Sitting on the bench by the fire Aunt Patsy Weaver held herself by a hickory stick, as brown as she and as wrinkled. She was smoking a pipe of strong tobacco. She had refused to retire to the dark room with the other members of the family. "Somebody'll have to show the neighbors whar the herbs and seasnen air," she had said. But in truth she was too old for grief or work. She was too old, even, for

memory, that last flowering of the blood before it runs thin
and dries. In her youth she had been carried off by friendly
Indians at the time of the Massacre of Fort Mims and kept by
them for five years in a small Creek village until her brother,
happening through on a trading expedition, bought her freedom for a dry cow and ten pounds of tobacco. There was
something of the strength of the earth in her character, for in
a long life she had buried nine children and outlasted two hus-
bands, and this in the days when the women were the first to
give way before the hard demands of the frontier. So when
the two men, one of them her great-nephew, had been brought
in from the knoll where they had fallen, she had shown no concern and but the most casual interest. She hobbled toward
the bed and looked at the wounds. "Right smart shooten fer
Injuns," she said.

yeoman farmers agrarian virtue

"Tain't Injuns, Aunt Patsy. Outlaws done it," her seventy-
year-old nephew shouted.

She shook her deaf head, looked at him from her watery
eyes and answered in a quavering voice, "You might pore a
leetle turpentime in, Davey. But I've never seen nobody
carry lead in thar belly and git up agin." She shuffled toward the kitchen after the turpentine, and her nephew had to
shout again that the men were already dead. "Thar now,
what'd I tell ye?" And saying this, she hobbled back to her
place by the kitchen fire.

Damon saw her watch the young woman by the kettle.
Directly she spoke:

"Ready to jug the pigeons, child?"

Damon had heard the tales people told about her, and as he
looked at the old woman, he found it hard to believe that anything had ever happened to her. But he didn't linger over
his misgivings. He glanced once more hurriedly about the
kitchen. Ruth was nowhere to be seen. He could not hide
his disappointment. He stopped in the middle of the floor
with the buckets.

"Here, sonny, hand me one of them buckets. I'll empty it
and you can fetch us more later on."

The other women ceased talking as he entered, but Aunt Patsy's voice went on, "Scald the livers and put'm on the fire for a minute or two. Then take them out and mince'm small and bruise'm with the back of a spoon. I ginerally use that-ar pewter spoon. . . ."

And then he saw her standing in the doorway with two lighted lamps. The soft light from the chimneys warmed her light brown hair, and as she saw him, her eyes brightened and her cheeks flushed.

"Here, boy, don't stand there gaping. Pour that bucket in this kittle."

"Yes'm." He hurried forward, and the woman noticed the change that had come over him.

"I'll just leave this other bucket in here," he said shyly.

She looked from boy to girl, and a mischievous twinkle wrinkled her eye.

"Boy, you stay out of this kitchen. You might spile the victuals."

"Yes, ma'm."

He turned and reached the table with the bucket as Ruth put the lamp down. She smiled. He nodded toward the porch, and his face had a desperate appeal. She nodded back. When he left the kitchen, his heart was light and gay. He hung about the well waiting.

"Aunt Patsy, I'll bring another lamp," said Ruth to her aunt.

She spoke in guilty haste, but the old woman didn't hear her. Aunt Patsy's voice went monotonously on:

"Now when you git done with that—Ruthy, git the pepper, salt, and nutmeg, air we got any grated?"

Shouting, "Yes, Aunt Patsy, it's been grated."

"Air the eggs biled hard?" Not waiting for an answer, Aunt Patsy continued, "Chop the parsley fine, bruise the yolks and mix all the seasnen together. Put as much suet as liver—shave it fine—grate the bread, as much again."

Ruth set the condiments on the table and slipped away. As she left, she heard her great-great-aunt's feeble voice intone with the cadence of an ancient high priest reciting a familiar ritual, "Work all these hyar together with enough raw eggs tell hit's crumbly, roll it in fresh butter. . . ."

"Hold on thar, Aunt Patsy," interrupted the young woman. "You're a-goen too fast."

"Put a piece in the crops and bellies; then sew up the necks and vents."

Ruth walked lightly onto the porch.

Damon saw her the moment she stepped through the door and glanced about the dark. He whispered as he came forward, "Here I am by the well." He took her by the hand and led her into the yard. As his hand closed over hers, he felt a timid answering pressure.

"I can only stay a minute," she said in a close breath.

The touch of their hands made him feel strong and confident. He let his fingers slip through hers until their bones pressed together in a tight clasp. Leaning forward, he whispered in her ear:

"Remember what you promised?"

"I . . . I think I do."

"Meet me tonight?"

"Oh, I can't. That is, I don't think I can."

"Don't you want me to talk to you?" His mouth brushed her ear, and she could feel the breath warm and tickling.

"Do you want me to?" she asked, teasing.

For an answer he turned and looked squarely at her. She drew back, and he reached for her other hand. It lay still and cold by her dress.

"Do you reckon I ought to?" she repeated.

"Please. We won't get a chance like this every day."

"I don't think I better," she answered.

At that moment somebody called her name.

"I've got to go," she said. She was seized with sudden panic. As she pulled away, he held her a second longer.

"I'll wait for you around the corner of the house"—she broke away—"after supper."

She ran toward the porch and disappeared in the house.

When she returned to the kitchen, she was carrying another lamp. It seemed as if she had never left it. Everybody was stirring about, and the old woman's voice still intoned in its halting rhythm, "Dip the pigeons in water and drap'm in the jugs. How many jugs air they?"

"Three, Aunt Patsy."

"How many?" The woman pointed to the three clay jugs.

"Tain't enough, but we can make out. Divide the pigeons eq'al, and season like you would fer a pie."

Sally Botterall came in, and the women greeted her. She took off her bonnet and they could see she was distraught.

"I'd 'a' been here sooner, but I had to git the youngest boy to drive me over. Lem ain't been to the house since the killen. I was halfway feared for him to bring me. With a barn full of critters we ain't got ary one fitten to drive."

"Lawd, Sal. Hit don't matter none. We've made out right well."

"I know, Betsy, but I wanted to do what I could at sich a time."

There was irritation in her voice. Betsy caught it at once, and her heart understood and was troubled that her friend should suffer and be mortified, for instinctively she could tell Sal's disappointment was not trivial. Her words had soaked long in the bone, where the sweet marrow had turned dry and bitter. Because of their girlhood together, because they had set up housekeeping at the same time and had boiled the water for each other when the children came and for the sake of old friendship, Betsy answered in an offhand way as if the thing that afflicted Sal was their common lot.

"They all git alike after the chillurn come, Sal," she said sympathetically.

"Yore man brought you, Betsy."

"You might say his belly brought me. If he hadn't come by to grease it, I'd 'a' not got hyar."

"I reckon you're right, Betsy. That Lem don't study nothen but horses."

"Cover'm close," spoke Aunt Patsy, "and set some tiles

atop the jugs. That's hit. Now they're ready to bile."

The old woman watched the younger carry out her directions. She knocked out her pipe, and her shaking hands went down to the pocket of her apron, shook there, and brought out some dry brown leaves. As she crumbled the tobacco in her hands, the movements of the women at their work quickened. There were spurts of conversation, pauses, long silences, and the close feminine communion that settles over a kitchen at such a time. The voices were freer. They took on the peculiar tones of intimacy, at moments almost of conspiracy, that is never heard in mixed company. Tonight there was an element of excitement of higher tension than usual. The relief from the strain of the last few days, the mark of death in the house, gave to their occupations a special meaning, and they moved in an atmosphere that was close and private.

The young woman stood up from tiling the jugs. She spoke up shyly but in some defiance:

"My man's not changed any since the baby come."

The older women chuckled. "Her fust one."

"Yes, May Lou, child," said Sal, "you're eaten yore white bread now."

"What about bread? Tain't baked done yet?" asked Aunt Patsy.

"We was talken about the men, Aunt Patsy." Sal shook her head. "Not bread, the menfolks."

"Men?" Aunt Patsy repeated the word as one who remembers a name but has forgotten its implication.

Sal was busy at work now, and the frown over her brow had softened. She was pouring the coffee grounds in sacks and tying them up.

"I'll declare," she said with a touch of pride, "the older men git the bigger fools they air. That Lem of mine, it's God's mercy he ain't broke his neck on them wild horses. He's so tubby he can't git on'm from the ground."

"I'll be bound the bed don't stand too high fer'm," said the woman whom Damon had met on the porch.

"Lawd, Em'ly, he done quit studying sich."

"I'll be bound he has," Em'ly said. It had been long since Sal had blushed. She spoke with fresh animation:

"All Lem studies is horses. Why, two weeks ago the old fool come in late and drunk, and fust thing I knowed I heard a commotion in the run and he was trying to stable his mare in the house. Had her in the run."

"Don't say."

"He led her in our room and hitched her to the bed post. Made one of the chillurn fotch an armload of fodder."

"What'd you do, Sal?" Betsy's voice was scandalized.

"Do. What could a body do? With him heavy drunk and the crittur nervous and skeered. Sayen his crittur was as good as anybody and by-Goden around. What was good fer me and the chillurn warn't too good fer his mare."

"Well, Lawd, what'll they do next?" Em'ly shook her head, as if to say there were no limits within her knowledge.

"I got in bed with mammy, but I couldn't sleep. Who could sleep with him a-snoren drunk and the mare a-tromping and you know what in my bedroom? He et humble pie in the mornen," Sal said with a firm set to her chin. "I seen to that."

"What'd you do?" Betsy asked.

"I never give him a bite to eat, no sir, not a God's bit, ontell he cleaned and scrubbed that room himself."

She looked at the women with pleasure at the memory of her defiance.

"I'd 'a' made him buy me a purty too." Betsy turned around to speak.

"He got me a barrel of white flour. We needed it, and I never said nothen."

There was a silence after this, and Aunt Patsy puffed in the corner. Directly she took out her pipe.

"I buried two of'm. The fust one—it was sw'are, sw'are, sw'are. The last one—pra'er, pra'er, pra'er."

Through all the moving about, through all the conversation, Ruth was thinking of Damon. She at first decided not to meet him, then she would remember how tenderly he had looked at her and how she felt when he was near or touched her. Then

she decided to slip away.   But her conscience rebuked her in
the form of her Cousin Alfred lying dead in the front room.
She told herself she should be thinking of him and sorrowing
for him and Aunt Tildy, his mother.   And for a little while
she felt sad.   And then she thought it might have been Damon
instead, and her heart almost stopped and she wanted to rush
from the kitchen and tell him she would be there.   Maybe she
could slip away without anybody knowing it.   But no, that
wouldn't be right.   The look of distress she imagined in
Damon's eyes started the round of argument all over again.

II

Damon came into the sitting-up room with the water.   He
could hear the pot bubbling over the fire and the steam sizzle
upward to vanish into the chimney.   He glanced covertly at
the bed, and there lay the forms of the two dead men under
the stiff folds of the sheet.   Abner Buchanan was setting the
jug down.

"Pass her around ag'in, Ab," said Botterall.

"No, I've had enough.   I mout make a mis-take and wash
myself."

There was gruff laughter, and Damon sensed an atmosphere
of gaiety, too boisterous and unrestrained, he thought, for the
occasion.

"Oh, I don't reckon a washen would come amiss," said
Botterall.

"Yes, Abner, you do smell sort of goatish," said another.

"That, gentleman, is from the something to eat I get."

He walked over to the bed and lifted the sheet and
dropped it.

"You are right, men.   I do need another drink."

So the jug went around again.   Botterall turned it up first and let the liquor roll down his gullet. He let out his breath with a wheeze, heavier than usual, wiped his chin on his sleeve, and passed the jug.

"They shore shucked that green," he said.

Joe Beatty threw it over his arm and turned it up. He had a long red neck and an eye with a white spot in it. As he drank, his Adam's apple moved up and down like a piston.

" 'Y God, boys, look at Joe chew his cud. Some of his folks mixed up with a cow shore."

"Come to think of, Joe has got a muley look," said Abner. He was feeling fine by now.

The merriment increased and was heard through the closed door, out into the run. Damon set the bucket down and went out. He slammed the door slightly with the hope that the noise might remind them of the proprieties. The jug went the rounds twice again. Some drank quick. Others pulled long on the neck. Abner shut his eyes and chewed the mouth.

"All right, men," he said, wiping his chin and setting the empty jug by his chair, "I'm ready for Brother Macon."

Beatty and Simmons drew back the sheet.

"Where do you want him, Ab?"

Abner stepped back unsteadily and looked at the body.

"Well, now, you've got me stumped. I'm new to this kind of a trade."

"Somebody git the wash tub," growled Botterall.

"You ain't figgering for me to set him in the tub, Lem?"

"Hell, no. But what's to keep you from standen him up in it?"

"That's an idey. I deputize you to hold, sheriff."

"You can't deshutize the sheriff."

"That's a fact. Well, Joe, you hold him."

Joe looked at the corpse.

"He'll lean ag'in the wall," he said.

The tub was brought, and the corpse of Brother Macon, after the clothes had been clumsily stripped, was lifted in. At this moment Damon returned with another bucket of water. He saw the grayish-brown figure leaning grotesquely against the mantelpiece. The body was thin and drawn, and it had the cold shine of death. The icy eyes stared into the room, and the beard hung softly down. From the hole in the stomach a black stream of dried blood had spread down the inside of a thigh, streaking the calf, to the twisted toes. The hands were clenched, and at the corner of the mouth dark stains turned down like tusks. A look of fear and horror spread over Damon's smooth features. He felt his scalp tingle, and when he spoke, there was hatred and disgust in his voice.

"Here's the other bucket of water. Be enough?"

"A bucket of water? Dump it in the tub, my boy," Abner said gaily, rolling up his sleeves.

Damon's face lost its color and he hesitated; but, looking down, he did as he was told. He could not help but see the water splash around the still, ashen legs. As soon as he had emptied the pail, he picked up the other one and left the room.

"The boy's got weak guts," said Beatty pleasantly.

"That's a sight to turn stronger guts to jelly," answered Botterall.

The assistants began to look a little grim.

"You boys ain't white-eyed on me?" Abner asked cheerfully.

"Hell, no," said Beatty. "He won't bite."

"Pitch the soap in that ar bucket and swing out the pot."

It was done in silence, and Buchanan picked up the broom. He dipped it in the kettle and swung the scalding water on the corpse.

"Ain't you a-goen to mix the water?"

"If it's too hot fer'm, he'll holler."

He ran the broom into the water, over the soap, then over the legs of the corpse.

" 'Y God," he said, "but I believe the dirt's set on him."

For a while there was no sound in the room but the sloshing of water and the noise of scrubbing.

"I always wondered how come Brother Macon to move into these parts," Simmons said, as he watched Abner work. "There ain't any of his faith in this country, and he set so much store by it."

As Simmons spoke, there was no light in his cold eye. His callous face looked like a rough block of sandstone, with a big chip knocked out, for his mouth was weak.

"I never heard him talk about his folks," said Beatty.

"That's a fact now."

"A man that don't have a woman gits cur'ous as he gits old." Botterall shook his head like a man who has the secret of wisdom. "And besides," he continued with the tone of a man that knows more than he lets on, "sometimes folks have to strike the road."

Beatty looked toward the sheriff, and a glance of understanding passed between them.

Buchanan set the broom in the corner.

"Well, gentlemen, I've done what I could for him." He pulled out his handkerchief and wiped his forehead. "Now wipe and dress him."

His assistants protested, but he turned to Botterall as moderator. Botterall sided with Buchanan. As the difficulties of his three assistants grew, for the dressing was slow and troublesome, Abner's spirits rose. When at last the body was laid back on the bed, Beatty said:

"I'd as soon dress a saw log."

"You ain't done yet, gentlemen." Buchanan spoke soft and purling. "Comb his ha'r."

Beatty and Simmons looked rebellious.

"That's right, boys. Comb his ha'r," commanded the sheriff.

"Shorely, men, you wouldn't begrudge sech a little favor to the man who had saved your ornery hides."

At these mock tones of reprimand from Abner, Beatty looked vicious, but he kneeled on the bed and brushed until a gentle knock was heard on the door, and Ruth's soft voice said:

"Get ready for supper."

Buchanan looked slyly at the men by the bed, walked over and inspected their work. He looked very solemn. "Well, here's one Campbellite that'll be buried a Christian." With that he went out of the room, reeling jauntily.

Damon, in the crowd and confusion about the supper table, had been able to catch Ruth's eye but once, and he couldn't tell what she had made up her mind to do. He had now been waiting half an hour at the end of the ell, and every minute of that time he had listened for her footfall. He had waited until the people had stopped moving up and down the run, until they had settled in the two front rooms. The muffled gaiety in the front part of the house sifted vaguely through the warm evening. Once his mind wandered to the ugly rites he had witnessed, and it made him feel strangely depressed. He could not get the sight of Brother Macon, leaning grotesquely against the wall, out of his mind. He shifted his thoughts back to Ruth, but somehow he was always seeing the frozen fury on the old man's face and the thin billy-goat beard. Once he was sure she was coming, but as he stepped out to meet her, he saw a shadow of a man disappear around the porch. He drew back to cover, not thinking how strange it was for a figure to be lurking about the outside of the house when all the guests had settled for the night.

At last she came. But she stayed only a minute, just long enough to whisper that she was going to her room and pretend that she had gone to bed. After everything quieted down, he was to tap at her window and she would slip away. After she left him, Damon reached in his pocket and brought out a finger full of tobacco crumbs, dropped them behind his jaw, and ambled into the woods back of the house to wait.

Only Botterall, Joe Beatty, and Simmons were with the remains. Theirs was the first watch. The rest of the neighbors who had come to sit up had gathered across the run. Into the room where the dead lay drifted the hum of subdued pleasure, the steady rise and fall of busy voices, with, now and then, a sudden laugh sounding sharply through the house.

Simmons looked at the sheriff.

"Ain't no worry over the way, from the sounds they're maken."

"No," answered Botterall, and he shifted heavily in his chair. "They air feelen mighty easy." He lapsed into silence.

There was a somber look upon the faces of the three men who sat back from the empty fireplace. The food was sogging in their liquor and upon the bed the dead men stretched quietly beneath the sheet, but it was not sodden piety that drooped upon their jowls—it was the sign of fear, sullen, suppressed, unmistakable fear.

"Them pigeons et fine," said Beatty, absently like a man who is thinking of something else.

"I don't reckon a one of all them folks has stopped to figger——" Botterall's voice broke off in the midst of the sentence he did not need to finish.

"Figger what, Lem?" Beatty faced him squarely with the air of a man who means to have it out.

"How one man could have done all them killens—jest the way they happened."

"Three Wiltons, Dee Day, and them"—nodded Simmons toward the bed. "Ever man of'm was with us the night we killed Old Man McIvor."

"Six for one," answered Beatty without raising his voice.

"Mighty pore average." Botterall leaned forward and spat in the fire. He drew back and folded his hands across his stomach. "Mighty pore."

"I'm like you all. I don't like it a . . ."

Before Simmons could finish, the three of them were on their feet and reaching for their guns. They dropped their hands reluctantly. A gray cat had leaped into the window. She was yowling and looking hungrily toward the bed.

"Kick that . . ."

Beatty flattened his boot against the animal and it fell, howling, into the yard. At once it leaped against the window, screaming now like a thing possessed. It stood upon the sill and pressed its face against the pane, scratching the sash.

"Kill that thing," Simmons cried.

Beatty grabbed the poker and rushed from the room.

There was a loud, persistent, angry cry followed by silence. Beatty returned, but the men were slow to settle themselves. Botterall's hand shook as he wiped his bulging neck.

"I've always heared them things was bad after dead meat."

"I've heared my mammy say her pappy was sitten up with a neighbor and they left the room and when they come back a old Tom had et a big hunk out'n the side of his face." Beatty spoke in awed tones.

"I've heared of sich things," Simmons admitted reluctantly.

"Set down, everbody," Botterall commanded. "Reach under the bed, Simmons. I set a jug of fine, extry fine, liquor Quint Harrison give me to bring over."

Botterall put the stopper back, gave it a stroke with his thick palm, and set the jug by his chair.

"I saw that'ar cat slinking around when I rode up," he said in a tone that pretended to explain its behavior.

"Well, I never saw it." Simmons spoke nervously, glancing furtively toward the window. He dropped his voice. "That warn't no common cat, men." He moved his chair closer into the circle.

"You'll be seeing ha'nts if you ain't keerful," Beatty laughed, but he failed to relieve the tension.

The laughter—for a laugh must be fed like a fire—died away, rasping his throat.

"You sure you killed it, Joe?" Simmons looked earnestly at his companion.

"No—no, I didn't kill it, but I knocked the far out'n it."

"Never did like no gray cats," Simmons complained. "The black'uns are bad enough, but it's them old grays——" Simmons shook his head. "My grandmammy, I've heared her say when Old Scratch wanted to prowl he took a gray cat's hide." He was leaning forward and speaking rapidly. "You heared him. No cat makes any such noise as that. And he warn't a-skeered of us neither. I tell ye . . ."

"Shut up, Simmons." Botterall spoke angrily.

"Well, then, who killed them six men, I ask ye? Who killed'm, I ask ye that." He half-rose in his chair.

Botterall lifted the back of his hand, as if he were going to strike Simmons. Simmons slunk back into the chair. Botterall lifted the jug and handed it over.

"Well, it warn't no cat. Here, take a swig out of this."
Simmons pushed the jug aside.

"I'll tell you another thing, Lem Botterall. I never said nothen about it before, because I thought maybe I was seeing things. But I saw a face, a brown face, brown as an Injun's, with white burnt ha'r jest after we come in from supper. It slid up from the ground and when it saw I was a-looken, it slid down agin."

"Better take that dram, Simmons." Beatty reached for the jug and handed it to him. "You need it."

Botterall looked at the charred back stick in the fireplace, and for a long while no man opened his mouth except to the jug, which at regular intervals passed from one end of the circle to the other. At eleven o'clock the three who were to take the next watch came in.

Squire Bascom, a little man with a high voice, said affably as he entered the room, "We lowed you all must be dead too. Ain't heard a sound in this room for quite a spell."

Botterall, including the others, was middling drunk; but he made no amiable reply to the squire. He tramped out of the room a little unsteadily, waving his confederates before him. The door slammed to behind them.

"Lem acts like something stung him," said the squire. He picked up the empty jug and smelled its mouth. "No use shaking it. Dry as a pea pod." He settled himself in a chair. "Arch, step out to the kitchen and pick us up a snack. If we can't drink, by God, we'll eat."

In the meantime after Damon had been wandering in the woods for what seemed to him a long time, he found that gradually he had been circling until he stood as near the house as the paling fence of the garden. He waited there and listened to the pounding of his heart. Was it too soon? He lingered some moments in this state of irresolution, then slipped to the corner of the ell, along the log walls, to her window. He raised his hand and knocked softly, drew back and listened— there was no response—and rapped again, more sharply. Suddenly she appeared behind the glass. He could see her hands clasped tightly in front of her dress. It was made of some dark material and, merging in the deeper shadows about her, its edges blurred the neat lines of her firm body until her face and hands seemed to hang doubtfully upon the edge of night.

Almost desperately he motioned to her to raise the sash. As her fingers reached timidly forward, he thrust his own under and threw the window to the top. She drew back and a little gasp caught in her throat. Nothing now stood between them. As his eyes reached through the opening, a sense of possession, strange and exciting, seized him. For a moment she could not meet his stare, but inevitably her eyes lifted and she saw him there, blocking out the heavy blue darkness. This frightened her a little, for he had never seemed so large by daylight.

The moon was not yet up, but the stars were out, and the Milky Way smeared the sky with its dull imitation of light. They moved through the woods in silence with her hand in his. At first it had felt cold and damp, and he had wondered at it, but now the blood was returning to loosen her tight hard grip. As the woods deepened and closed behind them, she felt its dark secrecy, at once protecting and menacing. Unconsciously she moved nearer to his side, to its sure protecting warmth. His arm slipped about her waist. His confident fingers pressed her side, drawing her between his chest and hard, pliable shoulder. Soon they were walking in a single rhythm, and she wondered vaguely how, in the room where she had waited cold and afraid, she had wished he wouldn't come.

Damon looked down at her hair and face to make sure it was she. This shy yielding was so unlike the bold teasing girl he had seen running swiftly across the meadow after the bees or before the gate as she handed the water bucket around to the posse. He wanted to tell her, but he was afraid the sound of his voice would undo the charm and make her flee. He tightened his arm, and she lifted her round shoulder and let it settle closer in answer. They passed like this through the great trees, choosing no way but the natural aisles marked by the stand of timber, thinking only of themselves, wandering in the strange delight of new, common sensations, hearing the tread of their shoes upon the soft floor of the forest, and never believing the long night would come to an end. Once Damon thought he could hear the sound of something stalking their trail. They stopped for him to listen, but no foreign noise jarred upon his ears, only the night sounds that bring the woods alive. Upon a rise, where a spring dripped constantly, they saw a pleasant grove with a heavy moss floor running away from an old water oak. He led her there, and they sat down upon its cool, spongy sward.

The sky paled as the copper moon lifted beyond the forest top. Damon leaned against the water oak and drew her against him.

"It's pretty here," she said after a while.

"An't it?" he replied. He let his hand run over the moss. "Just me and you together." He turned as he spoke, and when she looked up, he leaned over and kissed her quickly. She withdrew her small tight lips almost as soon as they had touched his, and they were silent for a while before first love's promise of unknown and secret pleasure. She felt him tremble, and he said:

"Will you be my girl?"

She answered softly, as if she dared not trust her words to breathe, "If you want me to, Damon."

A rock fell tumbling into the spring. She started and he held her close.

"Just a rock; nothing to be afraid of," Damon said. But he knew better. A rock doesn't fall that way of its own accord.

"Damon, do you reckon anybody has followed us?" Ruth whispered against his cheek.

"Why?" He meant to reassure her, but his voice showed he was listening. He stood upon his feet. He thought he heard the light fall of padded feet retreating. "It's some varmint. Suppose I go see." And when she was slow to answer, he asked, "You're not afraid for me to leave you?"

"No, I'm not afraid." But her voice trembled ever so slightly.

"I won't go far," he said. "If anything comes near you, stay quiet. It'll not bother you."

He handed her a stick. "If it's a varmint, this might come in handy."

Damon climbed the rise and looked about him. The stand of trees was thick, and he could not see any distance, but the moon was beginning to throw some light through the high tops. As he slipped forward, around the big trunks, through the tangled grapevines, dodging thickets, he remembered suddenly that figure he had seen prowling about the front part of the Weaver house earlier in the evening. For the first time he realized it hadn't belonged there. His suspicion was thoroughly aroused now. Every few paces he stopped to listen, but he heard only the steady hum of the secret movement which comes alive with the dark. Before, as he and Ruth swung along together, it had seemed friendly and comforting, but now the woods were hostile. He felt a loathing for the things crawling beneath his feet, hiding under the leaves to bite or sting, or climbing the bark in the hunt which meant death. There were the blood-suckers, and the things that lived on the dry bodies of insects, the heavy hunters, soft of foot but lithe and powerful in the spring. Behind the blotches of gloom lurked a thousand invisible eyes measuring from ambush the risks of hunger.

As he stalked the darkness, Damon caught this feeling of fear and hate charging the air. Everywhere about him he sensed danger, invisible and sinister; but as far as he hunted to track it down—he dared not get out of calling distance of the girl—he found nothing to justify his fears. Afraid that whatever it was might get between them and bring Ruth to harm, he turned back toward the grove. It might have been, he tried to think, a varmint after all. But this thought did not set his mind at ease. He was all stirred to fight. The lack of an object put him in an ugly temper, and his booted feet trampled the ground angrily. He neared a tree whose heavy trunk was bulging with a strange growth. He looked at it, but his thoughts were elsewhere. Then the growth fell away from the tree and, before he could collect himself, he felt a dagger touch his ribs.

"You've made enough noise, Damon Harrison, to wake the dead."

The voice was low, distinct, and sharp. The next words, tight with fury, stung the dark. "But you'll never raise Cameron McIvor from his grave."

This voice and its sudden slap of hate brought Damon comfort. Here was something to whip to a focus the scattered turbulence of his own feeling. He had found his enemy, and on the moment he knew he should spend the full measure of his fresh strength in her defense. He felt the pitiful weakness of the knife pressing his ribs. Its threat was lost in his own exquisite desire to fight. Intuitively he sensed that it was in his power to hurt his enemy. If it had been light, the other would have seen in Damon's eyes the cold pleasure of the power to torture. He sought the man's face like one who has waited a long time for this particular moment; then coolly, with deliberate contempt, said:

"If I could I wouldn't raise that old son-of-a-bitching nigger stealer from his grave . . ."

The dagger struck his side and drove him against the tree. At first didn't feel the wound—only the running warmth down his leg and the sickening smell of fresh blood. The fury of the attack told him how well his words had gone home, but even as he triumphed, once more the slick steel found his ribs. On the third thrust he shifted and it plunged through his shirt deep into the body of the tree. Before the other one could draw the blade, Damon kicked him into the bushes. He came back like a cat, but Damon had worked the dagger free of the wood. Damon charged this time, and the shirtless figure fell back toward the grove, sullenly, trying at every moment to close. For a while Damon's short jabs, never very deep, kept him at his distance, but he could not help but feel how fast his strength was flowing out of his side.

As his enemy saw Damon's strength fail, he changed his tactics, leading Damon forward, but staying always out of his reach. Through the dim light Damon could see the hungry eyes watching him for signs of exhaustion. This enemy was bleeding nowhere deeply and Damon knew that he must find a vital spot while he had strength left to drive the blade home. He closed, but as he felt the other's springing grapple, Damon knew it was too late. He would never be able to drive home the blade. He tripped and they tumbled to the earth. As he fell, Damon threw the useless knife into the bushes. For a few moments they rolled and kicked, then around his throat Damon felt an iron grip. His chest swelled to break for air. Black clouds covered his sight, and he sank in darkness.

The next thing he knew he was hearing his name called at a great distance, then the cool air on his face, and then, as he opened his eyes, the blackness faded into a murky blue, which grew finer by the moment, and the stars sifted out, while riding high, the round copper moon lay flat against the sky. He looked at it in wonder when, sharply and in fright he heard Ruth calling. Pressing his hand into his side, he got up and stumbled toward her. She was not far away. She saw him and ran into his arms.

"Oh, Damon, are you all right? I was sure I heard scuffling."

He made her no answer, but let his arms tighten and bring her close against his side. Her embrace was no longer chaste and shy. Passionately she held him as if unconsciously the promise of her body was trying to replace the life he had lost.

"Oh, Damon, Damon," she cried, "I'll love you all my life." Then he felt her relax and the fear return to her voice. "You're . . . you're wet, honey."

"Ruthy!"

She remembered the tenderness of that word all her days, and the frightful change to his voice, flat and strange, as he said, "I'm a dead man, Ruthy."

He shivered once; his body grew heavy, and he slipped from her arms to the ground.

12

Pleasant stopped at the edge of the woods, in the full light of the old moon, to look at his wounds. He was cut in several places and slashed behind the ear. The gashes were not deep, and already they were drying. He wondered if he had got away before the girl saw him. He shook his head. Never again would he let his anger fly so to his head. He had almost bungled his work. He had left Damon with some life left in him. Even now, as he remembered the insulting words, they pained him afresh. He closed his eyes and whispered, "Pa, I'll hunt them down, if I have to go to Africa." And then his lips trembled in his impassive face. "Give me a little time, pa. Give me a little time, and you'll rest easy."

He waited until he was calm, until he no longer heard his heart thumping, until the weakness left him. He slunk toward the fence where the horses were hitched and untied the reins of a young mare. He led her quietly down the road. Several hundred yards from the house he mounted and slow-walked away; then when he was out of sound of the Weaver house, he lifted the reins and the mare moved off in a fast trot.

Overhead the leaning arms of the forest spread their claws, and the shadows of the drying leaves quivered above the road or were still. Underfoot the sandy bottom muffled the steady glump of iron shoes, as horse and rider sped down the corridor of the crisp fall night. Quickly Botterall's clearings washed into view, his house and barns swimming in the cold white light, spectral objects in the visible gloom. Pleasant pulled steadily on the reins, and the little mare came to a stop with a toss of her head. He sat and looked long at the barn stabling the wild horses. When it seemed that he might never move again, he lifted his bridle hand and horse and rider disappeared into the forest.

A gust of wind rose, shivered for a moment among the branches, and died away. Then, thin and ghostly, as if mocking the mare's gait, the sound of other hoofs echoed through the still hot night, grew louder, and the heavy beats of Lem Botterall's mount galloped along, kicking the sand in the road. The sheriff reeled slightly in the saddle. From behind, man and mount looked like a horse running away with a feather bed strapped to its back. By the time Botterall neared his place the rhythm of the gallop had somewhat sobered him. The clear air, the feel of the animal beneath him, had restored his confidence. He looked at his house and remembered it was empty—Sal would be sure to sleep at the Weavers'. As he thought of his wife, a mood of saturnine gaiety seized his spirits. He raised his voice in snatches of her favorite hymn, keeping time to the steady beat of the gallop:

> "As the saints go march-ing in,
> As the saints go march-ing in,
> Oh, I want to be of that number,
> As the saints go a-marching in."

He took the fence in a clean jump and pulled up at the stock pen. He slid to his feet and stumbled toward the gate. Under his breath now that there was no accompaniment he hummed:

> "As the riv-er flows with blood
> As the riv-er flows with blood,
> Oh, I want to be of that number . . ."

Taking a deep breath, he walked more surely toward the barn. His thoughts were now all of pleasure. He would sleep the night out with his wild critters. If a body didn't have to eat, he thought, he would like to set up his bed in an empty stall. By God, he'd do it anyway. If Sal raised hell, he'd whup her. He'd never raised his hand agen her, but if Sal Scrimpshire thought she could always stand in the way of a man's pleasure, he'd show her who to respect. Now that her chillun were about growed she didn't have nothen to do but pester him. The sweet smell of the barn cut short his resentment, and he led the horse in and put him in his stall. He shelled him a good bait, and the slick grains ran through his rough fingers into the bucket. Nobody'd ever catch him feeding rotten corn to his horses. He chuckled as he remembered the hiding his pap had given him for feeding the seed corn to his own colt that year of the great drought.

He poured the grain into the feed box and stood by to watch the animal eat. After a while, with the pleasant crunching in his ears, he walked up and down the hall of the barn, sinking heavily in the litter, pausing before the stalls for his eyes to caress in the dim light the forms of his critters. There was Lady Doll, trim from nose to hoof, and Spider with his long mane, with feet and legs made for speed. The young filly with her reckless eye sniffed the air suspiciously as he passed. He stood for a long while by the stallion, and the animal pawed the litter until the smell of ammonia, sharp and bracing, struck the sheriff's nose. "You don't know your marster, sir," wheezed the man. "But I'll larn you." He repeated with rough affection, "I'll larn you." After a few minutes he turned and, in his curious waddle, pulled down some hay and threw it by the gear room. He unbuckled his pistol belt and tossed it to the floor and lay down beside it. The straw dust tickled his nose, and he sneezed. He sighed and, after a little, fell into a quiet sleep.

An air of peace settled over the barn, falling gently like a dry dew through the stalls, down the racks into the troughs, over the coats of the animals, sifting to the floor and into the damp and acrid cracks at the base of the building. The most restless of the horses were silent and the old work mules stood in their sleep. The rats had humped to their holes with their nightly theft and the late moon, a few minutes before diluting the darkness with straw-colored light, faded into the shadows of the sky. For one moment there was everlasting gloom. Then a rooster crowed in the far distance, and one near by answered. Softly, a pale tallow chill spread over the world and penetrated even to the thick walls of the barn.

Botterall's breathing sounded gradually heavier, irregular until, snorting, the air caught in his nose like a death rattle. In the loft the hay moved and a head lifted through the falling straw, the shoulders and chest, then the full length of a man.

Pleasant leaned over the edge of the loft and glanced at the sleeping figure near the gear room. He swung silently to the floor and still without noise swung toward the sheriff. He stooped and slipped the pistol from its holster. Here was the man who had put the niggers in the smokehouse, had led his father to jail, had gathered the posse which trapped him in his bed. And he was now in his power. He looked at him for a moment, then out through the big doors, standing ajar. Morning was in the air. He must hurry. He raised his foot and kicked Botterall in the thigh. The sheriff grunted like a stuck hog. He kicked again. Botterall sat up in the faded darkness and grabbed for his pistol.

"Who's thar?" he growled, half-awake.

"Get up!"

Pleasant took him by the shoulder and punched the pistol in his side.

The sheriff reached his feet and pushed back against the gear room. He opened his mouth to speak and, as his eyes came awake in the faint light, dropped in a whisper, "Old Man McIvor's ha'nt."

"No, Mr. Botterall, his flesh and blood."

The flesh about Botterall's mouth went to pieces. "But I seen'm blow your head off."

"I'm his son Pleasant, the one you had chained in the church house."

The sheriff was shaking all over. Suddenly he backed away into the hall of the barn, "No you ain't. Git away. Git away." He stumbled against the door of the wild gray's stall and crouched there, shivering. The stallion whinnied like a frightened mare and plunged at the log walls. But the sheriff didn't hear him.

Pleasant shot his neck forward like a snake. "You've moved just where I wanted you to." He raised the pistol to strike, but before it came down, Botterall slunk to his knees and rolled in the litter. His flesh shook and then he lay still.

The boy unlatched the horse's gate and, lifting with great difficulty the inert body of the sheriff, rolled it inside. The stallion backed away, rose on his haunches, and drove his front feet down so near the head they kicked the straw upon the drooping mouth. The golden strands hung to the slobber that drooled into his beard. Pleasant surveyed the senseless mass and, holding to the posts, pushed it with his foot nearer the center of the stall. The horse quivered with fright and he could see by the graying light the fear in its nostrils. He slammed the gate and fastened it, picked up the whip and swung easily to the top of the fodder rack. He hung there out of reach of the maddened hoofs, raised the whip. It curled and cracked. The animal dropped to the floor. Down flashed the thong with regular lashes, now about the wild gray's neck, now across his back, clutching, stinging. The stallion kicked, plunged, tramped the floor, but nowhere could he get free of the long black thing that struck and bit.

At last Pleasant lifted his burning eyes from the floor of the stall. He threw down the whip by the body and swung down to the floor and unlatched the gate. To guard against being seen, he climbed to the rafters and let himself down through the high window that opened toward the woods. The day was breaking. He stood for a moment and listened. The walls of the barn were shaking as they had that night he had parted from Eli. In front of him he could hear the Staircase. He took a deep breath and ran toward its deep steady roar.

13

Quintus Harrison sat at the foot of the long banquet table. There was no sound or movement but the tallow flames sputtering in their silver holders, throwing a dull reflection upon his empty plate. The servant offered the food with an extra dignity, carrying upon his black face, out of respect for the occasion, the marks of formal grief. He lifted the tops of the steaming dishes, waited the proper time for the silent refusal, replaced them, and with hushed movement left the room, leaving his master as he had found him, the empty image of himself. Quintus sat alone, huddled forward in the chair. There was a droop to the shoulders that old men have and his face, as if it had been hastily chalked, looked ghastly—white and pinched. After a while his wife entered the dining room. She passed her usual place and sat down at his side. He took no notice of her entrance.

Two long furrows of agony ran down her face, but her eyes were no longer hard and bright and possessed. She placed her hand upon the table and called Quintus's name with the tone a woman uses to soothe a sick child. He did not hear her and she thought as she looked at his huddled body that if she shouted, he would crumble before her eyes and disappear as she had seen her long-dead brother do at the touch of air. With the patience of sorrow she leaned back in her chair and remembered the long day. How the news came. The tale of a girl, found at dawn half-frozen, holding Damon's still head against her waist, chattering an inarticulate account of what had happened. Then the discovery of the sheriff trampled in a stall of his horse barn. She saw again her husband sitting in the wagon, holding Damon in his arms, saw him bring him in the house and lay him upon the bed, saw him the moment after go suddenly to pieces.

At that moment she had felt a spasm of pain, then relief. And as she closed the door and went about the last rites for the dead, she felt all the hate for her husband wash from her heart. He must suffer now what she had suffered since they had moved to the hill country. She saw clearly what few see only before death, how all along she had known this country must take her son, and how all along this secret knowledge had made her hate almost to madness. She remembered the sweet white body as she washed it, the still childish face, the hair as she combed it and how he looked as he lay dressed for the end, gay and innocent, as if he were ready to spring forward to meet the promise of the day. Then she knew that in this darkness he was hers again, and that she could wait for its ending as she had waited through that other darkness when she had felt him stirring at her side. This knowledge was denied the man now balanced beside her in the great chair. She reached her hand forward and gently took the cold fingers and covered them with her own. Quintus shuddered and turned his head.

"Mr. Harrison, forgive me," she said.

Very slowly the intelligence returned to his sight. After a long while he repeated her words aloud, in that way giving meaning to their unfamiliar sound.

"I've tortured you these last years," she said gently. "You must forgive me."

He looked at her, and the tears broke down his cheeks. She lifted him from his chair and put her arm about his shoulders.

"Come, Mr. Harrison, you'd better rest yourself."

Strong and erect, she led him from the room, and he held to her like a man who has lost his way. The candles were left to burn until one by one the wicks flared, sputtered, died away.

But in all the other cabins, dog-runs, and big houses around Buyckville the lights burned late. With the night, fear settled over the hills and people drew close together and talked in low voices. Little had been said about what was on everybody's mind until after the funeral. But at the churchyard the mourners noticed that several who had sat up with the dead were missing, and it was whispered that they had packed up and left for Texas. There was no loitering about the fresh graves. Almost before the preacher had consecrated the bodies to the ground, eyes had begun to look toward the vehicles hitched to posts and tree limbs. In the broad daylight the most reckless men looked pale and uncertain. People hurrying home from the burying asked if Simmons' house didn't look deserted, and now after sundown others were silently saying farewell and slipping out the back ways to disappear from the neighborhood.

To the north of Buyckville, Pleasant, astride a long-stepping blue mule, picked his way through the trailless forest. Since early light he had traveled, always north, avoiding the roads and paths. Not a man had he seen or heard. He had been now sixteen hours in the saddle and, coming to a cane break, drew rein. He felt reasonably safe from pursuit, and the mule was pretty well blown. He hobbled the animal in the cane, threw his saddle under a tree and stretched along the ground. He lay there with his eyes stretched wide. After a while he murmured softly in the dark:

"Too slow," and then later, almost with pain in his voice, he repeated, "too slow, too slow."

The cool fall air pressed heavily upon his eyes, and he felt the dry lids closing, yielding up his exhausted senses to the quiet night. No. Not yet, not yet could he sleep. He jerked upright and drove his fists into the spongy earth.

"I will not," he cried aloud, "I will not be at their mercy."

The still night replied, "From now on I'll strike alone."

He lay back down and, almost before his head struck the saddle, he was asleep.

14

Pleasant sat in the mouth of the cave waiting for twilight. Earlier than that he dared not venture abroad. It was two years now since his first sally into the hills above Wetumpka. In that time he had pursued his enemies, over many states, and always he had returned to his secret hiding-place unfollowed. He had chosen it well. He had left it now for a special purpose. After two years' absence he would not be expected

around Buyckville. Since establishing himself in the neighborhood, he had spied on Lovell's place until he knew all about
the habits of his people, when they rose, when they went down
to the fields, when they ate. He was at last sure of the dogs.
It had taken him two weeks to make friends with the pack.
He had let them see him the first two days when it was light,
had fed them. Then he had got them accustomed to his wandering about at night. At first they had barked, running out
to attack him. But when they discovered who it was, they
jumped all over him, asking to lick his face in pardon. He
barely had time to quiet them and slip away before somebody
came onto the porch to see what the noise was about. After
that he decided the little bitch had to be got out of the way. It
was a simple matter. She came to him, dragging in the dust
and beating the ground with her tail. She seemed to know
what he was going to do. As he picked her up, her flanks were
trembling and her eyes pleaded with such humility that he did
it as quickly as possible. She gave only one yelp. Lovell
would never know what had become of her. She lay in the
bottom of a sink hole, far enough away not to worry about
anybody finding her.

It was time!

He stood up and looked through the pine branches. A
misty darkness was rising from the river. He dropped down
the pine and went to the place where his skiff was sunk, emptied
it of rocks and water, pushed out into the river and paddled
softly to the other bank. By the time he could reach Lovell's
farm, it would be good dark and Lovell's people would be eating supper. He could slip to the barn with no trouble at all.
The world is never so still, so off guard as at supper time, unless
it is just before day. He pulled ashore, sank the boat and
hurried up the tree to the top of the bank, then set out in a
trot. It was growing dark faster than he expected. His trot
broke into a run and, in the gathering dusk, he sped through
the forest, skirting the edge of fields until he reached the woods
lot opposite Lovell's house and barn. He walked around for a
few moments and listened to the wind pumping in his chest.

That time he had burnt out Lovell the house was close enough to the woods for a quick get-away, but this woods lot was a thousand yards from the barn, with nothing but a few trees for cover. A man running from tree to tree would give himself away. As he looked at the house, it changed before his eyes into a solid shadow. Night came suddenly, without warning, as he waited and pondered what to do.

At that moment he ceased to think and, without knowing why, began to walk down the road, like a man coming in late from the fields. He never took his eyes off the house, off the sickly yellow light shining through its windows. In the darkness he was never at a loss what to do. Here he was walking down the road like a neighbor. If anybody was about, if Lovell came out for a breath of air, he'd pass the time of day, ask him how he did, for Lovell couldn't see, he couldn't know what was reaching after him through the night. He'd bring him the message in a neighborly way, and Lovell would raise his hand and say, "Good evening," not knowing that he would never again pull on his boots at crack of day and walk out into the bracing air and shout good morning to his people.

He slowed his pace—he must look more like a man tired after a hard day's work. The two front rooms on either side of the run were dark. There was light from the ell, showing they hadn't left the table. But he must be careful. He had already heard a chair scrape back . . . it might be to let a man undo his belt while he smoked but then it might not be that at all. The pale light reflected from the kitchen ran through the dog trot and made it gape like the mouth of a grave swung up on end.

He could not move his eyes away. Not once did he look at the barn, where he had intended to hide until near day, but walked steadily toward the mouth gaping in the dark, walking like one led by the hand. Then he knew that he was being led, led in his doubting moment. He could tell by the air. It was fresh and bracing like air after a storm. No longer did he hesitate or turn aside to hide and wait for his enemy to play into his hands. He let himself be led straight toward

Lovell's dwelling place. Such boldness was not of this world: another's boldness drew him on.

He opened the gate. It clicked to behind him, and the air grew still, as still as dust sifting down. No sound from the house. It was as still as death. He walked up the gravel path like a man trying not to move. His right hand hung down with his finger caressing the tongue-like trigger. He looked at the house. In thirty seconds he might touch it. There were lights in the ell but no sounds. His eyes darted from window to window, to the places where men like to lurk in ambush. Had he become over-eager, had he for the first time pushed too fast? If he had, it was now too late to turn back. If Lovell's men were ready to shoot him down, his one chance was to charge the house. To make for the barn was ruin. He moved on, reached the porch, swung lightly up and pressed his back to the wall, out of line of the run. And waited. Still there was no sound from the kitchen, no noise from the rooms. If men lay in ambush, why was he still alive?

He listened and heard only his heart thumping his ribs. Perhaps Lovell had gone away, but there was the light in the kitchen. He had distinctly heard chairs move back from the table. It was now past supper time, time for the men to take the air on the front veranda, to lie in the run with their backs against the walls. Every evening they did this. He had reckoned on this when he made his plan to hide in the barn while they were at supper. But the porch was empty. For good or ill he must now go forward. If the cook was in the kitchen getting supper against the master's late return, the chairs might have come from her setting the table, the stillness might have been her putting the bread on. That must be it. People don't make traps that fail to snap to.

He looked once around and slid softly down the run, stopped before Lovell's office. Lovell slept as well as kept his accounts in there. Slowly he turned the handle, and the door gave. Its hinges were greased, and it fell before his hand as if another hand pulled. He never turned his back nor made a sound as he entered. He couldn't prevent a slight click of the lock.

Although he knew it must come, at the noise he raised his pistol on the darkened space before him. Disgusted, he was lowering it when a voice said very quietly:

"I've been expecting you."

Pleasant froze in his tracks. There was no light in the room, but he managed to make out an object in the chair before the secretary. He held his pistol on it, as the moisture broke out over the hairs of his trigger finger. He first thought: this is the trap. He waited, waited to spend his life dearly. But in the following moments nothing happened. The voice near the secretary said no more. It, too, was waiting. For what? Gradually it came to him it was waiting for him to make the next move. What was it expecting him to do? To whom . . . or to what the voice might belong he had no way of knowing. He'd been too startled to recognize the tones. It might have come from a man, or it might have been . . . a voice out of darkness. He waited, but he couldn't hold frozen in action, forever ready for something, he didn't know what, to happen. He would bring the suspense to an end.

"Who are you?" he asked boldly.

Without the least hesitation the answer came, "The one you're looking for."

Whose company was this he kept inside these four walls, with the door shut at his back? If he could only see, but his eyes were slow to grow accustomed to the room. As if the voice had followed his thoughts, it said:

"You've just come in out of the night. In here it is much darker."

Very softly Pleasant moved until he touched the wall. He felt the need of some physical support. "Why don't you make a light?" he asked at last, in a voice hoarse and strained.

The room was so still that he could hear the other's breath draw sharply in. Afterward there was a pause, a slight one, but enough for him to think he could hear a suppressed chuckle, grim and sardonic.

"There can be no light between you and me," the voice said. And then, "You know that."

[handwritten margin note: does not know who is]

There was a shade . . . at least Pleasant thought he could detect a shade of contempt and impatience in the statement. Moments were wasting. He must make that voice declare its body, or he could not act. . . .

"Is your name . . ." he blurted out but never finished for, harshly, imperiously, his query was cut short.

"Your business is not names. Your business is blood."

Sullen now came Pleasant's words:

"I know why I'm here."

"Well, then, are you ready?" Biting, commanding.

Yes, he was ready. He was always ready. But by this time the blackness in the room had thinned. The copper-backed moon, swelling full, crawled viciously before the window and let its tongue play along the sill, tremble across the floor, dart upon the figure in the chair and lick his head and face. In that moment he recognized the yellow features.

There was a silence, and in the pause Pleasant saw the look of hatred in the curious eyes until, leaning forward, the figure escaped the light. It said once more:

"Have done and answer me: Are you ready?"

Pleasant waited a full moment, a full moment of joy; then softly, almost purring, his lips spat out the word:

"Yes."

"Good. Where are your hounds?"

"Hounds?" Pleasant's voice went hard, on its guard.

"Yes, hounds," said the other. "The bloody dogs of Hell. You know . . . with noses sharp enough to pick out a man's scent and track him down through the world's richer smells."

"I've got no dogs," Pleasant said, advancing. "I don't need dogs to smell you out."

"What's that!" the figure cried, springing to his feet, an old leopard surprised. And then, "Who are you, sir?"

"Who am I?" The words almost purred, and Pleasant slipped over the creaking floor to stand before the other. There was just enough light to sharpen the degrees of blackness, and in that shade which is neither light nor darkness each seemed the shadow of the other.

"Who am I?" repeated Pleasant. He paused and when he spoke, his voice was low.

"I'm God's judgment, Tyson Lovell."

The figure, with a barely audible gasp, sank back into the chair.

Pleasant waited a moment, waited for his enemy to deliver himself, spent and broken, into his hands. But something was wrong. The moment lengthened and Lovell showed no signs of fear. There he sat, perfectly still in his chair. He might have been asleep, but for the tension in his neck and in the eyes, watchful in the semi-dark room. Finally, with less confidence Pleasant spoke:

"You weren't looking for me, were you, Tyson Lovell?"

"Yes, I must confess it, I was looking for you. But not so soon." Lovell's voice was almost pleasant. "Not so soon."

At this reply Pleasant felt his control of the situation weaken. All he could say was: "So you were expecting me?"

"Yes, for the last two weeks. Ever since your reappearance in the neighborhood."

Pleasant could feel the other's evil crooked smile. He blurted out: "You have two minutes to say your prayers." The sound of the familiar ultimatum restored his confidence. "Make haste. I won't tarry."

"My dear, my excellent young enemy. Pray? But I've never said a prayer in my life." Then Lovell chuckled outright, hard rolling sounds. Slapping the arms of the chair, he leaned forward and thrust his head upward. "Besides, what will you do, sonny, when I'm dead and gone?"

Pleasant raised his pistol arm.

"Hold on, McIvor, hold on." Lovell drew back in the chair. "I've still another minute to waste."

Pleasant stepped back. "Well," he said, "shut your God-damned mouth and pray."

"Come, come, my young savage. Let us behave like gentlemen. One may be brutal but never rude before the dark portal. I, who have sent so many through it, should know the amenities."

"You can't talk yourself out of this, Tyson Lovell."

"Nor can you," spat Lovell, "talk yourself out of failure."
He raised his hand. "I don't mean that you may not send
me to my reward. That is possible"—he looked at the pistol
barrel poised in the moonlit room, bowed his head—"even
probable. But, you see, that's to be expected. My career is
over anyway. Fort Sumter brought it to an end just as Fort
Sumter brought you here. A stupid blunder. Had I been
in Beauregard's boots we should not have been guilty of such
tactics. Or even at Montgomery." He paused, and then continued in tones of revery: "The man and the hour have met.
Magnificent words, magnificently spoken by Yancey. I was
in the streets below looking up. I heard them boom out over
the crowd. But I should have been up there." He rose to his
feet and thrust his hand through the darkness. Pleasant was
so taken a-back that he merely watched. "I should have been
on that balcony. The hand of fate should have pointed to
me. The man and the hour!" Then sadly Lovell shook his
head. "The hour, yes. The man, yes. But they did not
meet." He dropped silently back into his chair.

Pleasant thought that Lovell's mind was wandering. But
he remembered that he had been out of touch with the
world for six months. Something might have happened to
threaten his plans. He asked as a measure of caution:

"What are you talking about?"

"War, sir. Where have you been? Ah, yes. You've been
in hiding. Quite proper. But while you have burrowed in
your hole, great things have happened. The Southern States
have seceded and formed a Confederacy at Montgomery. In
Charleston Harbor they very foolishly fired on Fort Sumter.
Lincoln called for troops. The Border States seceded, and
we are now at war." He paused, looked sharply at
Pleasant. "That's why I thought you had returned for me,
for surely you had intended saving me until the last. Surely
you would do me that courtesy. I calculated that you knew
the armies would swallow my men, the objects of your
vengeance, just as they have ruined my profession, and that,

if you must be thwarted of the others, you would have me at least. But even in that you have failed, for there is nothing left me in this changing world but death, the perfect death to finish a great career—the perfect instrument to give it. That instrument is you. In the whole wide world there are no two men so filled with grit as you and I." *common!*

Before Pleasant could answer, there came clear-ringing down the night the voice of a lone hound . . . then another, and another. The rapid yelps plainly told the scent was fresh. Pleasant listened, barely whispered: "Bloodhounds."

Lovell's voice returned as soft as any lover's, "Yes, my enemy, the dogs of Hell. I was afraid their master had forsaken me." His voice filled with triumph. "Your life for mine. You didn't think you could outsmart the old fox, did you?"

Almost before Lovell had stopped speaking, Pleasant was before him, and so close that he could feel his enemy's breath, its rapid flutter upon his face. "You think you've trapped me?"

"You didn't think, McIvor," Lovell whispered, "that I would leave the world without you"—the voice was almost a caress—"leave you to rot away, year after year, when together we might corrupt Hell."

Pleasant looked at the other's unmatched eyes, spoke coldly and rapidly, "I'm not going to kill you now, Tyson Lovell. But I'll return. If you are speaking true and there is war, I'll comb every company in the army. When I come back, you'll know all the others are dead but you. It may be months, it may be years, but every day of those years, you will think of death. And now, when you wake up, you'll know your hounds have lost their man."

He raised his pistol butt and struck Lovell over the head. The man slumped into his chair, Pleasant stooped over and listened to his heart,—yes, it was beating,—moved rapidly to the door, closed it behind him, and slipped away into the night. The baying of the hounds, growing ever nearer, filled the silence of the room.

4

I

IT was the second of April, 1862.

At Corinth the gusty winds blew through the Confederate camps, shook the white-sheeted tents, made them suck and pop across their poles. The sun was bright but chill and without comfort, for the wind came, like the disaster to Southern arms in the West, from every quarter. It slapped all the thaws of winter through the shivering cotton shirts of the soldiers. It shook the windows in the houses of the small railroad town, and in the commander's quarters the panes rattled ominously, like a distant battle.

Lieutenant Ellis waited in the small room which was army headquarters. He stood withdrawn near the mantel in the pleasant warmth of a slow fire, out of the way of the staff. He had been told to wait, that General Johnston was occupied. For the first few minutes he was aware of the pens scratching in the hands of the headquarters clerks. An officer, with a look of sad concentration on his face, was seated before a small table in the corner. With automatic hand he lifted papers from one stack, read them, made a mark with a pencil, then placed them face down on another stack. Ellis wondered what that had to do with war. But for his uniform the man might have been a factor going over his accounts. He turned his eyes abruptly away. There was something mechanical, almost inhuman in the officer's look. He suppressed a shudder: the factor-officer disposed of the regimental reports exactly as if they had been inventories of cotton bales or hogsheads of sugar. It was at that moment that he saw a gentleman standing in the window—he was obviously a gentleman. A slight movement, a sigh, had betrayed his presence.

As Ellis let his eyes travel over his form, immaculately

clothed in Confederate gray, he wondered how he could have been in the room so long without seeing him. He was tall, square-shouldered, and built of bone and muscle. He was perfectly still. He seemed to be listening to the wind, as if he might decipher from its sudden bursts some message he had long expected. There was something familiar about the square gray back, the carriage of the head. Could that be he? He had only seen him once . . . that time after the fall of Donelson, in the driving storm, on the road from Nashville to Murfreesboro. Ellis was sitting, he remembered, his little bay Nellie, with his head on his chest to keep the stinging water out of his face: their brigade had marched for three hours in the face of the storm, and the pelting rain had beaten his skin until it was tender. At the moment they were halted for a ten minutes' rest, and he was asking himself if he could stand the cold for another hour, for it would be at the least an hour before the army would halt for the evening. Soft cold mud spattering his face made him look up, angry and chilled afresh. An officer of rank, followed by an orderly, had just trotted by. He got a side glimpse of the long square face under the wet and drooping hat, stiff and glassy from the ice, then the great body seated squarely in the saddle. He remembered thinking that such a body could never tire. The rain had turned the officer's overcoat the color of granite, and the storm spattered him exactly as it does a rock. He drew rein before their brigade commander, and Colonel McIvor turned to call the column to attention.

"Never mind, Colonel," came the sure even voice. "Bivouack your brigade this side of LaVerge. Pick up all stragglers. We must bring as many people as we can to Murfreesboro. I'm concentrating there."

Without more ado he rode away. Not until then did it flash over Ellis that he had just seen Albert Sidney Johnston, the commander of the army, or what was left of it after Donelson. Upon those shoulders balanced Confederate fortunes in the West. Well, they were broad enough. General Albert Sidney Johnston, once the pride and hope of the South;

now the people in their terror were calling him betrayer, Judas.

The officer in the window turned and walked toward his desk. Ellis knew now that he was in Johnston's presence. There was no marked grace to his movements. They were solid, almost ponderous, but without any stiffness in his carriage. His neck and head lifted from his shoulders with great dignity, self-poised and calm. His dark brown hair a little mixed with gray, fine and wavy, curled above his broad forehead. His erect body was slightly bent, and his head leaned forward in thought. At the moment, the eyes, deep-set and looking small in the large face, seemed slow and dull. As he halted by the chair, the whole look of the man was strength: the square face, deep chest, the healthy fullness of bone and muscle, which without hardness would have appeared gross, the broad fair face, now slightly tanned, the mustache which failed to hide his gentle mouth, and the compact jaws. There was almost too much of him, too much strength, too much fairness for his size, too much moral suasion, as if nature's lavishness undid its purpose. In the small room, and Ellis thought that large rooms must look crowded when he moved about them, it was impossible to reckon with his complete character. Men, in self-defense, would seize upon some trait and pretend that Albert Johnston was thus and so. Then it came to Ellis like a revelation that he must always, at close quarters, remain unknown. Like a carving on a mountain he was seen in right proportions only at a distance. Only in the field, on parade, wherever there was pageantry or action on a large scale, could he seem real. He was made for charges.

Ellis snapped out of his reverie. A major, with haste in his coattails, bustled into the room and presented himself before the commander. Johnston raised his great head and the eyes became kindly inquisitive.

"Ah, Major Benham, I'm glad to see you." He extended his hand, and the two men sat down. "Your mission, was it successful?"

Benham was a man of no particular size. His was a restless,

nervous face. He leaned forward and spoke rapidly. "A complete failure, General. I got together, as you said, the prominent men in the surrounding districts and they visited the planters personally. But, sir," Ellis expected him to rise to his feet, "we got the promise of only fifty niggers."

Johnston's eyes went dull, but there was no change to his voice. "That's too bad," he said as if closing some routine detail. "I could have put the negroes in place of teamsters and cooks. That would have given me an extra brigade for the coming battle"—he paused for one slight moment,—"an extra brigade might mean the balance between victory and defeat. You told them we would pay?"

"I did, sir." The face thrust forward and shook vigorously. "They'll send their sons to get killed, and they an't stingy with money. But you just try to get a nigger or a mule out of them."

"Don't they realize," asked the general rhetorically, "that if we lose, there won't be any slaves?"

"Where slaves are concerned, sir, they don't realize anything."

There was a short silence. When Ellis saw the general's preoccupation, he prepared to withdraw. An aide entered.

Johnston raised his head, asked, "What is it?"

"A man to see you, sir," said the aide briskly. "He's been hanging around headquarters for several days. Hints at something mighty important."

"What's the name?"

"Tom Fox. He says a friend of mine sent him here. I don't know anything about him, though."

"I'd better see him."

Major Benham rose and excused himself. The aide went to the door and ushered in the stranger. Ellis noticed that the man had an evil look, was bent in at the stomach like a broken barrel stave. He slouched forward to the proffered chair, looking quickly at the aide through gold-rimmed spectacles. His countenance was at once acute, sinister, and malignant. He bowed to General Johnston, and began talking as soon as he was seated. As he talked, he would lift his eyes, cast them with sharp calculation upon Johnston, let them fall and shift about for some neutral object. Upon the desk lay a pile of official papers. He chose them as a base from which to assault the general's eyes. He would speak, look at the General, retreat to the papers, look again with more confidence, feel insecure, turn away to the stack, and from there stealthily creep again upon the other's attention. This maneuver continued for several minutes, until he began to feel more at ease. Then his voice changed. It had been rapid. It dropped in tone, ran smooth, rising to glib persuasion. Johnston watched him steadily from his dull sight.

"Yes, General," he said, "above all earthly things I have the Southern cause at heart. There ain't a man in the Confederacy, unless it's yourself or General Beauregard, who loves his country better. And I don't believe," here his voice slowed with hesitation, then rushed with words, "I don't believe we've got a worse enemy in Tennessee than Andrew Johnson, or for that matter in the whole South. Now I know somebody who can git at him, who's about him every day." He stopped significantly; looked cannily at Johnston's face. "He can be disposed of for a trifling sum of money." He abandoned his base of papers and waited.

Johnston rose slowly to his feet, and his eyes were kindling. "Sir, the government I serve meets its enemies in open and honorable warfare." The words were concise, measured, slow. "It scorns the assassin's knife and the scoundrel who would suggest its use."

Fox batted his eyes behind the gold-rimmed spectacles, curved around the chair, and, before the clerks could look up from their papers, was gone from the room. The general remained upon his feet with the anger gathering beneath the light tan of his skin. He was still standing when the aide returned with a young soldier.

"Private McIvor, sir. On that outpost matter."

Before Johnston recognized Pleasant, Lieutenant Ellis stepped forward, saluted, and handed him a note. The general collected himself, nodded, and read it through in silence. He lifted his head.

"Tell your good colonel, Lieutenant, that we have no muskets. Some are expected. As soon as they arrive, he shall be issued his share."

Ellis saluted and left the room. His departure brought Pleasant to himself. He was vaguely aware of the large soldier with the stern face sitting down. That was all he noticed at first. He was slow to collect his wits, for he had seen Fox slink hurriedly through the adjutant's office. He was upon his feet and almost following when the aide called sharply. The grave voice brought him to his business.

"Excuse me, sir," Pleasant said.

"While on outpost you were attacked, a sergeant and four men killed. Is that correct?" The general crossed his arms.

"Yes, sir."

"Tell me about it."

Pleasant looked at the general. He understood that he must be careful. He felt a watchfulness behind the open dignity, the kindly speech that would set him at ease.

"It was soon after sundown, sir. I was sentry. I saw something moving to my front. I called out, and it stopped moving. I told it to come forward, but it ran away. Then I fired. About that time I heard shots behind me. I withdrew thinking we had been surprised. When I came to the picket, I could see we were overpowered. There must have been ten of the Yankees. Two of our men were already down. I pulled out my pistol, beat about the bushes, and ran forward shooting and hollering, 'Come on, men, we've got'm!' "

"How is it all your companions were killed when you arrived, and you escaped?" There was a hardness to the question Pleasant didn't like.

"I didn't go in directly. I ran zigzag, so as to make them think there were lots of us. I'd shoot ten paces or so apart, as I advanced. That slowed me down. I got one Yankee, for they carried him off as they left."

Johnston looked steadily at the private, and Pleasant re-

turned his gaze. His look was frank and fearless—and innocent, but he was watching the effect of his words on the other,
and he saw he was believed.

"General Bragg trains good soldiers," said Johnston at last.
He smiled, and Pleasant found himself at ease before the commander of the army. "Always do your duty with as much
intelligence." He asked a few more questions, rose and dismissed Pleasant with a handshake.

When Pleasant was on the open streets again, his first thought
was what a fine soldier General Johnston was. He began to
regret the need to trick him with lies, for the general was so
honorable and direct, so simple in his greatness—any fool
could see he was a great man. He didn't strut like their
colonel, always damning and cussing the regiment for not
knowing how to drill. He couldn't tell General Johnston why
he was in his army, but he would make it up to him when the
time came to fight.

It had taken him two months to get on friendly terms with
the five men he had brought to justice. At first they were
suspicious of his name, but he let it drop he was a Kentuckian.
They believed him. He was a good forager. He often
swapped things he had picked up and let them get the best
of the trade. They got to thinking what a foolish good-hearted
fellow he was. Once he had slipped liquor into camp stopped
up in his gun barrel. This led Beatty to take him under his
protection. He pretended to be always in a good humor,
easy-going. This had worked. Daylight men don't see beneath the skin. After that all he had to do was wait for the
right moment. Beatty was a sergeant, and when the time
came to go on outpost duty, he always took Pleasant with him.
At other turns some innocent men were on duty, but Beatty
liked to take those along he could cheat at poker. So this
time, just the five of his father's murderers and himself—on
outpost duty in the thick bare woods.

He laid his plans. He was careful to bring along his Navy
Six. When the sentry was posted, the poker game commenced.
He played his hand well until it began to get dark; then he

lost, a little at first, then big bets. Pretty soon he let them clean him out. He knew what this meant. Beatty would send him to take the sentry's place. He begged the sergeant to lend him a stake. He wanted to make a comeback, he said, but Beatty gruffly ordered him to take Simmons's place. He buckled on his side-arms slowly and looked at the cards on the oilcloth. "Git the hell out thare," ordered the sergeant. It always gave him pleasure, a sense of the fitness and rightness of things, for his enemies to order their own deaths. Silently he disappeared to the front. He told Simmons he had come to relieve him. Simmons was glad to go—he knew what it meant—and Pleasant watched him until he walked out of sight.

He was alone in the green forest. He looked at the tender leaves hanging from the dark, solid limbs, at the ground that looked bright even toward the close of day. His eyes traveled down the long crooked avenues, for they knew where to look, and he knew no Yankee patrol was near. He smiled at the other awkward sentries who wore their eyes out straining because they didn't feel at ease in the forest. In the spring the woods are open as a road, but when he slipped up on Simmons, he could see that Simmons was afraid of ambush. He had put himself to the rear of a large tree. No eye could see beyond a two-foot trunk.

Pleasant hid himself and watched the squirrels play, until the grass began to look like snuff, and the darkness came out of the ground. He liked it best this time of year, because the night was not too black and the blackness was never still. He liked it because he could feel it quiver, and the quivering gave him a quickness and a sureness he never had at other seasons. He gave the doomed men time to build a fire against their fears, waited for that moment when the army would be eating—his best time, since the least likely time for inspection of outposts: he had remembered nigger Jim told him the best time to steal chickens was at supper time or just before day.

He waited a moment to cure his impatience, then slipped toward the brightness that was the fire. Tonight was the

time. Yesterday God gave to his enemies. Tomorrow might
be too late. Tomorrow the authorities might not believe his
lies. The demoralization of the army was disappearing, but
the fear of an enemy advance was still real. He crept behind
the low blackjacks. The fire was burning brightly behind
them. Sergeant Beatty had his back to it, and his dark form
stood sharply upon the red glow. Pleasant thought they might
be cooking, but the game was hot and the betting high. They
would not be playing if Beatty was losing. Beatty's head hung
belligerently over his cards. He was pretending to bluff. How
many times had Pleasant watched him do that. The muskets
and rifles, with the side-arms hanging down, were stacked
at a safe distance. He had slipped upon them at that moment
of close silence when every player is lost in the strength of his
hand and his tactics.

This was the moment to act. Without waiting another instant, Pleasant stepped quietly before the stacked arms. The
gamblers' interest was so tense and his movements so swift
and silent that Beatty, as he raised his head to speak, caught
the wind in his mouth. He just sat and stared, with his mouth
hanging open, while understanding collected and fear set behind the shadows on his face. One by one the players glanced
at the sergeant, in dumb play looked around their shoulders
until their eyes came to rest upon the barrel of the sure-shooting
Navy Six. Slowly, as if the distance was great and the effort
tremendous, they looked from the gun to Pleasant. He saw
the quick grim smile of relief on their faces, but before the
smile could spread, it twisted into a fearful grin. And they
saw as men see in a dream: the mark of doom was real, but
deep in their consciousness they felt that at its stroke they
would be torn from sleep. Then the fiction Pleasant had so
carefully built in their minds snapped. The truth was on them.

Beatty was the first to regain his self-possession. He laid
his cards upon the oilcloth—very carefully, where he might
easily pick them up and go on with the game. Pleasant could
not help but admire his courage. Beatty said:

"Boy, put that pistol away and go on back to your post."

The firelight played along the blackness of the iron in Pleasant's hand, lighted fitfully his face, made bright the hardness of his pupils. Very quietly he spoke: "You'll call no more bluffs, Sergeant Beatty."

Beatty stood up. "This is a hanging matter, McIvor. I'll give you one more chance to get back to your post."

Beatty advanced slowly, holding out his hand. Pleasant allowed him to get half the distance, when he said,

"I know, Beatty, this is a hanging matter; but hanging's not the only way to justice."

Without haste Pleasant raised his pistol arm, leveled it, and, as the sergeant charged, fired. The man leaped high in the air with a shout, spread-eagled his arms and legs, and fell against the gun stacks. After the clatter, there was no other sound. The bullet had found his heart.

The other men stood up in terror. "Don't run," came the same steady voice. "It won't do you any good."

Simmons began to mumble his innocence, but he was cut short: "And don't argue. I'm not justice. But I'm going to send you where'll you'll get justice. You have one minute to prepare yourselves." And then Pleasant began to count out loud.

Two of the men sank weakly to their knees. A short, compact, redheaded man began cursing. Simmons wrung his hands and said over and over, "O God, O God, O God." The redheaded man's voice was dry and cracked, but it grew smooth with violence. He had reached the stage of shouting when Pleasant called, fifty-nine . . . sixty.

He dragged them in different positions to make them look like they had been killed in a struggle, fired off some of their guns, emptied his own weapon, stamped the fire, wiped his shoes, and afterward ran to the rear, for in the distance he could hear the guard turning out.

2

There had been some suspicions, or was General Johnston just trying to find out something about the enemy . . . probably he'd never know. He'd have to tell himself to be careful, for it was easy to kill men in the army. It was too easy. All the time he was turning these thoughts over in his head and wandering the streets of Corinth, his eyes were open. He did not hurry. There was no need for hurry. When Fox's time was come, he'd find him. He moved along through the bright chill of the April day. The companies were at drill, but he was free until he reported back for duty. He searched every face that passed, mechanically searching as he had done ever since he had joined Bragg's army on the coast. There were twelve in Bragg's corps alone, that is, there had been twelve; and now that the whole army was assembled he would find more. He moved on, hungrily searching, but hiding the hunger in his heart, keeping it out of his face. He could not help thinking what good luck the war had brought, gathering his enemies in such confusion in the presence of his vengeance.

He made his way in and out of the crowded walks, brushing shoulders, following the strongest drift of the mingling human currents. In the streets, cut deep by the wheels, the wagons rolled. Those heavily loaded rumbled slowly along, a solid body of sound around which all other noises in the streets seemed to gather. The empty wagons rattled insolently by, their drivers standing upright and quivering from foot to jowls with the vibration, cracking their whips and shouting as if they wanted to shake the wagons to pieces for pure pleasure. Four oxen, under their white oak collars, swung in slow rhythm down the middle of the street, their mysterious necks, timeless in their swinging, set to the beat of the earth's pulse. Their feet sank gently, without effort, into the mudholes and slippery ruts, while their soft eyes, round like a doll's, stared with blank patience, forever remembering the sudden act of violence. Behind them the long wagon rolled easily, as if of its own accord and as if there was no ton of supplies stacked on its pole bottom. The driver walked by the rump of the rear ox, his knees bagging, the mud splashing his boots. His coat was hoisted on his sloping shoulders and was brushed by the black greasy hair. Pleasant could almost see the lice from where he walked . . . and from the driver's slow mouth came the easy calls, whoa . . . whoa-ee. Over his shoulder fell his plaited whip, as restless as a snake, tapping his boot tops. Squads of cavalry trotted by the outfit. Staff officers, their faces in a frenzy of some crisis, galloped to the right or left. All traffic, heavy or light, broke about the steady march of the four oxen and their heavy burden.

At a street corner Pleasant stopped. Men were scurrying and teams were pulling out of the way of a section of artillery galloping by, scattering mud from the hoofs of the animals and the skidding wheels. A young lieutenant, riding a blooded mare, led the way looking very efficient and dapper. His metallic voice, shouting "Right! Left!" swung his cannon and caissons without collision through the crowded way. Pleasant wondered if he would crash into the oxen, but at command the weary animals stopped. Upon the last caisson sat a private in rough dirty clothes, with a battered campaign hat, looking sallow and bored.

"That's a right peart outfit, now ain't it?" said a voice at his side.

Pleasant turned and saw a young boy in rumpled butternut, too large for him. His round curious eyes had brightened, and the soft fuzz on his cheeks and tender chin gave him an unkempt look.

"Right peart," answered Pleasant.

"Them guns'll shore talk to the Yankees, now won't they?"

The road was clear, and Pleasant crossed. The boy followed. A long dirk hung from a belt strapped about his jacket. He patted it and looked proudly at the other. "Hit's a-itching to taste blood ... Yankee blood," he said.

Pleasant looked at the dirk, at the oversized jacket sticking out like a petticoat around the belt, at the large collar about his frail and sickly neck. The youth was pleased at this close inspection and said:

"Mammy didn't want me to go to war, but this hyar ain't no time fer menfolks to be lolling around the doorstep. My mammy's a widdy-woman, and I wouldn't of left her, but she's got Myrtle's man to make the somethen-to-eat. He'd ruther plow than eat. Now as for me, I don't take much stock in plowen. That's all right, eff'n they ain't no fighten to be done." And he threw his head back as if to say that when the time came to fight, he was the man to do it.

"You'll need a better weapon than that," said Pleasant quickly. "Here take this pistol."

The boy fingered the Navy Six with precious care. There was so much joy in his eyes that he didn't see when Pleasant walked off and left him. He had gone a good piece before the boy could forget his good fortune and remember his manners. He ran after him.

"Thank ye, mister. I'm beholden to you. Burt Conry's the name, from Arkansas. Your true friend, Burt Conry."

They parted at the edge of town, and Pleasant wandered through the camps. He leaned against a tree and idly watched a company form for drill. His eyes ran slowly down the line. The men were standing at ease and bantering one another as recruits will do in ranks. Their bearing was gentle, their uniforms neater than most, and their linen was dirty. But their weapons were bright and clean. Besides his rifle, each private had a knife and pistol in his belt, and over the right shoulder a blanket was folded. Small groups of body-servants hovered about in groups. Just as Pleasant was about to move on, for he had quickly seen that nobody was hiding from him there, a private in the front rank said:

"Here comes the governor, Jeems."

Jeems, the sergeant, faced about and called the line to atten-

tion. A slight gentleman in middle years stepped out of the
woods with firm but unmilitary tread. Under his broad-
brimmed hat stringy black hair fell about his shoulders. His
fine gray coat was a trifle too large, and his light-colored
trousers looked like pantaloons as they stuck into the tops of
polished boots. He bore himself with the air of accustomed
command, judicial not military. Taking his place in the center
of the line, he drew his sword and surveyed his men.

"Gentlemen of the Morgan County Guards," sounded his
grave voice, "is it your pleasure to drill up the road or down
the road today?"

He waited a few moments, standing quietly in his boots,
leaning slightly forward, courteously waiting for an answer
to his question. A youthful voice, easy and familiar, sang
out from the ranks:

"We'll be proud to drill anywhere you say, Governor."

The captain inclined his head courteously to the speaker,
waited, and when there was no further comment, said, "Then,
gentlemen, we will drill down the road today."

The company wheeled and stepped briskly off. Pleasant did
not notice the line of guns, which was badly dressed. His
eye followed the uniform swing of the squads as they marched
and wheeled. From all sides the shouts of command struck his
ears: far down the road they came like muffled speech, under-
tone to the staccato voices around him, and through the trees
the tread of thousands of heels striking the roads and beating
down the open fields. Everywhere, as he listened, he could hear
the peculiar hum of life in the camps. Instinctively he noticed
the change in the tone of the army. The spirit of his own
corps, Bragg's, had always been high; but as the dirty, weary
regiments straggled in from Tennessee, they had for a while
been sullen and listless. Even now they mustered less than
two-thirds their strength, weakened by sickness and desertion.
But rest and food, he knew, had raised their spirits, if it had
not improved their equipment. They still looked like a loose
gathering of many citizens who had left their business and
their plows to meet a public peril. Pleasant had the feeling

that the plows still leaned in the furrows, that the storehouses were shut up, as for dinner.

He turned in the direction of his own mess. But suddenly he pulled up short. He had not gone in the right direction. He had allowed his thoughts to wander, and his feet had brought him to a brigade camp he'd never seen before. He realized with a shock that he had not been watching for his blood enemies: he had been thinking about the army and wishing for it to meet the Yankees and drive them out of the country. He quickly put such thoughts from his mind and looked about to get his bearings. In a clearing stood neat rows of tents, muddy and torn, some of them, but set out in straight lines. Behind the tents the wagons of the brigade stood in park. This was real order, and he found himself curious to know whose command it was. He walked toward a group of tents set back from a large fire. The ground was steaming for several feet about the brush crackling and burning above a pile of logs. The staff was clustered about a large middle-aged officer seated in a chair with his feet spread out toward the fire. He was giving orders. There was something familiar about the officer's back. As he drew near, Pleasant saw who it was: it was his Cousin Armistead. He walked forward and drew within the busy circle. A major held the morning reports in his hands. The colonel was rumbling:

"I want to know what in the God-damn-hell made my brigade look so ragged at inspection."

"Twenty per cent is on the sick list, sir. That's what made it look so ragged, sir."

Armistead McIvor dropped his eyes to the fire for a moment. When he looked up and spoke, it might have been to a man at the far end of a ten-acre field, not one two feet away.

"Publish me an order, sir," he rumbled, "I won't have it. I'll give them until Monday to get well. Then only two men in a company will be allowed to get sick at a time."

As the major hesitated, he sharpened his eyes, "Well, get along, Major, get along and draw it up and have it read before the companies."

He dismissed his adjutant by shifting his attention to the private who had just come up. "What can I do for you, young man?" Then he recognized Pleasant. He shouted and slapped him across the shoulders, "Well, now if it an't my pistol ball. Where'd you come from, boy? Gentlemen," he took the staff in at a glance, "here's a young man that will just naturally eat a Yankee up. My young cousin from the cotton country."

At that moment a courier interrupted with the information that Colonel McIvor was wanted at General Hardee's quarters. Swinging to his feet, Armistead called for his horse, for his cape, for his sword and pistols, leaned on the shoulders of two aides while a servant pulled on his boots and fastened his spurs. All the while he was giving booming directions about the entertainment of his young cousin—"You can stay and have a snack with us, sure you can"—about the slippers he had just taken off, about the dressing of a pig for the barbecue, about the coals in the pit.

The horse arrived, as stout as his master, part Norman, and with spirit enough to shy as the colonel's blue-gray cape bellied out in the wind and showed its red lining. He pulled on his gloves and mounted. The gelding, feeling the honor done him, shied around and put the staff at its proper distance. But before the colonel could leave, a dirty group of horsemen rode into camp. The corporal saluted. Mounted and tied to his saddle, a youth rode in the center of the detail.

"What is this, Corporal? If it an't important, I must be off."

"Deserter, sir," replied the ruddy-cheeked corporal easily.

"Deserter?" The colonel repeated. "I must be off. . . . From whose command?"

"Yours, sir."

"Impossible, sir. Impossible."

"Yes, sir. He was picked up near the lines this morning."

Colonel McIvor looked around him in bewilderment, and his adjutant questioned the corporal.

"The deserter from McGinnis's command?" he asked.

"Yes, sir."

"This is the man, Colonel, reported by Captain McGinnis.

I request to bring to your attention, sir, that he willfully and deliberately quitted his post in the presence of danger."

"Is it possible?" asked the colonel, puffing and looking about for some way of escape from the prospect of an unpleasant duty.

"That an't so, Colonel," said the boy with indignation.

"It an't?" repeated the colonel with some relief. "Now, you see the boy says tan't so."

"I just went home to see ma. You can ask Bob Pearsoll if that's not so. Brother Bill come through the lines at Murfreesboro and told me she was powerful bad off and wanted to see me. . . . I told him where I was going and that I'd be back as soon's I saw how she was. And I did, too. I been ten days on the road, and these fellows"—he looked with contempt at his captors—"picked me up after I'd purty nigh got here."

"Untie him," thundered the colonel to hide his feelings. "Come forward, sir."

The boy rode toward the commander, with the flush of indignation still on his cheeks but awed by his superior's ferocious manner. Pleasant noticed the staff officers winking at one another. The inspector slyly held out a gold coin behind his back to be covered.

"Young man, are you the sort of fellow that runs from a fight?" asked the colonel.

The private's indignation returned at the suggestion.

"Well, sir, if I let you go back to your command, will you promise to kill me two Yankees when we meet them?"

"I sure will, sir."

"And remember, you are never to leave your company again without permission. Public duty, when your country is in peril, comes before private. Do you understand, sir?"

"Yes, sir; but ma was bad off . . ."

"I know, sir," came the hurried interruption. "But you must be punished in some way. . . . Chop me up a cord of stove wood. That'll make you remember to apply for furlough in the proper way. Turn him loose, boys."

The detail was glad to free their prisoner. As they left, the boy was talking freely to his recent captors. There was a short silence. The adjutant broke it: "That's bad for military discipline, Colonel."

"Discipline be damned. I regard such things as the decrepitude of the military art."

With that Colonel McIvor, as if to forestall argument, galloped off toward Corinth.

As he was passing out of sight, the adjutant sighed and spoke at large to his brother officers:

"I make you a standing offer, gentlemen, to eat the man Colonel McIvor has shot for a military crime."

"You forget this is a volunteer army, Major," came the quiet voice of Lieutenant Roswell Ellis. He was standing with one foot on a stump, his right arm propped carelessly on his knee, resting his body in that way. "Colonel McIvor may seem unprofessional to a regular army man like yourself, but you must admit he knows how to command men. I, for one, haven't forgotten the retreat from Bowling Green."

He paused and looked into the fire. Pleasant made a rapid inspection of the tall, rangy figure, the voice with the sound of flint on tinder, the eyes the color of scorched linen. Pleasant had the feeling that he had seen him before . . . it was probably one of the many faces he had searched and dismissed.

Ellis continued: "There was no brigade with so high a morale as ours when we finally pitched camp here at Corinth. And it was because Colonel McIvor looked after his men. We used to complain bitterly of overwork, but he never went to bed on the wet ground until he had seen his men well fed and made as comfortable as it was possible to make them. It may not be official discipline, but it serves for our people, and I'll bet any man we give as good an account of ourselves as any other brigade when the time comes."

He stopped, and there was silence for a moment. The adjutant cleared his throat.

"You take me too seriously, Ellis. I know the colonel's good points. But I know what war ought to be. We've got brave men, but brave men don't make an army. Just yesterday I sat on a court for some privates from the Mississippi bottoms, great big powerful men, excellent material for soldiers. While on outpost duty they had romped around the woods shooting squirrels. When put under arrest, they were indignant. I explained carefully, as carefully as I knew how, that the safety of their comrades depended upon their alertness, that they had risked the life of the army, and that they must be punished. But do you think I made any impression? Not the slightest. They just stared, and one of them said he'd come out to fight and didn't see no use in scaring the Yankees away."

The officers smiled, and the quartermaster spoke up: "Remember the Southern wool speech, gentlemen?"

"What was that," asked Pleasant.

"Give it to us, Captain, for the benefit of the colonel's young cousin here."

The quartermaster was a small plump man burning with energy. His face was lined with wrinkles breaking, or ready to break, into smiles. He looked as if he had never missed a meal in his life.

"It was at a temporary halt on the retreat," he began, moving up and down rapidly, making nervous gestures with his hands, throwing his words out of his mouth as if they cluttered up his thoughts. "And the colonel demanded and got clothes for the brigade. All the men were poorly clad. Many were almost naked. One regiment, Deas's, had three hundred and fifty barefooted and not over a hundred blankets for seven hundred men. General Johnston sent a thousand suits, with hats and shoes. When I issued the clothes, I noticed the men examining with suspicion the peculiar color and texture of the cloth. They had expected wool, as well they might in winter, and they were getting cotton. When the colonel saw the look of dissatisfaction spread over their faces, he stood up on the end of a supply wagon and made this speech."

The captain jumped on a stump and his flesh shook. He swelled out his chest, cocked his eye, a favorite habit of the colonel's. Pleasant recognized the familiar habits and smiled.

"Defenders of homes and firesides, sacred guardians of household altars, patriots! Not since the days when Hannibal crossed the Alps has any commander seen greater courage, greater endurance, more lofty patriotism than you, my soldiers, have shown on this retreat—no, I will not say the word, hateful to the senses of true patriots—on this retrograde movement. As yet you have seen no enemy; but that other enemy, the weather and the march, you have seen and conquered. That enemy, my fellow compatriots, is the most trying, the most deadly of any war; and you may truly say that soldiers who overcome the crusty road, the wet Heavens, and the frosty dawn, may laugh at powder and shot. Your government is sensible of your patriotism and your hardships. Its civil officers have suffered in spirit, General Johnston has suffered in the flesh, and in their thoughtful care of you in your privations have sent splendid new uniforms, which I have issued, woven out of the best quality of *Southern wool* with which, doubtless, many of the Kentuckians are not acquainted."

The little captain got down, and the audience of officers applauded his performance. In the embarrassment which comes to a man when he knows he has spoken well, he ended with, "The colonel said the words nearly choked him, but that something had to be done.

"One Kentuckian said," the captain continued, "that it must be a strange country, where sheep grew on stalks like cotton." And with that he waved his hand, winked, and bustled off on official business.

3

Presently Pleasant and Roswell Ellis were left alone together. They walked about with some constraint, speaking occasionally. It was not because one was an officer and the other a private, for in the Southern armies every man took for granted his equality with every other. The officers were simply men with superior talents whom the soldiers chose willingly to follow. It was rather that the two young men were feeling with care for some common sympathy as strangers do who meet, and meet with pleasure, but lack the key to break the hostile door which hides the thing they believe is behind. Pleasant told him with directness that he liked what he had said to the professional officer, but this was too direct for Ellis, and it brought only a few words in reply, and a longer silence.

They drifted toward the open kitchen and the smell of food. The headquarters cook was a large negro, with a carriage and gestures faintly burlesquing his master. He was moving sullenly between the rough, makeshift table and a large iron pot and two ovens squatting over hot coals, with piles of ashy coals heaped on their iron tops.

"What are you mumbling about, Edward?" asked Ellis. "It smells like things are cooking mighty well to me."

The servant was slow to reply. He turned the pig over in its long bark bowl and scraped the pinkish-white carcass where a few hairs bristled. "Dey ain' nobody gon-n talk to me like dat. . . ."

"Like what, Uncle Edward?" asked Ellis pleasantly.

"Dat adjitunt. Come over here and talk rough to me, like I was a free nigger and didn't have no marster to look after me."

"What did he say?"

"'Tain't what he say. It's how he say what he didn't have no call to say. I takes my orders from a colonel, jest like him. And the next time he come around here telling me how to barbecue a pig, I'll speak right out and tell him."

This was spoken as he lifted the pig and set it on a grate of split white oak staves in the center of the spit. There were two other pigs already lying over the coals. He picked up a ramrod bent like a hook and lifted the top from an oven, let it down with a clatter.

"I'll be glad when marster whups dem Yankees and me and him can go back to mistiss and my kitchen. She tole me to take keer of'm and see that he got plenty of good somethen-to-eat. You can't ca'y no seasnin to the woods, and they ain't nothing fitten to eat in this craw-fishy country noway. You can't even git poke sallet, wid de army trompen around. I'm going tell marster to send me back to mistiss. I ain't no campaigner, me big as I is, retrograden in de mud and snow and freezen and that yallow Marthy in my kitchen burnen up de mistiss's victuals."

Pleasant looked at Ellis, saw the smile around his grave eyes, and suddenly they were no longer strangers.

"But just think, Uncle Edward, we'd starve to death if you left," came Ellis's gentle bantering voice. "We can't get along without you."

"I can git along without you all. Dat's certain."

Ellis chuckled and dropped down on a saddle. Pleasant straddled a stump. Soon they were whittling and smoking. After a pause Ellis brushed the shavings off his breeches.

"I reckon," he said slyly, "I'll just have to buy you from the colonel. That's the only way I see to keep a good cook at headquarters." He cocked his eye at the old negro.

Supreme contempt settled over the old servant's face. "You ain't got money enough to buy me," he grunted.

Ellis gave a long sigh. "Maybe not. I'll see if I can't get the colonel to put you up in a poker game. He was saying last night he'd like to stir up a little game."

Deep concern now filled the elephant eyes in the heavy black face.

"Now, look here, young marster, don't you go projecten with marster and kyards. He's bad to gamble and bad to lose. Mistiss made him promise her he wouldn't game no more'n he had to in the army and wouldn't cuss more'n he had to. He already in danger of hell fire. Mistiss prayen for him, but she might not pray at de right time. You won't tempt him, and I won't say nothing about going home."

Ellis seemed to consider the problem deeply and finally

agreed solemnly to let the matter drop if Edward would promise to stay in camp.

"I ain't going to promise nothen outright, but if you go projecten with marster, I'll shore burn your victuals."

"Looks like you'll have to retrograde, Ellis," said Pleasant.

"I know when I'm whipped," he replied.

The two soldiers laughed and ambled away from the neighborhood of the rich odors that seasoned the air above the pits. They walked the soft ground toward the boisterous messes and on the way met the colonel returning from his call on Hardee.

"Get you a wagon, Ellis, and go to the depot and draw a hundred of those new English rifles. Here's an order. I got it out of Hardee. Make haste, or somebody'll beat us to it."

Ellis drew himself up, saluted smartly, and hustled off. The colonel threw the reins to his body-servant, Alfred, asked the adjutant if there was any pressing business, discussed the sauce with Edward, who was now all smiles, felt the heat coming from the pits, considered it wisely and directed a few more coals to be dropped into the end of one pit, shouted to Alfred to help Edward when the horse was put away; then, putting his arm over Pleasant's shoulder, led him into his tent. He dropped the flap and brought a jug out from under a bundle of clothes and poured two glasses of peach brandy.

"Fine stuff, boy, fine stuff. I don't see how this pestilential country can make it."

They sipped the yellow liquid in silence, and the colonel looked across at his kinsman.

"I need an orderly," he said. "How'd you like to join our family?"

"I'd like to, Cousin Armistead."

"I'll arrange for your transfer tomorrow. And now, boy,"—he dropped his voice to a stage whisper that shook the tent—"tell me what I want to know." The rest of the question came from his steady eyes.

A sudden change passed over the smooth square features of the younger man, the warm genial light congealed in his eyes, the appearance of youth vanished. For a while it seemed that Pleasant might not answer; then he spoke the one abrupt word, "Fifteen."

The colonel silently emptied his tumbler, as if it were necessary to restore confidence to the flesh and melt the cold word. "I found me a hiding-place in the hills of Winston, a good piece to the north and where nobody goes," came the voice, low and cold, yet filling the tent. "I found me a wide cove, took Eli there, and we raised a cabin. Cleared some ground. From there I'd slip back to Coosa County. There are caves on the Staircase where I can hide for days, and an island in the river full of canebrakes. I turned my horse loose in the cane until it was time to strike out for Winston again. That's the way pa told me the Indians used to fight. When they wanted to raid, they would travel several hundred miles, strike some distant settlement; then disappear. Nobody could follow fast enough, so they nearly always got away. I kept this way of doing things until the guilty were all dead or got scared and left the country.

"Then I'd get wind of where they had gone, mostly from their families. I tracked some of them as far as Texas. There was one I was bound to get . . ." Pleasant paused, and the way he said the next words made a chill pass down his cousin's spine. "I tracked him to Texas and back to Louisiana. When I reached the town where I thought he was, I was careful to scout around some. I found he had taken up with an old gentleman by the name of Champion, that is, he'd taken up with the old man's daughter, Miss Emily. He put out he was a big mule trader, but it didn't take me long to get on to him. I knew what kind of trading he was doing. Old Man Champion got suspicious, not that he thought he was a nigger stealer but that he warn't the man for his daughter. He forbade Miss Emily to see anything more of him.

"I was working in a grocery, and with men coming and going and toddying back by the stove it wasn't long before I knew what I wanted to know. One day I saw an oldish-looking maiden lady go by in a buggy. I asked who she was.

Why don't you know—that's Old Man Champion's daughter. They say, and the man lowered his voice, she and this fellow Osborn are having dealings with one another. I looked at her good, and she had a pinched face and a hungry eye. Right then she was looking out for Osborn. You don't mean it? I said. Yes, but young fellow, if you know what's good for your health you won't go say anything about it. Old Man Champion is a jealous old fellow and he's plumb crazy about that gal of his'n. Why, he lets her draw any sum of money she wants at the bank. That piece of information gave me my clue.

"One evening I went up to the old man's house. He was on the porch, sitting in his chair like an Injun, with his black hat on his head, tapping his boot with his cane. He looked at me sharp and I told him who I was. He invited me in, looking sharp all the time, and offered me a chair. We talked about the weather, and about his stock—I knew he was having trouble with'm and I let on how much I knew about work stock. After we had passed the time of day and made our manners, I asked him if he wouldn't board me, that I couldn't eat the food where I was, I said I'd heard what a good table his wife set. I made out a strong case for myself, and he narrowed his eyes and said that he'd take me if I'd look to the care of his barns. I wasn't long in agreeing, for I knew he was a sharp trader and since it wouldn't cost any extra to feed me, he figured he had pulled a smart one. I let him think what he wanted to think.

"It hadn't been a great spell before the old man and the old lady took a strong fancy to me. It was a mighty pleasant place to live. I'll tell you the old lady set a good table, and she had feather beds in every room in the house; and her bed-clothes smelt sweet and clean. She kept'm in a chest, with little sacks of lavender dropped about. After supper every night Mr. Champion called the servants in and read a chapter out of the Bible. Once, I remember, he read from the prophets, 'I have pursued mine enemies and overtaken them; neither did I return again until they were consumed.' Then we knelt and prayed. Sometimes I could see Miss Emily crying a little as the old man's voice called on God to keep sin from his house. I got to feeling awful sorry for her, for she was a suffering woman. She had that lean raw-boned face that most men-folks don't fancy, and eyes that were dry all the time from what was burning her up. I've always noticed that women and horses with such an eye are dangerous and take a heap of petting and care, or they'll bite and kick, and when you're not looking for it. She loved her pa, but she'd had a taste of the real thing, and I could see she was eating her heart out for that lowdown man. She'd got along for thirty years without living, and here he comes and gives her a big bait of it, and she has to give it up, or is afraid she will have to, account of her pa. But she didn't mean to go back to quilting and pre-serving and such-like. It was such a trick as that Osborn would play on a lady. The longer I lived with the Champions the more desperate she got. It wasn't that she took a fancy to me, it was that I was about as far from her in age in one direction as the old folks in the other. Just to have me around reminded her of what she'd been missing and didn't mean to miss no more. We would gather around the fireplace in the old folks' room, with her pa sitting on one side smoking and her ma on the other, with nothing to break the stillness but him or the old lady knocking out their pipes, or yawning, or nodding, or maybe popping corn for a change, or maybe some night reading the Bible aloud by the candle, or something stirring out of the *Democrat*. Then Miss Emily would get fidgety and look at the clock and get up and kiss'm good night. I know she couldn't help but think of how much time already she'd wasted that way. I felt sorry for her and almost made up my mind to leave the country, for I knew if I stayed there I had to kill that man, and I couldn't have stood to see the look on her face when she heard it. And I'd have left, too, because there warn't no chance of him getting away from me for good. But I decided that he would up and leave her any-way, or devil her into doing something she'd never get over. He did, but I had no idea it would be as bad as it turned out.

"The old man had a habit of taking long trading trips, and one morning at breakfast he told us he was going away and would be gone for quite a spell. I looked out of the corner of my eye and I saw Miss Emily flush up, and when she kissed her pa good-by, I'll be bound but I thought her eyes would melt and run out of her head. The old man was touched, and he watered up the least bit, for him and Miss Emily had just been congressman-polite to one another after he told Osborn he'd whup him like a stray bitch if ever he set foot on his place again. Pore old man, it just goes to show that folks study themselves so much they don't really know what's going on in their own families, right under their noses.

"But I knew what was buzzing around in Miss Emily's head, and I said now if I watch her close, I'll find that Osborn's hiding-out place. The ell was two-storied. My room was in the front part upstairs and Miss Emily's was next to it, but there was no connection. I came down through the main part of the house, and she had a stairway all to herself that was boarded up so's the men couldn't see her ankles as she came down in the morning. Under my room was the old man's, that is, the room he slept in when he had the white swelling in his leg; behind that the dining room. Well, sir, one night I heard something jar the house. I didn't pay it any mind at first, but in a little while I heard whispering in Miss Emily's room. I stuck my head out and saw a ladder leaning against the house, and right against her window. Directly a man climbed down it, and Miss Emily after him. I put on my breeches as fast as I could and followed them. They had set the ladder by an old pear tree. But they were gone when I got down. He had tied his buggy a piece from the house, and before I could get dressed and down, they had driven off. I heard the horses' feet strike the road. He drove a blooded span.

"I waited the next night in my clothes, and I hid a mare in the bushes. They were so quiet about it I slept plumb through, but I knew they had been out together because her eyes were as bright as two pennies the next morning. After breakfast she told her ma she had to go to the bank, and I had her buggy hitched up for her. I'm suspicious by nature—I reckon it's because I'm thinking of one thing all the time—so I figured she was going after money for him."

The colonel leaped to his feet and paced up and down his tent.

"Why, the scoundrel, the scoundrel. Oh, sir . . ." and his voice quivered like a bull getting ready to bellow. "Oh," growled Cousin Armistead, "if I could only get my hands on him. To abuse that sweet, that gentle lady, to soil her innocent love, to betray a virgin in any such way!"

Pleasant waited quietly until the colonel plopped back in his seat, pulled out a cigar and bit it half in two, threw it away with an oath, and pulled out another. He yelled through the tent flaps:

"Alfred, oh, Alfred, bring me a chunk!"

The servant knew by the tone of voice that he would stand for no delay. He came running, throwing a hot coal from hand to hand, until he stood within the tent flap. The colonel usually leaned over to meet the coal, but he was in such high dudgeon that he sat stiffly erect and let Alfred press the chunk against the cigar end. In a moment a cloud of smoke whirled about the colonel's head.

"It's lit, sir. It's lit. Begone. Begone, sir."

Alfred scuttled out of the tent. Pleasant continued:

"I made sure I wouldn't sleep again; so the next night I followed them to a cabin about two miles from town. When I slipped up to the window, she was in his arms and they were kissing. I felt downright mean spying on Miss Emily that way. 'Oh, I can't let you go,' she kept saying in a desperate voice, and she reached after him again and they set in kissing afresh. After a while they stopped and cooled down, and Miss Emily sighed awful pretty. They drew up in front of the fire, for it was a coolish night in November, about as cold as that country ever gets, I reckon. I could see he was looking for her to say or do something, but he was too smart to ask about it. Directly she reached in her placket and pulled out a fist full of bank-notes. 'Here's a thousand dollars, Ronald.

Promise me you won't gamble any more. I don't know what pa will say when he finds out I've drawn so much. He's bound to ask questions when he comes back. But I don't care. Yes, I do, too. You must take me away before then. You must take me away.' He smoothed her hair and petted her and pulled her in his lap. I couldn't hear what he said to her, but she turned on him and desperate-like said, 'Ronald, if you ever leave me, I don't know what I'll do. I believe I'd kill you.' And he laughed and soothed her and kissed her. And then they commenced to make love in earnest, and I could see he warn't no rabbit man. I'd got what I came to find out; so I left. I just couldn't spy on Miss Emily any more."

"You did right, sir. You did exactly right, the proper and honorable thing," blurted out the colonel. "If you'd stayed another minute, I'd not claim you for kin."

"Mr. Champion," continued Pleasant, as if there had been no interruption, "came back before anybody was looking for him. He sent his body-servant ahead of him with two fine pair of gold ear-rings, one for the old lady and one for Miss Emily. He had some business at the bank, he sent word, which would keep him in town until after supper, to put his supper up, that he'd be in after dark. Miss Emily turned as pale as she could—her skin was dark—and right after supper she complained of dizziness and went up to bed; leastways she claimed to go to bed. When the old man got home, I could tell he had learned about the money being drawn out, for he looked mighty grave and right away he asked for Miss Emily. When the old lady told him she warn't feeing pert and had gone to bed, he started up to her room but thought better of it and said, no matter, what he had to see her about would keep until morning. . . . How much better it would have been if he'd kept to his purpose. . . . He was so worried he forgot to ask how things had gone while he was away. But he got cheerful after a while and told us what a fine trade he'd made, and by bedtime he asked me to come have a toddy with him. He had a fire made in his white-swelling room, and that showed how worried he was and he didn't want his wife to know it. When we went through to open the dining room door, it was locked. He sent me to find the key but called me back; said he didn't reckon he needed the drink anyway.

"Now, there wasn't any good reason for that door to be locked; so instead of going to bed, I set out for Osborn's cabin. When I got there, the fire was out in the hearth and the place empty. I hurried back as fast as my mare would carry me, for I was real uneasy. When I reached the house, it was lighted up and there was a great stir inside. People ran to the door as soon as I rode up, thinking I was the doctor. The old man had been robbed and stabbed, they said, stabbed with a butcher knife. I went right away to his room, and there was a great mess of things: chairs kicked over, blood on the bed and floor, *and the dining room door wide open*. The old man was lying on the bed groaning, and the groans warn't the kind that a man makes from a slit in his side—I've heard too many of that kind to know—his side was too fresh stabbed to hurt him. Those groans came straight from a broken heart.

"I sent for some hot water and had 'm tear up the sheet— the old lady was standing by the bed twisting her fingers, plumb dazed—and I stuffed his side and cut down the flow of blood. He let me work on him, but he was indifferent and looked like he didn't care whether I helped him or not. The doctor came and complimented me on my bandaging, said I had saved Mr. Champion's life. The funny thing about the whole business, Miss Emily didn't once come into the room, and her pa didn't ask for her.

"As soon as I could talk to the old lady, I asked her if Mr. Champion had any notion who it was. 'He woke up,' she said moaning-like, "with a man holding him in bed and a woman with a sunbonnet tied around her face. The woman had a carving knife, and she stabbed him. She stabbed him again and again, until he fought them off.' Then the old lady recollected what she had said, and I couldn't get anything more out of her. I nursed the old man for three days, and I heard the doctor tell him the wounds weren't necessarily fatal. But Mr. Champion just shook his head and turned his eyes away.

On the fourth day his head bent back over the bolster, and I saw he was dead.

"As soon as they laid him away, I took my gun and went out to Osborn's cabin. I tapped light on the door, and he hurried to open it like a man who's expecting someone. I held a pistol in my hand, and he fell away from me. Without taking my face off him, I shut the door.

" 'What is the meaning of this?' he asked with a show of innocence.

" 'You've killed Old Man Champion,' I said without raising my voice, 'and I've come to give you two minutes to make your peace with God.'

"Then he tried to get haughty with me. 'Young man, for your own good you must learn not to meddle in things that don't concern you.'

" 'Half a minute's gone,' I said.

" 'Do you know you'll hang for this?' He was trying to bluff.

"I waited with my watch out. 'One minute.'

" 'Listen, kid, I know you mean to avenge the man you loved, but you don't know all about this. I didn't kill him . . .'

" 'Minute . . .' I cut him off. I didn't want to hear what he might say.

" 'Look here,' he said eagerly, 'I've got a bag of gold.' He was getting sweatified.

" 'I'm not killing you account of Mister Champion,' I said easy-like.

" 'Then in the name of God what . . . ?'

" 'I'm Pleasant McIvor.'

"Then he went all to pieces. He dropped back, and his mouth fell open. I put a bullet through it."

" 'Bravo, my boy. Bravo,' " whispered the colonel with feeling. Then he sighed.

"I took the money and carried it back to the house. . . ."

Colonel McIvor said, "Let us draw the curtain on this sad and tragic scene, my boy. I don't want to know any more."

"I forgot myself, Cousin Armistead. I was so upset I killed him without letting him make his peace. I've had to do that three other times, once in the gulf off Mobile."

Colonel McIvor got up from his chair. He looked grave. "You must forget this thing until the war is over and our country is free. It's every Southern man's duty to put away his private life now."

4

Pleasant closed his mouth. He remembered how he must walk alone, and he was sorry he had taken this kinsman into his confidence. His cousin Armistead wasn't the same. This war had changed things. It threw a man off his guard. In the woods he knew how to handle himself. The ways were secret, and it was easy to hide and slip about. But in the camps rubbing shoulders with thousands of men, not being able to get off by yourself, it was hard to keep your thoughts. There were so many ways to be tripped. But Pleasant was learning. There was such a haste in things, such a recklessness. Now that he had found this out, he would take hold of himself. He saw the colonel sniff the air.

"Son, there's only one thing can travel so sweet and so far . . ." He lifted the tent flap. "Let's join my guests. Tain't fitting I should be so unmannered." As he stepped into the open, his lusty voice reached the barbecue pit and the circle of officers standing about it. "I might have known, Colonel Rob," he shouted, "if the wind blowed south, you'd follow the scent. How's that pig turning?"

The junior colonel, with a mild slow speech coming strangely out of his hatchet face, said, "Armistead, that's as saucy a sauce as I've smelt since I left old Kaintuck."

"Well, it's my granddaddy's mixture, and it's seasoned a

many a gullet. Sit down, Rob. Sit. Boys, you shame me. Fetch the colonel a chair or a stump, or something to rest on."

"No, no, Armistead. I prefer to stand. These young bucks won't understand it, but I've got to the age when there's no greater pleasure than roasting my butt."

"That's right, Rob," said Armistead, as he drew the circle about his friend. "Us oldish fellows an't fit for camping out any more. We'll get this war started, let these young-uns cut their teeth on a few more lead balls; then we'll take out and go home to our fires and our toddies."

The servants had placed a long plank across two oak stumps and were busy setting this makeshift table when the rich April sky grew suddenly dull, the sun lost itself behind the forest, and dark shadows streamed from the woods. Now that the pig was done fresh wood was heaped on the fire, and it leaped crackling and steaming, shooting sparks high above the company's heads. The soft air grown heavy with rich smells from the red mouth of the pit, like some light wine too heavily spiced, brought the conversation to a drowsy halt, and the officers let slip their weary duties in the pause that comes over the world at first dark, before the general weariness is broken by the evening meal. Far down the line, as far as his eyes could see, Pleasant watched the low sky light up with the fires from the company messes. Drifting on the light winds or falling away, he could hear the cheer of close comradeship, the noisy banter of the soldiers who had already come to think only from meal to meal.

As he listened, Pleasant thought he could make out his own fire, not so far away, and he was sorry that he had promised to join his cousin's staff. He thought of Eli who shared his blanket and of Long Boy Taliaferro bending over the skillet frying flapjacks, the red flames scorching his steady eyes, and of Old Man Long from the swamps of the Alabama, sitting in the shadows of the circle, pulling at his scrubby black beard, looking after his boys, taking their gibes with good humor, but putting them in their places if they went too far. He had arrived in camp to nurse his only son who had come down with the measles; and when the boy died, he had stayed on to take his place. The ground was too hard for his old bones, he complained, and often he would sit up in the night and tend the fire that first hard winter to keep the boys from freezing. He refused to do any of the cooking, saying that was the young men's business; but he would mold the bullets, dropping them deliberately into the water. Nothing could hurry or ruffle him, and very quietly he taught the mess many things about living in the open which kept it in tolerable good health. If a boy got sick from the greasy flapjacks, the old man would go into the woods and come back with a sack of herbs, sit on his haunches and boil them; then gravely hold the sick man's head and make him drink it down. There was Arthur Clay, no more than a frolicsome kid who already had learned how to forage. He took naturally to it, as if he had been born for nothing else. Pleasant smiled as he remembered the time they had put their pockets together and sent Arthur out with a dollar to buy supplies. He had returned with five cents' worth of bread and ninety-five cents' worth of liquor, and some of the boys complained that he had spent too much on bread. Seven of them there were altogether, a lucky number as long as luck lasts.

His cousin's voice, calling his guests to table, interrupted his reverie. Ellis sat down beside Pleasant. After they had got adjusted, he turned and said:

"You know, McIvor, I'll bet I know what you were thinking about just now."

"What?" asked Pleasant. As he turned, he saw a wistful look cover the other's rugged features. Ellis was a curious fellow, he thought as he looked him over. There was always a contradiction, always a surprise. The soft dark eyes in the hard, raw-boned face. Then to hear the gentle persuasive voice, when the ear expected rough words, or harsh words gently put. Pleasant listened uneasily, feeling that Ellis might in some way know his secret.

"I'll bet you were thinking about your girl," Ellis said intimately.

"I an't got any girl." Ellis's statement, so unexpected, caused Pleasant to speak with too great relief.

"Then you don't know what you're missing, fellow." Ellis sighed.

"You got one?" Pleasant looked curiously at his companion for a moment, as a traveler watches a native of some distant land. *— Have a those who live normal life —*

"You bet your bottom dollar I have," said Ellis. He was surprised at the tone of his voice. It was almost defensive.

At this moment the pig, its juicy vapors rising to the colonel's nose, was brought and set before him. All conversation came at once to a halt. There was a silent feasting of the eye as the guests watched the long sure strokes of the colonel's knife, the tender slices fall to the dish, and the comical snout that never changed its leer, no matter how much meat fell away from the bone. The servants quickly passed the heaping tin plates, the spirits of the table instantly rose, and the two young men listened respectfully while their elders talked.

"Well, Armistead," spoke up Colonel Rob, and his eyes gleamed, "I hope we pitch into Grant's army with the spirit you've cut that pig to pieces."

"Well, Rob, if we just gobble'm up like you are doing now, our independence is sure."

"That'll be easy," said Captain Reins dryly, "if Grant is just as uncomplaining." He picked up his knife and removed a spot of gravy from his coat.

Armistead looked complacently down the rough table. "I have no doubts, gentlemen. We've got our army together. We've got Beauregard, Bragg, Polk, and Hardee . . . and we've got General Johnston."

"Johnston is a noble man," said the inspector, "but he's got to prove he's a general."

"Come, Captain Naylor. He an't responsible for Donelson." The colonel frowned.

"Maybe not. And the army's morale has improved."

"Of course it has," boomed the colonel. "You just give Johnston a chance. He'll lick the boots off of Grant."

With that Colonel McIvor steered the conversation from a subject he considered bad for discipline, a discussion that, at best, must not be made in the presence of the younger men.

"Speaking of General Johnston, gentlemen," said Colonel Rob, "you can go a far piece and never see as noble an animal as his steed, Fire-eater. How proud he goes. He knows he is carrying the commander of an army."

Colonel Rob's voice rang as he spoke. Armistead looked across at his neighbor and was warmed by memory as he saw the familiar signs of the only enthusiasm that ever crossed the old bachelor's stern face, for Colonel Rob had been too occupied with his stables ever to find time for courtship. To hear him talk, the handsome matron and the blushing miss were always in his thoughts, his heart a broken vessel. But, in truth, as his friends knew, he had come no nearer love than the ladies' pavilion at races. The pavilion, the ladies seated in their gay costumes, was to him a part of the setting, the necessary parade to dignify the race. Always he must drink of their beauty before he could settle down to the serious business of the day. Nothing more. But he would have dropped the acquaintance of a friend who dared to hint that they were no more to him than the roll of the starting drum or that he admired more the finished gloss of a thoroughbred's coat than all the finery and plumage across the track.

"In general build Fire-eater reminds me of Wagner," he resumed, pushing his plate away and crumbling tobacco to fill his pipe. The moment his pipe was properly filled and patted, his servant ran forward with a coal. The servant knew exactly how many pats to wait before bringing the fire. Colonel Rob took several puffs, just the time to get the attention of the table and, looking around his nose at his host, asked:

"Armistead, were you by any chance at the Louisville Jockey Club the time Grey Eagle and Wagner ran those memorable two races?"

"Why, I was still in didies." Colonel McIvor winked broadly at his staff.

"You mean, sir," came the quick retort, "that sainted lady, Miss Evelyn, threatened to put you in didies against the coming of your second childhood?"

The table laughed loud, as men will laugh when a good meal lies well against their ribs, and Colonel McIvor's voice was loudest of all.

"No, Rob," he answered with good heart, prodding his friend to go on, "I didn't get there. It was in September, warn't it?"

"The thirtieth of September, 1839, if my memory don't fail me."

Colonel Rob rolled the words reverently over his tongue as an old man recalls the sweetheart of his youth, to whose memory he has ever been faithful.

"I kept at home looking after my crops," said Armistead, carrying the by-play further, "and probably yours, too, while you were gallivanting all over the country, besporting yourself and breaking hearts."

Colonel Rob smiled with pleasure at the allusion. "You needn't try to show off here, Armistead McIvor. We all know who holds the reins at your house. If you didn't go, it was because Miss Evelyn had an errand for you to run. Eh, Roswell?" And he glanced across the table at Ellis, his eyes twinkling under their heavy lids. "But whatever kept you away, Armistead, you missed a performance that has never been equaled in Kentucky—and when I say Kentucky I might as well include the now disrupted country—never been equaled for the excellence of the sport and an attendance unparalleled in numbers and respectability. The Oakland course was in the finest possible order, the stewards in uniform and well mounted, and the arrangements of the proprietor, Colonel Oliver, and of the club, were not only in good taste but complete in all respects.

"I shall not recount the variety of circumstances on the occasion of this, the first race between the champions of Louisiana and Kentucky. But I know I'll be pardoned for alluding to the unusual number of distinguished individuals there and the blaze of beauty reflected from the ladies' pavilion. Their number was estimated at eight hundred, while nearly two thousand horsemen assembled on the field. The stands, the fences, the trees, the tops of carriages, every eminence overlooking the course, were crowded. Probably not less than ten thousand persons altogether. The gentlemen were unmatched for variety: the Bar, the Bench, the Senate, the Press, the Army and Navy, and the entire Kentucky delegation in Congress. Good breeding forbids a numbering of the throng of belles: the young miss just from the trammels of school, flushed with joy and fears, the budding, blooming girl of sweet sixteen, the more stately and elegant full-blown woman—and she, too, with a face as faultless as Neæra, in the Suliote cap and bodice, lives she not last, as well as first, in my remembrance? But the night wastes." Colonel Rob threw his head back and looked at the stars. He sighed ever so gently. "It was such a day to be remembered when we pledge our warmest friends in the generous wine-cup."

"Hold on there," came Armistead's rumbling voice. "Alfred, fetch me that jug from under my quilts."

The negro was back with the jug in a flash, and the staff and visitors stood and pledged, first, President Davis, then Colonel Rob, and last the memory of two noble steeds. With his throat and heart thus warmed the speaker stepped away from the fire.

"On the morning of the race," he continued, "it being understood that Wagner, Grey Eagle, Queen Mary, and Hawk-Eye only would start out of the ten nominations, betting commenced in earnest. Wagner was offered against the field, and as freely taken. Grey Eagle was backed at small odds for the first heat. At a quarter to one the call for the horses was sounded." At this point the old bachelor's voice became deep and vibrant. "Soon with stately step and slow the proud champion of Louisiana, surrounded by a motley group, approached from Mr. Garrison's stable. There was a pause. Wagner was stripped and a finer exhibition of the perfection to which the trainer's art can be carried I have rarely seen.

His coat and eye were alike brilliant . . . a light gold chestnut, with a roan stripe on the right side of his face, white hind feet, about fifteen hands and a half high, with a head singularly small, clean, and bony, set on a light but rather long neck. Forehanded, he resembles the pictures of his sire. His shoulder is immensely strong, running well back into a good middle piece, which is ribbed well home. One of his finest points, I should say, was the depth of his chest. Few horses could measure with him from the point of the shoulder to the brisket. His arms heavily muscled like Mingo's, with the tendons standing out in bold relief. Uncommonly strong hips, a good loin, remarkably fine stifles and thighs, with as fine hocks and legs as ever stood under a horse."

Pleasant looked around the circle. He could see that all but one, Captain Reins, were devoted lovers of horseflesh. From their mouths came sounds of approval and admiration at the technical description of the champion's points. But Colonel Rob waited only a moment, pausing dramatically, looking off into the night as if his eye had caught sight of unbelievable beauty:

"A murmur, then a suppressed cheer from the multitude, the crowd parted, and Grey Eagle came up to the stand. His flashing eye and lofty carriage brought a burst of applause which told better than words the hopes of the sons and daughters of Kentucky. The trainer stripped off his sheet and hood. And there he stood! And there he stood, gentlemen, a magnificent gray, nearly sixteen hands high, with the step of a gazelle and the strength of Bucephalus. No son of Whip ever had a finer set of limbs under him. I will not attempt his description, except to say that he looked ready to run for a life.

"At half past one the judges cleared the course, gave orders to the jockeys. Cato, called Cate, in a richly embroidered scarlet dress sat upon Wagner. The rider for Grey Eagle lost the confidence of his owners just before the race, and at the eleventh hour they had to hunt another. Stephen Welch, a three-year-old rider, was selected. The friends of Grey Eagle had entire confidence in his honesty; and it is clear that he did his best, though weighing but eighty-two pounds he had neither the strength nor the stamina to hold and control a powerful fiery horse like Grey Eagle. The president dislodged the band from their seats over the judges' stand, and Mr. Clay, Judge Porter, my friend Colonel Whetstone of the Devil's Fork of Little Red and I were invited to occupy them. It was a fine view, not only of the race but of the ladies in the pavilion opposite."

Here Colonel Rob drained his glass and threw it to the ground. He grasped his lapels, threw one foot forward, and proceeded with rapid voice.

"All being in motion and nearly in line, the President gave the word and tapped the drum. Grey Eagle was last off. Wagner went away like a quarter horse, with Queen Mary well up second. They were taken in hand at once, which allowed Hawk-Eye to take the place of the Queen on the back stretch. Wagner came first to the stand, and at the turn Cato held up his whip as a signal to the rubbers and boys of Garrison's stable that the old sorrel stud was going just right. They gave a slight cheer, at which Wagner broke loose and made a spread-eagle of the field. The other jocks were startled at this show of speed, and each called upon his nag, so that near the three-quarter post the field closed. But here Stephen let out the phenomenon he so gracefully bestrode, and like twin bullets the gallant gray and Wagner came out of the mêlée.

"At the head of the quarter Stephen was told to 'pull him steady.' So before Wagner reached the stand, Queen Mary changed places with Grey Eagle, notwithstanding her saddle had slipped on her withers. Hawk-Eye was already in difficulty, his pace getting no better very fast. On entering the back stretch Grey Eagle set to work in earnest, outfooting the Queen and challenging Wagner. At the half-mile post Cato called upon Wagner, but Stephen collared him with the Grey, on the outside. The critical moment had arrived. For three hundred yards the pace was killing. Once Grey Eagle got his head and neck in front, and a tremendous shout went up, but

Wagner threw him off so far in going around the last turn that, halfway up the stretch, Mr. Burbridge ordered the gray pulled up, and Wagner won cleverly, Queen Mary dropping just within her distance, one hundred and fifty yards. Hawk-Eye was nowhere. Time: seven minutes and forty-eight seconds.

"The mortification was so great that the first twenty minutes after the heat Queen Mary was freely backed against Grey Eagle. As for Wagner, it was considered a dead open and shut. Before the second heat, however, a reaction took place in favor of Grey Eagle. *Not a Kentuckian on the ground laid out a dollar on Wagner,* although their judgment prompted them to back the Southern champion. Talk about state pride in South Carolina! Why, the Kentuckians have more of it than the citizens of all the states in the Confederacy. But to the horses."

At this point Colonel McIvor held up his hand. "Wait, Rob." Then, shouting, "Alfred, fill up the cups."

As the negro moved quickly from cup to cup, Pleasant noticed that to one side of the servants a large audience had gathered, standing or squatting on the ground. It was long past call to quarters, but Colonel McIvor, if he saw the soldiers, gave no evidence. He rose to his feet:

"Gentlemen, I give you Grey Eagle."

The cups were raised, nor taken away until the last drop of liquid stung the tongue.

There was a moment to let the officers resettle, then the speaker continued easily:

"All cooled off well, but more especially Grey Eagle. He appeared not to mind his run a jot. He extended himself with such ease in the second heat that I was convinced the sweat had relieved him. Great odds were staked on him, but small amounts only were taken. His noble bearing and game-cock look excited universal admiration, so much so that a cargo of laces, gloves, and bijouterie must have been required to pay the wagers in the ladies' pavilion.

"At the tap of the drum they were off, Wagner leading

with a steady businesslike stride, Grey Eagle close up. It was evident that Mr. Burbridge had changed his tactics: the moment Stephen got Grey Eagle into straight work on the back side, he made play for the track, and after a terrific burst of speed for a hundred and fifty yards came in front. Holding his stroke, he soon made a gap of four lengths, and though Wagner drew upon him a little in coming up the rise toward the stand, passed safely beyond with cheers. As if inspired, Grey Eagle kept this terrific pace through the second mile. Wagner lay close up, and there was no faltering, no flinching, no giving back on the part of either. The distances were unchanged to the half-mile post on the third mile, and the pace seemed too good to last. But there were links yet to be let out.

"Near the Oakland house Wagner set to work to do or die. 'Rowel him up,' shouted his owner to Cato. The rally to the turn was desperate, but Wagner gained not an inch. As they swung round the quarter stretch, they were lapped. 'Spur your proud coursers hard and ride in blood' were the orders on this as on Bosworth Field, and both horses got a taste of steel and catgut as they charged up the ascent. Grey Eagle was the first under the cord by a head and shoulders. At the turn Stephen maneuvered Wagner on the outside and soon drew clear in front, looking so much like the winner that the crowd sent up a cheer that made the welkin ring for miles around.

"The group in Wagner's stable bid him go on, but Cato was calmly biding his time. If he could bottle him up for a few hundred yards, there was still another run to be got out of him. He took a bracing pull on his horse, Wagner recovered his wind and came ahead at the quarter stretch. Stephen, long ere this, had become so exhausted that he was unable to give Grey Eagle the support he deserved. He rode wide, swerving considerably from a straight line, and was frequently abroad in his seat.

"From the Oakland house home it was a terrible race! As they swung around the turn in the quarter stretch, Wagner got up neck and neck with the gallant gray. Over the stands the silence was profound—and painful. Both jocks had whip-hands at work. Each spur, with a desperate stab, was buried to the rowel head. For the first hundred yards Grey Eagle was clearly gaining. But in an instant Wagner was up with him. Both were out and doing their best. It was anybody's race yet! Now Wagner—now Grey Eagle. It will be a dead heat! See, Grey Eagle's got him! No, Wagner's ahead! A moment ensues—the people shout—hearts throb—ladies faint—a thrill of emotion, and the race is over! Wagner wins by a neck, in seven minutes and forty-four seconds, the best race ever run south of the Potomac. And Kentucky's champion throws into the shade the most brilliant performance ever made in his native state."

Colonel Rob stood in the shadows of the fire in the silence which followed his words. For a while there was a warmth and a brightness to his eye; and the circle of listeners, especially the youths, hung upon his mouth as if there were secrets and brave stories yet to come. Armistead dropped his eyes to the fire and from the dying embers sought the threads of who knows what memories. Through the town and the forest a hush had spread over the camps, warning at last the brigade headquarters that sleep must come against the morrow, that peace was dead, that the things of peace were no more. From the edge of the group of officers the white eyeballs of the servants shone in the demi-light. A lean negro stepped quietly forward and threw a cape over the speaker's shoulders. "Hit's time to go, Marster."

The soft words broke the spell.

There was a sigh, barely audible. The host pulled himself together and reached his feet in a businesslike way.

"Yes, we'd better turn in. We got a heap to do in the morning."

Colonel Rob and two other officers quietly took their departure, followed by their body-servants. Colonel McIvor watched them go, turned and said, as if he were thinking aloud:

"I was with him when Abe Lincoln's proclamation reached Kentucky asking for troops to subdue her sister states. He didn't do anything but walk out to his stables and order every animal, from brood mare to colt, got ready for sale. He didn't

invite me to go with him, and I didn't offer to go. I would
as soon have intruded where the bridegroom stands in the
darkened room, before the empty marriage bed, while the
mourners walk on toes and whisper in the hall. Not a colt did
he keep. He cleaned out his stables and equipped a battalion
from the sales."

Armistead paused before the memory of the sacrifice; then
briskly, almost hoarsely, ordered:

"Turn in, gentlemen." To the soldiers who were lingering
beyond the fire: "You boys get to your tents or I'll court-
martial every mother's son of you." To Pleasant: "Son, stay
and share my cover."

"I'd better get back, Cousin Armistead."

"That's right. Military discipline. I'm glad you respect
it. There an't enough around here that do. I'll get your
transfer tomorrow. Good night."

As Pleasant turned to go, Roswell Ellis followed him away.

"I think I'll go a piece of the way with you," he said hesi-
tantly. "Somehow I don't feel much sleepy."

"Fine," said Pleasant.

The two young men walked off into the night. On the
edge of town a mounted officer passed them rapidly. Pleasant
and Roswell drew back to keep from being spattered. In the
flash of the street lamp, dim as it was, they both saw the gaunt
face, the eyes straining, filtering the darkness.

"Hell of a hurry." Pleasant spoke with anger. "These staff
officers got to look like they're doing something. I don't mind
being splattered in daytime, but there's no excuse at night."

"Wait a minute. McIvor, you know who that was?" There
was a breath of excitement in Ellis's voice.

"No, and I don't care."

"That was Jordan, the adjutant-general of the army."
Ellis pulled out his watch. "It's a quarter to eleven. I wonder
where he's going in such a hurry this time of night." And he
followed the slushing thud of the horse's feet until the rider
turned a corner sharply.

"Well, it's time he was in bed," grumbled Pleasant.

"It's time we all were in bed," replied Roswell after a pause. "I think I'll turn back." He held out his hand. Pleasant took it. "I'm glad, McIvor, you're going to join our family. I'd be glad to have you share my blanket."

"Much obliged." Pleasant's voice seemed none too eager. He had accepted his cousin's invitation because he thought it might offer a safer base for his own operations. Now he would have to get out of it some way, for the colonel had made it plain that there was no room for private vengeance, at least in his brigade. If Cousin Armistead thought he would waste his time, the opportunity this war had given him . . . Ellis was withdrawing his hand, and he felt a coldness pass between them. It struck him that Ellis thought he was rejecting proffered friendship. He pressed his hand and said warmly:

"I'd like to. I . . . I was thinking of something else."

"Fine," came the reply; and he noticed how quickly Ellis's voice could be warm or cold. "Good night."

"Good night."

The two youths walked off in opposite directions. Quickly the shadows covered them, and the night smothered the distant sounds of the horse's muddy trot. There was silence in the streets of Corinth, broken now and then by the sentries' startled challenge, the sudden voice crying from sleep; then the deeper quiet and the few street lamps sputtering feebly against the darkness.

5

Colonel Jordan drew up at General Johnston's headquarters. As he tied the reins to the hitching post, his hands fumbled with haste. His boots struck the porch arrogantly, he scarcely returned the sentry's salute, as he passed through the house, into the room where the commander-in-chief sat

with his staff gathered about him. Jordan saluted and handed
him an open dispatch. The general took the telegram and
read it. It was from General Cheatham commanding the outpost at Bethel some twenty miles away. It had been sent to
his corps commander, Bishop Polk, and gave the information
that the Yankee General Wallace had been maneuvering in his
vicinity all day. At the bottom was this indorsement in
Beauregard's handwriting:

"Now is the time to advance against Pittsburg Landing."

Johnston read through to the end without comment. Of
his staff, some were working, others sat before the fire. They
glanced at Jordan with annoyance. His manner, they showed
plainly by their looks, was too officious and they had not liked
the way he came into the room.

Johnston laid the dispatch aside and raised his eyes to
his subordinate. They did not reflect the eager haste in
Jordan's glance which bored into him. Very calmly he
asked several questions about the brigading of certain regiments, if the new arms had been issued to Breckinridge's division. Jordan suppressed impatience as he replied. It was
plain he thought the questions irrelevant. One of the staff
showed open hostility at Jordan's impatience, but the general's
features remained serene. He received the answer to his questions as if they had been given in a routine way. In the dim
light his eyes looked dull. Then after a few moments of reflection he got up and picked up the dispatch. He turned his
heavy shoulders and said quietly:

"I'm going across the street and speak to General Bragg."

At the door Jordan asked, "Shall I accompany you, sir?"

"Certainly," came the even reply.

The two soldiers walked onto the porch, through the four
small columns, down the steps, into the yard.

Bragg had gone to bed. On their entrance he was rising
and throwing a military cape over his nightshirt. His face
was covered by a well-trimmed and bristling beard which
failed to hide his firm, slightly cruel mouth. His thick hair
was rumpled with sleep and under the heavy shaggy brows

running together at the nose his dark impatient eyes looked across at the men. Johnston, without remark, handed him the dispatch.

Bragg leaned over to the light, read hastily. He looked up at his commander. His eyes had come to a focus. They no longer seemed haunted.

"I agree with Beauregard," he said eagerly. "The enemy has divided to operate against the Mobile and Ohio. Now is the time to strike. Buell is advancing from Middle Tennessee. We must strike before he effects his junction with Grant."

Jordan gave quick agreement. Johnston's eyes sank into his head, became sharp and gray. He listened to the two men; then slowly, deliberately, almost as if he were thinking aloud, began to speak.

"Let us weigh the chances. First, let us look at ourselves. After reverses almost beyond repair we have reassembled our forces. The reorganization of the army has got barely under way. The brigades, divisions, and corps are in name only. Your corps, General Bragg, understands regimental drill, but your regiments have never acted in brigade formation. We are short of officers, and those we have are almost as ignorant of their duties as the men. The men are badly armed, many of them entirely without arms. Our transport is inadequate, inefficient. We are making an army. Dare we risk battle before it is ready?"

He paused and looked across at his chief of staff; then at the adjutant-general. Jordan spoke:

"We are as well organized now as we can hope to be for some time to come, sir."

Johnston had watched his subordinate like the director of a puppet show. The string was pulled, the mouth opened, the words came, the string pulled it to. Johnston nodded professionally.

"That is true, Colonel Jordan."

"A battle is necessary to revive the spirits of the people ... and the army, sir." Jordan argued his case with vigor.

"Perhaps, sir." Johnston replied as a man thinking far ahead of the question at hand. "A battle must be fought for the Southwest, but it must be won when it is fought. I doubt whether the state of the country will sustain another reverse, whether the army which is no better than militia will hold to- gether under defeat. It is true the spirit is reviving. If we could only give it time . . ."

"Give the word to advance, sir, and you will see what spirit is in the men." Bragg shook his head as he spoke, and his eyes gleamed.

Johnston, as if fitting the words to a puzzle, said without comment, "And the enemy is now divided three ways. If we make this hazard, we must strike before Buell brings up his army. Can I move my raw troops by two narrow roads and throw them on the enemy at the proper time?" He hesi- tated. "The country is rough. We lack topographical infor- mation of the terrain around Pittsburg Landing. We don't know, even, Grant's exact strength. And where can I assemble a reserve in time? Van Dorn is on his way, of course; but we don't know when he'll get here." He looked at Jordan.

"The brigades under Breckinridge can be assembled in Burnsville for a reserve," Jordan said crisply and with con- fidence. "For a week, sir, General Beauregard has been map- ping out the advance of the army, the ways of assembling a reserve. He believes it can be done. We have only twenty miles to march. It should not take more than two days, even, for a raw army to march it. General Beauregard thinks we may surprise Grant."

"Do you think we may surprise him, Colonel?" The com· mander's voice was soft, seeming to ask confidences.

"General Beauregard thinks so."

Johnston listened carefully as Jordan disposed of his ques- tions. He finally asked what he had returned to several times in the conference:

"Does General Beauregard think we may risk our raw troops against a victorious enemy?"

"It is the risk, sir, he believes we must take. It is now or never. The union of Buell with Grant, to be looked for any day, will make the offensive out of the question."

"And a battle is necessary," Johnston returned gravely, "to save us?"

Jordan looked to Bragg, and they nodded assent. Johnston remained silent, ignorant of the men in the room. He loomed in the shadows like a dark and fatal judge, offering the two sharp horns of decision. The two subordinates forgot for the moment that he was not offering but must choose between them.

Johnston had known from the moment the thin slip of paper had been put in his hands what he had to do. From the very beginning at Bowling Green he had been at the mercy of forces he could not command, would not obey. And these forces had allowed the enemy to take the initiative from him. He was made for command. He knew it, but now that he must lead an army into battle, disaster, bad luck, or something more sinister made it difficult for him to act, to do what he could do better than any man in the Southwest. Already he had suffered defeat without battle. He had lost Kentucky and Middle Tennessee. Upon his shoulders fell the blunders of his incompetent generals. And that was right. Yes, in some way that was right, because he was responsible for everything in his department. He had been set over the states and the people for one thing—Victory! And it was his failure when his generals lost Donelson and the army there. And now that he had done what had seemed impossible— brought his scattered and demoralized forces together again— the feat went unrecognized by all except his friend Davis. His throat tightened at the thought of the president's support. He had never doubted, when all were crying for his removal. But, perhaps, that was right, too. The people are not supposed to understand such things. The army, even, is blind to everything but victory. It is a hard rule, but it is right, for without victory there will be no liberty. And then Johnston thought of the ways he might have avoided this bitter retreat. He might have gathered all his forces and advanced. Taken the

risk. But it was a madman's risk. He was no magician, over-
night to turn a people into an army. He could not strike the
ground and make arms spring forth, divert the channels of
rivers. Nor could he whistle gunboats upon their waters.

On his arrival at Corinth he had tried to restore confidence
by offering Beauregard the command of the army, limiting
himself to his departmental duties. But even that move had
got twisted in some way and brought his purpose to worse
than nothing. Beauregard had refused, but Johnston could
not forget the pause, that significant pause, before Beauregard
declined the proffer of responsibility. They then agreed upon
a nice balance. Beauregard would take over the reorganization
of the army, on his own terms. In this way Johnston had
thought to effect the same purpose and use Beauregard's powers,
his name, for the good of the cause. He had thought that he
knew how to use men as well as command them . . . but that,
too, had been a mistake. Had Beauregard misunderstood his
motive? *Had he believed that the commander had lost confidence in himself?* Had this blindness, or Beauregard's vanity, deluded him into the belief that he was actually in command of the army? And was he now asking for a perfunctory
consent to let it advance? What a curious blindness! What
a dangerous condition for the state of command. Did Beauregard think he could assume the direction of the army without
also assuming the responsibility for its fate?

What is this thing that makes what is strong in me weak?
That at every turn neutralizes my powers? This thought
struck him with such agony that his mask almost cracked before the room. When the people were slow to flock to the
standard, it was his blunder. When the governments failed
to arm what forces he had, it was his fault. When he lost
the confidence of the people and had the army's faith shaken,
he was blamed. When he had tried to remedy conditions, restore confidence in the only way he could, by the sacrifice of
himself, he had been balked, misunderstood, pushed into a
more difficult dilemma. Somehow, the clearer he saw his duty,
the more confused it turned out in performance. And now

the enemy, as if he had slyly read his mind, had forced the issue just at that moment when he was most embarrassed, but when he saw the end to his embarrassments. The gauge had been thrown down. He would pick it up. Alone, whatever the end, he would take it and hurl it back in his face.

Very quietly, with a peculiar resonance to his voice, he said, "Colonel Jordan, you may draw up the order for an advance."

6

Pleasant opened his eyes. He opened them with a start and a sharp ringing in his ears. The morning haze hovered above the ground. The vague light dripped damply upon his face. He thought: I am trapped by the day. But at once he remembered. He was no longer in the woods above Wetumpka, stalking his enemies. He and they had been hurled into a close, new world. He was no longer free to draw the cloak of darkness. The pain in his ears was the morning bugle. It was giving him orders. Already Eli was awake. He sat on the blanket yawning, looking vacantly at the ground through swollen eyes. Old Man Long was stirring the dead ashes of last night's fire, piling brush, blowing at the few live coals. For a moment Pleasant watched their soft gray flakes go spattering ever so gently against the hard leather of his face, cling to his eyelashes. In a flash he realized Mr. Long was a very old man. The flame leaped at the steady eyes, and the white sticky smoke curled low to the ground. In the half dark, as he sat back on his haunches, squatting by the fire, Old Man Long looked like a rotten stump. Pleasant sprang lightly to his feet and stretched. Dropping his arms suddenly, he shook the sleep from his shoulders and stood for a moment very quietly, thinking in a puzzled way how this could happen, how he could sleep like other men. . . .

From all sides the clear gay bugles sang in the forest, sharp and peremptory close by, soft and sweet from a distance, answering one another like roosters. When the last brassy sound had cut thin through the heavy air—that was the bugler in a Mississippi regiment, the strongest chest in the army— the hum of thousands of voices rose, swept over town and camps. Bodies rolled from under blankets; and the stale odors, sharp and familiar, swept once by the nose, met the damp air, turned the garments strong and brassy. Reluctantly men abandoned the warm earth and stood shivering, alone or in groups. Then, with a roar, the camps came alive.

Long Boy Taliaferro had straddled little Arthur Clay and was teasing him awake. He goosed him, pulled at his curls, and the boy shut his small eyes tighter and struck out like a child. He flopped over on his stomach, pulled the blanket over his head.

"Git up, baby chile," said Taliaferro, "and let mammy feed it."

Several of the mess drifted toward them.

"Come on. Git up and let mammy scrub his little ass, and then he kin have his great big old black teatty."

From under the blanket the small voice, outraged but heavy with sleep, said, "Go to hell, Taliaferro."

Taliaferro winked at his audience and together the men picked Arthur up, blanket and all, and threw him high in the air. He fell hollering and kicking. With a shout Taliaferro caught him in his long, taut arms and held him struggling and cursing.

"God damn you, Taliaferro, I'm going to . . ." The iron arms squeezed him.

"Going to what, little-un . . . going to what?"

"Let go, you hurt," Arthur said fiercely.

The bugle sounded fall in, and there was a scramble to get in ranks. The company dressed, and the sergeant called the roll.

The men stood in line looking blankly into space, bored but submissive to this foolish formality, answering to their names as if they were playing some stupid game. The sergeant was hurrying through his duty with an unusual briskness. Pleasant watched him and wondered idly what made him look so blown up with importance. And there was Captain Bob Curtin on time, and looking bright and eager. Something unusual was afoot. In the distance a great shouting came booming through the camps. Pleasant's first thought was, as he noted the way the sound traveled, it's going to rain; then he felt an interest stiffen the ranks. Another shout. That must be a whole brigade. Every eye was by this time fixed on Bob Curtin. He spoke, and his uneven voice rang with excitement.

"You men will cook up five days' rations for your haversacks. You'll be issued forty rounds of ammunition after breakfast. . . ." He did not finish.

Pleasant felt his throat strain and tingle. His mouth flew open, and his ears cracked with the rising shouts.

The men broke ranks and crowded about Bob Curtin. They pelted him with questions, rushed off to the quartermaster's wagon to draw their rations. Old Man Long sat down and very carefully, unmindful of the flurry about him, melted lead, dropped the molded bullets into the company kettle. There was a sizzle, a little rise of vapor; then in dropped another. Pleasant ate a small snack for breakfast and put the rest of his fried meat and flapjacks in his pocket. He rolled up his blanket, put an extra shirt inside, and tied both ends of the roll. Then he sat down and cleaned his gun. He drew his cartridges, counted them, feeling the heavy little balls at one end of the greased paper, then dropped them in his cartridge box. He was ready long before the others had settled down to their business. From one group he heard bursts of laughter: it was Arthur Clay swaggering about, telling how many Yankees he was going to kill. Long John moved more quietly than usual, whistling under his breath, and looking every now and then at Clay with concern in his eyes.

Eli brought his boots over and sat down on a log near Pleasant. He began rubbing tallow on his feet and toasting them before the fire.

"What are you doing that for?" asked Pleasant.

"Well, nephew," he answered gaily, "I'm getting my feet into condition. When the enemy begins to run, I want to be able to run after him."

"You better grease your boots, then. It's going to rain, uncle."

"Now that's right. I always like to see a young man respectful to his elders."

Pleasant had never seen Eli in such fine humor. He was always one to catch the spirit of a group of people: he was sad when you were sad, gay when you were gay, he'd drink or not drink as the occasion demanded; be ready for a frolic or . . . for what they had been doing together.

Eli pulled one foot away from the fire, felt its bottom. "Yes, nephew, a little action's what I need. Something to tone me up for the spring. It's better than rhubarb or sassafras tea."

Bob Curtin strode through the messes, looking very important.

"Hurry up, men. Assembly in fifteen minutes. Hurry up."

"Bob looks happy for the first time in two weeks, since he and Major McGoffin had that tussle." Pleasant spoke reflectively.

"Yes, Bob's just like me. Salt's too weak for us. We've got to season with black powder."

"Well, get your tallow feet in those leaky boots, or you'll be left behind."

Pleasant felt a little irritated with Eli's gaiety.

7

The fire had died on the hearth. The dim yellow light from the lamp fell on General Beauregard's bed. An aide tiptoed into the room. The general was sitting up in bed writing. Around him, on the covers, lay envelopes and telegrams. Several had fallen to the floor. The aide looked at his superior: he was bent over, and the pencil traveled rapidly over the back of an envelope. Tiptoeing over to the window, he drew the curtain. The pale morning smothered the yellow flame from the lamp. Beauregard looked up and nodded. His sharp, brown face was haggard, and there was a look of sustained weariness in the clear brown eyes. He finished the last note, sighed, reached his hand to his throat and rubbed it. Glancing toward the window, he said:

"Ah, it is morning."

"How do you feel, General?" the aide asked solicitously.

"This bronchial infection," he answered, "it has Union sentiments."

"Can I bring you some coffee, sir?"

"Yes, Chisholm, and will you fetch Jordan? I have here the orders for march and battle." He waved his arm abruptly over the covers at his feet. "He must draw them up as quickly as possible."

When Chisholm returned with the adjutant, they found the general dressed and assorting his papers. He spoke briefly to Jordan and handed him the envelopes.

"Here is the sketch of the terrain, the roads between here and Pittsburg Landing. These notes relate to Hardee's march, these to Bragg, and these to Polk. Breckinridge will concentrate at Farmington and march from there."

He spoke in his brisk nervous voice. When he was through, Jordan hesitated over the papers.

"It will take me some time to draw these up, sir. Hadn't you better give the corps commanders oral directions?"

"Good. Chisholm, my compliments to Generals Bragg, Hardee, and Polk. Ask them to meet me here as soon as possible."

The two officers stepped briskly out of the room.

Beauregard was left alone, and his mind went blank with weariness and the long sickness in his throat. It was a little better, but early in the morning, these sharp mornings, it still troubled him. The servant entered with coffee, black and strong as it is made in New Orleans. He picked the cup up and watched his trembling hand lift it to his lips. Hastily he ate the bread and meat, and at once felt stronger. That moment of doubt, of depression, that he had felt after Jordan stepped through the door with his orders had passed. The die was cast. The chances were good for a surprise; but if anything went wrong, if he found Grant alert and ready, the attack could be turned into a reconnaissance in force. The army could be brought back to Corinth and Grant tricked into some blunder as he followed. Corinth could be fortified.

As he thought of the fortifications which he could make rise about the town, Beauregard took comfort in his sure knowledge of engineering. Yes, the risk was not so great. If the worst came to the worst, he could fortify. Bugles blew sharply across his reverie. He heard shouts in the camps. Then from the hall outside came the sound of heavy footsteps. He looked up almost as if he had been surprised.

The large gray form of Johnston stood in the doorway.

Beauregard bowed, spoke briskly: "Good morning, General."

Johnston returned the bow. "Good morning, General Beauregard," he answered, gravely courteous.

Johnston moved across the floor with heavy precision. For one moment the two men faced each other. Johnston's face glowed with health. His eyes were bright and steady and very grave. Beauregard's cheekbones stood high above his brown, hollow cheeks. His eyes, too, were bright but dry and burning, the lips dry above his combative chin. Johnston spoke, after the slightest pause:

"What are your logistics, General?"

Beauregard with incisive clarity began to explain the dispositions he had made for the march and battle. He drew the roads on his camp table—Jordan had taken the only map—pointing out Monterey and Mickey's, where the roads crossed, the place of rendezvous. Then he sketched the triangle of land that lay between Owl and Lick Creeks, the base made by the Tennessee River, and then his pencil made a dot.

"This is Shiloh Church. The assumed position of the enemy is about a mile in advance of this position, his right resting on Owl Creek, his left on Lick Creek."

Johnston nodded, listening carefully to the explanations, asking questions, weighing the answers, following the rapid movements of the pencil.

"We will attack in three lines," continued Beauregard, speaking rapidly, "Hardee the first line, Bragg the second, Polk the third, one division marching from here, Cheatham joining on the field from Bethel, if he can elude Wallace. It is about the same marching distance. The reserve coming up from the right."

Johnston interrupted: "These orders, General, throw the different corps in successive lines along the whole front of the army. I had in mind entrusting a part of the front to each corps. In this way the reserves can be assembled better and there won't be the confusion of mixed commands."

Beauregard demurred: "The country is rough and broken, the roads are few and narrow, our troops so raw, I believe it is safest to throw each corps upon the enemy as it reaches the field. The success of this movement depends upon surprise. Hardee is more proficient at marching. None of Bragg's brigades have acted together."

There was a pause. Johnston remained silent.

"I have assumed," continued his second in command, "that the enemy cannot break through three lines."

"Very well, General," said Johnston slowly. "It may be as well. The main thing is to hammer him . . . to hammer him. We'll drive in his left and throw him into the river."

Johnston's voice reverberated through the small room.

Beauregard, with the querulous tones of a man who has been sick, but with all respect, said, "This was Napoleon's formation for Waterloo."

8

Roswell Ellis rode his horse at a walk through the streets
of Corinth. It was late afternoon of April third. The streets
were crowded with wagons, artillery, and men under arms.
To move at all, he had to pick his way. The men had been
standing in ranks, or squatting on the sidewalks, or lying
spraddled on their blanket rolls, since before noon. Their
high spirits had lost some of their early eagerness. As he went
through the congested streets, the men hurled pleasant insults.

"Say, Mister, thar's something in the road up thar. Git it
out fer us, will ye. I promised Gineral Grant I'd meet him
by sun, shore." Then rough laughter, and Roswell blushed
to his ears.

Near a battery the officers and men lounged with studied indifference, looking suspiciously at the infantry as if it were a
sort of verminous rabble which must be kept at a proper distance from the precious guns. Most of the artillerymen were
gentlemen, but there was one humped over on a caisson whose
face was marked by a dirty leer. Without lifting his insolent
eyes or raising a shoulder, he called to Roswell:

"Hey, purty boy. Hey, ain't you one of Gineral Johnston's
little fellows?" Roswell flushed, looked injured, and rode on
without answering. You could not fight every man in the
army.

"Run tell him," came the voice, "you ain't lost. So we kin
git along. I'm wore out setten."

He turned into a side street. There was great commotion.
Some ordnance wagons were trying to pass another battery.
The horses shied, got tangled. Officers were shouting, teamsters
cursing. One long thin driver was standing with marvelous
balance in his seat. Through the rearing team Roswell could

see in his yellow eyes the abuse ready to pour from his mouth.
He rode on. At the intersection of this short street he had
to wait for a whole regiment to pass. The men marched in
ragged line, with a swinging step. Some had haversacks, but
most of them carried only a blanket wrapped over their
shoulders. Their faces were gaunt, scraggly beards grew from
their chins, and, sunk back of lean cheekbones, blank eyes
smoldered in dry sockets. Roswell turned to a major mounted
on a flea-bitten gray.

"What command is that?" he asked.

The officer turned his square face. "An Arkansas regiment,
Polk's corps. He has been blocking our movement since
twelve o'clock." The major pulled out his watch and Roswell saw his eyes snap at the heavy gold piece, the plume in
his hat bend and quiver as he jerked his head. "It's now a
quarter to four," he spat out his words. "My battalion has been
under arms, ready to march, for six hours."

A gap formed between two companies. Roswell lifted his
hat, and spurred his horse through. Slowly he reached the
edge of town, where the road leading to Monterey led off.
Lying by the roadside, or standing in groups as far as he could
see, brown figures moved restlessly or lay still between the
dun-colored trees, trampling underfoot the tender grass. At
intervals the batteries and wagon trains waited in the road.
Groups of officers, mounted and on foot, waited impatiently,
casting their eyes upward, squinting them before the sun. He
inquired for General Gladden's brigade. Nobody seemed to
know exactly where it was. He rode on. Finally, about a
mile from town, he came upon it. He presented himself before a group of officers standing in the road holding their
bridle reins. He saluted and handed an order to a flat-faced
man in middle years on whose collar were the gold wreath and
three stars. Ellis took him for a colonel, a homespun colonel
smoking a corncob pipe.

The field officer took the pipe from his mouth and said in a
slow, well-modulated voice, "Captain Curtin's company is
about three hundred yards down the line." Turning in his

tracks he spoke to a young officer beside him, "Lieutenant, order Private McIvor, of Company C, for detached duty."

Roswell saluted, and the Colonel with mild interest watched him ride away. When Roswell found Pleasant, he was lying on the ground with his back to a tree. He was idly pulling at the tender shoots of grass. He looked up gravely, and, when he recognized Roswell, a smile slowly spread over his features.

"Hello, Ellis," he said.

Roswell thought that in some way McIvor had changed. He got up, came over and laid his hand on Roswell's saddle.

"What are you doing way over here?" Pleasant asked.

"I've come with an order for you."

Pleasant looked at the ground; then squarely at the other.

"Tell Cousin Armistead I think I'd better not transfer now. After the battle, maybe."

"Oh, it's not that," Ellis replied hastily. "You've been detailed with me to make a scout in the enemy lines. General Hardee wants to know how they lie, and Colonel McIvor says you are the best scout in the army."

Pleasant's expression changed at once.

"We'll get back in time for the fighting?"

"Sure." There was a shade of envy in Roswell's voice.

"All right, then, I'll go."

"Not now. At Mickey's. You're to meet me at Mickey's when your corps gets there. I've got to get more information from a guide to Hardee's corps. You'll report to Colonel McIvor's brigade."

A bugle sounded, sharp and peremptory. It was taken up down the columns, ringing, bounding through the forest. Pleasant's hand tightened on the saddle. Roswell straightened up. Staccato voices shouted, "Fall in. Fall in." In a rush men sprang to their feet, tumbled out of the woods. The trees seemed to shed them. Officers mounted pitching horses, and there was Bob Curtin running to his place, calling like a boy at play, "Take your places. Fall in." Pleasant hurried off, saying, "See you at Mickey's." The colonel rode by with his staff, splashing the gray, gluey mud from the slippery roadbed.

Roswell pulled his animal around to clear the way. It had caught the excitement, reared and leaped into a sassafras thicket, knocking a wild-eyed youth against a tree. There was a moment of confusion, men milling and churning in the center of the road, twisting backward and forward, with their gun barrels held high. When it seemed that the mass would never untangle, its center stiffened, the fringe wavered; then the whole seemed to shake itself into a pattern, suddenly grow quiet. As far as his eyes could carry, Roswell saw a long grayish-brown column, four men abreast, jagged with gun barrels and, at intervals, with folded standards. Far down the column he heard a faint shout. It was taken up, hurled backward, growing louder, more distinct. Curiously it seemed not many voices but one bouncing down the air. He turned in that direction. The head of the column quivered, pulled out like sorghum on a cold day, slowly, reluctantly. A booming voice at the head of the regiment at last called, For-wward. . . . It was repeated by puppet voices of the captains. . . . Mar-rch. The men moved, the guns leaped up, and Pleasant's regiment was on the move.

It passed slowly. Then behind him Roswell heard a whip crack. Over the swinging infantry the team of the first wagon settled down to their collars. He saw the lead horse move, the harness tighten against the flanks, the wheels roll over. The regiment passed. There was a break, and the line of wagons rolled by, rumbling with their heavy loads, harness squeaking, the drivers slouched over, molded to their seats, with indifferent faces, shaking with the jolts like figures glued to the seats. There was a sharp war-whoop up front, and a gun went off. As if it were a signal, the woods shook with one mighty yell, a weird savage yell that brought a lump in the throat. Roswell felt his heart swell, and the water ran through his eyes. He turned his mount's head into the woods, in the direction of the Bark road, roughly parallel, as he knew, to the direct route over which Bragg was marching. There Hardee's column should be unwinding its slow body.

9

All through the fourth of April showers fell, and all through that day the butternut columns crawled slowly forward. The rains made the bad roads worse. Those soldiers who had blankets untied one end of the roll and fastened them about their necks, managing in this way to keep dry from neck to knees. The caisson wheels cut deep into the mire. Thousands of feet trampled it into mush, a sticky, slippery, gluey mush. The heavy ordnance wagons slid about, hunting bottom. Men in the rear columns took off their shoes and tied them about their gun barrels, rolled up their pants and waded through the mud. The horses, their heads down, straining at their collars, the red and gray mud plastered to their bellies and tails, strained under their heavy loads, the heavier going underfoot, splashed or plunged when the wagons or the dark-mouthed cannon sank up to the axle, wearily responding to the crack of the whip or to the monotonous, hoarse commands of the drivers, the monotonous profanity.

Pleasant trudged along, or stood in the mud every mile or two, waiting until the road ahead unblocked itself. His division had got only a short distance beyond Mickey's when the sun began to fall. He reported to his sergeant and fell out. Hardee's corps was much farther ahead toward the Landing. He settled down to a long stride and left the straggling columns behind him. He must try to make connection with Roswell Ellis before dark. The short march from Corinth had tired him more than a whole day of steady going in the woods. Occasionally he would watch the ranks straggling along, but the haggard faces made him weary. He stepped over knives and pistols that had been thrown away to lighten the load. Here and there lay a haversack. Here and there he would pass a group of men laughing and talking, but mostly the dun-colored columns were silent. Once he passed a great man in ranks, heavily loaded with knapsack, skillets, blankets, his own musket and one belonging to a comrade. Just as Pleasant passed him by, he broke into song. And this cheer made those to the front and to the immediate rear pick up their feet. Overhead clouds gathered to mask the failing light, and the woods turned drear and clammy. But Pleasant swung toward the front, light of heart, alone as he preferred to be, free from the sluggish straggling march of his regiment.

First dark fell suddenly, when he reached a brigade halted to the rear of an ordnance train. The command was given to move into the woods and go into bivouac. He heard it, as he passed the wagons, counting them. There were twenty-three, all of different sizes, farm wagons, some government wagons, but wagons mostly pressed in the country about Corinth. The teams stood quietly with the resignation of beasts that have been over-pulled. As Pleasant neared the wagon which was holding up the train, he could make out several mounted officers riding around in the semi-darkness. Rattling out orders, their voices rose, sharp and worn. Then from the front a large horse and large rider trotted into the confused group. His voice rolled in the gathering darkness with a familiar lustiness. There could be but one such voice in the whole army, Pleasant thought: it was his Cousin Armistead's.

"The last two squads fall out and cut me a stout sapling. Step along now."

The ax thudded in the heavy atmosphere, the chips fell on the sodden ground. In no time the small tree fell and was quickly cleared of limbs.

"Now, gentlemen, bring it over here. Put it under that rear axle. Now, boy," to the sullen negro driver, "ready! All together!"

The mules, without unison, attempted to settle down to the pull. They splashed sideways, leaped up in their harness at the long cracking thong, at the guttural Hep! Hep!, the grunting Git! Git! Dar! The soldiers slipped in the mud, strained under the sapling. The small tree bent, the wheels sank deeper into the mire, rolling an inch or two forward.

"Tain't no use, marster. These ornery critters . . . " The negro sounded desperate.

"Let them rest," cut in the full and irate tones of Colonel McIvor. Pleasant saw his cousin, with his head bent over on his chest, sit for some minutes, sit heavily on his mount. The darkness grew. Throwing up his head, Colonel McIvor ordered torches, and soon the red-smoking flames cast strange shadows upon the dispirited faces gathered in the road.

"All right, gentlemen, to your places." The colonel spoke confidently. The sapling slid through the greasy mud, into the thick yellow pool, found bottom. Twenty hands grasped the slick bark, ten bodies dropped to a squat position. Colonel McIvor opened his pistol holster and brought out his weapon. He leveled it at the negro's head. The black man's eyeballs grew wide and yellow, and fear splashed from the torches over his sweating features.

"Now, you black scoundrel, you get this wagon out of this hole," he said calmly.

The driver had been shouting angrily, curling the black snake whip over the animals' backs. "Yes, sir, marster," he said hurriedly, sat erect in the wagon seat, tightened the reins evenly in his hands; and then, very gently, with soft persuasion, called, "Now, Kate, old gal, steady thar. You, Jim, pull up, whoa now. Whoa! Sam, Gray, listen to me. No-oww . . . HEP! HEP! UP THAR."

With one steady pull the mules moved forward, settled against their collars. Their feet seemed to prance in the slosh; they found bottom; their legs swelled with the strain, moved in a running walk; and the wagon groaned, gave a leap, and with the wheels dripping mud, stood clear. Colonel McIvor put his pistol back in its holster and called to his impressed pioneers:

"Cut me some logs and lay'm across this hole. Now make haste, gentlemen. Make haste."

Pleasant felt a tap on his shoulder and a voice, "Well, you got here." He turned; it was Roswell Ellis.

"Yes, I got here—by the hardest."

"Well, come on before the old man makes pioneers of us." The two young men were soon away, going toward the brigade headquarters in silence. There seemed little to say now they had met for their adventure. They picked their way through dark forms moving ghoulishly through the forest, talking in undertones. Many were sprawled wearily on the wet ground, or leaning against tree trunks. Others were dragging brush for beds. Roswell scarcely noticed them, but Pleasant let his eyes, now well accustomed to the dark, inspect everything to his front. He looked at the dark forms of daytime men with sweet contempt. For the first time since he had joined the army he began to feel the old confidence, the easy freedom of his habits in the country about the Staircase. At last the two scouts came to a tent raised between trees. There was no light, and in the gloom they sat down to eat a snack. His Cousin Armistead's body-servant, when they had finished, came forward with two horses. "What are these for?" Pleasant asked abruptly.

"They are for us," said Roswell.

"Take them away. We're going afoot."

Roswell hesitated before answering. He felt sharp resentment—he was tired anyway—at the short command. Suddenly he had the feeling that he must go on this adventure with a stranger for companion. The quiet, square-faced, but gentle youth he had met around Colonel McIvor's campfire had disappeared. This form—he began to have the feeling that Pleasant was only a force, a hard voice—that moved about with the easy rhythm of a cat he did not know. And he had no way of judging the sudden change in Pleasant's character. If he could only see his face, Ellis thought, he might make fresh acquaintance, combine the familiar with the strange. But it was too dark. He answered, and his voice sounded peevish; he had hoped to make it cold:

"How can we cover the distance between here and the

enemy lines, reconnoiter, and return before morning if we go on foot?" As an afterthought, "Suppose they give chase?"

"We'll never reach the lines on horses." Pleasant spoke impatiently.

At this moment the adjutant strode up with his hands before him, as if he were pushing the darkness aside like a curtain.

"That you, Ellis?" he asked.

"Yes, sir."

"Hello, young man"—to Pleasant. "Well, I see you are ready. I've been sent to give you final instructions. The enemy is somewhere to the front, about two miles forward. Do you hear those bands playing?"

The two young men listened. They heard what they thought were bands in the Confederate Army.

"Well," continued the adjutant, "they are Federal serenades. You see how close we are to their lines. I can't believe we have got this close without their knowledge. That music could be easily a ruse. At any rate, you are to proceed to our left until you reach Owl Creek. From there proceed to the front, until you make contact with the enemy; then you will go from left to right, noting his positions, state of preparations. Return before light. Late this afternoon a cavalry reconnaissance ran into his advanced posts. There was a spirited skirmish. We captured several men, and from what information we could get they are not expecting us. But the skirmish was so noisy it may have put them on guard. The general particularly wants to know if there are any breastworks." He paused. "If there are, God help us."

There was a slight silence. The adjutant spoke again: "Now have I made everything clear?"

"Yes, sir," came Pleasant's abrupt reply.

"McIvor thinks we'd better go on foot," spoke up Roswell.

"It is Colonel McIvor's orders that you have complete freedom, but I suggest that you take horses as long as you keep to the road."

Roswell looked toward Pleasant in the dark. Without hesitation Pleasant gave his crisp agreement.

"Good," said the adjutant. "I'll send an orderly along to bring the horses back."

In another minute Pleasant and Roswell had mounted and were slowly picking their way to the road. As soon as they struck it, they went at a steady pace for forty minutes. Roswell soon found himself following his companion's lead. He decided that Pleasant's horse was surer of the road. He could see Pleasant leaning forward in the saddle, peering through the blackness. Roswell had the curious feeling that Pleasant was traveling down a well-known thoroughfare; and yet he knew that his companion had never been in this country before. The road was very narrow, and the forest rose up on either side, a solid darkness, pitted with heavier shadows, rising to a cloudy ceiling. As they went along, the clouds rolled over the lighter strip of night through which they were speeding. Roswell had another strange sensation. The night settling in the roadway seemed a liquid daubing holding back two oppressive walls. Gradually the darkness grew heavier. The atmosphere pressed hard against a man's chest. But for the steady fall of their animals' feet in the soft roadbed, the bands and some shouting in the enemy camps, the world was still. Its very stillness made the few noises, even the music, ominous. Roswell wondered if it were playing them into some trap. He looked at the sky. Through thin edges of drab light he could see the clouds bank and pile. He thought, it's going to storm. As the words formed, there came a slow distant rumble. Suddenly, a stream of lightning ripped through the threatening sky. Pleasant pulled up his horse's head.

"Here's where we get off," he said.

Pleasant's voice was warm and eager. His strange excitement puzzled Ellis more than ever. In the chill air, in extra darkness, with a storm threatening, going on a dangerous scout, there seemed little in such prospects for eager cheer. He lowered his voice and spoke:

"We haven't reached the creek yet."

"It's about thirty paces ahead," came the answer.

"How do you know?"

"The lightning."

"Oh."

They pulled up and dismounted, gave the bridle reins into the orderly's hands. The orderly said, "Well, fellows, take care of yourselves." He looked in the direction they were to take. "That's sure going to be worrisome." He waited a few moments before leading the horses back down the road they had come.

After his departure Pleasant stood for a moment on the edge of the forest. Roswell saw him throw his head up like an animal catching a scent. In a moment Pleasant said, "Let's go." They stepped through the first wall of darkness. They picked their way slowly at first, but Roswell noticed that Pleasant always got through the thick undergrowth before he did. Soon Roswell found himself falling in behind him, and the going became much easier. It was not hard to realize why Colonel McIvor had chosen his cousin for this particular scout. Roswell had been on possum and coon hunts, and he thought he knew something of the woods; but Pleasant traveled these strange woods with the surety almost of an animal. The pace—a slow swinging stride, rarely varying and very steady.

This kept up Roswell couldn't tell how long. There were no words passed. He watched, now that his eyes were getting more accustomed to his surroundings, the easy swing of Pleasant's hips; heard the soft fall of his foot on the spongy leaves, the brush and slap of undergrowth on their clothes, the occasional splash when they struck a pool of water. Once Pleasant hesitated, looked right and left, and swung straight to the front into a long stretch of back-water. They seemed to be making enough noise to wake up the whole Federal Army, splashing and lifting their boots through the deep muddy bottom. Halfway across they both stopped in their tracks. Bugles sounded from their front, clear and near through the heavy air. Roswell felt himself tremble with excitement. He believed they would never reach dry land again and unconsciously he hurried forward, bending over, expecting any moment a hot bullet to drop him into this still pool of water.

He could feel the water closing over his head, sinking and choking to its slimy bottom. At last they reached firm ground. He stood a moment and wiped the heavy beads of sweat from his forehead.

Pleasant turned to the right and increased his pace, stopping every now and then to listen. He beckoned to Roswell to be more silent; then they bent over from the waist like monkeys and crawled for a long distance. When Roswell stood up again, he could see through the thick woods a long line of flickering redness and gray monsters moving in the dying firelights. Pleasant whispered, "The enemy camps. We've slipped between the outposts." They squatted like Indians and faced each other across the darkness. For a while Roswell heard nothing but his heavy, rhythmic pants. He looked at Pleasant—he could now—saw him with mouth closed and head cocked on one side listening. The words "slipped through the outposts" sent a thrill to Roswell's heart. He realized suddenly what expert knowledge his companion had for this kind of business, and he felt ashamed of his early resentment.

Then, not two hundred yards to their left front, they heard steps, underbrush crackling, the rough noise of men walking through the woods. Were they discovered? They jumped to their feet and ran to trees standing close together. Quickly they unbuckled their holsters and drew their pistols. Roswell held his breath. He heard Pleasant hiss, "Don't shoot unless you have to." They waited, it seemed, an interminable time. At last something broke through a thicket. Roswell cocked his pistol; then dropped it to his side. A small cow swung toward them, stopped, wandered off toward the west. They both faced each other, laughed quietly with relief. This incident drew them closer together.

"We'd better get closer." Pleasant spoke in a businesslike way.

As long as it was safe, they slipped from tree to tree. Finally, dropping to the ground, they crawled until they came to a creek. Across it stretched the company streets of an enemy brigade. The camp was quiet, and the fires were dying. In their shadows the sentries walked to and fro. There were no breastworks, and under the white tents men lay sleeping, all ignorant that scarce two miles away forty thousand men were gathering in the forest to strike. Without speaking the two scouts turned away toward the right and crept for hours, behind ravines, through difficult undergrowth, until a camp was reached, silently inspected, and so on to the next. The camps were still in sleep and unknowing of what the morrow might bring. Very carefully the boys skirted three outposts. In two there was no movement, but the guard at the third was alert. They lay reclining about the fire and talking of the skirmish of that afternoon. Roswell wanted to slip up and hear more, but Pleasant pulled him away. The information was not worth the risk. As they felt their way along, it grew darker. The thunder rolled heavier, the lightning became more frequent. Then there was a moment when the world seemed to be sucked empty, and in a great cracking the storm fell. Pleasant and Roswell piled what brush they could—there was no time—and sat down on the eastern slope of a ridge, wrapped in one blanket. The other blanket they threw over their heads. In this fashion, huddled together, they took the storm.

It came in such sheets of water and wind that the bare forest, in spite of the thick stands of timber, proved little shelter. In five minutes their blankets were soaking, and the rain beat sharper than hail against their faces. Blankets of fire flapped across the night like battle flags. Chains of lightning bolted from the clouds, trembled for a moment, shattered and bloody standards hurled by a giant hand; then a clap of thunder and they were gone. At such times the rain glistened in the air, and water ran down the slick dark bark of the trees. At any moment Roswell looked for the wind to tear the forest up by its roots and break the backs of the hostile armies lying so close together, one in the shelter of its tents, the other sprawled in the mud and torrent, sullen like a moccasin.

Water rolled in streams from their heads into their boots. It raced in tiny streams under the brush beneath them. Roswell shifted and stuck himself with a broken branch. He shouted to Pleasant, but his voice fell dead at his lips. Pleasant shook his head to let him know he couldn't hear. Once when the sky seemed to explode, Roswell looked up. Bending and dashing together, the empty tree tops beat their branches until the tenderer limbs fell to the earth with the water. Soon Roswell found he was shaking with a chill, and nowhere was there any warmth in his body. He moved closer to Pleasant and put his arm around his waist for warmth. Pleasant reached out and fixed the blanket, and they sat close together, soaked to the skin, keeping each other warm as best they could until the storm broke. The thunder rolled into the distance, the lightning grew less frequent, and the heavy rain stopped suddenly, as if it had been cut off.

Or so it seemed for a moment. The pounding downpour had slackened, certainly. It had followed the thunder away. But a gentle rain set in as steadily as if it meant to wash away the storm's violence. After the last half-hour it seemed to the two boys no more than a mist. They stood up and stretched, being careful to hold the blanket about them.

"I think some rations would do us good," and Pleasant reached in his pocket and brought out some corn pone and thick fried slices of bacon. To Roswell, after the fury of the storm, his voice sounded faint and strange.

"An't you hungry, Roswell?" he asked, for Roswell made no move to forage in his pockets.

"Hungry as a bitch with pups."

"How come you don't eat then?"

"I'm afraid I'm not as good a campaigner as you." There was a certain humility in his voice.

Without saying anything, Pleasant divided his pone and meat.

"No," Roswell spoke hurriedly. "I'm not going to rob you."

"Go on. Take it. It'll lighten my load."

Roswell shook his head. "It'll teach me a lesson." And he looked away from the food. His voice was almost gruff.

There was a short silence, and Pleasant looked at the pone and thick meat in his two hands, as if he were inspecting the division to make sure it was equal.

"What's mine is yours," he said simply, holding out the meat and bread.

Roswell no longer hesitated. He reached for the food, and as he took the sodden pone, the cold fat meat, he held the other's wet hand for a moment. In this way, briefly, almost casually, the two young men declared their friendship. No more was said about the food; but as they ate it in silence, the fresh sense of close comradeship, as well as their sharp hunger, made it taste rich and sweet.

As soon as they finished eating, they squatted back down on the brush pile to wait for the rain to hold up. All around now they could hear the rising noise of flooded streams, as the water poured from the ridges into the lowlands. Directly Pleasant said, "If this rain keeps up, it's going to wet the caps and powder."

"I know it," answered Roswell. With sudden passion he said, "We've got to win this battle tomorrow."

"I figure," returned Pleasant slowly, "that we've covered about half the enemy camps. I figure, when it lets up, we'd better split. You go back and report. I'll cover the rest of the front."

Roswell protested. "But how'll you get back?"

"I'll get back all right. And our people'll need to know what we have found out. They may attack tomorrow. The whole rear of our army is mired down. I walked along it for two miles."

"Don't you think we've seen enough? The enemy's not expecting anything." Roswell began to argue, although he did not know that his chief concern was for Pleasant's safety.

"No, I'd better see everything." Pleasant's answer was given absently, but each word was evenly stubborn.

"All right," agreed Ellis. "You know what you are doing." After a while he said, "If I should—you know—if I should get killed tomorrow, I want you to do something for me."

"You're not going to get killed tomorrow."

Pleasant heard himself with surprise. He had spoken with the same feeling of certainty which the communion with his father's spirit inspired. With a little start he realized that he hadn't thought of his father or his father's enemies since that afternoon in his Cousin Armistead's tent. This was the first time he had even gone so much as a day without making some plans to trap them. It must be the confusion of the army moving toward battle. But as soon as the fighting was over, he knew what he would do. Roswell's voice cut across his thoughts.

"You see—this girl, Miss Martha Menifee, I love her."

"Yes, I see," but Pleasant didn't see. He was thinking how he might slip by the next outpost.

"And if anything happens to me, McIvor, if you would go to her——" He put his hand over his chest. "There's a locket under my clothes. If you'll take it to her."

"Sure I will," Pleasant spoke lightly, "but you'll get through tomorrow."

"I think so, too, but . . ." And his voice trailed off.

10

Saturday morning, in the dim light, Hardee's corps deployed in the drenched forest. Slowly the muddy columns extended to right and left, reaching like crooked fingers around the neck of land that lay between Owl and Lick Creeks. Softly the Confederates slipped over the sodden ground, splashed in the streams, slouching forward, winding among the trees. At last in line they leaned from behind trees, peering from under their flopping hats at the morning mist boiling up through the blackish-brown trunks and limbs.

General Johnston, followed by one or two of his staff, rode

down the lines and watched them unroll. He had just left Bragg's quarters, where the report reached him that Hardee's corps would not reach from creek to creek. He ordered Bragg to send Gladden's brigade forward to make the extension on the right. Soon after there had come from the front the sound of heavy skirmishing. Ordering Bragg to form his line in the rear of Hardee as quickly as possible, Johnston galloped in the direction of the firing. He discovered that his men, anxious to know what the rain had done to their powder, were firing off their pieces. Ordering a stop put to this gross carelessness, he began the inspection of the first battle line.

The men saw him coming. On the retreat from Bowling Green he was no more than a name to most of them; but now, on the field of battle, they saw him, the man who held the threads of their destiny in his hands. Like one piece of marble come to life, man and beast moved along the crouching butternut line. The men opened their mouths to shout, but he held up his gloved hand for silence. His voice, low and measured, but clear and confident, echoed through the deep woods: "Sight along your guns, men, and fire low." Stopping before an Arkansas regiment, he surveyed them quickly; then, "Men, you have boasted of your prowess with the bowie knife. Today you wield a nobler weapon, the bayonet. Let's see how you use it!" And he passed on.

By eight o'clock Johnston took position in Hardee's rear and waited for the attack to begin. Bragg's right under Withers had deployed on time. But as Johnston looked to the left, the division which was to form there was nowhere to be seen. He had expected the storm to delay the movements—the storm: nature seemed to be conspiring against him, but in spite of nature and men he would throw this army upon Grant and drive him into the river. The soldiers, the straggling regiments that his will, and almost his will alone, had pulled through the mud, the chilling rains, the black depression of army and people—through all that he had pulled them. Now these men were in line and waiting. Where were the others? Where were those that Beauregard held under his eye for the same weeks? He pulled out his watch. It was nine o'clock.

"Colonel Munford, my compliments to General Bragg and ask him why the column on his left is not in position."

Munford mounted and galloped off to the left. In twenty minutes he returned.

"General Bragg's compliments, sir. He has sent to the rear to learn why the missing column has made no appearance. As soon as he finds the reason, he will notify you."

The commander received the report in silence. His face showed no sign of disappointment at the precious loss of daylight. But at ten o'clock he began to pace the spongy ground. Without hurry, deliberately, his large feet fell and rose as he trod his post like a sentry. His staff, at a distance, watched him. Turning, he said again, almost abruptly,

"Colonel Munford, go to General Bragg and ask him *why* the column on his left is not *yet* in position."

Munford returned with the same answer. Minutes passed into hours. As the sun rose high in the sky, Johnston glanced more and more frequently to the left, to the vacant woods, and still no sign of the missing column. Suddenly he turned. His face was flushed, and the deep-set eyes looked angrily at the sun. He pulled out his watch, looked at it, again at the sun overhead . . . then, with passion exclaimed:

"This isn't war! Come, let us have our horses!"

The mounting was quick. General and staff galloped to the rear and at last came upon the missing column massed with its head in an empty field. General Polk's reserves were in front of it, his wagons and artillery blocking the road. In a glance Johnston took in the situation, cleared the road and put the missing division on the way to its position. But by the time the corps could deploy, it would be too late to deliver battle. It was already afternoon. Breckinridge from Farmington had been reported near and Cheatham was almost joined, but neither general could reach the field until a few hours before sundown. Johnston, hiding his chagrin, spent several hours putting troops in position or inspecting them as they reached the line, encouraging them, getting their temper.

Everywhere he noticed an eagerness for combat, the nervous tension, the drawn faces. About four o'clock he turned his horse's head toward Bragg's headquarters.

As Johnston hunted for that officer, he discovered Beauregard, Polk, and Bragg standing in the road. It was apparent that everything was not in accord. He could see Polk's well-known stubborn look, the haughty head, the square shoulders drawn up. The declining sun struck Beauregard's square chin as it jabbed the air. His head kept turning from Polk to Bragg. Now Bragg was talking to Polk. Johnston could hear the sound of their words but he was too far away to catch the meaning. There was accusation, cold formality. Now Beauregard was waving his hands, and his head moved again, this time from Bragg to Polk. He shrugged his shoulders. Withdrawn at a respectful distance, staff officers watched the conference. This was bad, Johnston thought, it will get through the army that there is discord in the high command. He spurred his horse, dismounted, and strode toward the group of generals.

Beauregard's overwrought voice was saying, "General Polk, I am disappointed in the delay that has occurred in getting the troops into position."

The bishop-general's cold and well-modulated tones replied, "So am I, sir. But so far as I'm concerned, my orders are to form on another line, and that line must first be established before I can form on it."

Beauregard paused a moment; continued with that peculiar tone which ignores an explanation as if it were subterfuge— Johnston knew how irritating that would be to his friend Polk:

"The delay has made it impossible to surprise the enemy— and the noise of yesterday's reconnaissance"—this was directed to Bragg. Beauregard spoke sharply, biting off his words, jerking his head nervously. "Our hope of success lay in surprise," he repeated. "That hope is now dissipated. Grant will be entrenched to his eyes. We must return to Corinth."

"What's the trouble, gentlemen?" Johnston asked, walking into their midst.

The generals were so engrossed that they did not see him until he was among them and speaking. Although he stood with them in the road, Johnston was withdrawn enough to seem apart, almost like a judge in the dispute. His eyes were very grave and, Polk thought, showed fatigue and a loss of his habitual poise.

Beauregard repeated himself, finished by saying that the army must return to Corinth. He spoke as if there were no alternative, as if the issue was settled. The state of confusion he had witnessed on the road made him, for the moment, forget the amenities. If Johnston noticed this breech of etiquette, he did not show it. He listened quietly until Beauregard had finished; then spoke:

"General Beauregard, this will never do."

Beauregard interrupted: "Wellington, you remember, marched out against Massena in the Peninsula, hoping to take him by surprise. When he found Massena intrenched, he counter-marched to his old position."

Johnston said a little sharply: "Our army is raw, but it is eager and willing for combat. A retreat will have as bad an effect as defeat."

Johnston was now completely himself. He did not argue. He seemed to present the situation. He saw that the effect of his words on Bragg and Polk was good.

Beauregard resumed the argument with great politeness. Johnston's manner had recalled his own. "Soldiers," he said, "do not fight well on empty stomachs. Polk's men have eaten or thrown away their rations."

The bishop flushed, and Bragg spoke up, "My men have enough to share with the First Corps."

"What about the reserve?" Beauregard persisted. "We don't know its condition."

As Johnston turned to send a courier to find that general, he saw Breckinridge riding toward them.

"Here he comes, now," said Johnston with some relief.

"I suggest, sir," Beauregard did not wait for Breckinridge's arrival, "I suggest, sir, that we turn this movement into a reconnaissance in force, draw Grant away from his base and fall upon him when he blunders."

Very quietly, Johnston replied, "But Grant first must blunder."

"It's not possible, General Johnston, that the Federal army is unaware of our presence here."

Very firmly, master of himself but alone, Johnston answered slowly, "I still hope to take the enemy by surprise. But whether he is waiting for us or not, since I've put this army in motion for battle, I will venture the hazard."

At this moment Breckinridge presented himself. His boots were painted with mud, but his dark blue blouse hanging loosely about his shoulders was immaculate. The large protruding eyes seemed tireless, and the color of his blouse made his dark skin look weathered and hardy. He sat astride a blooded mare. In a swift glance Johnston inspected man and mount.

Breckinridge saluted. He had ridden ahead of his command, he said, for orders. Johnston asked him the condition of his men. The condition was good, he replied. The reserve had rations enough and some to share.

Beauregard seemed not to hear. With that peculiar freshness and brittle ring which the will imparts to the voice he insisted that the army must fall back and replenish from their depots at Corinth. Polk interrupted. He managed to be both polite and curt.

"The enemy's supplies are much nearer," the bishop said.

The discussion appeared to be moving in a circle. The council was drifting into uncontrolled talk, with tempers growing short. Johnston drew himself up, caught their eyes. He paused a moment, paused for the fatal words; then said firmly but quietly:

"Gentlemen, we will attack at daylight tomorrow."

II

Since Pleasant had parted with Roswell Ellis, he had slipped with increasing ease through the strange woods. All day Saturday he kept his ears alert, waiting for the burst of the Confederate attack, but his eyes were rarely turned to the rear. They swept the woods clean or from some ridge or swamp searched the enemy camps. Never did he move until he saw that the territory within the radius of his vision was empty and safe. For hours he squatted on a stump in the midst of swamp land, still as rotten wood, hidden by the twisting vines. From there he could hear, see a little. No disquieting rumor disrupted the daily confusion of camp-life. A continual stream of army wagons came from the rear, unloaded their supplies and returned with a hollow rattle. He could hear the clucking of their wheels, the yells and oaths of the drivers, the cracking whips, the braying of the mules mingled with horses neighing. On the parade grounds officers drilled their companies. The drums rolled, the bugles blared. All of these noises rose and fell in an incessant hum, and they told Pleasant the Federals were still ignorant that at any moment thousands of brown and gray-backed men were gathering in the thickness of the forest to spring, at the signal, upon their innocence.

But were they? Had something happened? This was yesterday. Now it was Sunday. Saturday had passed, and nothing happened to shake the enemy's composure. Saturday he had watched the sun drop slowly behind the sullen woods. While it still hung in the forks of a dead sycamore, darkness streamed out of the swamps and drowned the low ridges, rose like a flood upon the trees, filling the undergrowth with solid shadows, lapping the black-green bark. Then the forest around Shiloh church swelled with blackness and bred the night. It was so dark that even he had to move dangerously close to the enemy camps. At last, near midnight, he found on the left of Grant's lines a long break between two camps. Here, after reconnoitering, he crawled into a thicket and went to sleep.

The next thing he heard was a redbird in the tree over his head. He realized that he was awake. Then bugles blowing reveille—almost in his ear. He lay still for long minutes, timing the men as they tumbled out of their beds, took place in line, answered to the roll call. He crawled into the open. Not two hundred yards to the left the woods were crowded with the enemy, but immediately about him there was nothing but empty forest. For the first time he had got lost in the woods. There was one thing he knew: he could not linger here. He hurried away to the right. The sun was now up, shining brightly upon the feathery green bursting from the tangled limbs. Not a cloud marred the blue sky. It was a beautiful, peaceful morning, what a Sunday morning should be. But it was strangely still. There was no sound but the plaintive mourning of the turtledoves. A rattling noise broke the peace, and he fell to the ground. The keen look of caution passed from his face; and he got up silently, shamefaced. A woodpecker in a dead post-oak had thrown him off his guard. That went to show how upset he was. Something had gone wrong. Had the evil woods swallowed Johnston's army?

Worried, not knowing whether to skirt widely and return to Corinth, he wandered through the bright, solemn forest. He must have gone a quarter of a mile before he reached the outskirts of the next camp to the right. Just to make sure, he'd give it a quick inspection; then try to find his way back to his own lines, if they were still waiting. He followed the northern face of a ridge several hundred yards, crawled to the top and looked through a bush down upon the company streets of the Yankee camp. The men were scattered about among their tents, or in front of the parade grounds, polishing muskets, brushing their shoes, cleaning jackets and trousers, shining buttons. They were talking easily, or bantering one another. The wagons were parked, and the mules stood in their corrals, peacefully crunching hay and swishing their tails in steady rhythm. The camp was getting ready for Sunday morning inspection.

Suddenly, off to the right, in the direction of the little log church, there came a dull, heavy *Pum!* Then another. For a third time this dull, sinister noise broke upon the air of the quiet, bright morning. At the first sound, as if the earth had heaved, the blue-breeched men leaped to their feet. They stood in a trance, with faces frozen. Their eyes rolled in their heads, looking blank and startled as dolls' eyes do. Their mouths parted with a question. Shoes, guns, jackets hung still, molded in the jelly of the thin clear air. The heavy booms came thicker and faster; then from the southwest, rolling along the ground and rising as it rolled, there came a low, sullen, continuous roar. There could be no mistaking that sound, even if a man had never heard it before. That was musketry. The attack had begun!

Pleasant was brought to his senses with the long roll beating in the camp. He was standing in view of all eyes. Quickly he dropped behind a tree. Nobody saw him, for in the desperate haste below nobody saw anything: buckling on cartridge boxes, getting into jackets, loading guns, officers saddling or trying to saddle plunging horses. Pleasant's eyes fell hard on a corporal seated on a cracker box. Abstractedly he was trying to put a shoe on. He fumbled at it for an endless time. He would look at the shoe in a dogged hopeless way, raise his head toward the increasing roar, then with a painful effort back at the shoe. From the right a staff officer dashed into the company streets, looked at the confusion with wild eyes, and in a loud and desperate voice shouted, "My God, this regiment not in line yet!" Wheeling his horse, he disappeared through the confusion in the direction of the colonel's tent.

Finally the companies were drawn up in line on the parade ground. The command was given in high voices, deep or sharp tones, "Load at will: load!" By this time the roaring musketry was getting louder and louder, sweeping from the right to left. The colonel, wearing a short gray beard, directed his

skittish horse to the center of the line. The sun caught his blue
coat and polished boots. Fine and bright, he sat alone. His
saber sparkled. Pleasant thought: what a pity to spoil that
fine shiny polish. The heads of the men in ranks cocked unconsciously to the right as they watched him for commands.

"Gentlemen," the colonel said, and his voice was heard by
every man in the regiment, "remember your state and do your
duty like brave men today."

That was all. The regiment marched at quick step across the
field and formed on the colors, in battle line, at the edge of the
woods. The men stood at order arms and waited for the attack they knew must come. The ridge ran along the edge of
this field and Pleasant followed the regiment forward, although the cover grew thinner and more open. The roar on
the right had now become terrific, the blue ranks were strained
and nervous. As if he were overhead and could see it, Pleasant
followed the Confederate Army unfolding its front, steadily
toward the enemy's left. On the right, blue rings of smoke
curled suddenly through the treetops. The air changed. One
breath was clear, the next made his nose and throat tingle.
He swallowed, and his saliva tasted sweet and acrid, as if the
honey flow on the trees had soured and blown into his mouth.
He vaguely noticed that his throat had gone dry, that his jaws
were tight and set. He could do nothing but lie still and listen
to the roar sweeping nearer and nearer. It sounded like the
sweep of a thunder shower in summertime over the hard ground
of a stubble field. He thought: now suppose I get killed here,
behind the enemy lines, killed by my own companions. Suddenly panic seized him. He jumped up to run but forced himself back to the ground. Quickly the life at home in Georgia
flashed over his thoughts: his dog, Bounce, lying on the porch
in the sun; the warm wind rustling the greasy corn; his father
riding among the hands, his mother knitting or moving about
the house with her keys jingling from her waist; hens pecking
in the dusty yard.

Suddenly, obliquely to the right, there came a long waving
flash of bright light. It was the sun catching the Confederate

bayonets. His people had come at last! A long brown line, with muskets at right shoulder shift, in excellent order, swept out of the woods. Pleasant leaped to his feet and shouted until his throat cracked. But his voice was drowned as soon as it opened. The Federal regiment had fired. The advancing Confederates halted and returned the fire. Smoke leaped up and covered the woods. It hung to the limbs like thick festoons of gray moss blowing in a light wind. It thickened into a mist and completely hid the Confederates. The rattling musketry had changed into a steady roar. Pleasant could hear nothing and see very little. Twigs and small fragments of bark, limbs, began to fall around him, and he wondered vaguely what was making them drop. Then, over his head came an incessant humming, like the flight of many swarms of bees. He looked up, wondering if the battle had driven the bees before it. Then he discovered what the sound was. Bullets were striking the trees from twenty to a hundred feet overhead. He dropped quickly behind a dead log. If the Confederates weren't shooting any better than that, no need to hug the ground. Then he saw men in blue fall back out of the smoke. First, one or two fell back, fired, reloading or trying to reload their guns as they retreated. A few threw their muskets away and bolted to the rear, looking neither to right nor left but fixing their eyes on some remote object. Finally the whole line appeared suddenly out of the smoke and fell back in good order across the field to the ridge, the lower edge of which he occupied. As far as he could see to the right, the blue line was falling back. He thought it queer. There was no reason, so far as he could see, for it. No Confederates followed.

Then in the camps on the far right, through the acrid haze, he saw men in gray and brown running about with trailed muskets. They kept pouring into the woods and disappearing. A few stopped and then began running toward the camp at Pleasant's feet. He saw an officer wave his sword in this direction. Others followed. He would lose them in the smoke; then see them again as they leaped through it. Some knelt, took aim, and fired; but others kept running and yelling as they ran. He thought they were yelling. Their mouths were open, but he couldn't hear anything come out. Every now and then a man would turn, loose his musket and jump at the ground. Somehow he expected to hear the sound of the fall, but nothing ever made any change in the steady roar of noise. Then suddenly there was a sight which sent a tremor all through him: it was the stars and bars of the battle flag. Flapping above the smoke, it moved jerkily forward as if without human aid, although he knew by the way it snapped that the bearer was on the double quick. A great anger seized him. His hands clutched for the throat of any Yankee who might touch it. Then breaking all around him, thousands of men seemed to be calling hogs all at once, only their yells were hoarse and frenzied. On the edge of the woods to the front the smoke hung low to the ground. Out of this smoke he had seen the enemy run. Now he saw why. In ragged line the Confederates were charging and yelling, dashing toward the ridge where the enemy had gone. Their mouths were open, and they bent forward and ran as men run against a high wind. One in particular he watched, at least twenty paces ahead of his comrades. He was long and tall and his rawboned face was set in battle fury, with long teeth extending like fangs through the opened lips, his stiff black hair flying over his shoulders. He lifted his lunging legs over the soft field, running like an outcast. Soon he was gone, and the main line followed. Here and there the runners stumbled, fell. Pleasant waited for them to get up, but they lay on the ground like dirty sacks of grain.

A riderless horse charged cross-wise over the littered parade ground. Its head was up, nostrils distended, and he could see its eyes rolling in fright. It galloped madly through the advancing line, toward the ridge, with stirrups flying and saddle guards flapping. It dashed in among the bushes, the scrubby blackjacks, and turned toward Pleasant. In a moment he knew he must catch him and deliver his information to General Johnston. This settled in his mind. It did not occur to him that, now the battle was raging, his information was useless.

On came the horse. He ran out, raced beside it, snatched the flinging bridle reins and leaped into the saddle. He tried to calm the animal, but there was no calming him. He did manage to turn his head toward the rear, where General Johnston or General Hardee or his Cousin Armistead would be.

At the edge of the woods the horse stopped suddenly, threw up its head and whinnied. Pleasant could feel the animal trembling all over, and he remembered later feeling a sort of pity for his fright. All at once the horse dropped on his legs and bolted through the woods with fresh terror. In a daze his rider dodged limbs, jacksawed his legs as they grazed by heavy oaks, clung to his neck. Pleasant passed in flashes strange shadows of men with frozen faces, wandering in a dream— one he long remembered, a white-faced boy with his back to a tree, pressing hands full of last year's leaves against his shattered leg. In a disinterested way the boy stared at his hand, until the slow blood pushed upward, staining the dull brown leaves, painting his dark-clotted fingers a fresher red; then with a sly look in his eyes, as if he were about to steal a move in a game, he reached for more leaves. A deer stuck its head out of a thicket, stared a moment with its round, soft eyes. As it turned to flee, the horse made for a tree. Pleasant tried to turn him aside, but the animal, with the bit in his mouth, went headlong against it.

He picked himself up from the ground, some twenty feet away. He looked for his mount and saw four legs quivering upright, the great body flounder for a few moments, the legs give three convulsive kicks, grow still and, with the smooth iron hoofs exposed, point stiffly upward. Soon he found that he was wandering through the woods without aim. He remembered that he had started somewhere, but he couldn't remember why or where. He looked at the sky. The bright morning was gone. A sweetish-sharp haze drifted through the roof of the forest, and a dull light fell down the leaden dust, yellow shafts of sun cut through it. In the fury of sound he could hear the several attacks strike with the rhythm of a powerful machine, the lull in between, the renewed fury. He now set his will toward finding the battle. Anything was better than wandering in this torture of sound beating down the ravines. It was no noise that man could make. He knew what it was. It was this forest turning loose all its sullen vicious strength on the men who had come to trample its rank and twisted ground. He could smell what a wood was like, and the time he had pried about it told him what an evil place it was. It was not like the wood above Wetumpka: the quiet stealth, the secret ways, the hidden life—that kind of forest had taken him in, protected him. Friday night and all day Saturday the slimy swamps and hard ridges lay in a terrible silence. He knew then what it could do if it ever got loose.

At the foot of a dying black gum a dead soldier lay, a full grown man with sandy hair and mustache of the same reddish color. He had been struck, while firing, square in the forehead, killed instantly, knocked on his back at the foot of the tree. He had been in the act of biting a cartridge. His teeth were still fastened on the cartridge paper; his right hand grasped the bullet end. The teeth, long and snaggy, were tobacco teeth. His eyes were stretched in a furious glaze, in the rage and lust of battle. Pleasant did not stop: he saw this as he stumbled along. The dead were becoming thicker, but he could see no regiments crouching. The forest had swallowed them, all life in it, and left him to wander forever through its emptiness. There was only that noise that was no noise.

He stepped aside, just missing a boy lying stretched before him. He was at the end of a long, thin line of fallen men. Must have made a stand here. Pleasant looked at the dead soldier. He was fair, not over eighteen, with regular features, light blue eyes, very blue now in his pale face, light brown hair. It was the hair that didn't look right. It was glossy as if it had just been brushed. He lay on his back, his right arm straight in the air, rigid as a stake. Suddenly Pleasant knew what the noise was. It was the cracking of this empty woods. He began to run. As he sped along, dodging brush and trees, he thought he heard his name called. He slowed down and listened. McIvor! McIvor! He looked over his shoulder, and there was little Arthur Clay jumping up and down, shouting to him. Then he realized that he had come upon his regiment lined up, in double rank, waiting in the woods of Shiloh.

Eli was leaving ranks to meet him. "Come on," he said. "We're about to go in."

His face was pale, and he talked wildly. Automatically Pleasant leaned over and picked up a gun at his feet. He had the curious feeling that he had done all this long ago. There was silence through the butternut ranks. He noticed this as he took his place. The world had become real again. The officers were sitting their horses looking to the right. Their heads were up, and they looked as if they were expecting a signal. Even the horses caught the general tension. Their necks were arched, their heads raised. They looked ready to bolt. A shell flew over the regiment and burst in the rear. The men crouched, the ranks quivered, and a major's horse got out of hand. Then the old colonel with the flat face wheeled about and brought the regiment to attention. Long Boy Taliaferro was in the rear rank. He touched Arthur Clay on the shoulder.

"Let's change places, buddy. I don't want to get shot with a dirty bullet."

Taliaferro smiled with a sort of glum cheerfulness. When Clay protested, he picked him up and set him squirming into the rear rank. At once the command to go forward was given, repeated down the line. The two ranks, after one nervous moment, moved as one, their guns at a right shoulder shift. The trees soon broke the alignment. It grew ragged, but the regiment managed to hold some sort of formation. Pleasant looked once to the right, very quickly. As far as he could see, the faces of the men looked all alike. They were white and drawn, resolute but bent as if they expected to receive a blow.

At the foot of a rise the regiment was halted and dressed. At command, it swung steadily up the rise until it reached the crest. Pleasant stopped dead in his tracks. He felt others to his right and left give little grunts of surprise. Not a hundred yards away he saw the tents of a Federal camp, with something like a picket fence around it and long lines of blue men drawn up and waiting. He stood fascinated as the enemy muskets, flashing in the sun, came to position: then a solid flash of fire and smoke, a crack and roar, sharp and above the general noise. As he watched the smoke rings spread and vanish, twigs and limbs fell softly to the ground. Suddenly the ground shook beneath him, and he realized that his regiment had returned the fire. He raised his musket, took careful aim, and pulled the trigger. He aimed at an officer half-covered by the smoke and missed. Before he could reload, the officer had disappeared in the spreading smoke. Out of it he could see the enemy ram-rods flashing. The men all around were lying down under cover. Those fellows had been ready for them. It was going to be hard to carry this camp. He and Eli got behind a log. Pleasant fired until the gun scorched his hands, until he ran low on cartridges. How long he and Eli stayed in that position he had no way of knowing. It didn't seem any time before he was crawling around and emptying the cartridges from the boxes of the dead and wounded. He reached through the legs of a frail-looking man to pick up a handful of cartridges some-body had dropped to the ground. The man shifted and put his boot on Pleasant's hand. Pleasant looked up to tell him to get off. The man's face was wild and contorted and the edges of his mouth were very white. He was loading his gun as if each charge would be the last and firing straight into the air. He would ram the charge home, look toward the enemy, shoot straight into the air. Pleasant waited until he had fired a round and jerked his foot off his hand. The man looked at him with hatred, but Pleasant realized he couldn't really see, for at once he turned away to reload. As Pleasant crawled back to the log, he saw others shoot their ramrods away. The pieces of iron looked funny dodging crazily through the air.

As he slipped behind the log, Eli said, "They're putting up a stiff fight over there."

Pleasant didn't answer at once. He was loading. In a little while he said, "They sure are."

But this time Eli made no answer. When Pleasant turned

his head, he saw Eli slumped down behind the log, with the blood pumping slowly out of his forehead and soiling his shirt. He dropped his gun and picked his young uncle up in his arms. A glancing bullet had caught him in the right temple, tearing a long, ugly hole. Pleasant tried to make him speak. He leaned down and deliberately shouted in his ear. Once Eli rolled back his eyes, the warm flesh quivered, and he straightened out. Pleasant looked up to tell somebody to do something—he saw Bob Curtin out in front waving his sword over his head. He knew he couldn't get any help from him, and he shouted to those nearest him; but they were measuring the piece of field to the front as if they were trying to estimate how many acres it held . . . and fixing their bayonets absent-mindedly. All at once the soldiers crouched, pulled their hats low over their eyes, and leaped forward. Then as far as his eyes could reach and that wasn't very far, Pleasant could see the rusty gray lines charging, and the woods ringing with that savage hog-calling. He laid Eli softly against the log so that nothing could trample him, picked up his gun and ran after the line. All of a sudden his voice tore at his throat. He didn't have any bayonet. But if he could just reach that blue line . . . he prayed to reach it . . . he'd be willing to die if he could just get that far and beat their brains out.

12

It was the smell of coffee that made Roswell open his eyes. When he realized what he had done, he came awake all over. He had overslept on the morning of battle. What would General Johnston think of him? He reached for his boots and pulled them on, fastened his spurs. It took him twice as long, his hands trembled so. Last night when he finally reached headquarters—he had got lost after leaving McIvor and hid out in the woods all day—the general had received him at once. He would never forget the great man's kindness, with all that must have troubled his mind on the eve of battle. Johnston had questioned him closely on his report, then put his hand on his shoulder: "My son, you have done well. I will need just such a head about me tomorrow. Do you think your good colonel can spare you?" And Roswell was so flustered, he stammered and said something about how he thought his colonel could spare him: thought his colonel could spare him. What a conceited fool General Johnston must have thought him. Now he'd think he was lazy as well. He buckled on his sword, felt the hard lump of pistol at his elbow, and walked through the tent flaps into the fresh morning.

General Johnston was gathered with most of his staff about the small fire. They had coffee and a biscuit for breakfast. Not far away the general's horse was saddled and pawing the ground. The spongy sod flew in little ragged balls against his hind legs. Colonel Preston, his brother-in-law, was near him talking. Preston's eyes were still swollen with sleep. Others of the staff stood back in little groups. They drank their coffee with haste, lifting their eyes surreptitiously to the front. Roswell gave one glance at the thick timber and advanced apologetically. Colonel Munford passed him, buttoning up his blouse. He, too, had overslept. The general turned. His face had its usual composure, but no longer seemed heavy. As he spoke, he could not hide the grave eagerness of his voice:

"Colonel Munford, you and Lieutenant Ellis had better eat something. We will move upon the enemy in a few moments."

They mumbled something about having overslept, and he said, "Your horses are ready."

Roswell picked up a biscuit; the servant poured coffee into his cup. As he was draining it, several muskets went off in rapid succession somewhere to the front. There was an instant pause around the fire: the lifted cup caught in mid-air, the crunching teeth parted. Then a sudden, heavy report, the sullen growl of a cannon.

"There," said Colonel Preston, "the first gun of the battle." Johnston looked toward Preston and Munford. "Note the hour, if you please, gentlemen."

Colonel Preston pulled out his watch. "It is precisely fourteen minutes after five o'clock, sir."

"Let us have our horses." Very calmly Johnston spoke, as he pulled on his gloves. The staff respectfully waited for orders, and Roswell knew, as he fastened his eyes upon him, that Johnston was invincible. There was a pause, then the deep, resonant voice:

"I'm going to hit Grant today and hit him hard."

The horses came up. There was the flurry of mounting. Roswell was near the commander's blooded bay, Fire-Eater. Johnston's face was slightly flushed, the deep gray eyes were bright and confident. He ran his gloved hand down his animal's neck, patted it gently.

"Tonight, gentlemen," he said, "we will water our horses in the Tennessee."

At this moment Beauregard dashed up with his staff. The two generals withdrew and talked for a few minutes. Roswell saw the commander point once toward the firing. Beauregard inclined his head, and then together they rode to a small rise, their staffs following. They made quite a body, Roswell thought. The small rise gave a good view of the advance. In quick step the long rusty columns swung by. They deployed as they advanced. The step was elastic, the faces of the soldiers set and earnest, and Roswell thought he could see upon some the glancing shadow of death, or maybe it was the way the light fell through the woods. Then suddenly the sun rose from the treetops, and the half-green forest turned sparkling bright and gay. Someone whispered, "The sun of Austerlitz." The sharp, spiteful skirmish which had announced the contact of outposts had ceased. There was no sound but the heavy tramp of thousands of feet, the tramp of horses, and the clacking roll of cannon and caisson wheels. Of all the troops who passed the artillerists alone seemed not to have any human emotions. Holding to gun carriages and caissons, their bodies shook from the rough bumping ground, but their faces were wooden.

This resolute step, this eagerness to close with the enemy, how different from the straggling march and the confusion there, thought Johnston as the troops swung by. And then his mind began to reach forward, decipher the mystery of the deep woods. What is beyond? What is beyond? he whispered. And his eyes remained open, but his sight was closed; and through his ears came sound to feed that other sight, the cold mind which must see without being able to see: the stealth of forty thousand men moving in ambush, the three lines—Hardee sweeping forward; Bragg at eight hundred yards distance in column of brigades ready to fill the gaps; the third line, Polk massed on the left, Breckinridge on the right. The enemy's forces might be larger, but Grant could present no greater front between the creeks than he could. Owl and Lick Creeks, with the Tennessee behind, the deep-flowing Tennessee. He would hammer him! He would hammer him and drive him into the spring floods, those floods that had done such damage at Henry and Donelson. A greater army than his couldn't be well handled in this tangled wood, and the more men Grant crowded on his front, the more targets there would be for his huntsmen. His own flanks were safe—the creeks and the cavalry protected them. His general officers had caught the spirit of the men. Even Beauregard showed animation and eagerness for the fight. He would leave him in the central position in the rear, leave him to send forward the reserves as they were needed. But he himself must go to the front.

The army was raw, men and officers alike. It would be difficult to mass the brigades for crushing blows from the rear. If the army knew its business—but the army didn't. That's where Beauregard had made his mistake. An army must bleed before it can stand many strategic retreats. At last he had triumphed over the things that would pull him down. Alone he had done it. Alone he had given the order for advance. The suggestion was Beauregard's, but the decision was his. That order would settle for all time the dispute as to his military skill; it would settle the fate of the Confederacy in the West. He had done all he could beforehand to make victory sure. It was he, when Beauregard grew dispirited, who had kept the army to its purpose. And now the army was moving forward to the execution of this purpose. . . .

His sight returned, fixed upon the face of a lad who couldn't be over sixteen: he had lost his hat, his thick curls were dirty; but as he passed the rise upon which the generals sat their restless mounts, he turned his eager face upon *him*, the army's chief; and there was the look of worship in the innocent blue eyes, the parted mouth, and the smooth unformed chin. Suddenly maps, rounds of ammunition, batteries, regiments of foot, lines of attack fled from Johnston's head; and he saw that not only this lad but thousands of others were marching to the execution of his orders, moving not only to resolve the great questions of a nation's destiny, but for many all questions, solving the dark mystery of life and death.

Quickly, almost brusquely, he said: "General Beauregard, you will remain in the rear, in the central position, and feed in the reserves. I'm going to the front."

Roswell put spurs to his horse and followed. In the clear bracing air, under the cloudless sky, he could not help seeing the triumph on the commander's face. The men saw it, as he rode among the regiments like a lord of the clans. They dashed across the front of Colonel Gibson's brigade, and the young officer brought his men to attention. The general returned the salute and took the colonel's hand. "Randal, I never see you but what I think of William. I hope you get safely through today, but we must win a victory." And Roswell remembered Randal was Preston Johnston's friend. They ran suddenly into General Hindman. He had been put over a division. "You have earned your spurs as major-general," Johnston spoke loud enough for his ranks to hear, "let this day's work win them." Young Marmaduke explained with pride that his regiment held the center of the first line.

The general put his hand upon his shoulder. "My son, we must this day conquer or perish."

Then, all at once, the silence exploded. The rusty gray line had struck.

13

The battle was now rising to a climax. Roswell had heard General Johnston say it was well joined. But still he couldn't tell much about it. He with the rest of the staff had raced after the general toward the sound of the first clash, had arrived to see a lot of Confederates swarming around a Yankee regiment and driving it back. A staff officer had ridden up and reported Hindman had knocked a hole in the enemy line. Two camps were in their hands. But a lot of the Confederates were drifting to the rear and looting. That didn't look like success to him. He had followed the general into the camp, saw him show anger for the first time. The rebels were wandering about, marveling at the wonderful luxury they saw, pots smoking with whole lambs, wonderful tents, wagons loaded with canned goods. Johnston's voice rang out, stern and indignant:

"None of that, men. Your place is there." And he pointed toward the rising smoke of battle.

Johnston had organized the men he found drifting to the rear and sent them back in. It must have taken the general and staff three-quarters of an hour to do it. Then he sent Hindman an order to charge again. Hindman—Roswell had seen him walk lumbering like a countryman—slowly and deliberately got his brigade in hand and charged, with help knocked one Federal brigade to pieces. Johnston, without waiting, began drawing brigades from the second line. Roswell was sent to lead Chalmers against the Federal center.

After success there Chalmers was shifted farther to the right, and Jackson was thrown into his place. Struck front and flank, the Federal brigades crumbled, gave way, and the whole line, fighting sullenly, fell back. In the confusion and noise this was what Roswell had learned. He could see very little, but General Johnston seemed to understand it all.

"All goes well on the center, the attack is unrolling properly to the right, now let's see how things are on the left." There was almost levity in his voice.

They rode at a fast walk, sometimes at a trot, and reached the left just as Cleburne was marching his brigade across a field. In Cleburne's front lay a morass and a creek. Beyond, there was a rough-looking ridge. The enemy had withdrawn behind it after the first surprise. They now lay sheltered behind trees, logs, and bales of hay. The assault would be doubtful. Johnston lifted his glasses, examined the position slowly. As far as he could see, he caught the glimmer of metal. He dropped his glasses and spoke tersely:

"Preston, ask Beauregard to send two brigades to Cleburne's support."

Without waiting for the attack to develop, Johnston turned his mount's head to the right and retraced his steps. The wounded drifted by to the rear; ambulances dashed forward through the trees or returned slowly. Stretcher-bearers passed. Skulkers slunk by. Knots of soldiers seemed dazed, wandering about as if they didn't know what to do. Roswell caught glimpses of all this, but Johnston saw none of it. He sat perfectly erect in the saddle, listening, watching the ebb and flow of struggle, drawing through his eyes and ears the moving, variable front of battle, fitting its hot and noisy sectors to the cold pattern in his mind. When they did not match the route to victory, he stopped long enough to fling the hoarse and passionate regiments against some part of the gloomy woods. At last they drew rein upon a hill near the left center. Here the Confederates were still struggling for a camp. On the left the fighting was heavy. Johnston could tell by the noise and shouts from that quarter. To the right he heard the rebel line swing slowly around like a creaking door, pushing the Federal left to the rear, hammering it back upon the river.

Just as the lead pellets were swarming from the woods like bees down a high wind, stinging the air about the hill, Jacob Thompson galloped through the storm and saluted. General Beauregard, he said, wanted to know the condition of things at the front and to know of the commander what order he had to give as to the disposition of the reserves under Breckinridge. Not until this moment did Roswell know that the whole army had been drawn to the front line.

Johnston, self-possessed and cool, turned in the shaking air.

"Say to General Beauregard that we are sweeping the field before us. In less than half an hour we'll be in possession of all their camps, and I think we shall press them to the river. Say, also, that I've just had a report from a scout that the enemy is moving up on our left in force. General Breckinridge had better move to our left to meet him."

Thompson put spurs to his horse. The general called him back.

"Don't say to General Beauregard that this is an order. He must act on what additional information he may receive. Reports to him are more to be relied upon than to me."

Thompson galloped his shivering horse to the rear; and Johnston, as if nothing had marred the soft spring day, turned back his eyes to the scene before him. It was not long before the camp was carried. The enemy withdrew, fighting stubbornly, falling back on the second line that Johnston knew was being formed some half a mile to the rear, covering Pittsburg Landing. The enemy had now recovered from his surprise. He was posted, waiting behind ridges, in sunken roads, smarting from the first blow, but resolute. Scouts, upon lathered beasts, came up in quick succession and reported: heavy masses of Federal infantry about Pittsburg Landing; a heavy column marching from that point down a road which would turn the Confederate right. To each scout Johnston said:

"Tell me, sir, what you have to say as briefly and as quickly as possible."

It was soon evident that the Confederate attacks everywhere were spending, that they had made no appreciable dent in the new position of the enemy. Nowhere had the fighting stopped, but over the forest there came an ominous lull. After the last scout had been sent on to Beauregard, Johnston looked at his watch and continued chatting with his staff for twenty or thirty minutes. Roswell looked at his chief with wonder. Here he was upon this rise, with a few of his staff gathered near, perfectly collected, when it was obvious to all, even to him, that the fury was dying in the thick forest. The débris of battle was growing, drifting in larger numbers to the rear. But for one fresh attack and the splitting batteries on the left center that quarter was settling into exhaustion. And here they were, the general and a few of his staff, gathered on the hill like fox hunters, chatting to waste the time until the chase would begin in earnest. Twice Johnston leaned forward, as if he were listening for the clear-ringing music that says the chase is getting sweet; but each time, disappointed, he returned to his leisurely chatting. As for Roswell, he felt himself getting pale with anxiety. Surely the general could not be certain of what he was doing. How could anybody be certain of what he was doing in this deep, broken woods, where you could see nothing but smoke swallowing men?

Suddenly the great shoulders lifted, the general stiffened in the saddle. He pulled out his watch. Without lifting his eyes from its face, he said, "It is now time to move forward." This was spoken casually, too casually Roswell thought, as if the commander was inviting his staff into dinner. But then, tersely, clearly he began to give orders to the horsemen about him:

"Order Gladden forward." This to Colonel Munford. "Captain Wickham, the attack will unfold from the center to the right. The brigades dressing on Gladden. In column of brigades, at half distance. If Generals Bragg or Polk are at hand, give them these orders. Otherwise deliver them direct to the brigadiers. That's all, sir." And then he turned to Roswell, and Roswell had the feeling that he no longer existed as a person. "Lieutenant Ellis, go to that battery parked on the road. Order them to that hillock and enfilade that line."

The staff galloped away to left and right. Only Doctor Yandell was left with the commander. When Roswell returned, the troops on the center were in motion. When it was, he could not tell, for there is no time on a battlefield; but as far as he could see, the troops advanced in compact form but so arranged that every man, horse, and gun carriage had the necessary room. He did not know that all but two of Breckinridge's brigades were being drawn to the front line, filling gaps left open by the first advance or by those regiments which had been broken, crippled and were now limping toward the rear. He did not know that Bragg and Polk, meeting between ten and eleven, agreed that Polk should command the left center and Bragg farther to the right. He did not know these things because he could know only what he saw, and at the moment he could see only that part of the advance to the right of the hill. Nor did he realize that neither the commander-in-chief nor Beauregard in the rear at headquarters could know of those thousands of things which would decide the day, nor that the commander's will would be felt but weakly on this part of the field.

Gladden's brigade, with orders to close with the enemy to its front, opened the second stage of the battle. Gladden had already been killed. The Senior Colonel, Dan Adams, gave the word. With a shout his butternuts leaped forward, and their standards popped with the motion. Suddenly a poisonous flame licked the ridge top to their front, sopped the gloomy thickets, and death blew through the forest like a blight. Roswell saw the very moment it touched the sweeping line. Its momentum broke. The swinging, tramping stride of gray-breeched thighs crumbled, stopped. The regiments slowed abruptly, paused upon the pestilential ground and shook with chills and a fever. The gray men withered where they stood and fell, rotting, about the feet of their companions. Those who were left fell back, weak and spent, to reform. Again and again they leaped to the charge until at last, with most of their field officers struck down, they drifted to the shelter of the trees and dropped panting to the earth. Some cursed, some wept, others wandered about calling in strained voices the names of friends.

Johnston sat upon his hill, aloof, waiting for the attack to develop all along the line. He sat immobile, like a piece of stone, moving his head or his great body in short direct movements, receiving reports from couriers and members of his staff as they arrived and departed. And all the while the gray smoke drifted about the hill. Roswell, returning from moving a regiment "promptly into action," saw him thus: a gray compact body smoldering on the hill, covering the whole forest in smoke.

All through the woods around Pittsburg Landing brigades, alone, at times in concert with others, hammered the ridges of the enemy. Trickling through the pale green branches, the first sweet smell of death soaked down the acrid air and swept toward the river. More exciting than musk, it filled the lungs of the youthful ranks until, quivering with battle lust, they charged wildly toward the sprawling enemy, many dropping in their innocence, others making lodgment in wedges of the blue lines; or, spent and weary, falling back to keep up a steady fire from what shelter the woods gave.

For hours the battle raged with little decision. For four hours regiments and brigades had been thrown by Bragg against the Federal center, but it had not been moved. The right had been forced back, but at such cost that Hardee and Polk had, for a long while, no more charges in them. On the left and left center the enemy had frequently retired to correct his alignment. But there he stood dealing slaughter. At one o'clock Johnston received a message that the extreme Confederate right had run into such resistance that it could no longer advance. He left his high perch and rode into a little depression, drew rein, and dropped his head upon his chest. He remained in that position for some minutes, as if he were disgusted with the whole bloody business and had washed his hands of it. Roswell, for the second time that day, felt a sudden terror. Then slowly Albert Sidney Johnston raised his shoulders, cast his eyes to the right. There was little to be seen: the fantastic forest, the small ravines, the tender green shivering upon the dark limbs.

Roswell saw the spurs dig into the flanks of the great bay, Fire-Eater, and before he knew it, he and a few other officers were galloping to the right, following the general, leaping streams, dodging trees. They drew rein on the extreme right of the Confederate attack. Somebody reported that the last of the reserves were going in. At the double quick the gray regiments had just reached the crest of a slow ridge. The colors hung for a moment on the top, then dipped out of sight. Johnston said softly, almost gaily, "That checkmates them."

Colonel Munford and Roswell were near. Munford replied: "You must excuse so poor a player, sir. But I don't see it."

The commander laughed, replied: "Yes, sir, that mates them."

After a while Captain Wickham returned with news of the attack. Chalmers' brigade had forced the enemy back. The two lines now faced each other at an angle of about forty-five degrees. This meant that a wedge was being driven between the enemy and the river. He also reported that Breckinridge, with Bowen's and Statham's brigades *en echelon*, was advancing to occupy the front between Chalmers and Jackson. Johnston spoke to Munford:

"Order Breckinridge to advance and engage."

Before Munford could return, the regiments were deploying and marching up the slope of the ridge. The soldiers could not see, but facing this ridge was another, some seventy-five yards away and across a deep depression. Here the Federals were massed in heavy lines. They were especially strong opposite the position Statham would occupy, near the point where the Confederate right joined its center. An ugly angle protruded through an uglier-looking thicket. This angle was the key to the position. Until it was broken, Bragg could make no headway at the center. The afternoon was upon them. The final blow must be struck, and here it must fall.

The butternuts were trotting, all unknowing, up to the crest of the ridge. Roswell saw a soldier drop his shoulder to pull up his suspenders. As the hand reached for the strap, the man lost his balance and stumbled. In the bursting air, for the enemy had let go his full venom, Roswell idly waited for the man to rise. When at last he realized that he would never get up again, Roswell lifted his eyes. As far as he could see, the line was wavering upon the top of the ridge. Finally, except before the angle, it took position. There the men ran up singly, or in squads, took post behind a rail fence or what protection they could find, fired, then ran back down the slope to safety. Three times the colonel and brigade officers rallied the raw troops, but the officers could not make them stand on the ridge.

Then someone began to speak. It was General Breckinridge. Roswell had not seen him ride up. His olive skin was flushed; and as he spoke, his voice, usually ringing so clear and confident, was thick and almost desperate.

"General Johnston, I have one Tennessee regiment that won't fight."

Governor Harris, who was standing by the commander, spoke briskly:

"Show me that regiment, General Breckinridge."

The commander of the reserve had not seen the governor in his preoccupation. He bowed apologetically and indicated the command.

"Let the governor go to them," said Johnston.

The group around the commander waited for Harris to rally the Tennesseans. He finally, with great difficulty, brought them to the ridge top and put them in line of battle. Johnston now closely watched the ridge. The thing that counts so much in battle, the shoulder-to-shoulder courage, was slow in traveling through the line. He saw it stagger, not give back, but waver along the whole length like small grain when struck by a breeze. At this moment, Harris galloped up with the glint of triumph in his eye.

"The Tennessee regiment is in line, sir."

Johnston nodded and said absently, "Those fellows are stubborn over there. I'll have to put the bayonet to them."

Hard on the governor's arrival, Breckinridge returned. Roswell noticed that the wavering had increased. Put the bayonet to them. They'd be lucky if the enemy didn't put the bayonet to the reserve. All along it was shaking like an immense ragtail of a kite.

"I'm afraid I can't get that brigade to charge, sir."

"Oh, yes, General Breckinridge," said Johnston evenly, "I think you can."

Breckinridge hesitated, and Roswell saw shame spread over his handsome features, into the dark blue eyes. Bitterly he said: "I have tried and failed."

Cheerfully, in pleasant tones, Johnston rallied his subordinate.

"Then I will help you."

At that moment a shell from a Confederate battery to the right flew over the heads of the gray ranks, past the commander and his staff, exploding between the first and reserve line. Johnston paused an instant:

"Colonel Munford, correct the position of that battery."

When Johnston told the commander of the reserve that he would help him, his voice took no notice of that officer's baffled state of mind. It refused to recognize that there was such a possibility as a brigade refusing to charge. It merely said a little more help and the difficulty will clear away.

Breckinridge received his final instructions and galloped back to prepare the lines for their work. Governor Harris sat his horse restlessly. His head was large and handsome. It was carried with such grace that his imperious eye, moving restlessly, could not shake it from its balance. Johnston now turned his eyes upon Harris, held them with strict attention. For one short moment he held them fixed as if the riddle to the whole business lay somewhere upon that intelligent face over which, like a flash of powder, the mark of everlasting impatience had scattered.

"Governor," he said, "go to that regiment you have just put in line . . . and encourage it."

The words were courteous, saying that the regiment had behaved with caprice, purposely and obstinately, to draw their governor to them.

Harris whirled around and galloped away. Soon he was seen among his people delivering a sharp harangue. Then he dismounted and, with pistol in hand, brought the uncertain regiment again to its line. Breckinridge was riding through the whistling air, and his fine voice could be heard above the steady roar and bursting thunders. But it was his manly bearing that told the men what they had to do: that and his young son, Cabell, who followed his father, serene and confident, wherever he went. But it was plain something was missing. There was an impatience, perhaps, in Breckinridge's manner. In his very courage the men read a lack of confidence in theirs. The order was given to prepare for a charge, but the ranks were uncertain. They lacked the stiffness which carries the day, and what strength was in them they had drained from their officers. But it was only enough to hold them, irresolute, upon the rise.

At that moment Johnston moved to the front and rode slowly down the line. His hat was off. His sword rested in its scabbard, and in his hand he held a little tin cup. It was a peace offering to the men he had, earlier in the day, reprimanded for looting. He twirled it now between his fingers. As he went along, his words were few. He touched the bayonets with meaning gesture. "These must do the work," he kept saying over and again, as if that had been the trouble all along. Not once did the proud animal under him increase its nervous step. Nor did the master notice the thick storm that sped across the narrow hollow. The lines stiffened as he passed. His voice, now encouraging, now compelling, dropped upon the ranks like invisible links in a chain, tying them together.

He was inviting men to death. As they saw the light in his gray eyes, his splendid presence full of the joy of combat, life became suddenly unreal, a mean and ignoble thing. He reached the center of the line, turned about with studied slowness and faced his men. Then, as if the temptation to share this precious adventure had overborn his will, he cried:

"I will lead you!"

The line was already thrilling and trembling with that irresistible ardor which decides the day. As he turned toward the enemy, those near rushed about him with a shout, their bayonets stabbing the gray air, their faces bright and hungry for this exquisite promised thing. The shout traveled the whole length of the rusty lines, gathering in violence until, shrill and wild, it swept forward through the ravine, cut through the heavy musketry rolling from the opposite ridge and thickets. In its wake the solid ranks bulged forward, sweeping down the slope. The flashes of fire increased on the other side of the short valley. The smoke boiled like heavy steam. The scorching air split apart, and death seized the gray ranks like a spasm. Men dropped like flies after the first frost, but they did not pause. Thin and leaner, they surged over the wooded crest, into the treacherous thickets. There was a short struggle. The enemy broke and fled. Spiteful shots spattered the hoarse cry of triumph, whistled impotently over the small valley and over the dead and dying huddled about its rough floor.

General Johnston sat alone, a few feet in the rear of his new position. He had broken in the arch that for so long held up the advance. Now the enemy was swinging back on his center, away from the river, toward Owl Creek. To gather his whole strength and follow this up, hammer away until the crumbling of the enemy was beyond repair . . . Governor Harris galloped up for orders. He was flushed and for once his impatience seemed tamed. He looked upon his friend and would remember that he had never seen him more bright, more joyous, more happy. It was the look of victory and vindication that he saw, although that fierce bird, hovering over the field, cast as yet only the shadow from its wings.

"Governor," he said playfully, lifting up his boot heel, "they came very near putting me *hors de combat* in that charge."

Harris bent over in sudden alarm. "Are you wounded? Did the ball touch your foot?"

The general shook his head, almost with surprise at the question. Didn't Harris know that Death was his black and faithful slave? The moment of the question, an enemy battery opened and enfiladed the new Confederate line. Johnston broke off in the middle of a sentence:

"Order Colonel Statham to wheel his regiment and take that battery."

Statham was only two hundred yards away. Harris galloped quickly to where that officer stood; in a few moments he returned.

"General," he said, "your order is delivered and Colonel Statham is in motion."

As he spoke, Johnston reeled in the saddle. Sharply, with accusation: "General, are you wounded?"

Very deliberately, emphatically, as if he were reporting the discovery of some remote, impossible fact:

"Yes, and I think seriously." At that Johnston lurched forward.

Harris pushed his horse against Fire-Eater and, putting his arm around the general's neck, caught him by the coat collar and righted him in the saddle. Captain Wickham rode up, and the two men led the commander to the rear. They had gone only a short piece when the bridle reins slipped from his hands and fell gently to the neck of his charger.

In slow state the two aides went on to a small valley. Harris got down and pulled the general upon him. He gave him brandy, but it gurgled strangely in his throat. The aides and members of the staff gathered from different parts of the front, but Albert Johnston never spoke, nor opened his eyes again.

Harris mounted Fire-Eater and turned his head toward Shiloh Church, where Beauregard might be found. But the animal lumbered slowly over the ground. His rider soon discovered four dark and ugly wounds from which the blood ran. Seizing a fresh mount, he hurried, his old impatience taking hold of his face with new fury, toward the rear. At last he found Beauregard in the disorder that gathers in the rear of every battle. He was looking nervously toward the front. Harris lifted his hat and said:

"I must report the death of General Johnston, sir."

Beauregard expressed his regret, asked, "Everything else seems going on well on the right?"

Harris assented vigorously.

"Then," said the new commander with studied patience, "the battle may as well go on."

14

There came a lull over the woods. The smoke lifted, the ceiling to the forest grew thin, and more light fell down the sullen ravines. There would have been quiet but for the scattering fire which rattled spitefully across the hollows and the few cleared fields. It might be rowdies breaking the peace on a Sunday. It might be but for . . . Pleasant looked around him. He lay panting behind a stump in the corner of a rail fence which his regiment had seized in its last charge. He could see to the end of its ragged line. That was something he couldn't have done at the beginning of the fight. Another series of such charges and the regiment would be no bigger than a company. Then he realized that he had thought of it as always being the same size. He had known that men would be killed, and killed in his regiment, but somehow these losses were to have nothing to do with the looks of the companies; they were not to make them shrivel up, make men he had seen every day for a month look strange. Long Boy Taliaferro was squat-crouching behind the fence, taking aim through the rails and firing deliberately, as if he were out squirrel hunting. But the grime of powder and sweat had painted his face, and his set dry eyes looked fierce and unnatural. His sleeve had been torn away, and it flopped strangely against a long mark of dried blood on his arm. Even little Arthur Clay had lost his brightness. He lay beyond on his back and panting. A dark line made of spit and powder ran down one corner of his mouth. It looked like a tusk, making his boyish face leer in a curiously evil way. Then Pleasant thought suddenly of Eli. He knew he had put him behind a tree where he could find him later. Or had he? Hadn't he covered him up with leaves? No, that was some other fellow hiding his comrade. Then very deliberately he said aloud, Eli is dead and I won't see him again. He waited to feel something; then said, He's dead and I'll never hear him speak again. He stopped, but the words carried no meaning. He felt nothing, and the more he spoke the less meaning his words seemed to carry. He sat up in a panic.

Crashing through the woods to his left, horses galloped forward, the foam dashed like a soft meringue against their necks. They were drawing artillery. The heavy wheels bounced over the rough ground, spun in the air. The drivers shouted; but the cannoneers, holding tight to the gun carriages and caissons, said never a word. When a wheel struck a stump and swung the carriage in a wide ark, throwing the dirt in Pleasant's face and knocking in a piece of the fence, the cannoneer never changed expression. He was astraddle the gun. His thighs tightened, his body inclined slightly, as if it had been astride a bucking horse. Before he could turn his head away, Pleasant saw a battery of four guns unlimber not fifty feet in advance of the infantry position. For a moment there was confusion; then the rapid gallop of horses to the rear, and the four guns stood in line just below the brow of the slope. The caissons were in line and withdrawn to the rear. Officers and men ran about for a moment, froze stiffly at their posts and waited about the iron pieces with jealous attention. A large, red-bearded officer sat his horse somewhat to the rear. He looked carelessly to the left and Pleasant followed the turn of his head. As far as he could see other batteries were rushing forward and unlimbering. Somebody was massing artillery for something. He got up and walked to the rear, counting the guns. There were twenty-six of them, stretching from the left of his regiment to the hill rising out of the woods.

When he got back to his position in line the signal gun fired. Almost at once, first smoke rings, then whirlwinds of sound that shook the earth, sprang from the twenty-five muzzles. The cannoneers in fury served the guns. Orders came down from mouth to mouth, shouted from the rear by lieutenants, for the infantry to increase its fire. Soon the steady roar of musketry rose through the forest, a solid body of noise supporting the plunging, cracking artillery. It would not be long now, Pleasant knew, before the lines must charge again. The ramrods flashed. Faces, black and creased by sweat, leaned against their gunstocks, sighting down the barrels. The triggers pulled, the guns kicked, and the long muzzle-loaders slid back from the rails to be loaded and primed. Soon smoke covered the lines afresh, and men moved like figures in a dream. As Pleasant rammed home his charge, he glanced over his shoulder. The smoke parted for a moment, and he saw the far battery caught by a shaft of sun. The men had stripped to the waist. Running with powder, swinging the black iron balls to the cannon mouths, the swinging arms ramming home, the pause, the leaping gun, and swinging again into action, washing out the lingering smoke, the men danced on the far hill. The sweat on their white bodies flashed in the light. He raised his voice to cheer; then he felt every tooth in his head shake. A shell had struck the piece nearest the infantry, sweeping the entire gun detachment to the ground. He forgot his own business as he watched the cannoneer coolly disengage himself from the wreck, stepping to one side where he was free from the dust and smoke, stoop to take his observations and make his calculations of distance and time. With ringing voice he turned and shouted to the man at the limber, who had got to his feet in a daze, "Three seconds." Pleasant saw him come alive and cut the fuse. By the time this was done the gunner, stepping over dead and dying comrades whose flesh hung dripping about the spokes, bent over the trail spike, doggedly aimed the strained and half-disabled piece, gave the signal for the fire to touch the fuse. . . .

An elbow rammed into Pleasant's side. A hoarse voice, strained and whispering, said, "Load and hold your fire." He could almost hear the word traveling from man to man by the silence that followed, a silence that could be heard above the greatest roar of battle. All knew what this meant, long moments, maybe hours of waiting, taking the enemy's fire without striking back, with nothing to do but listen to the bullets sing and think about where they were going to hit next. Pleasant bit off the cartridge end, dropped the charge slowly down the barrel, rammed it home. He stuck the ramrod into the ground; then remembered. He pulled it up and idly cleaned the dirt from its end and ran it in place. He turned over on his belly and hugged the earth. The firing from the smoke across the way had redoubled, and splinters from the cedar rails scattered through the air like needles. The bullets and bursting shells all but grazed his back. He held his breath. To breathe seemed death, and he could feel the whole regiment straining and quivering against the earth. He began wondering if he could rise and face the charge. In this air it was certain death. Then he heard Arthur Clay sing out in his high gay voice:

"Oh, I wish I was a baby, and a gal baby too, so I wouldn't have to go to war."

Pleasant leaned on his elbow and smiled at Taliaferro. He saw their fat corporal shaking with laughter. All around the nervous tension was gone.

He saw Bob Curtin crawling along the ground shouting something. Pleasant waited, waited patiently, to hear what it was. Curtin crawled right up to him and his head nodded wisely as he said:

"Who's number four here?"

Pleasant pointed to himself.

"At the signal, rise and take that corner of the fence and push it down."

Pleasant nodded, and Curtin swung his head over the ground and crawled away. At the command he rushed to his post. There was a common push, and the fence went down like paper. Then for a moment he stood alone. Fear seized him, and he looked behind him. The whole line was rising. He saw the men pull their hats down, leap the rails and, bending before the storm of lead, run forward. Through the thin smoking air, toward the heavier banks, the rolling clouds, the men yelled and charged. To the left and right he could hear the renewed sounds of clashing bodies. Then for some reason the regiment stopped in the middle of the field and fired. There followed a stand-up duel for several rounds, but Pleasant ran forward to a fringe of trees. The space before him was clear of men. He took his time and loaded. Then coming through the trees from the right he saw several blue soldiers drifting to the rear. One had a large tear in his breeches, and his shirt tail hung through. Pleasant raised his gun and fired. He saw the little puff of dust rise from the broad blue back. The man stumbled and fell forward. That was one Yankee he could account for.

He had shot two rounds and was capping his piece when his arm went numb. There was no pain, but the blood ran profusely from his hand. He looked at it and didn't know what to do. Bewildered, he walked back to the rear and stood about, wondering what he had better do. There was not much the matter, he knew, but he felt peculiarly helpless. He was a useless machine, of no further value in the fight, and he didn't know how to get out of it. The sergeant came over and took a handkerchief from his neck and calmly tied up his hand and told him to go and lie down behind a swale of ground. Pleasant obeyed him like a child.

But this place soon filled up with other wounded until they were all piled together like hogs sleeping in the corner of a pen. An officer came among them, shouting and kicking. Pleasant raised his hand and showed the bloody bandage. The major passed on, and he heard him say, "My God, if the officers skulk, how can you expect to keep the men in the fight. Get up"—

a kick—"you coward, and go to the front." A pale face turned up from the ground and whimpered, "I just . . . can't go out there." The major raised his boot, tramped and kicked; but the man hugged the ground, groaned, and took it. After a while the wounded and the frightened were left alone together. Then men passed running to the rear. As he watched them pass by, fear of capture took hold of Pleasant and he got up and followed them. He jumped across a small ravine and lay down in a gulley, behind a dead rebel who made a sort of breastwork for him. He heard several bullets strike dully against the cold not quite solid flesh. Men continued to pass him in rapid flight to the rear. He heard one of them say that the lines were breaking. In fresh panic Pleasant got up and ran far to the left, until he was sure he was out of danger. It seemed to take an eternity before he could get out of reach of the bursting shells. Finally he turned to see how the battle was going. He could see very little for the smoke, but by the charges of small arms and the whirlwinds from the cannon he learned to interpret the changing front. The sound was withdrawing toward the river.

As the red sun dropped closer to the forest rim, a Confederate brigade moved out of the woods on the far left. This surprised Pleasant, for he thought the whole battle front had moved forward. He could see that the brigade had already been torn by the fight, but it marched gallantly through a level field. Suddenly, a northern brigade stepped from the opposite woods to meet it. The sun struck and quivered along the points of the bayonets, and the foemen marched with quick step toward each other, as if they were brothers eager to embrace. All at once both lines stopped. Their guns were leveled to a man. The blue brigade got in the first volley. Some of the Rebels fell, a few ran to the rear. Pleasant waited breathlessly, wondering if all would follow. Staggered but a moment, they returned the volley and rushed through the smoke they had made. All was hidden now, but soon out of the woods and across the fields the wounded limped by, going to the rear, with staff officers dashing in every direction, and ambulances bouncing over the rough, stubby ground. Gradually the firing and the shouts of the men grew more distant, and he knew that his people were winning the day.

A sense of loneliness came over him, and he wandered aimlessly through the woods and the wreck of battle. He was a broken wheel, with no companions and no food. Everywhere the débris of battle littered the fresh green earth, and he was a part of it. Suddenly, in an open place he stumbled upon a surgeon cutting off a leg. He walked up to the wagon bed where the patient lay. The doctor was sawing at his leg, and the man lay there grinding his teeth against a musket barrel. Pleasant asked the surgeon if he would dress his hand when he got through. The surgeon turned his ferret eyes upon him, looked fiercely, never speaking, and returned to his sawing. Stretcher-bearers jostled Pleasant out of the way. The sight of the pile of arms and legs, the smell of warm blood made him sick and he turned to leave. He felt some shame that he had troubled the surgeon with his hand. He had scarcely got out of sight of the field hospital when a soldier passed him running, shouting crazily, "Prentiss division surrendered." He took hold of Pleasant's shirt, "Whar could a body find hit?" Without waiting for an answer, the soldier ran off among the trees. Prentiss division surrendered—then the army must be winning a victory. The thought, somehow, gave him no pleasure. It wouldn't be long till sundown, and he would be left alone in the darkness. He could not bear the thought. To be lost in the night ... if only he could find his comrades. And Pleasant remembered something that made him stand perfectly still. It was Long Boy Taliaferro swinging through the smoke, lost, carrying a lifeless form in his arms. Pleasant looked at the white face hanging backward, at the hair falling toward the earth, and the bald spot, deep and red, in the center of the head. Was that Arthur Clay? For one moment Taliaferro paused, as if everything depended upon which way he turned. In that moment Pleasant saw the hurt in the rough man's eyes, the dull uncomplaining hurt of an animal. And then Taliaferro went away, across the field toward the thick line of trees which bound the clearing. He walked like a man who expected, when he reached the woods, to step out of the world.

Pleasant stumbled along, but even as he went, he knew he couldn't find what he was looking for. There was no more comfort in Shiloh woods. He saw a pond and remembered that his throat was rough and dry. He hurried toward it, but there already men were lying around it, their heads upon the rim, their feet flung backward in the mud. He found an opening and got down to drink, but the water was bloody.

"How can you drink it?" he asked of the man next him, but the man made him no answer. Slowly Pleasant let his eyes travel around the uneven edges of the pond. From body to body he shifted his eyes. Some were dressed in blue, some in gray, one wore a hat, another's head was bare, some grew hair as black as ink, falling long about their shoulders, others were fair and blond. One with rigid arm clasped his fist over the dark red water. But all their faces, fair or dark, were set, were marble-smooth and still.

Pleasant stood up, faint with nausea and walked away. After a long while wandering, he came to the place where his regiment had waited for its last charge, but there were only the flattened rail fence, the lumpy dead, and emptiness. The thundering artillery was gone from the long slope, and the chill that comes before dark had risen from the ground and was blowing through the woods. He turned away. It began to rain, and there was nothing for him to do but walk among the numerous dead, who covered the fields. After a while, out of sheer loneliness and wretchedness, he walked up to a group of wounded Federals. One was a major from Ohio. His ankle was shattered, but he had hands, coffee and rations. Pleasant had one hand and two legs. He brought wood and water from a stream near by, and they soon had coffee boiling, in spite of the rain. Food revived the group and, sitting under the wet sky, they talked over the happenings of the day and then lay down to sleep. All through the night, at regular intervals, the gunboats shelled the forest and the rain came down in floods, but Pleasant slept as a man sleeps who has no cause to wake.

While it was still dark, he felt somebody shaking him, saying, "Get up. Get up."

He opened his eyes. It was the Ohio major. He was telling him to get up and leave, or he would be captured. The Federals had been reinforced. Pleasant needed no second warning; he could see the solid shadows, the dark ranks advancing, hear the gruff subdued commands. He grasped his enemy's hand, said a few words, and slipped away as the blue sky in the east began to split and tear. He found that his old habits were returning, and he retired easily from cover to cover. But his wet clothes bore heavily upon him, his shoes made enough noise to wake the dead, and his hand throbbed with sharp pains, especially when his foot slipped on the slick earth. He could hear through the noisy streams the sounds change in the world: one life withdrawing into hidden places, another opening up to meet the day. Half-heartedly he listened to this change. It was both familiar and strange. It promised him cover, but the cover in some way was distant and threatening. His old life with its clear sure purpose lay somewhere lost in this confusion, and he would never reach it again. There was a sickness in the air, the heavy stifling smell of powder and blood and corruption. He could no longer think. He must get out of it, or he was forever lost. He ran into a sentry sleeping against a tree, butt propped against the trunk, head hanging against the rifle barrel. He slipped noiselessly past him.

The day came, and he felt easier. He stumbled into a hospital tent and a surgeon dressed his hand and ordered him to the rear, to Corinth. He would have to walk, the doctor said. As he turned away, a sudden crash of thunder shook the ground at his feet. He looked at the sky, but it was blue ribbon blue. Then the unmistakable rattle of small-arms, the heavier reply of the artillery, both blending into a steady and dismal roar. . . . Another battle, as if there had been no conclusion on yesterday's field.

Wearily he stepped down the muddy road to Corinth. Marching to Pittsburg Landing three days ago, he had thought how much faster he could have gone, if he had been free to move alone and through the forest. But now that he was alone and returning, he felt no call to strike out by himself. He did not lift his eyes from the road. He drifted with the skulkers and the wounded, on the edge and always in sight of the liquid clay route through which the army had so slowly crawled. And then as he listened to the sound of battle, which he thrust ever in the distance, he said aloud, "Yesterday the enemy was broken, driven back, and now it is beginning all over again. Is there no end to anything? Can the day's victory be tomorrow's defeat? Can friends die for nothing, and all yesterday's blood and sweat be wasted?"

As if for answer he raised his eyes to the forest for comfort. But there was no comfort there. The heavy-topped trees, the black-jacks, the stubborn thickets stood up from the ground glistening with the early morning dew, but darkly glistening, close, hostile about the narrow road that stretched its thin way between Pittsburg Landing and Corinth.

5

From Chattanooga to Murfreesboro the cars rattled and bumped over the thin iron rails. They moved slowly all the way. There had been several breakdowns: once the engine jumped a bad place in the track; out of Cowan it had stalled, and the passengers cut up a man's fence rails to stoke the boiler, and he had cussed and cussed. Whenever the train labored climbing grade, convalescent soldiers who were returning to the army at Murfreesboro got out and walked or frolicked beside the cars. Only on the downgrade from Tullahoma did the train pick up any speed. Pleasant was glad of the crawling pace. He was glad, for when the cars rolled into Murfreesboro, his mind had to be made up . . . not made up, it was already that. It was that, once arrived, there could be no turning back.

You could cut the air in the car with a knife. The seats and aisles were crowded, and the waves of October heat set the sweat to rolling. The still hot air hung about the cars without entering. What little sucked in through the windows, instead of cutting the odors, blew them together until they swapped like juices in a kettle: the stiff layers of dried sweat, sopped by the butternut pants and jackets, stealing from the rotting shoes and down from the tight hat brims . . . sixty days of marching along the hard turnpikes, sixty nights by the cool roadside, with the dust of a strange country sprinkling under the hard copper moon and settling surreptitiously, ghost-like, over the army; the salty sweat of thirst on the road, the stench of fear that overflows the body as men stand and wait for the charge, the sweetness turned sour of wasted blood, the rancid odors drying under folds of fat men's bellies; and that odor, stronger than musk, that comes from the livers of the sick, whose weakness still remembers the grave; and strongest of all, the sharp, pissy smell of men crowded together. Pleasant watched it roll down the cheeks of a large officer crowding him next to the window. The man's collar had wilted into the red creases of his neck. Automatically he raised his handkerchief and went through the weary motions of mopping his face and neck. He turned his sodden eyes.

"By God, sir, don't it stink!" The ruffles on his dirty shirt rose and fell with full and regular panting. "Don't soldiers never wash?" he asked querulously.

A private across the aisle examined the officer carefully. Pleasant saw the glint of hard bright humor in his two gray eyes, eyes that looked almost transparent in the sallow face, still marked with fever. "My friend," the private said, "that's the stink of battle gut. A body can't wash that away." He looked directly at the officer. "Shorely you've smelled it before."

"I'm in the commissary," the large officer mumbled and looked away.

The soldier's gray eyes widened innocently. "That's a different kind of stink, I reckon."

Pleasant smiled and turned again to the window. The brown fields swung slowly by, corn cut and stacked, snake fences outlining row after row of canelike stalks, with the fodder all pulled and tied in neat bundles between the ground and the heavy ears. Shrilly the engine's whistle sounded. The cars, after a series of jerks, rolled to a quiet halt. Between the sky and the earth there fell a peace in which all things grew forever still and such quiet that he was able to hear the slight wind rustling the fodder bundles. The engine, panting down the long line of cars, broke the moment's pause. Somebody spoke. The strange voice reckoned that the cars had been put on the siding to let an empty supply train pass on its way to the depot at Chattanooga. The army at Murfreesboro had to be fed. Pleasant turned away from the window. In a few hours he would be a part of that army again . . . a part of the Army of Tennessee. Then he remembered he could never belong to it nor to any other army again.

Chattanooga . . . Murfreesboro, the beginning and the end. From Chattanooga Bragg had started on his Kentucky campaign where, for a few weeks, it looked as if the states of Kentucky and Tennessee might be returned to the Confederacy. Those miles of marching over the hot dusty roads, the dry dust in the throat, high living in the blue-grass country, fighting for water-holes at Perryville, and afterward the army's withdrawal through the mountains to Knoxville, to Chattanooga, then to Murfreesboro, and halting there. This did not make up many months as time goes. But how much had happened, how the world had changed since the spring in Shiloh woods, when he had walked away with a bullet in his hand. Brother William was wounded at Perryville. He had been wounded in the spring of '62, Brother William in the fall. It was still the fall, gathering time for those who were left to gather. And he was on his way back to the army and Brother William was on his way to the ground.

Pleasant's eyes came to a focus on the soldier facing him. He was young, about sixteen; but the roundness of plenty, the softness was gone out of his face. It was lean and hard, like every other face in the army. The men were now all alike. There was the same purpose in every eye, the same appetites, the same thoughts.

The boy lifted his mild blue eyes, but behind their mildness lay a hard blue film. "Pardner," he asked, "you ain't got any bacca crumbs on you?"

Pleasant reached in his pocket and handed him over a twist. The soldier bit off a chew, pushed it against his jaw with his tongue.

"I'm obliged to you. I was plumb worried to death for a chew," he said, handing back the twist.

As the tobacco swapped hands, Pleasant noticed the boy had a finger missing.

"Minie ball tuck that off at Perryville," the young soldier said with careless pride. "I didn't know nothing about it until I tried to pull my trigger." He inspected his hand carefully. "A body's hand don't look the same, now does it?"

"It sure don't," Pleasant agreed. There seemed nothing more to say, and he glanced through the window and saw an old man walking down a fence row, kicking up the dry dust from the brown stubble. It rose in little clouds, spread out, settled gradually to the earth, clung to his feeble legs like a swarm of blow-flies. It settled like the red dust around the clods that fell from the shovels in the soldiers' burying-ground at Chattanooga.

Pleasant's thoughts washed suddenly clear. He must remember exactly how it had happened. He was standing on one side and his mother was standing on the other, beside the grave being dug for her sons. When she got word that William's wound had turned gangrenous, Susanne set out to fetch him home. She got the word one afternoon and, without waiting for another sun, hitched up the only team left on the place and set out alone, taking time to put on her bonnet and wrap a little silver in her handkerchief. It was a long journey for a lone woman in troubling times. She followed the ridges over Sand Mountain, passed through the lines of two armies, camping sometimes in the open, sometimes sleeping on the rough floor of a hospitable mountain cabin. Out of Huntsville a Federal sentry told her she couldn't pass; when she tried to, raised his musket. She looked at the man. Her son could not rest in a strange place, she said. She was going to fetch him back to lie with his own people. She popped the reins over the mules' back, and the wagon rolled past the leveled gun.

She waited in Chattanooga for Pleasant. She waited because he would be sure to know where William lay. There was some sort of record, but she wouldn't trust it. When Pleasant arrived, he had to tell his mother that little Levi, too, was dead. She already knew, she replied. The doctor at the hospital told her about him. He got up too soon from the measles to attend his brother . . . there had been no holding him, they said. He sat without sleeping by William's cot, with his hand on William's forehead; and when the fever left suddenly, driven by the cold damp chill, it was sometime before Levi knew what had happened. In three days he followed his brother. Pleasant put them in the same coffin. Levi had asked it, but he would have done it anyway.

Pleasant remembered that his mother had said nothing when he told her these things, he remembered this very distinctly as he faced her at the shallow grave, as the men threw away their picks and shovels and stepped down to lift out the box. It was then she spoke.

"Open it first," she said deliberately.

The burial detail straightened up, looked with bewilderment at the slight woman, at the drawn face and the bright eyes shining hard and dry from under her bonnet slats. "Surely, ma'm, you don't . . ."

"Open the coffin," she repeated steadily.

The soldiers, standing in the open grave, their bodies bracing against the heavy lift, appealed silently to Pleasant.

He said, "Ma, I'm sure."

"I must see." Her voice sounded strained and tired, with a slight crack that might break any moment. The men heard it and bent hastily down and pried the lid open. Pleasant gave one glance and turned away. After a pause in which there had been no sense of time, he heard his mother say: "All right, you may nail it down and set the coffin in the wagon."

And then somehow he and Susanne were standing on either side of the wagon. Her eyes rested upon the long rough box, bulking large between them. At last she lifted her head, a moment too soon, because it was not until she looked steadily at him that the bitterness withdrew into her dark pupils. And he knew, too late to drop his eyes, that she did not mean for him to see. He felt a sense of shame, as if he had tricked her, had discovered a hidden thing that no eye should have ever seen. But in a moment her sight was clear, and it said, These I have lost and it is a loss that you cannot understand, but you are left, and I could better lose them both than you, for my oldest and my youngest have wasted themselves on foolish adventures. You will never turn away and spend yourself on things that do not matter.

Not until that moment, with her dead between them, did

Pleasant realize what he had done. He scarcely knew when she said good-by, when he untied the bridle reins and put them in her hand, for the knowledge that he had turned aside, that he was failing, came like a blow too great for man to stand. Not since Shiloh woods had he attended to what he had to do. For months he had held his hand, had let his father lie uneasy in his grave. All that time his father's blood enemies skulked in the army. He had let them, he had left them alone to die like other men, like Brother William and Levi. There was the shame. He remembered now that in camp at Tupelo he had kept close to his mess. Without thinking he had done it to keep from seeing them. And on the road to Kentucky he drank from the same water barrel with two of them. He told himself that after the battle they would get attention. At the moment they were needed for the cause. The cause! There was no cause for such as they: there was death and judgment. The cause was for men like Roswell Ellis and for . . . he had almost said for himself.

He had been a good deal on scout duty. That would be the easiest way. He could slip between the lines and kill them while they were on outpost. In that way his messmates would never find out. It would be more difficult to hide it from Roswell. Roswell could tell almost what a man was thinking, and ever since Pleasant had returned to the army, they had shared blankets. He remembered the day Roswell joined the mess. It was the day he was leaving the hospital, and Roswell had come over to see him and say how glad he was he hadn't lost his hand. As they left for camp, he noticed his friend was unusually sober. Then Roswell let out what was on his mind—he spoke very quietly in his gentle way—he said that he had come to a conclusion: he felt he ought to join the ranks and fight with the men, too many gentlemen were doing staff duty, and he wondered if Pleasant could get him into his company. Pleasant told him of course he could and introduced him to the mess. It had changed since Shiloh. Of the seven men who had dipped their hands in the skillet that last morning at Corinth, only three were left—Long Boy Taliaferro,

Old Man Long, and himself. Not many, but somehow they had not felt like inviting others to join. The mess had been mighty close, and they knew as they sat around the fire and talked about Eli or Arthur Clay or Old Man Long's boy that just anybody who wanted to join might not understand. The three of them had an understanding that no stranger should intrude. So Pleasant felt some uneasiness about the way they would take to Roswell. But he had no cause to. Taliaferro had mighty fine feelings about certain things. He came forward and extended his hand and said that any friend of McIvor's was a friend of his. Old Man Long was a little slower. He looked Roswell over from head to foot; finally said, "Draw you up a stump, young man, and make yerself easy."

Taliaferro now was gone. He would never forget his bearing on a scout. Once, a mere handful, they had sallied into the woods to engage unknown numbers. Taliaferro was as gay as if he were entering a ballroom. Twelve enemy cavalry charged them—they were five—but Pleasant, Taliaferro and the others stood their ground in the center of a country lane. Taliaferro's head was cut by a saber just as a horse knocked him into a fence corner. His thick wool hat and the blow from the horse's shoulder saved his life that time, and he was up and back into the fray before a dude could brush his hair. What a man he was! Once Pleasant saw him eat thirteen roasting ears and "damn a government that wouldn't furnish fodder." Old Long Boy, fearless before an enemy, cautious on the scout, lying somewhere in Kentucky. He could never forget him, for himself and for the way he had welcomed Roswell that time.

For he and Roswell had become like brothers. That same night Roswell told him what had become of Cousin Armistead. The first day at Shiloh the old gentleman had been wounded in both legs. No persuasion could get him to leave the field and he couldn't ride a horse. Doctor Yandell dressed his wounds and ordered him to the rear, but he sat stubbornly on the ground with his back against a tree, bellowing out his orders in a voice that sounded as strong as ever, rising above

the heavy rolling musketry. Only for a few moments did he
seem to draw away from the battle, when the message came
that Colonel Rob and his mount had been blown out of the
world by a shell. He dropped his eyes to his boot toes, but the
senior captain soon roused him. The captain asked if he
should lead the charge—it was the last one around Prentiss's
flank—and the colonel raised his shoulders and by-Godded and
by-damned him back to his company, he'd lead what charges
were to be led. Then he sent Roswell for his two black servants. They made a pack saddle for him, and in this way
Colonel McIvor put himself at the head of the brigade. For a
minute he faced the ranks, waiting for them to get into position, with his arms as large as hams clamping the necks of
his two black men. Their faces were the color of ashes, but
they stood and walked with pride. There was no complaint.
He told them what he was going to do, that if they got out alive
he would grant their freedom, he couldn't force a slave to take
a freeman's risk. Suddenly the colonel raised his voice and
sang the opening line to "We shall march away to battle," and
the weary, shattered regiments stiffened to a man, picked up
the tune, and followed him through the smoke. Just before
the abattis Roswell saw the slaves stumble and sink slowly
with their load. He saw them try to rise, falter, pull feebly
as their hands caught under their master's buttocks, and then
stretch out quietly around him. The colonel threw open his
mouth as if to shout; then his head fell forward and rolled on
his shoulders. And there he sat through the short, hard
struggle. The lines once bent around him, but the officers
would point to him there, sitting peacefully, with his head on
his chest and his hat over his eyes, like an old gentleman taking an afternoon siesta.

Pleasant sat perfectly still in the bumpy train, thinking of
these things. Then his mind opened suddenly like a trap and
lost everything that was in it. There was the steady beat of the
wheels against the rails. For some minutes there was nothing
but the monotony of this sound in his head. Every time he
began to plan how to strike his mind wandered. If this kept

up, he would bungle all he had to do. This frightened him.
Before Shiloh there had been one thing in his heart: love for
his father, hatred for those who had come slipping through the
night to trap him. But now he felt a fresh bitterness and, he
had to admit it, the old hatred had gone a little stale. He
had never known that there would be anything more to lose.
But it was plain that he had come to have other loyalties. This
was why his father had not come to him during all these
months. It was because he had deserted Cameron McIvor.
The engine's sharp whistle screamed its warning. Pleasant
looked up. The cars were rolling into the depot at Murfreesboro.

He swung off the cars. He didn't see Roswell at first, but
he was there to meet him. They shook hands and said a few
words, but his friend referred in no direct way to his trip,
nor did Pleasant say he was glad that Roswell had come to
meet him, but each man understood the other's mind. They
set out for their camp on Stone's River. On the way Pleasant
asked:

"Everything all right?"

"The rations are more plentiful."

After a pause of eight swinging strides, "Good."

Then after another silence, "Anything else?"

"Phil Nelson's got the seven years' itch."

"That'll be hard on Dan."

"Dan says maybe his lice'll catch it. Anyway he's not
going to desert the top blanket with winter coming on."

They kept on out the Franklin dirt road, stepped aside once
to let a troop of cavalry trot by. The thick lime dust rose in
clouds from the road, and after the troop had passed, the two
friends stepped back and walked through it waist high. Suddenly a shaft of the afternoon sun fell through a cedar thicket
and set the small white particles sparkling on their way to the
ground.

With the tone of a man whose mind is on something else,
Roswell asked, "Remember that Georgia captain?"

"Which one?"

"You know. The one with the long curly hair and six feet tall."

"Oh, the one who was so reckless at Corinth."

"Yes, who would stand on the works and look through his spy glasses at the enemy, with the bullets flying all around him."

"I actually saw that man stoop over and dig in the dirt for the balls. Said they had been meant for him, and he reckoned he'd better get them." Pleasant paused; said as an afterthought, "I never saw a man so contemptuous of Yankee marksmanship."

"Well, he's dead."

"Dead?" repeated Pleasant slowly.

"Yes. The day you left he cut a little piece of flesh out of his thumb. Whittling."

"What's that got to do with it."

"Well, he died this morning. I went to the burying."

"Died from what?"

"From that little hole he'd cut in his thumb."

Pleasant stopped in his tracks. The two friends looked at each other.

"Roswell"—he spoke suddenly—"let's go out and sit on those rocks where that creek empties into the river. I brought rations from Chattanooga."

Roswell answered, "Fine."

They turned off the road and struck out through the woods. As they walked over the dry earth, through the hot afternoon, Pleasant felt his heart grow heavy. If he could only tell his friend what was on his mind, what he had decided to do. But that couldn't be. There was no way for him to travel now but one way: he must go alone. It was almost treachery to keep his thoughts from Roswell, and the full force of the sacrifice he must make came over him. Sacrifice! To think that he would ever, for a moment, weigh the price of serving his father. But it was so. They walked along in the late afternoon, Roswell chatting easily, thinking Pleasant's sadness due to the cause for his journey, the last farewell in this world to his brothers.

They came to the river, and it was running low and sluggish, but there were deep blue holes stirred by a slow current. "Let's go in washing."

Roswell had turned and, as he spoke, his voice carried the old familiar ring of affection. They tossed off their clothes and jumped in. The water was warm, and the waves made by their bodies lapped against the hollows in the clay banks. They swam around and then stood waist deep in the blue pool. The light was gold, running over the surface of the river like oil, but the western sky was every color. "I've got a piece of soap," said Roswell and swam to the bank and got it out of his pocket. He pitched it to Pleasant, and Pleasant lathered his hot brown body, threw the cake to Roswell and dipped into the water and afterward rubbed his slick skin, and his hands ran over the hard corded muscles, the hollow ribs; then he waited until Roswell was through.

As he waited, standing in the sluggish water on the quiet afternoon, he thought how many times they had come down together to wash their dirty clothes. Then he heard his friend say, "Had enough?" Pleasant nodded and they climbed up the bank and stretched out on a limestone ledge to dry. The slick rock was still too hot for comfort; so he reached for his clothes and stuffed them under him. The stale odors rose about his clean body and struck his nose with familiar staleness. Both Roswell's staleness and his own, for when people sleep under the same blanket, their smells are bound to swap. He thought of the intimacy of their life, of all the chores, the hardships, the dangers they had shared and would now share no more. But it was those little things that you never thought much about at the time that made it so hard. Once he remembered, when they were foraging together, how Roswell had let a woman's calf out of the barn and while she was trying to hold the calf off, Pleasant had stripped two teats into his canteen, milking through the fence. It was about dark or he'd never have been able to do it. What a feast they had that night. Cooked three days' rations, all they had, and washed them down with the milk. And then at Perryville in that nervous moment just before the battle opened. Roswell had come over and put his arm around him, saying with the only emotion he'd ever seen him show:

"McIvor, if you dare to get yourself killed, I'll never forgive you."

But there weren't many things like that. It was those hundred common things that you did every day in camp or on the march. The stirring in the dark, the hasty breakfast, and the marching before light, racing for position and knowing the enemy is doing the same. The halt at noon, the crowding around the roulette or chuck-a-luck boards as soon as arms are stacked, or pulling out a pack of cards around a blanket, betting whatever a man had. The way they had learned to read the weather signs! If the day was foggy and the mist rose, one end of the blanket was unfolded and tied around the neck, because a good campaigner knew it would rain before the morning was over; but if the mist went into the ground, the blankets were always rolled, tied, and thrown over the shoulder. And those halts for the night in the wet woods, with a man wondering how he could light a fire. Somebody would take the dry inner bark of a dead tree, cedar twigs, or dry leaves, and a glimmer would appear, the small flames be carefully fed. A hundred hands would bear away a lighted twig—fireflies spreading—and soon campfires sprang up through the army.

Some gathered wood for the night, others hung six or eight canteens over their shoulders and went hunting water, others went about the meals. That sorry moment when the commissary wagon drove up in the dark wet woods after a hard day's march and dumped the flour for a whole company on somebody's oilcloth or a blanket. Then the cooks would mix it with cold water, often without salt, and bake it in ovens or skillets, or wrap the dough about a ramrod and turn it over the flames. Corn meal was harder to manage than flour. You couldn't bake a hoe-cake in a fresh fire on the damp earth, nor could you cook it on ramrods. You had to wait your turn on the skillet. But after the short meal was over what shouts of laughter rose about the fire! You could look around and see the good marcher bathing his feet in cold water, rubbing the bottoms with tallow and toasting them before the fire to harden them against tomorrow's tramp. Always somebody was busy with his lice. How many times had he seen Roswell stripped to the waist, standing before the fire, holding his shirt over the flames. Taliaferro said there were marks on his back— I.F.W.—in for the war. In for the war . . . there was marching, fighting, going into camp, but where was Taliaferro now?

What would happen to Roswell when he deserted him? Pleasant didn't answer this question. He opened his eyes and it was dark. Roswell was dressing, looking down at him:

"You been asleep, McIvor? I've called you several times."

Pleasant got up and began pulling on his clothes. "I must have dropped off," he said hastily.

They made a fire and boiled coffee in a cup, and Pleasant divided the rations he had brought from Chattanooga. It was a rich feast—fat bacon, hardtack, a tin of canned beef, and coffee. They lingered over the meal until the flames fell away, until the gray ashes mounted the live coals and there was only a faint glow topping the dead fire . . . then darkness. The two friends walked through it, back to camp, spread their blankets and lay down between them.

Roswell fell quickly to sleep. Pleasant listened for a while to his gentle breathing, raised up once and, under the late moon, looked at the repose on his regular features; then lay back down. Tomorrow he would go on a scout. He knew a cave to hide in, not too far away, just the distance to let him slip back among his enemies. His mind grew sharp with plans, and he lay awake for hours waiting for dullness and sleep.

In the night Roswell cried out. He woke up grabbing Pleasant's arm in a convulsive grip.

"What's the matter with you?" Pleasant's voice was thin and distant.

"It is you, then." Some terror still haunted Roswell's voice, and he shook with a chill.

"Yes, it's me," answered Pleasant. After a slight pause, "Who the hell did you think it was?"

"I don't know. I must have been dreaming. I thought I was lying not on this hard ground but in a soft bed, with white stiff sheets. And that you, sometimes it was you, sometimes somebody else, were on the other side. I thought how nice it was to sleep in a bed again and to have clean cover. But something was wrong. The cover was clean but there was a smell coming out of it, I couldn't tell quite what it was, except that it made me sick. And then I reached out to touch you, to ask you if you noticed something was wrong with our fine nice bed; and, as I looked at you, your eyes were closed, your face was set, and you looked like a dead man. I shook you, but the moment I touched you your face turned black, the whole room went black; and from where I thought you lay the smell of corruption rose thick and stifling, two long bony arms reached about my waist, with hot rotting chunks of flesh falling, and wherever they fell scalding me. I must have screamed out. God, but I hope I never have any more such dreams. They shake a man."

"Well, I'm still here," Pleasant answered quietly, "and no more corrupt than when we crawled in together. Go on back to sleep."

2

The November air was chill. It blew through Pleasant's gray jacket until his teeth shook like dice. He was tempted to put spurs to his horse and gallop down the Wilkerson turnpike into camp. His scout in the direction of LaVergne had been dangerous and tiring, enough in itself to promise a man rest. But his real work was just beginning. These scouts were the price he had to pay for freedom to move between the lines, and his information for headquarters had to be valuable enough to give him this freedom. In the last five weeks he had been only three times in camp, but those three times had been enough for Roswell to feel his coldness, to be hurt. One night they had fought, had to be separated for pulling cover. Other people might pull cover, but they had never done it before. He ought to stay away altogether. These bickerings would take away even the memory of this friendship.

Pleasant pulled up his horse and, by the light of the moon, quickly got his bearings. Awsumb ought to be on picket two hundred yards ahead. He knew every position along the whole front of the army. Going and coming these weeks he had taken pains to learn them. There were always minor changes, but the general positions were always about the same. There was no way to slip up on Awsumb on horseback. He dismounted. His hands were so cold it took him twice as long as it should to tie the mare up and mask her. He patted her neck and then pulled himself together. Now what next? Awsumb would be mounted and withdrawn from the road, just on its edge and hidden, more than likely, by some suitable clump of bushes . . . but which side? He would try the right-hand side first. That kept him covered all the way; and if anything miscarried, he could reach his bay without having to cross the pike.

He swung along just far enough back from the road to stay hidden. The movement warmed his body, and he felt better, surer. With long familiarity his eyes snapped at the shadows, at the pools of light. This was such a night when the shadows were safer, were easier paths of travel, than the more ghostly open splotches of light. He had the feeling, a common feeling now, that his mind stood off and tracked his body like a hound. An open field stopped his advance for a moment. He dropped over and took the risk of crawling in the cover of its fence until he reached the cedar grove on the far side. From here on he would move more slowly. Every ten paces he stopped dead still and listened. He stopped four times without discovering a sound foreign to the night. But on the fifth time he noticed a shadow, large and shaking in the cover of a tree, right by the pike's edge. He moved forward, bending over and holding his breath, although God knows his boots made enough noise to wake the world. If he could only get a pair of moccasins. He ran from tree to tree, in silent rushes. There sat Awsumb—fifteen paces away and sound asleep on his mount. The animal was a more worthy foe. He had long ago discovered the danger. He was flinging up his head, stamping, trying to warn his master. It was almost impossible to slip up on a horse. If Pleasant rushed him, the animal would turn and gallop away. If he tried to slip up closer, he was sure to shake Awsumb to his senses. Pleasant calculated three seconds; decided to wait behind a tree, hoping the animal would grow quiet. He drew himself against a black gum's trunk and waited, still and silent, for ten minutes or so. What little warmth he had worked up was gone in five minutes. The chill covered his body like a plaster. His feet lost all feeling, but he dared not stamp the blood down. His eyelids closed over the balls as wet as ice. When he began to feel that he might never be able to move again, he broke the stiffness and bent his neck around his heavy, useless body . . . but there stood the horse, neck up and curved—Pleasant could almost see the distended nostrils—alert, watching the tree behind which he was hidden.

The ruse had failed. There was no way to take that intelligent animal by surprise. It made him feel a little foolish. There was even less chance of making a rush than before. He thought a few moments . . . it gave him pleasure to be checked by this fine animal . . . but he would have to act. He couldn't play out the game as it deserved. There was this: he could shoot Awsumb off the horse, or he could shoot the horse and rush the man. On the other hand, it seemed a pity to shoot such a noble animal in cold blood. Of course, he might wound Awsumb, taking the chance on the horse whirling and throwing him to the ground. He could rush him then and tell him who had killed him . . . he couldn't bear to think of Awsumb dying, believing that a Yankee bullet brought honorable death. But, then, suppose Awsumb didn't fall to the ground? Suppose the horse carried him to safety?

Pleasant pulled out his pistol and leveled it squarely at the animal's forehead. He expected him to get even more restless. But the horse stood there with head up and looked him straight in the eye. Pleasant shifted his aim. He'd be damned if he'd kill such a fine beast. He'd take the other chance.

Steadying the pistol against the tree, he took deliberate aim at Awsumb's waist. Then his trigger finger went numb. His hand shook so he had to lower it. But it was not the chill of the November night which made it shake. His will had snapped. He had forced it until it could be forced no longer. As he stood behind the tree, shivering with nausea and the cold, he accepted the truth: it was not in him any longer to kill in cold blood. These last weeks he had tried, nobody knows how he had tried, to return to the old loyalty, to carry on what he had sworn never to lay aside until it was done. But his nature had at last rebelled. His private vengeance had been swallowed by something greater than his love for his father— no, not greater, only more overpowering. It had taken him as the flood current takes the great tree, torn up by its roots. Even now, when the truth was on him, he tried to rally and bring himself to knock Awsumb out of his saddle. He thought of Lovell, he tried to think of Lovell, of all he had done, hoping this would make the old hatred flare again. But that evil man's features did not appear before his sight. He spoke Lovell's name, the name so hateful that he had never dared whisper it even, and it brought no echo to his heart. He knew then that all was over. The rod of vengeance was broken. Nothing he could do would mend it.

He looked once at Awsumb's mount, then slipped back the way he had come. The horse, as if he understood Pleasant's defeat, shook his head and then dropped it. The master slept on, all unconscious that he had ever been in peril. Pleasant found his own mare waiting quietly in the bushes. He fumbled at the reins, mounted and took a path through the woods that would put him on the Murfreesboro-Nashville turnpike. He rode slowly along, wondering what there was left him in this world. The rhythm of his little mare's stride restored his calm, and he began to consider which way to turn. There was Roswell. He would go to him. Roswell could lead him back into this world which had taken him in spite of himself, whose violence had made nothing of his, whose blood was spilled by the rivers' full. This was his only course. As he thought of his friend, he felt the first peace he had felt since that time he stood before his brothers' grave. Roswell would understand. Their old comradeship would return. And if all was not well, at least he might throw himself into the war, lose himself . . .

He rode on, struck the pike, and turned toward Murfreesboro, was challenged, gave the password, and rode toward headquarters to report. He could wait until morning, but the concentration at LaVergne might have some meaning, and he'd better turn in his information. He'd gone through this routine so often that he felt he was doing the same thing over and over again. He passed through the camps, the rows of dog tents, huts, and the men wrapped up together on the ground, looking like hogbacks glistening in the frost. The whole world was still, with nothing to break the stillness but the sharp challenge of an occasional sentry. He reached the adjutant's tent and roused him from sleep. The officer cursed wearily, lighted a candle, and turned his swollen eyes through the dim flame. Pleasant gave his report in a few words.

"Brilliant, McIvor. Brilliant. You'd wake a man up to tell him that."

Pleasant's temper was short, and he asked if the concentration to the front had no meaning.

"Plenty—yesterday. You are just twenty-four hours too late, sir."

"What do you mean?"

"I mean that a brigade had to be sent out to test the enemy's purpose. Your brigade, by the way."

The adjutant blew out the candle and crawled back to bed. In the dark Pleasant asked, "Do you know the casualty list?"

"Get out of here and let me sleep."

Pleasant stood perfectly still for a few moments. He told himself there was no need for alarm. Reconnaissances in force were too common. But he left the tent shaken. He hurried to his company's camp. Everybody was asleep, and Roswell wasn't where he ought to be. He stared at the empty ground, then went from one end of the company to the other. Still no Ellis. He strode through the still night until he came to the nearest sentry post, scarcely waited for the sharp challenge, and asked where Lieutenant Ellis was.

"He was wounded this morning," the sentry said.

"How bad?"

"Bad, I think."

"Do you know where they took him?"

"No, I don't."

Dan Germain would know. Pleasant hurried away and dragged Dan from under the covers. It was hard to get him awake, to make him understand who was talking, but finally he got some sense into his head.

"Oh, Ellis. He was wounded at LaVergne. Didn't live to get back to Murfreesboro."

"Didn't live?" Pleasant's voice sounded cold and disinterested.

"No. I helped carry him off." Dan's thick sleepy tones cleared up as he went along. "He took an unnecessary risk—the brigade was only on reconnaissance—he was in charge of the company and rushed some artillery, two isolated pieces . . . and took them. It was beautiful work, the sort of thing a man would have done in '61. He got a lot of canister in his guts." He stopped; then said, "By the way, he asked me to give you something."

Without moving, Pleasant watched the sleepy man fumble in his pockets. At last Germain brought out a locket and put it in his hand.

"He said you'd know what to do with it."

After a long while Pleasant asked, "Did he say anything else?"

"No, I don't believe he did." Germain got back under his

cover; then ". . . I believe he did say he hoped everything would be all right with you, or something like that. I'm sorry, McIvor."

Germain held out his hand. Pleasant automatically took it and returned the pressure.

"He was a fine fellow," Germain said, pulling the cover over his head.

Pleasant stood without motion, alone in the still dark world. He could hear the slow blood, its labored strokes against the bone. Never again would it quicken for Roswell Ellis, for he was dead. Dead by his hand. He had killed him as certainly as if he had pressed the cold blade into his heart. Thirty-six hours ago he had discovered the activity about LaVergne. Thirty-six hours! If only he had come in, the brigade wouldn't have gone out. Or if he had talked with Roswell, told him. But Roswell would have said with Cousin Armistead that there is no time for private vengeance. Now there is no time ever any more for vengeance. Vengeance—the dark way. Into Shiloh woods he had gone, had carried it there. On that field where the living died and, dying, came more alive, he had lost it and had found himself. . . . But where now was Shiloh, its dismal woods, the sudden ravines? Where was Corinth or the hot dry fields of Perryville? Where was . . . life? Roswell who was to lead him back, away from the will, the brittle will which had broken out there between the lines . . . where was he? As a mourner before the open grave Pleasant dropped his head to the ground, where Roswell should be sleeping, waiting, and the ground was empty, as empty as his heart. Then suddenly he knew what he had done, what no man in this world may do. Twice he had loved—once the dead, once the living, and each by each was consumed and he was doomed. In the partial darkness he raised his eyes to the river. Stone's River, icy-cold and black, turned between the town and the cedar thickets across the Nashville pike, broke over the shallow rocks at McFadden's Ford, fell again into deep chasms, flowing north, silently flowing through the long night.

Pleasant straightened his body, looked once about him. The camps were still asleep, only the sentries walked their posts, frozen shadows in the darkening world. He looked to the south. Far to the south the hills of Winston rose close and stubborn out of the lowlands. The hills of Winston. It was no long journey to a man who knew the way, who had lost every other way. There he would go. There, in the secret coves far away from the world and vengeance, a deserter might hide forever. . . .

THE END